Dime

Books by Luis Figueredo

Dime

COMING SOON!
Breaking Arrows

Dime

Luis Figueredo

SPEAKING VOLUMES, LLC
NAPLES, FLORIDA
2022

Dime

Cover design by Hannah Linder

ISBN 978-1-64540-609-9

Chapter One

SAINT MAARTEN

Juan Carlos Laporte took a long drag of his cigarette and listened intently to the Saint Maarten police force scamper just outside his bedroom window. The first police car swerved into the driveway of his oceanfront condominium at approximately three in the morning. Twenty minutes later the entire property was blocked in by patrol cars and surrounded by uniformed police. Juan Carlos considered his options as the police moved with purpose just outside his front door. Ordinarily, Juan Carlos would have a contingency plan. However, with each passing second, the notion that he didn't have one became more deeply rooted in his thought process. At thirty-nine, Juan Carlos was already a twenty-two-year veteran of the drug smuggling business. When he was seventeen, Juan Carlos began his career in the drug trade by unloading marijuana shipments in remote swamps in the Florida Everglades. By the time he celebrated his twenty-eighth birthday, Juan Carlos Laporte was a financial advisor to one of the most powerful drug cartels in the world.

* * *

The swirling blue and white lights sliced through the drawn blinds. Juan Carlos's eyes moved down to his watch. Thirty minutes had now passed since the first patrol car pulled into the driveway. He raised the cigarette to his lips and took another pull never thinking that in the end his demise would come at the hands of the Saint Maarten police force. The United States Drug Enforcement Administration and Interpol had been trying unsuccessfully for years to connect him to the South American drug cartels and ironically in the matter of the next few minutes he would be arrested on a small island that had built its economy on servicing tax evaders and criminals.

Given the local police force's reputation for severely beating prisoners, Juan Carlos figured that his chances of winding up with a fractured skull in a remote sewage canal were about as good as being brought before a magistrate. To complicate matters further, there was the predicament of his employer. If the cartel suspected that he might cooperate, his family would become targets. Juan Carlos raised himself up, his eyes fixated on the front door and waited for what now only lay a few moments ahead.

As the precious seconds ticked away, Juan Carlos cursed himself. Finally, the door at the end of the hallway exploded off its hinges as a sudden wave of armed men overwhelmed him. Before he could blink a second time, a revolver was pressed firmly against his temple. "If you so much as flinch, you son-of-a-bitch you'll be wanting a coffin," the officer shouted in a heavy West Indian accent.

Juan Carlos dropped slowly down to his knees. His arms were jerked behind his back so hard they felt as if they were being ripped from their sockets.

"You are charged with criminal conspiracy to import and distribute methamphetamine," the arresting officer's voice bellowed.

At some point during the arresting officer's statement Juan Carlos's eyes unfocused on him and shifted to the other police officers that were gathering anything that could be concealed in their pockets and later sold at the underground markets. It was during all the commotion and nervous chatter that Juan Carlos gained clarity. He realized that they were not going to kill him. He was a trophy to be displayed to the United States and Interpol which had been working for years to penetrate the cartel. Once he was fairly certain that he would make it through the night alive, Juan Carlos's thoughts turned to the cartel and his family's safety.

* * *

PIERCE EVANGELISTA FIRST met Alexis Laporte in the large conference room of his law office in downtown Miami. When he first laid eyes on Alexis, Pierce took a deep breath and just stared for a moment awed by her beauty. His pulse quickened and his thoughts drifted. Her almond shaped eyes, long black eyelashes and perfectly sculpted eyebrows possessed a seductive quality that Pierce found intoxicating even under these dire circumstances. Alexis was accompanied by her mother-in-law, Laura Maria, a ruddy cheeked, heavy-set Cuban woman in her early sixties. Laura Maria slumped back in her chair as if her legs had been cut out from under her anxiously waiting for Pierce to enter the conference room. Alexis stood leaning lightly against one of the perfectly translucent windows that created the illusion that there was nothing between the viewer and the view.

The real reason Pierce agreed to meet with the two women was his ex-wife Jordan. She called him first thing Sunday morning and left him a message that she needed his help with a family problem. Nothing more specific than that. The fact that Jordan asked for his help made Pierce curious. Pierce knew that it bothered her that he was still the first person she thought of to call when she had a problem. When they spoke later that afternoon, he listened patiently to Jordan as she explained the facts surrounding her cousin Juan Carlos's arrest in Saint Maarten.

"I don't do criminal law," Pierce replied.

"I know you don't," Jordan fired back. "What they need is a "fixer" and you're one of the best."

Pierce stared at his reflection in the window. "Why would they need what I do?"

Jordan's answer caused his right eyebrow to shoot up a quarter inch. "Because this clearly isn't what it appears to be. The Dutch arrested Juan Carlos on the Dutch side of the island for a crime he allegedly committed on French soil. The American consulate was not officially informed that a U.S. citizen had been arrested and my cousin was transferred to a Maximum-security prison in Curacao before he's had any type of hearing. The official word is that the Dutch government is holding Juan Carlos pending an extradition hearing. But my gut tells me there's more to this," Jordan's voice was tight with tension. "If there's even a remote chance that it could be something, it wouldn't hurt to have you look into it . . . You've always had a talent for getting ahead of most problems," Jordan sneered.

Pierce picked up on the subtle dig about their failed marriage but decided to let it go. He could always tell when Jordan was dug in on something. "Fine," he said. "Have your aunt call my office and we will schedule an appointment."

"She'll be there at eleven tomorrow morning."

"And, checkmate," Pierce thought to himself.

* * *

Pierce studied the two women at the far end of the long conference room table, gazing unwittingly out at the view of Biscayne Bay as if it held some answer to their dilemma. They stared silently, never saying so much as a single word to each other. It was obvious that Juan Carlos's arrest was taking a toll on Laura Maria. Her sullen expression and sweaty brow painted a picture of despair. She was clearly a woman at the end of her emotional rope. Alexis seemed to have her emotions under better control. Her sad eyes alone managed the burden of her predicament. Alexis stood beside her mother-in-law's chair in her black linen pants with a silk blouse and matching linen jacket. Her long brown hair which possessed golden accents glistened under the Miami sunlight filtering in through the windows. Her tropical complexion and luscious lips, the type that make men immediately think about a particular sex act, initially flustered Pierce.

Alexis took a deep breath and let it out slowly as she fell into her thoughts.

"My, husband, Juan Carlos was arrested three days ago but he wasn't allowed to make a telephone call until yesterday. They would only let him talk for a couple of minutes. He talked so fast," she continued. "Juan Carlos tried to convince me that he was all right, but I could tell that he was scared."

Pierce thought about the fact that it took three days before Juan Carlos had been given telephone privileges as he tapped his finger on the table. "That's very unusual."

Alexis stiffened, her mouth tightening as if trying to suppress a horrible secret. Finally, something inside her broke and the words, "Juan Carlos was arrested for drug trafficking," poured out.

Pierce gave her a skeptical look. "That shouldn't matter. Seventy percent of Americans arrested in foreign countries get arrested on trafficking and possession charges," he said.

When Alexis was finished, Pierce didn't ask any questions. He moved headlong into what he thought needed to be done.

"We have a small window here, so I'm not going to sugar coat this for you. From what Jordan told me, Juan Carlos is facing very serious charges. The extradition hearing is not going to determine Juan Carlos's guilt or innocence. The panel only determines whether the country requesting Juan Carlos's extradition has presented sufficient evidence to justify a trial . . . However, I'm going to need to retain the services of a criminal attorney on Curacao." Pierce's voice was laced with concern. "This is going to get expensive. Since you're Jordan's family, I'll speak to my firm about waiving my fees but . . ."

"Please hire the very best criminal attorney on the island you can to work with you," Laura Maria interrupted. "And you don't have to waive or reduce your fee. We are willing to pay your full rate. Just, please help us," Laura Maria pleaded.

Pierce nodded. "I'll clear my schedule for tomorrow and start rattling some cages."

Laura Maria and Alexis shared a look. "Is there any way we can find out how Juan Carlos is doing?" Alexis asked.

Pierce looked at her slowly and sympathetically and smiled. His blue eyes lit when he smiled. "I will notify the State Department and request that the U.S. Embassy send someone to visit Juan Carlos as soon as possible."

Alexis forced a smile. "Thank you." Her voice flat from hours of crying.

"This whole thing is madness," Laura Maria blurted out in a fit of tears.

Alexis shot Laura Maria a disapproving look.

Pierce pretended not to notice.

"I can't imagine how hard this has to be on each of you. But I need both of you to understand that in light of the charges getting Juan Carlos back home is going to take some time."

A startled expression flashed across Laura Maria's face. She forced herself to take a series of deep breaths before asking, "How long will my son have to suffer in jail?"

Pierce shook his head. "Getting Juan Carlos released on a bond is not a realistic option. The extradition hearing will be our first opportunity to get him out. I'll go to Curacao and visit him and begin to gather whatever evidence and information I can to prepare for the hearing," he continued, his voice now had a determined edge.

Pierce could feel Laura Maria's anxious gaze." Please, go home and relax. I promise as soon as I have some information, I will call you."

Laura Maria nodded. "I just wish I knew that he was okay," she said numbly. Pierce looked at Laura Maria and regarded her for a moment. "I have a back channel I can use to get Mr. Laporte some telephone privileges so that both of you can speak with him."

"Thank you," Laura Maria blinked in a choked voice. Pierce could almost feel the desperation and horror that was grinding away at her very last nerve. When Laura Maria stretched up to kiss Pierce's cheek, the top of her carefully coiffed blonde hair tickled his chin. Laura Maria clung to every reassuring word that Pierce offered. Alexis being more reserved offered Pierce her hand and once again thanked him for his help. Pierce took her hand, momentarily spellbound by her watery gaze.

"How could I say no?" Pierce thought. After all, the unfortunate soul sitting in jail also happened to be his ex-wife's cousin. Pierce learned the hard way that marrying into a Cuban family was like being inducted into the Mafia, once you're in, you were in for life.

Chapter Two

BON FUTURO PRISON, CURACAO

Juan Carlos sat on the floor flush against the dark stone wall of his prison cell with his chin resting on his chest and head down between his knees. There was very little natural light filtering in through the small rectangular shaped window. The poor ventilation together with his permeating body odor made breathing an unavoidable burden. The sweltering cell made him feel like he was slowly roasting in a brick oven. Juan Carlos could feel the sweat running down every part of him as he tried to steer his thoughts away from the insufferable heat and his predicament. He thought about Alexis and his family, fantasizing about the time when he would be reunited with them. He had not spent much time with them over the course of the past couple of years. He would see Alexis and the rest of his family about once a month when he was passing through Miami. His business commitments made it impractical for Alexis to live with him in Saint Maarten. At least that was what Juan Carlos told her.

"Get up! You have a visitor," the prison guard yelled at Juan Carlos in a heavy Dutch accent. Without delay, Juan Carlos abruptly lifted himself out of his daydream and up off the scorching floor. His clothes drenched in sweat and covered in grime, Juan Carlos nervously stood in front of the open prison cell door waiting for the guard to tell him he could exit the cell. He had received a well-placed kick to his groin the first time he attempted to step through the cell door without first receiving permission to do so. Juan Carlos was a quick learner; for him, all it took was one lesson. He figured that by being white as well as American, it wouldn't take much provocation for the prison guards to beat him senseless. He also assumed that, if it wasn't for his rumored association to the Carraboca drug cartel, he would have been beaten more severely and frequently than he had been.

Juan Carlos was escorted to an interrogation room where a tall thin man whom Juan Carlos estimated to be in his early fifties was waiting. The man reached out and handed Juan Carlos his card. At first, Juan Carlos assumed that he was someone sent by the cartel. That is, until he read the card.

Lloyd Hogan – Special Agent in Charge
Caribbean Division
United States Drug Enforcement Administration

Juan Carlos placed the card in his shirt pocket. He was intrigued. Hogan sat awkwardly in the metal frame chair which was ill equipped to comfortably handle his six-foot seven-inch frame.

Hogan looked at Juan Carlos closely. "Mr. Laporte, I want you to know that I am not here in any official capacity other than to check in on your well-being."

"Not here officially?" Juan Carlos repeated under his breath.

Juan Carlos sat quietly. His eyes swept over Hogan like a searchlight looking for any irregularity, a nervous mannerism that would betray him. But Agent Hogan was unreadable.

Juan Carlos sucked in a breath. "So, Lloyd, let's skip the foreplay. Why would the DEA be interested in my well-being?" Juan Carlos pulled out Hogan's business card and stared at it as if it held the answer. "So, why are you really here?"

Hogan stared at Juan Carlos and frowned. "Mr. Laporte, you are an American citizen being held in a Dutch prison, and the French government has requested your extradition," he began.

"And why would any of that be of interest to the DEA? Are you working with the French?" Juan Carlos interrupted.

Hogan dismissed the notion with the back of his hand. "Small potatoes," he smiled. "The French police want you for conspiring to smuggle one hundred fifty pounds of methamphetamine with the intent to distribute on French soil. If they get their way, you will either rot away in a French prison on Guadeloupe or end up on the wrong end of a knife after you get there. It wouldn't make much difference to them." His smile didn't waver.

Juan Carlos gave Hogan a measured look. "And you. What do you want?" Juan Carlos asked already knowing the answer to his question."

Hogan stared at Juan Carlos and shrugged as if to say it wasn't worth acknowledging the obvious. "The same things you want," he replied.

Juan Carlos frowned at Hogan's answer. It was a cryptic response, and Juan Carlos was in no mood for cryptic.

There was almost an imperceptible pause and then Hogan said, "Right now, in here, you have to know that you are living on borrowed time."

Juan Carlos's face remained neutral. He adopted a relaxed posture that spoke of boredom despite the fact that he was irritated by Hogan's ability to accurately size up his situation.

Hogan locked eyes with Juan Carlos to make sure there would be no misunderstanding. "We can offer you a way out of this shit-storm you're in," he said.

Juan Carlos leaned forward, "I'm familiar with your offers," he said in a cynical voice. "I'd be trading one set of problems for a whole different kind. No, thank you."

"What about your family. Do they have any idea what kind of danger you put them in?" Hogan asked with an arched brow.

Juan Carlos didn't like the predicament he had put his family in. In a moment of greed and personal weakness, he had made them targets of the cartel. Juan Carlos could not mask the look of deep concern on his face. "They're only in danger if I agree to cooperate."

Hogan gave a slight nod as if Juan Carlos's answer was fine with him. "You know better than most what the cartel does to family members of those that betray them."

"I did no such thing," Juan Carlos snapped defensively.

"You got yourself arrested cutting a side drug deal. I don't think that is going to sit well with Dario Carraboca," Hogan scoffed.

Juan Carlos sat quietly, mentally running through the possible scenarios.

"When Dario tortures your family, their deaths will be on your head."

Hogan stopped talking letting the words hang in the air comfortably as he placed three photographs on the table. They were black and white surveillance photos of Juan Carlos's parents and Alexis.

"These pics were taken by someone working a freelance op that my men picked up."

Juan Carlos looked at the pictures. They appeared to unsettle as well as irritate him, which was just fine with Hogan.

"How do I know that your men didn't take these?"

"You don't. But you know better than anyone how the cartel works."

Juan Carlos felt a twist in his gut. He crossed his arms over his chest and leaned back in his chair.

"Okay, I'll bite. What are you offering me?" He glared at Hogan.

Hogan shook his head. "You have this backwards. You need to make me an offer if you want to keep your family safe."

Juan Carlos lowered his eyes to the pictures again. “I don’t know,” he shook his head nervously.” What you’re wanting me to do . . .”

“Is cooperate with the United States Drug Enforcement Agency before the Cartel kills you and your family,” Hogan cut him off.”

Juan Carlos mulled Hogan’s comment over.

“We need everything on the Carraboca Drug cartel’s smuggling and money laundering operations,” Hogan insisted.

Juan Carlos buried his face in his hands and shook his head. “I need time to think,” he said with some difficulty.

Hogan checked his watch. “You have twenty-four hours . . . after that we will have you moved to the general prison population.”

Juan Carlos looked up surprised, his lips parting slightly as if it had never occurred to him who had been responsible for keeping him in solitary confinement.

“Yes,” Hogan nodded. “As you can see, we are already looking out for you. You are in your own prison cell as an accommodation to the U.S. government. However, if you decide not to cooperate, we would have no reason to use up our political capital on you,” Hogan frowned.

Juan Carlos looked at Hogan, opened his mouth as if he intended to say something, then he seemed to think better of it.

Reaching into his leather valise, Hogan pulled out a manila envelope.

“This envelope contains letters that were written to you by your wife and mother. From what I know about the mail system in here, it would take several weeks before their letters would get to you,” he said as he slid the envelope across the table towards Juan Carlos. Hogan reached into his bag one more time. This time he pulled out some blank writing paper and handed it to him.

Juan Carlos grabbed the pieces of paper without thinking. Then he stopped himself in mid-thought and said, "I've only been in here a few days. How did my family know to get in touch with you so quickly?"

"Don't look a gift horse in the mouth."

Juan Carlos thought about it for a moment and then said, "Really Agent Hogan, I would like to know who put this together so quickly?"

Hogan sighed heavily, "You have a very persistent lawyer. I'll leave it at that."

Juan Carlos was baffled. "My family doesn't have a lawyer."

"Believe what you like," Hogan said with a shrug. "If you decide not to cooperate, you may want to say your good-byes. I'll see to it that your family gets them." Hogan looked like he took a perverse pleasure in pointing out to Juan Carlos that he was out of time and out of options.

"You've already made your point," Juan Carlos said with a tone of open contempt and then continued to focus on the contents of the letters. He read his mother's letter first. She wrote of the family's pain and frustration. She also told him that Alexis was working closely with a lawyer named Pierce Evangelista to help fight his extradition and obtain his release. Juan Carlos found it curious that, in light of all the praise his mother imparted to Pierce for his effort, never once did Alexis mention him.

When Juan Carlos finished replying to the two letters, he folded them and handed them to Hogan. Hogan's knees let out a cracking sound as he raised himself up from the small metal chair.

"You have twenty-three hours. You can reach me on the number on the card," he said.

Hogan stood a long moment and then shrugged as if it was a small thing. "The prison population here in Bon Futuro prison is sexually active and it has the highest transmission rate of HIV/AIDS of any prison in the Caribbean; just a friendly warning should you find yourself in the general prison population."

Juan Carlos shook his head and made a sour face. "I would like to see a doctor. I have been urinating blood for the last two days and I can't get any medical attention," he said anxiously.

Hogan didn't turn around. He simply remarked that he would speak with the prison officials on his way out and arrange for Juan Carlos to be seen by the doctor. Special Agent Hogan opened the door and closed it behind him before Juan Carlos could ask for anything else.

* * *

About twenty minutes passed before a prison guard finally came by to retrieve Juan Carlos. He used the time to put away the money squirreled away in his mother's letter. Juan Carlos realized that the news of Agent Hogan's visit would soon filter down to the general prison population. He could become a target for every ambitious prisoner and prison guard wanting to gain favor with the Carrabocas if he didn't make his peace with Dario. He also knew that Hogan would not be able to protect him as long as he remained in that prison. In the past, Juan Carlos had always proven himself to Dario to be very valuable and resourceful. Juan Carlos's only chance of surviving was to convince Dario Carraboca that he was still worth more to him alive. If Dario Carraboca wanted him dead, there would be no amount of money or drugs which Juan Carlos could use to bribe the guards. There was little doubt in Juan Carlos's mind that in order for him to have any chance of working a deal with Hogan he would have to move quickly and contact the cartel before they decided to eliminate him.

Just before the prison guard locked the cell door Juan Carlos flashed a one-hundred-dollar bill.

"There's a telephone number on this bill. Dial it and ask to speak with Rene. Tell him that I need to see him tomorrow. We will need some privacy. Do that and there will be four more bills like this one," Juan Carlos said, his voice was edgy.

The prison guard eyed him suspiciously before slipping the hundred-dollar bill into his shirt pocket.

"All right, I'll make the call and see to the arrangements. But there better be four hundred dollars for me by tomorrow whether or not your friend comes," he jabbed a finger toward him.

Chapter Three

VENEZUELA

The cool midsummer night wind sweeping off the Andean mountains ambled throughout Dario Carraboca's highland retreat. He liked to go there with some of his most trusted advisors whenever he had to sort out some of his more difficult problems. It was quiet there. The distractions were few. The piazza overlooking the Andean mountains was lavishly decorated. The polished Italian marble floors provided an exquisite backdrop to the rich Persian and Oriental rugs which were decoratively scattered. Dario watched the grey smoke from his Cuban cigar hover and disappear into the crisp mountain air. He brought the cigar up to his thin lips and inhaled deeply filling his lungs with the essence of rich Cuban tobacco. He was a man in his late sixties, but his small frame and dark hair graying only at the temples made him seem much younger. Dario's keen intellect was only equaled by his ruthlessness. He was a man that expected nothing less than absolute loyalty. Betrayal was dealt with harshly and swiftly. His dilemma, however, went beyond a simple error in judgment motivated by greed. Juan Carlos's mistake and present predicament could have grave consequences for the cartel and its business partners if it was not handled correctly. Dario deduced that the Americans, and even the Venezuelans, were watching him closely, expecting him to make a move. But Dario never did what people expected. He was unpredictable, shrewd and disciplined. He was widely regarded as a visionary, a despot and a modern-day assassin all rolled into one man by allies and enemies alike. When Dario moved, he did so decisively with no hesitation, but by no means impulsively or out of vengeance. Unlike his advisors who place little value on human life, Dario put a high value on it. The threat of killing someone's family or torturing them until they begged to be killed was much more effective than putting a bullet in an informant's head. Once a man was taken into custody, he could be convinced that he would be protected if he talked. However, even so, most would not cooperate if they thought their family members were at risk. His reputation of having gang raped a man's wife until she slipped into a coma or arranging for a video tape to mysteriously show up on the doorstep of a secret government safe house that showed the informant's mother and father being brutally sodomized by a large sharp instrument before cutting off their heads proved to be powerful deterrents. Fear was the only thing that kept people loyal in their business.

Dario didn't feel the immediate need to take preemptive action other than to gather intelligence. He didn't disagree with his advisors who believed that if the DEA got their hands on Juan Carlos, he would talk and divulge secrets. His advisors were all men he trusted. Men who stood beside him when he dared to smuggle drugs under the radar and giant shadow cast by the Colombian drug cartels. Together they built a formidable and sophisticated operation. When the DEA pressured General Noriega and the Panamanian banks to give the United States control of the Colombian cartels' bank accounts, the DEA froze most of their assets. The Colombian's operations suffered, and the Carraboca Drug Cartel seized that opportunity to morph into a major drug supplier. Juan Carlos was one of Dario's principal advisors in structuring and overseeing the cartel's money laundering operation and investments. Dario was keenly aware that if the DEA was successful in coaxing out of Juan Carlos what he knew, the Carraboca Drug Cartel could share a similar fate as the Colombians.

"Why not just kill him and get it over with?" Hector Espinosa, one of Dario's advisors asked impatiently. "That is the only way you can be sure that Juan Carlos will not tell them anything."

Instinctively, Dario liked the simplicity. If the Americans got Juan Carlos, he would eventually talk, just like everyone did, and then their exposure would be horrible. "If it was only that simple," Dario smiled politely. "If we kill Juan Carlos, we wouldn't know what information about our operations he may have already given the Americans until it was too late." Dario sat in rigid silence listening to and watching the heated debate between his most trusted advisors.

When he had heard enough, a simple hand gesture was enough to tell everyone in the room to stop talking and listen. "Killing Juan Carlos without knowing if he talked accomplishes nothing and unnecessarily exposes us."

Hector ignored the point and said, "If we kill him, we cut our losses."

"Do we?" Dario looked uncharacteristically grim. "Killing him now without knowing what he told the Americans is impulsive and is nothing more than an act of vengeance."

"All of you play chess," Dario looked around the room. "Tell me, when is it wise to sacrifice a valuable piece?" Dario paused as he rolled the cigar between his fingers.

"You sacrifice it when you are reasonably assured that the concession will yield a decisive advantage," he said, making eye contact with each man.

Manuel Trujillo, the cartel's liaison to the Mexican drug cartels rose quickly to his feet. "The DEA will try enticing him. When that doesn't work, they will threaten him. Juan Carlos is a game changer for the DEA. We all know that they will do whatever is necessary. They'll torture Juan Carlos until they break him, and he gives them what they want. If we kill him now, we put an end to that threat. We all know that a dead man doesn't talk," he let out a small laugh.

Dario's eyes locked on Manuel's with an all-knowing stare. "But you forget that he has already met with the DEA. We need to know if Juan Carlos told them anything."

Manuel gave an exaggerated sigh. "It was only one meeting. Remember who we are talking about. This is not a soldier or even a mid-level member of our organization," Dario said with an undertone of distaste in his voice. Dario hesitated as if he was trying to find the most delicate way to say something that was brutally indelicate. "If it was any of you, I wouldn't hesitate to kill you. But this is Juan Carlos, a man who has every detail of our smuggling and money laundering operations at his fingertips. Every detail! One meeting is all it could take to expose our operations," Dario stressed.

"All the more reason to act now," Arsenio Mendoza, a portly man who was renowned for his frankness and penchant for openly disagreeing with Dario scowled.

"Juan Carlos is too valuable to the DEA for them to let him slip through their hands."

Dario sat quietly for a few seconds and then nodded. "After a little feigned objection and resistance to their overtures, Juan Carlos will reluctantly agree to cooperate with the DEA. Only, we will control what he tells them to make sure that nothing he divulges poses any real threat to our operations."

Dario's eyes met Arsenio's. "That is the smarter move."

A rustle of exchanges broke out between Dario's advisors as they debated the merits and rattled each other with questions. Dario emphasized that Juan Carlos could be a useful decoy.

"That will give us the time we need to make some adjustments to our operations."

"And what about Juan Carlos?" Arsenio moaned. How can we be sure that he can be trusted?" He asked unrepentantly.

Dario's still face betrayed only a hint of his growing impatience. "No one can be completely trusted," Dario said in a deliberate tone and fixed his eyes on a man who was standing quietly in a corner.

"That is precisely why Juan Carlos must be convinced that we are doing the groundwork necessary to free him, but he must first fix the problem he created for us. He brought the Americans to our doorstep. Now he must lead them far away."

Arsenio threw up his hands. "Juan Carlos knows how you deal with disloyalty. He will never believe that you have miraculously decided to forgive him."

Dario stared down Arsenio. "That is precisely the reason why he must believe that I do not see his arrest as an act of disloyalty but rather a foolish mistake."

Arsenio made a faint sound of disgust. "Juan Carlos came into our inner circle as an outsider. He now poses a real threat to our operation, and you wish to show him more leniency than you would give any one of us . . . He needs to be eliminated now. We need to act decisively, or we are putting our entire operation at risk."

Those in the room silently exchanged looks.

Dario stayed calm, but there was something unmistakably ominous just beneath the surface. "We are acting decisively. We have an opportunity to disrupt the American's investigation and deal them a significant setback. Killing Juan Carlos only satisfies your desire for blood. The man plots on more levels than any of you are capable of comprehending and will do what he has to, to stay alive. Juan Carlos will cooperate if he believes that he can make things right with us by doing this."

Dario turned his attention to the man standing in the corner and gestured to him to join them.

"Rene, you are one of Juan Carlos's closest friends. You will deliver the message containing our offer to Juan Carlos personally," Dario paused reflectively. "He trusts you. You must be perfectly clear that by doing this Juan Carlos will not completely clean the slate. But it will be a step towards making restitution. Let him know that the information that he is to provide the DEA will be delivered to him by one of our people."

Rene started to mention that a prison guard on Juan Carlos's behalf had contacted him, but before he could finish the thought, Dario handed him a note. "Rene you are not to leave until you have an answer." Dario fixed Rene with an adamant stare. His message was clear.

Rene nodded indicating that he understood. He did not say another word about the phone call.

"There is a plane waiting to take you to Curacao," Dario told him.

Rene was the perfect messenger. While he was one of Dario's most lethal assassins, he was also one of Juan Carlos's closest friends. By sending Rene, Dario hoped that Juan Carlos would perceive his offer as genuine. He was aware that sending Rene could be a risk. Juan Carlos could view Rene as nothing more than a smoke screen. However, Juan Carlos was smart enough to know that if Dario wanted him dead, there would be no need for pretense. He would simply order Rene to kill him, and it would be done.

Dario and his advisors took a temporary recess from discussing business matters to allow a woman carrying a large silver tray to enter the veranda where the men were seated. She poured a measured amount of cognac into a crystal glass and handed it to Dario. She waited patiently for Dario to sample the cognac and gesture to her to serve the others.

Dario reflected on the plan while he continued to sip his cognac. The warm feeling of the cognac which he felt as it eased its way down his throat was a nice contrast to the mountain chill.

Arsenio's sour face told Dario that he was still skeptical about his plan. Juan Carlos knew too much about the cartel's operation and Arsenio made it clear to anyone who would listen that he didn't trust Juan Carlos, he never had. If the cartel killed him, the problem would be contained, and they would deal with whatever mess he left them.

"I think you're taking an unnecessary risk Dario. It would be smarter to kill Juan Carlos. He has already breached our trust," Arsenio persisted. He squared his shoulders and looked at Dario solemnly. "There is no reason to believe that he will not do so again. Why would you take such a chance?"

Dario's eyes gleamed like razors. His gaze seemed to cut away at Arsenio's resolve stripping him down to the bone. But instead of losing his temper, Dario smiled. In some ways his smile was as unnerving as his wrath. "One of the reasons we have succeeded where others before us have failed is because we're neither predictable nor do we shy away from taking calculated risks. What do we gain by killing Juan Carlos now?" Dario asked and then he exhaled. "I'll tell you; we gain nothing."

Arsenio shifted uncomfortably in his chair. He did not appear to relish challenging Dario, but when it came to matters that concerned Juan Carlos, he was not bashful about accusing Dario of having a blind spot.

"I know Juan Carlos is smart, but he's also reckless. In some strange God forsaken way Juan Carlos reminds you of you thirty years ago. But you were never a greedy, selfish little prick. Juan Carlos got involved in a street drug deal for a lousy three million dollars with no thought to what would happen if he got arrested."

Arsenio ran through a list of other transgressions that Juan Carlos got away with over the years.

Dario noticed a brief exchange of looks between his advisors.

"Only by killing him now, can we be assured that he will not testify against any of us," Arsenio said in an almost pleading voice.

Dario let out a tired sigh. It was his way of releasing pressure so that he didn't blow. "I don't cut my losses."

Arsenio tried to respond, but Dario shut him down with an open palm. "If Juan Carlos provides the Americans with false information, we will turn this situation into something positive." Something in Dario's voice told his advisors that he was no longer willing to consider a different opinion.

Arsenio shrugged. "And if we can't convince him?"

Dario pounded his fist against the small mahogany end table next to his chair. "We will!"

Dario rose to his feet and walked slowly towards the fireplace. He stood still for a moment, a dominant silhouette in the dim light of the fire. Although he didn't show it, he was angry with himself. He realized that when it concerned Juan Carlos, he did play favorites. When Juan Carlos was in his early twenties, Dario saw firsthand that he had a real aptitude for moving money so efficiently and elegantly that it stayed under the DEA's radar. In the drug smuggling business, it was much easier to smuggle drugs than to launder the profits. The amount of manpower and high-tech surveillance equipment required to monitor potential smuggling routes made finding alternative channels for moving drugs possible. However, the DEA could track bank transactions and the movement of money anywhere in the world with a couple of financial analysts from their offices in Washington. The cartel succeeded in developing a system for laundering their profits that escaped the DEA's detection and Dario had to protect it. Juan Carlos's skill set was rare and undeniable. He had a long list of talents which was why up until this last transgression Dario had been willing to overlook his short but potent list of faults.

When Dario addressed his advisors, his words echoed in finality.

"Juan Carlos has nothing to gain and everything to lose if he refuses us. He is a flawed man but not a stupid one. He knows that the Americans cannot protect his family. His only way out is to do what we tell him. The Americans expect us to kidnap Juan Carlos's family and hold them hostage. We will keep a close watch on his family and let the Americans see us doing it. That will only serve to further reinforce in their minds that our intentions are to keep Juan Carlos from cooperating. If Juan Carlos plays his role well, the DEA will have no reason to question what he tells them."

Dario's voice took on a brooding tone. "And then when the time is right, we will kill Juan Carlos."

Chapter Four

CURACAO

The blazing sun began to settle into the deep blue waters of the Caribbean by the time the twin engine plane carrying Rene touched down in Curacao. Rene checked himself into a modest hotel. It was off season, so the place was not busy. In the dining room, Rene ordered a light supper and washed it down with two beers. He decided against going for a late-night stroll, thinking that it would be wise if he kept a low profile. Rene opened the window to his hotel room to let in the evening breeze while surveying the street below for signs of anyone lurking that could be watching him. There was nothing unusual which he took as a good omen. Rene was intrigued by Dario's willingness to give Juan Carlos another chance. When someone doesn't follow orders to the letter or wanders off the reservation, Dario puts a bullet in his head. Rene lay in bed a long time trying to imagine how his meeting with Juan Carlos would go. He did not let his mind wander down any path where Juan Carlos refused Dario's offer, although that was a remote possibility. He couldn't help but wonder as he lay stretched out under a ceiling fan thrusting warm air down onto him, what could be going through Juan Carlos's mind. The man, as long as Rene knew him, was always plotting. If given the choice of earning a fortune honestly or stealing it from someone, Rene was convinced Juan Carlos would prefer to steal it. After about an hour, he finally began to drift off to the faint music of an old accordion and the myriad of voices of people engaged in conversation and frivolity on the cobblestone streets below.

Rene awakened the next morning to the shimmering sound of the rain as it danced across the corrugated rooftops. As he went through the motions of his morning routine, he couldn't completely ignore the thought hovering in the back of his mind that in a couple of hours, depending on how things unfolded, he might have to kill a good friend. However, if all went as he dared to hope for, he could be back in Venezuela in time for a late supper. Given Dario's history of brutality, Rene would not blame Juan Carlos if he had misgivings about the offer. However, if Juan Carlos refused, Rene would rather cut his best friend's throat than have to face Dario with bad news.

* * *

The road leading up to the prison was poorly paved. As Rene drove closer to the prison, the asphalt road turned into a dirt road, and for no apparent reason ceased to be a road altogether about fifty feet short of the prison entrance. Several tall cacti, thorny shrubs, rusty cans and bottles were strewn along the perimeter of a fence. Behind the fence was a wooden lookout tower in bad need of repair. It looked like it had been hastily propped up after the last one had been knocked down, perhaps by a hurricane or maybe a prison riot. There was a second tall barbed wire fence, and behind it was a series of yellow cement buildings that appeared to surround an internal courtyard. It was brown and dirty and dead. Rene waited about an hour beyond his appointed time before a prison officer in a voice devoid of any interest called his name and led him down a long corridor to a small room. There were two small wooden chairs separated by a small table. Thirty minutes later Juan Carlos walked through the doorway. He stood statuelike staring at Rene, barely breathing waiting to see Rene's reaction.

* * *

RENE SMILED RESERVEDLY at Juan Carlos and extended his hand to shake hands when it was abruptly brushed back by the prison guard.

"No touching," the guard ordered, his English tainted by a heavy Dutch accent.

Rene glared at the guard and reached into his pocket and handed him an envelope containing $2,500.

The guard's eyes widened.

Then Rene glared at him. "All you have to do for this is give us privacy. I assume you know who I work for. Are we going to have a problem or are we good?"

The guard nodded. "No problem."

"Now, please wait outside."

The guard shook his head and took a step towards the door.

"We'll let you know when we're done," Rene replied in a forceful tone.

They listened for the clicking sound of the door's bolt as it shifted into the latch. Juan Carlos wanted to tell Rene how good it was to see his old friend. But he sensed from Rene's stoic demeanor that he preferred to have the social pleasantries wait until after they had concluded their business. A moment of silence passed between them before Rene reached into his shirt pocket and slid Dario's note across the table. He watched Juan Carlos's eyes move from side to side as he absorbed the information. Juan Carlos could feel Rene's eyes on him, looking for any reaction no matter how small or seemingly insignificant for a clue as to what he might be thinking. He continued to read the note slowly and deliberately, all the while trying to deduce Dario's reasoning for keeping him alive. Rene spoke to Juan Carlos about unimportant matters while he read, just in case someone was listening. When Juan Carlos finished reading the letter, he folded it in half and smiled; not because he was relieved that Dario had no intention of killing him. He was still not convinced that he wouldn't wind up being stuffed into five-inch cylindrical cans and sold as cat food. He smiled at the hopelessness of his situation. Juan Carlos knew that he could not refuse Dario's offer. If he did, Rene would give the guards and inmates something to talk about by carving out several of his organs and leaving them laid out in the room for them to find.

* * *

Juan Carlos was no fool. He also knew that despite Agent Hogan's assurances, the Americans could only provide limited protection. After all, he was in a Dutch prison awaiting extradition. Despite being locked away from the general prison population, he was an easy target for Dario Carraboca. Sliding the note back, Juan Carlos shrugged his shoulders in a non-committal way.

"How's Alexis?" he asked.

Rene's eyes narrowed, and he looked at Juan Carlos disapprovingly. "Dario doesn't have her, if that's your question. He expects you to make things right without having to hurt your family."

Juan Carlos wondered out loud. "Why show me any clemency?"

Rene glanced down at the folded paper. "I'm an assassin. It's not my place to ask questions. I'm not into "whys." I leave that to Dario and people like you. The point to all this is you get a second chance."

"Of course," Juan Carlos nodded. "Please tell Dario I will do whatever he wants."

Rene looked relieved. "I'm glad to hear that. If you do what Dario asks, you should be fine."

Rene looked around the room for a moment before his eyes bored into him. "So, what the fuck were you thinking getting pinched?"

Juan Carlos let out an exasperated breath. "I didn't do shit. This small-time drug dealer, a fucking amateur, brings me three million dollars stuffed in a duffel bag and asks if I can set him up with a steady supply of meth. So, I took the money."

Rene's face darkened. "And that didn't look even a little suspicious to you?" He asked with a hint of sarcasm.

Juan Carlos shrugged. He didn't want to hear it. But Rene was not someone you told to shut up unless you were Dario.

Rene shook his head letting Juan Carlos know that he was extremely disappointed. "You already have millions why do something so stupid?"

Juan Carlos stared imploringly at him. "They got nothing. No drugs, nothing connecting me to drug trafficking. Nothing recorded . . ."

Rene cut him off. "They got you . . . hermano. And that's not nothing." Rene shook his head a second time. "For someone so fucking smart, how could you be so stupid?"

A look of intense regret flashed across Juan Carlos's face. "I was greedy. I figured three million in cash . . . I know I was careless."

"Even if it was a legit deal, they would have expected a delivery. You weren't going to walk away with the money without making good on the . . ."

"That wouldn't have been difficult to pull off," Juan Carlos interrupted.

"Difficult probably not," Rene said. "But stupid."

Rene met his look with a cool level stare. "Most in Dario's circle want you dead."

"I'm sorry."

With an icy voice Rene said, "You don't have to apologize to me. I'm just a soldier. If Dario gives me the order, it won't matter how I feel about you. I'll do my job."

Juan Carlos shot Rene an impatient look. "I will fix this."

Rene said nothing. He just stared at Juan Carlos with a look of stupefaction and anger.

"You're a banker not a dealer. You move the cartel's money around. You're not supposed to get your hands dirty," Rene's tone hardened.

"It's a bad situation. I know, but I will make things right." When Juan Carlos looked at Rene all he saw was a lifeless face staring blankly at him.

"Do exactly what Dario wants. Don't analyze it or improvise. Do what he asks no more or no less," Rene grunted. "If you don't, I will come back."

Juan Carlos understood Rene's meaning. "I will," he nodded. "But I'll need the information Dario wants me to give the DEA soon. The DEA Agent," Juan Carlos said referring to Agent Hogan "is a pushy bastard. If I don't tell him something soon, they'll move me into the general prison population."

"I'll let Dario know," Rene said.

"Does this conclude our business?" Juan Carlos asked, looking to move on to another subject.

Rene shook his head. "It does."

"I need you to arrange to get me a few things while I'm in here," Juan Carlos told Rene.

Rene eyed him strangely.

"I need some money and some good food, like a couple of steaks and fresh fish. Get me a bottle of Grey Goose Vodka and some fucking Cohiba Cuban cigars," Juan Carlos said.

Rene made a face. "This is prison motherfucker not the Ritz Carlton."

Juan Carlos's eyes brightened. He found himself suddenly smiling. "Speaking of the Ritz, what was that Russian bitch's name? The tall one she had to be over six feet tall."

"You mean the one that works for you?"

"She works for me?"

"She's a hostess at your club in Miami."

Juan Carlos's mind was drawing a blank. "What was her name?" he said under his breath. "Well you know where I'm heading . . . I want you to arrange a conjugal visit for me."

Rene cocked his head and gave Juan Carlos a long look. They were in prison discussing how he could avoid being killed by the cartel and all Juan Carlos wanted to talk about was finding a way to get laid.

Rene didn't answer.

"What is it?" Juan Carlos asked. He could tell by the look on Rene's face that something was bothering him.

"I know what I have to do. And I'll handle it," Juan Carlos assured him. "But in the meantime, I want a good looking blonde. If that is too difficult, as long as she has a nice ass, I will make do," Juan Carlos said with a fleeting look of satisfaction.

"How much money do you need?" Rene asked.

"Ten thousand should be enough to pay off the guards whenever I need them to do something for me."

"I'll make the arrangement for the money today. The woman might take a little time," Rene said.

Juan Carlos shrugged, "That's fine."

Rene stood up to leave.

"I want you to do one more thing for me," Juan Carlos said. "I need you to look into a lawyer."

Juan Carlos explained that his family hired an attorney in Miami to represent him in his extradition hearing. He told Rene that he didn't know anything about him and was concerned if he was qualified to represent him. Juan Carlos insisted on knowing everything about Pierce.

"I want to know who he represents; who he does business with; who his friends are; if he's married or seeing someone and what he looks like."

Rene gave Juan Carlos a dubious look.

"Why do you need to know anything about his personal life? Why does it matter what he looks like?"

Juan Carlos's jaw tightened. "It doesn't but you know that I am a stickler for details."

Rene gave him a knowing grin. "Fine, I'll let you know what I find out."

Juan Carlos took hold of Rene's hand and gripped it firmly. He wanted to hug him, but he could tell that Rene wasn't ready to forgive him until he made things right with Dario.

"Rene," Juan Carlos asked, "What do you want me to do if the DEA comes back before our people get me the information that I'm supposed to deliver to the DEA?"

Rene shook his head and said, "If that happens, then you'll have to stall them until we're ready."

When Rene rapped on the door signaling to the guard that he was ready to leave, Juan Carlos cleared his throat and said, "Tell Dario I'm sorry."

Juan Carlos was cognizant of the fact that Rene was not only there to get an answer but to gauge his attitude towards the cartel's offer and report back. So, he made sure that the face he put on for Rene in no way jibed with his thoughts. Dario's offer gave Juan Carlos time and at the moment that was as precious to him as air. Time was his greatest ally in working his way out of his situation. The food, cigars and the vodka would also help. They would provide Juan Carlos with a taste of civilization that would help calm his nerves and let him sleep. If Juan Carlos couldn't get some rest, he would make mistakes. Mistakes were not something he could afford to make the next few days. He thought again about his conversation with Hogan. He was ready to play the DEA against the cartel. He needed to be smart and methodical. And he needed to appear to each side that he was genuine and cooperating. Twenty-one hours after their initial meeting, Lloyd Hogan received a telephone call from Juan Carlos.

"I'm ready to talk," he said.

Chapter Five

MIAMI

The sky had not yet begun to pale when the alarm clock sounded. Pierce rolled to his right and out of bed in one fluid motion. He always jumped out of bed quickly knowing that if he even thought about it for a second, he would come up with at least a half a dozen excuses why he should skip his workout and sleep in. He lifted the pair of workout sweats he laid out on top of the dresser the night before and got ready to head out. It was almost five thirty in the morning when he pulled into the empty parking lot just in front of the gym's entrance. He waited by his car for Shane Hamilton who parked next to him a few minutes later.

Shane was Pierce's closest friend dating back to their days at Harvard. There was no middle ground for Shane in law or in life. He was a lawyer who took no prisoners in the courtroom. His specialty was defending white collar criminals such as bank executives and brokers from allegations of bank and securities fraud, embezzlement and Ponzi schemes and his scorched-earth approach to practicing law was more of a by-product of his hatred for losing than his desire to win. Still in his thirties, Shane's star was continuing to rise and his reputation as a persistent stone in the shoe of the Department of Justice was well deserved. Even in sweatpants there was an air of confidence about Shane that commanded respect.

After giving Pierce the once-over, Shane jumped right into the subject that Pierce knew was on his mind. "So how deep of a hole is this Juan Carlos guy in?"

Pierce's mouth quirked at the corner, Shane was never one for small talk or wasting time.

"It's difficult to say. The evidence I've seen so far is pretty circumstantial . . . but it may still be enough for the Dutch to extradite him," he said.

Pierce explained that the French police's investigation had no hard evidence. Their undercover detectives tried to set up meetings with Juan Carlos to discuss the details of the drug deal, but he was always a "no-show."

"So far, all I've seen are two sworn affidavits that say that Juan Carlos took three million dollars in exchange for promising to deliver one hundred fifty pounds of methamphetamine. They don't have Juan Carlos on tape, and he never actually made good on the drugs."

Shane gave him a dubious look, "And they gave your client three million dollars no questions asked?"

Pierce saw instantly where Shane was headed. "If you believe their story, Juan Carlos insisted on a good faith deposit before going to his supplier."

"Unbelievable," Shane cracked a small smile. He continued to ponder the facts while Pierce was busy taking his turn on the bench press and then said, "So all the French can really prove is that your client scammed them out of three million dollars."

Pierce grunted, jerking the weights up off of his chest. "The French can't even connect Juan Carlos to the three million dollars because the money is missing. All they have is a convicted felon's statement that he dropped off three million dollars at Juan Carlos's place. It's his word against my client's."

Shane frowned. "Okay let's assume that they don't have any hard evidence, from what I understand about the French legal system the presumption of innocence is not as strong as it is under our criminal laws. Prosecutors are given a wider berth than they are here. In other words, you can't pay attention to that burden of proof bull shit. You can't sit back and wait for the prosecution to prove that your client is guilty beyond a reasonable doubt. You are going to have to prove Juan Carlos is innocent."

Pierce took a moment and said, "That only applies if Juan Carlos is extradited."

Shane let out a short laugh. "Oh, you can bet your panties he'll be extradited. The Dutch didn't arrest him just to let him walk. They will turn your client over to the French."

Pierce nodded and was sullen for a couple of seconds; he had a hunch that Shane was right.

Shane wiped the sweat off of his clean shaved head. "Juan Carlos is going to need an alibi. The detective who worked the case and the informant's testimony could be enough to convict him unless Juan Carlos can somehow persuade a French court that they arrested the wrong man. Courts abroad typically come down hard on Americans accused of drug trafficking," Shane said frowning. "If I'm reading this right," Shane said, "and I usually do, the French desperately need a conviction to justify all the time invested in the investigation not to mention the three million dollars that disappeared. Someone has to pay, guilty, or not," he said with a hint of inside knowledge. Shane then balanced the bar over his chest and blew through another set. "Then again, you can't discount what your source in the DEA's office told you," he exhaled. "They know that Juan Carlos works for the Carraboca Cartel. If the DEA thinks that Juan Carlos can help them, he isn't going anywhere."

Pierce checked his grip on the weight bar before taking his turn. He drew in a breath. "What's your point?"

Shane shrugged as if to say it's obvious. "What I'm saying is that the weight of the evidence against Juan Carlos is irrelevant. If the DEA thinks that they can use Juan Carlos to help them build a case against the Carraboca Cartel they are going to hold on to him. If he doesn't work for the cartel, the French will get him. If he does, the DEA will snatch him. Like I said, either way he isn't going anywhere."

Pierce sat up on the bench. The look of determination in his eyes suggested that his mind was busy at work.

Shane did a few stretches before taking another turn. "What makes absolutely no sense to me," he muttered out loud, "if it turns out that Juan Carlos is in bed with the cartel, why would he take such a foolish risk for only three million dollars?" Shane asked before switching places with Pierce on the bench.

Pierce had no answer. "Something doesn't add up," he admitted looking dissatisfied as he reflected on the police surveillance reports.

Shane was breathing heavy. "What do you mean?"

"For starters, the surveillance reports claim that Juan Carlos spent thousands every night on gambling and women."

"What does any of that have to do with the alleged drug deal?"

Pierce shook his head. "It doesn't." Pierce explained that since the French police were not having any success in getting Juan Carlos to attend a meeting where they could get him on tape talking about the specifics of the drug deal, they followed him and detailed his activities hoping that it would lead to something they could use. The surveillance reports mainly consisted of nightly gambling and Juan Carlos leaving with one or two women in their early twenties that were described as looking like runway models."

Shane managed to contain his impulse to smile.

"Juan Carlos owns a small export business. The appliance export business just isn't that profitable, something else has to be bankrolling that lifestyle," Pierce continued.

"Maybe," Shane interjected with snarling amusement, "but that alone doesn't make him a drug dealer."

"It doesn't," Pierce agreed. "But what it does tell us is that Juan Carlos indulges his vices."

Pierce didn't realize that he was making a face.

"What is it?" Shane asked.

"His wife, Alexis," Pierce frowned, "is one of the most beautiful women I have ever seen." Pierce paused for a moment trying to find the words which would get across his point without making him sound provincial.

"Don't misunderstand me, I can look the other way on a casual fling but there's nothing casual about this guy. The guy acts like he's on a one-man crusade to sleep with every woman he can whether or not he hurts his wife in the process."

Shane shook his head. "Well if he's as reckless and selfish as you're describing him to be, he's exactly the type to take the three million even if he didn't need it."

Pierce sat brooding for a half a minute.

Shane still looked hugely entertained. "Then why not walk away?" He asked even though he knew Pierce was not the kind to run away from a fight even if there was little chance of success. In fact, Pierce was the exact opposite. He had rigid principles and fighting for the underdog had always been one of them.

Pierce looked down at the ground. He wasn't entirely sold on the reason himself.

"Laura Maria and Alexis need my help, Pierce said with a heavy sigh.

Shane gave Pierce a look that told him that he wasn't buying it. "That may be partially true, but my money is on the fact that you don't want to disappoint Jordan," he scoffed. Shane kept talking, but Pierce appeared to stop listening. "When are you going to come to terms with the fact that when Jordan left you and moved to Philly, she pretty much made up her mind that she wasn't coming back? You are way past a rough patch. You and Jordan are history," Shane said with a wake-up expression on his face.

Pierce thought back to his phone call with Jordan. He felt a small knot in his stomach. "This has nothing to do with Jordan," he shot back defensively.

"Bullshit, you're letting this get personal. Keep in mind that the Carrabocas are nothing like the Medellin Cartel. These guys are no cowboys; they're assassins. If Juan Carlos is involved with the cartel, they will use Alexis as insurance to keep her husband from testifying against them."

Pierce stubbornly shook his head. "We don't know that."

Shane threw down the dumbbells, looked up at Pierce with a seriousness that he usually saved for his clients and snapped. "Buddy, you need to get a hold of your ego. These motherfuckers are worse than terrorists. Once they sink their talons in someone, they own him for life. The cartel isn't going to sit back and let the DEA turn one of their own. They don't play by the same set of rules as most of us do. You may be great at what you do . . . fuck, the best I've seen, but you're in a whole different world here. If the DEA moves Juan Carlos into protective custody, the cartel will push back and probably take his family hostage as insurance. This battle is going to take place in a whole different arena than any you're used to." Shane gave an exasperated sigh. "You have to tell the family that, after reviewing the police reports, there is nothing that you can do for Juan Carlos."

"What about Alexis?"

"Fuck her! She made her bed. I'm thinking about you right now," Shane's clipped tone offered no hint of sympathy, or kindness; just cold, hard, grim determination.

Pierce realized that Shane was only trying to protect him. When he was a first-year law student, Shane was assigned to be Pierce's mentor and had been looking out for him ever since. Despite their different backgrounds, they quickly developed a strong common bond since both had to overcome significant obstacles to get there. For Shane, he grew up in a small mid-western town in Oklahoma. He attended Wichita State on a basketball scholarship and graduated Summa Cum Laude. While in college, he also moonlighted as an enforcer for Wichita's richest and most powerful people. If someone was being black mailed, they called Shane. If someone had trouble collecting debts in the rough areas of town, Shane collected for them. He took care of the dirty jobs discreetly so his clients wouldn't get their hands dirty. Shane never viewed his vocation as a career but rather as an avenue for gaining access to the inner circle of Wichita's wealthiest and most powerful. Even if he was regarded by most of them as "the help," he still had access and, more importantly, he knew their secrets. By the time he was twenty-six years old, Shane had grown tired of the life. He had broken enough bones and left so many people lying in pools of their own blood that a bottle of whiskey was the only friend he could count on for comfort. When he was ambushed and shot a second time, Shane decided that he was finished with that life and called in every favor and used the secrets he had collected over the years to convince his powerful clientele to use their considerable influence to help him get into Harvard Law School.

As far as Pierce was concerned, there was no one he respected more than Shane Hamilton. There were times he could do without Shane's blunt and in-your-face insight, but he'd been a loyal friend over the years, and Pierce trusted him.

Despite every effort to give Pierce the benefit of the doubt, the look of concern was plain on Shane's face.

"So, what are you going to do?"

Pierce shrugged his shoulders. "I guess I'll meet with the family and tell them what I know."

"And then you're dropping the case." Shane gestured forcefully at his best friend.

Pierce communicated his resolve with an icy stare that silently told Shane that he was going to see this through to the end.

Shane had seen that look before. He was done arguing with Pierce. "All right, I get it. Do what you have to do. But be careful. I don't want to read in the Miami Herald that the police found you dead, stuffed in the trunk of a car."

Pierce instantly set the troubling thought aside. "I'll be fine. But I need you to call Hugo."

Shane made a face like he had taken a bite out of a lemon and said, "Shit, Pierce."

"If you're right about the cartel, I'm going to need his help," Pierce spoke with intensity for the first time in the conversation.

Shane began shaking his head the moment Pierce mentioned Hugo by name." The one thing I never want to do again is piss Hugo off," he said. "This will probably do it."

Pierce wore a determined look. "I'll call him, if you prefer to stay out of this."

Shane nodded slowly. "No, I'll call Hugo and go see him. This is a conversation better had in person."

When they finished working out, Pierce found himself sitting on the hood of his car watching Shane as he drove out of the parking lot. He tried to picture himself sitting in Laura Maria's living room across from Juan Carlos's family as he calmly explained to them that their beloved Juan Carlos was suspected of being connected to Dario Carraboca, the most dangerous criminal in modern history. He felt a shiver run down his back when he realized that there was positively no way he could tell them. But Pierce had to tell them something and prepare them for the possibility that Juan Carlos might not be coming home.

Chapter Six

BON FUTURO PRISON, CURACAO

Juan Carlos visually canvassed the room. It was cramped with no windows. On the table was a laptop computer and a small video recording device. In the corner of the room there was a small white board propped up on an easel. Three men dressed in white starched shirts and dark jackets with bulges that concealed their gun holsters sat immediately to Agent Hogan's right. Juan Carlos's sunken eyes moved deliberately from one agent to the next in concert with Lloyd Hogan's introductions. He could see the distrust in their eyes. Suddenly, he was beginning to have second thoughts about helping the Americans. The creases in his face betrayed his growing concerns. As thoughts raced through his mind, Juan Carlos was sure of only one thing: that Dario Carraboca was going to kill him after he finished giving the Americans the false information. His entire body shuddered at the thought. Juan Carlos knew how Dario's mind worked all too well. What better way to convince the Americans that they were closing in on the cartel's operations than for the cartel to kill the DEA's new witness. Juan Carlos's death also guaranteed the cartel that he would not talk in the future. The DEA promised to place him in a witness protection program if he cooperated. But could the DEA really protect him from Dario Carraboca? Juan Carlos didn't have much faith. He gagged and vomited the remains of his breakfast into the wastebasket, scrambled eggs and black coffee. As Juan Carlos tried to regain his composure and to come to terms with his decision to help the Americans, the invisible fist that had gripped his intestines a few moments earlier gave another squeeze.

Lloyd Hogan and the other agents sat quietly, patiently waiting for him to begin. The DEA had been working for years trying to map out how the cartel was moving its money around the globe. They recently began to target Juan Carlos as one of the men responsible for making the cartel's assets and drug profits impossible to track. The topic of Juan Carlos was the source of fascination and debate among the DEA agents and financial analysts assigned to investigate the cartel. The financial analysts in Washington considered him to be nothing less than part genius and part magician. A few of the agents in the field who were acquainted with Juan Carlos viewed him as a mixed bag at best. Hogan was one of those agents who shared that opinion. He believed that Juan Carlos could possibly be brilliant, but he was a still a walking time bomb. One day the cartel would regret their decision to put their faith in him.

When Juan Carlos finally spoke, his voice had an edge that betrayed his concerns. "Where would you like me to start?" he asked.

Hogan's knees creaked as he dragged his chair closer to where Juan Carlos was sitting.

"Why don't we start at the beginning," he said.

Juan Carlos sighed as he felt a lump build in his throat. He began by explaining that the downfall of the Medellin and Cali cartels weakened their stranglehold on coca production.

"Guatemala, El Salvador and Honduras have vast coastlines, and ungoverned spaces in close proximity to Mexico. Geography was only part of what made those countries desirable," Juan Carlos said. "Armed conflicts in Guatemala, El Salvador and parts of Honduras for thirty years laid foundations for weapons trafficking. The routes that had been used for smuggling weapons were the same ones the cartel used for moving their drugs; the new governments were untested which made it easier for us."

One of the agents, Agent Roy glanced past him to Agent Hogan for permission to speak.

"We already know that the cartel moves shipments overland through the Central American rainforests. The dense vegetation makes the routes the cartel uses impossible to spot from the air. We want you to point out the routes," Agent Roy said in a friendly manner.

Juan Carlos hesitated, his gut gave another squeeze. He gestured vaguely in the direction of a carafe of coffee situated on the table in front of him.

Hogan nodded, "Help yourself."

He took several sips of coffee before he started to explain that knowing the routes that had been used by weapons traffickers had limited value because just as with the smuggling operations in the Caribbean and the southern United States coastline, the routes could be easily changed. Juan Carlos exhaled, some of the color returning to his face. He looked at Hogan: "I need a cigarette."

Hogan slid a pack of Stallion cigarettes and a lighter across the table towards him.

Juan Carlos continued along that same line of thought. "Even when the DEA and coast guard aggressively policed the smuggling routes used by the Columbian Cartels, they still got most of their drugs safely into the United States."

He concluded that the DEA had greater success when it began to target the cartel's money instead of trying to capture random shipments. "Cartels, like any criminal organization, are fueled by money. To run an effective organization and keep the supply chain moving, you need money," Juan Carlos frowned. "The Columbians didn't realize how vulnerable they were until it was too late. They had all of their money in Panamanian banks. When General Noriega caved under U.S. pressure, the banks gave the DEA access to the cartels' accounts. Right after that, the Colombian cartels' domination of the cocaine market came to an abrupt end." All of the agents nodded in agreement. "When the DEA disrupted the drug cartel's ability to funnel their profits back to Colombia, operations suffered, and they were never the same. Even their leaders went from untouchables to fugitives in their own native Colombia."

"And this opened the door for the Carrabocas," Hogan finished his thought for him.

Juan Carlos' eyes were fixed on the endless strand of smoke flowing from the lit end of his cigarette and nodded. "In a manner of speaking . . . yeah. Up to that point, we were too small a player to be on DEA's radar. The Mexican cartels stepped in for the Colombians, and we filled the void for methamphetamine being created by the DEA's crackdown on American made meth."

A look of intrigue passed across Hogan's face.

"Our laboratories were bigger and more sophisticated. We could manufacture a less expensive, purer grade of methamphetamine than was available in the U.S. markets." Hogan leaned forward. "We already know that the Carraboca Cartel is responsible for manufacturing and distributing some of the crystal meth that is being sold in the U.S."

"Not some," Juan Carlos shook his head, "most of the crystal meth smuggled into the U.S. through Mexico is made in our laboratories. We had an agreement with the Mexicans that we would not expand our cocaine distribution into their territories if they distributed our methamphetamine product," Juan Carlos said with a shrug and took another drag from his cigarette.

Hogan looked around the table at the other agents and raised an eyebrow.

Juan Carlos could feel them all looking at him with intensity. "So back to the smuggling routes and why they are not terribly important," he said. "I advised Dario against relying heavily on private aircraft to transport drugs. The U.S. satellites alone could effectively track all private flights leaving from South America . . . even late-night flights landing on isolated dirt runways were very risky. So . . ." Juan Carlos said before taking in a deep breath and letting it out slowly. "I found other ways to move drugs; better ways."

"Do you mean another route, in addition to the land routes through the rain forests?" The slow pace and careful enunciation of Agent Roy's words underscored the intrigue in his voice.

Juan Carlos's mouth was a hard thin line. "No, like I said, the routes became less important because we changed our tactics by integrating smuggling operations into legitimate industries. While the DEA was spending its vast resources to ferret out clandestine operations, we operated in plain sight." Juan Carlos took a small amount of pleasure in seeing a couple of the agents hang their heads.

"The northernmost Nicaraguan-Honduran border has a very large shrimp, clam, lobster, fishing industry. Boat traffic in this region is immense making it difficult to police and seize drugs concealed in fishing trawlers. So, we purchased several commercial fishing companies," Juan Carlos explained. "After that we discovered that by acquiring legitimate privately held business concerns worldwide, it would be easier to ship the chemicals we needed to manufacture meth such as ephedrine from places like Thailand and India. DEA and other law enforcement agencies didn't pay a lot of attention to routine commerce . . . The trick was to stay with the herd."

"And how exactly were you able to do that?" Another one of the agents chimed in.

Juan Carlos smiled the smile of a man who knew he now had the room in the palm of his hand. "The first few companies were acquired through privately held Trusts so there was no apparent connection to the cartel. In the beginning, I targeted companies whose sovereign governments were very receptive to outside investments."

"We need the names of the companies," the agent interrupted.

Juan Carlos nodded and took a long drag from his cigarette. "All in good time, you need to understand the big picture first so that all this makes sense. Then I'll give you names."

"We get the big picture. I don't need you to tell me how to build a watch when I ask you for the time," the agent fired back.

Agent Roy stared at Juan Carlos giving off the impression that he was measuring him, and he finally said, "I think you're stalling . . . In fact, I think all you're doing is spinning a story to get out of here. I don't think you ever planned on giving us anything we could use."

"No," Juan Carlos protested vehemently. "I already gave you the smuggling routes in Central America."

"We already knew about them," Hogan interjected. "It was only a matter of time before we pinpointed their exact locations."

Juan Carlos's expression hardened, and he shot Hogan a cynical look. "Agent Hogan," he spoke his name in a cracked voice. "We have a deal . . . Once I walked through this door, I had no choice but to tell you everything."

Juan Carlos glanced up at the clock on the wall. "I've been here almost three hours. By now, Dario Carraboca knows I am talking to you. So, if we both don't live up to our ends of the deal, I'm a dead man," Juan Carlos said, his voice empty. His eyes moved from Hogan to the other agents. "Unless anyone else has something to add, I'd like to continue."

Hogan nodded. "You can start by answering Agent Roy's question." Juan Carlos's face was once again tight with tension.

"Mr. Laporte, you are quite safe here in your private cell away from the prison population until we can move you back to the U.S. Now, if you wouldn't mind giving us the names of the companies," Hogan assured him while the other agents all nodded in agreement.

Juan Carlos reluctantly stood up and shifted past the agents towards the board. He began to draw a series of boxes and used arrows to illustrate how they related to one another. The chart was extensive but not overly complicated or hard to follow. It was a textbook example of vertical integration that would make any business school professor proud. "Each phase of the smuggling operation was handled by a different subsidiary corporation which could not be traced to the cartel or Venezuela," Juan Carlos continued.

It was Hogan's turn to ask a question. "How did you invest the cartel's money without leaving a trail?

"I initially funneled the money for the investments through Liechtenstein."

"Liechtenstein?" Hogan repeated, leaning back in his chair and squinting slightly.

"Yes . . . there are a number of safe havens that I could have used. But Liechtenstein is one of the better ones. There it's possible to bury money so deeply, to put so many legal fronts—attorneys, corporations, fiduciaries—between depositor and cash, that identification of the true owner becomes utterly impossible."

Juan Carlos took one last drag from his third cigarette before putting it out. "When we had acquired several legitimate companies," he said pointing to them on the board," we used those companies to invest in and slowly acquire a controlling interest in a few banks."

Agent Hogan's forehead wrinkled as he studied the board. Every corporate acquisition was strategic and facilitated in some form the supply chain used to manufacture and move the cartel's drugs.

Juan Carlos started to explain the roles the companies on the board played in the operation and stopped. Looking at the boredom in their eyes and at their body language, it occurred to him that a few of the companies he identified were already under investigation.

Hogan, however, wore a pensive look; a couple of the companies not targeted by the DEA that Juan Carlos identified would complicate his investigation. They were large contributors to some of the most powerful elected officials and had enormous political currency in D.C. Agent Hogan sat back on his heels. "What we are most interested in is how the cartel moves its money and where it keeps it."

Juan Carlos nodded, "I was getting to that." He continued to explain how all of the companies played some role in laundering the cartel drug profits.

"The cartel developed an expansive financial infrastructure to move its money," he emphasized at the same time as he scribbled down the names of several banks and investment firms. "All of these companies are owned or controlled by the cartel," he said, sliding the sheet of paper across the table.

Agent Roy's eyes widened. "This can't be right. With a grunt, Agent Roy rose from his seat. Hogan's cold stare told him to sit back down.

Juan Carlos resisted the urge to tell Agent Roy that he didn't give a fuck whether or not they believed him, but instead said, "Believe what you want but over 30 percent of the Eurocurrency deposited in the world's largest banks today is drug money."

Juan Carlos told them that not all of the cartel's money was deposited in institutions that they controlled. The cartel also used the same banks that the CIA used to funnel money to secretly fund third world coups and black ops missions. Those banks had sophisticated systems and personnel in place to move money and most importantly those were the banks that the U.S. government could not leverage.

Agent Roy gave a half-hearted nod.

Juan Carlos lit another cigarette and took a long pull. "Agent Roy, do you remember the bank crisis in 2009?"

Agent Roy looked like he had to think about that for a second.

"What saved several banks during that financial crisis was inter-bank loans funded with drug money. Hard to believe isn't it?" Juan Carlos cracked a thin smile.

Hogan tapped his pen on the table. Nothing Juan Carlos said appeared to catch him by surprise. The global drug trade was estimated to be roughly $380 billion annually; the only way to launder hundreds of billions of dollars of drug money with little trace would be for several major banks to be involved.

Juan Carlos leaned closer to Hogan to where Hogan could smell the nicotine and coffee on his breath.

"Today, there isn't a major bank in the world that hasn't been penetrated by drug money."

Hogan arched an eyebrow.

Juan Carlos picked up his cigarette and moved it to his lips before inhaling slowly. "New York and London are now the world's two biggest laundries of the cartel's drug money." Juan Carlos did not feel a need to go into any more detail.

He looked over at the clock on the wall. It was getting close to 5 P.M.

"This seems like a good place to stop?"

The agents seemed to be shrinking in their seats, but Hogan was too focused to notice. "We can stand a little more," Hogan said.

Juan Carlos nodded. "What your agency doesn't want to accept is that the war on drugs is over. Drugs like cocaine and meth are valuable commodities in the global economy regardless of what market they're sold in. Your government can't afford to completely put the cartel out of business without impacting its own economy. If the DEA goes after the cartel's legitimate business holdings, it's safe to say that such actions would ripple through the stock exchanges and have an adverse impact on the bank accounts, 401K's and retirement accounts of everyday people."

Juan Carlos gave Hogan a long look. The look on Hogan's face told him that he wasn't drinking the Kool-Aid, even a little bit.

"The cartel may control a few multi-national companies and have a couple Washington politicians in their pocket . . . but that doesn't mean the war on drugs is over," Hogan said. "We just need to bring the war to the cartel's doorstep."

Hogan directed his full attention to Juan Carlos and communicated his resolve. "We need the names on all the accounts, the account numbers and the pass codes."

Juan Carlos frowned and gave him a look that said that the DEA would not get them before he was out of Curacao and in protective custody.

Hogan expected that. With the cartel's account numbers and pass codes, the DEA could empty the accounts electronically and cripple the cartel's operations.

Chapter Seven

MIAMI

When the elevator doors parted on the fifty-second floor, Pierce peered around the corner to greet the receptionist like he did every morning when he caught a glimpse of Alexis sitting by herself in the corner. His eyes sparkled when he saw her. Living in South Florida, Pierce came across plenty of gorgeous women, but none of them hit him with this kind of lightning bolt. Pierce walked over and tapped Alexis on the shoulder. His friendly gesture was met with a warm smile.

"I'm sorry, I thought our appointment wasn't until later in the day," he said.

Alexis blushed, slightly embarrassed and confessed that she was very anxious and had run out of things to do, so she decided to wait in his lobby until it was time for them to meet.

Pierce gave her a relaxed smile. "Nonsense, we'll just meet now."

She crinkled her nose and said, "Are you sure? I don't mind waiting."

"Of course," Pierce held up his hand and waved at her to follow him. Alexis wore a black shirt and a beige skirt that clung to her tight, athletic frame. Her hair was pulled back off her face in a ponytail. She wore very little makeup but enough to accentuate her prominent cheekbones and almond shaped eyes. Her beauty so flustered Pierce that when he looked at her, he was grateful for the fact that she couldn't read minds.

He stared as inconspicuous as possible at her skirt and how it caressed her slender curves. He couldn't keep himself from stealing frequent passing glimpses which turned into prolonged glances when the situation permitted. Alexis and Pierce engaged in small talk as they walked into his office before finally getting to the subject of Juan Carlos.

"You mentioned that you have some documents concerning my husband's case," Alexis began with a hint of cautious concern.

Pierce broke free from her gaze focusing now on the painting of water lilies hanging on the wall just behind her.

There was a long pause. After his talk with Shane, Pierce wasn't sure how much he should tell her. Finally, he said, "I received some documents containing police reports. The reports claim that your husband agreed to supply a French undercover police detective with methamphetamine."

Alexis sat in stunned silence while Pierce told her about meetings with a confidential informant working as part of a sting operation and Juan Carlos's commitment to deliver one hundred fifty pounds of methamphetamine. Pierce mentioned that the French police also claim that they paid Juan Carlos three million dollars. Alexis closed her eyes as tight as she could as if trying to get rid of a bad thought. "Why would anyone give Juan Carlos three million dollars to get them drugs?"

Pierce tapped his fingers on the file containing the police reports which was sitting on his desk trying to think of a way to delicately answer her question. Looking for some way to soften the blow, but he couldn't think of one, so he cleared his throat and said, "Because your husband is suspected of working for or at the very least having access to drug dealers that work for the Carraboca Cartel."

His words sent a shiver down her spine and her face transformed into a mask of confusion. Alexis gripped the coffee mug tightly as if she needed to, to steady her nerves.

Pierce studied her for a brief moment and then asked, "Are you okay?"

It took Alexis a long time and then she shook her head numbly, but other than that she did not respond.

He gave her another moment before he tried to point out the weaknesses in the French's government's case. "I want you to understand something very important. The only evidence that the French police have is the testimony of an informant who'll say whatever is necessary to avoid being prosecuted, and one ambitious investigator who needs results. They don't appear to have any recordings of the meetings. And the police did not find drugs or the money in Juan Carlos's apartment or in his warehouse in Saint Maarten."

Alexis shook her head in semi-disbelief while Pierce did his best to throw her a lifeline after just telling her that the life she knew might be crumbling around her. What Pierce couldn't bring himself to tell her was that the lack of hard evidence wouldn't matter in Juan Carlos's case.

Alexis wiped away the few stray tears that had broken free and had been working their way down her cheekbones. She looked up at him with unfocused eyes.

"Do you think Juan Carlos is innocent?" she asked in a barely audible voice. Her tone sounded more like a desperate plea than a question.

Pierce measured his words carefully. He didn't want to lie to Alexis. It occurred to him that she had been lied to many times. He had no idea why this was suddenly important to him, but it was.

"Alexis," Pierce smiled at her. It was a sad smile. "We haven't heard your husband's side of the story. Remember this is the government's case. Of course, it's going to look bad. If it didn't, they wouldn't have any reason for holding him. What's important is not whether I think he's innocent but that I get your husband out of jail."

Alexis sat pensively for several minutes. Pierce wasn't sure whether she was in shock or trying to make sense of all the names and dates he had given her. After she absorbed all the information, she blew out an exasperated breath. "What about the woman he was having an affair with?" She said with a pained expression.

"What . . . woman?" Pierce stammered, stunned by her question.

Alexis's gray pallor deepened. Pierce could tell that she suspected Juan Carlos of being unfaithful and was looking for anything in the reports that would confirm what she already felt in her gut.

"Please Pierce, you are not protecting me by lying about my husband's indiscretions. Do the reports mention anything about his having a mistress?"

Pierce was aware of the fact that he instantly began concocting excuses for Juan Carlos's misguided activity the instant that Alexis accused him of having another woman as though he was bound by some unwritten male code.

"I don't see how any of this is relevant to the case," Pierce insisted.

An anger rose in her eyes. Alexis could no longer contain her tears. She turned away from Pierce.

"I should have known," she murmured under her breath. "All those excuses for being away and never letting me come visit him."

As Pierce watched her weep, a wave of protectiveness washed over him, and he did something that just a few moments earlier he told himself he would not do. He lied to her.

Pierce looked directly at Alexis. His blue eyes were luminous. "Your husband," Pierce struggled to get the words out, "was not involved with another woman." His eyes widened. "Let me rephrase that," he stumbled nervously. "There is nothing in the file about your husband and another woman," he finally got the words out.

He noticed her face muscles tighten a bit. She knew that he was covering for Juan Carlos. "Stop," she insisted. "Please stop lying to me."

Pierce stammered. "What I mean . . . I don't have any personal knowledge that Juan Carlos was unfaithful, but if by chance your suspicions turn out to be right, it wouldn't necessarily mean anything. That's what I mean." Pierce took a deep breath. His instincts told him to be quiet; that there was nothing he could say to make things better. Normally, Pierce listened to his gut. But for some inexplicable reason he ignored it. "Men have sex for a number of reasons," Pierce said, a tinge of panic creeping into his voice. Inside of his brain, he was screaming at himself, "Stop you idiot!" He meant his words to be reassuring; it was clear that they weren't. Instead of stopping, Pierce felt some irrational need to keep talking.

"Listen to me; men are just more physical than women. Men in most cases make up their minds within the first two to five minutes of seeing a woman, whether they want to sleep with her. Men more than women rely on physical attraction and plain old lust," Pierce said trying to somehow make promiscuity sound like a natural male response.

Alexis glared at him resentfully. "Don't be a sexist. You're better than that," she snapped at him.

Pierce ignored the voice in his head which was still yelling for him to shut up. "What I'm saying is that Juan Carlos was alone for weeks at a time, and from what you told me, on a few occasions you went as long as a month without seeing him . . ."

Alexis was irritated by the implication. "That wasn't my fault," She said, casting a defensive glance.

Pierce shrugged, "I'm not suggesting that it was your fault." He felt vaguely ashamed realizing that his logic was as absurd as someone accusing a rape victim of being partially to blame for wearing a sexy outfit.

Pierce's reasoning struck Alexis as a feeble excuse. She had heard enough from him on the subject. "Stop making excuses," she said bluntly. "What about me? You don't think that I have needs?" Her face was a picture of misery. "When he's gone for weeks at a time, don't you think that I also get lonely? I tried to move to Saint Maarten to be with him, but he wouldn't allow it."

Trembling, Alexis said in a low barely audible murmur: "Juan Carlos was my first and only boyfriend."

Alexis looked past Pierce, her eyes darkened by her memories. Pierce could tell that this wasn't the first time she felt the stabbing feeling that was playing havoc with her insides.

"Do you have any idea what it feels like to sit at home each and every night feeling like your life is slipping away while the person you're married to is sucking every drop of gusto out of life that he can?" There was no malice in her voice when she said this, merely regret.

"I think you're just a little upset right now . . ." Pierce started to say, trying to be comforting.

Her eyes were glassy. "Wouldn't you be? We made a commitment to each other." Alexis suddenly stopped herself. Her eyes widened as she looked to be struggling with what she was thinking.

"Just answer one question honestly . . ." Alexis took a deep breath, straightened her shoulders and asked, "Is he in love with her?" Her voice cracked with a mixture of sadness.

Her question hit Pierce like a bone jarring pothole on an otherwise smooth road. He didn't know how to respond. Was he in love with whom, which one he wondered? The surveillance reports identified a mistress in New York named Jessica Davis. But in light of Juan Carlos's numerous trysts, Pierce hadn't considered whether Juan Carlos was in love with her. He wasn't even certain about how Juan Carlos felt about Alexis. Pierce couldn't know Juan Carlos well enough from the reports to even start to form an opinion about any woman. The only thing he was certain of was that Juan Carlos was in love with himself and that nothing else mattered to him.

"No, I don't believe that he's in love with anyone else," Pierce said.

"Well, he's obviously not in love with me either," she huffed and turned away from Pierce. Pierce looked at Alexis with a thoughtful frown. He could tell that she needed to be alone and made up an excuse to step out of the office. When he returned, he asked Alexis if she was all right, but her face had closed like a door. It was as if she had decided she'd had enough and stepped through the iron gate of her prison. Gone were her shattered eyes, and the vulnerability on her face had also disappeared.

She took a step towards where Pierce was sitting and leaned over placing her hand on his shoulder. She tilted her head just enough to put her lips on his cheek and kiss it.

"Thank you, I don't know what I would do if I didn't have you," she said. Alexis pulled back and walked towards the door. When she got there, she turned back and put her hand on her hip and gave him an appraising look before heading towards the elevator.

Pierce could not take his eyes off her. The easy sway of her hips as she walked away captivated him. He felt powerless and completely drawn in.

Chapter Eight

FORT LAUDERDALE

Shane nursed a large cup of coffee while he waited at Lester's Diner off State Road 84 in Fort Lauderdale for Hugo Jackson. Hugo and Shane agreed to meet at eight in morning. It was almost nine by the time he waltzed in.

Hugo's deep voice boomed, "Yo! Home Slice, what brings you up this way?"

Shane watched all six foot five inches of him saunter towards the booth. Hugo took his job seriously, but he also had a casual air about him that said, "*when I'm not on the clock, there is no clock.*" Hugo could not be adequately described as a tall man. He was a mountain of a man that looked like he had been chiseled from granite and spray-painted nut brown.

"Damn Son," Shane grinned. "You need to put the brakes on all that working out. If you get any bigger, you're going to scare all the white people around here."

Hugo let out a short laugh. "You're probably right," he said with an impish grin.

"Seriously man, you're a fucking monster," Shane said.

"It's true," Hugo said, so modest and matter of fact about it that there seemed nothing conceited about it. "In the personal protection business, clients typically think that bigger is better," Hugo slid into the booth across from Shane. He looked over the menu and then winked at the server to come over to the table and take his order.

She gave him a polite nod.

Hugo licked his lips while reading the menu.

Just before placing his order, he twisted in his seat and took a good look at Shane. He had a playful gleam in his eyes. "By the way, are you paying?"

Shane glared at him. "Motherfucker, no matter how big you get, you still got alligator arms."

Hugo's lips curved into a smile. "Well you're the high-powered lawyer. I'm just a bodyguard."

"Stop right there, Shane cut in. "You've been sticking me with the check since we were fourteen years old."

Hugo chuckled in a boyish manner. "It's good to see you man."

He turned to the waitress and placed an order of ten egg whites, a skirt steak, a bowl of oatmeal, two large glasses of grapefruit juice and a cup of coffee. Shane shook his head at Hugo in mocking disapproval.

"Hey, this body needs a lot of fuel to keep running," he said. "So, how's the wifey doing?"

Shane rolled his eyes. "Mad at the world because she isn't as young and beautiful as she used to be," Shane said, winding down the small talk so he could get to the real reason for why he asked Hugo to meet him.

Shane folded his arms and thought long and hard before he spoke. With a deep breath he said, "Hugo, we got ourselves a little situation."

"Uh oh, I already don't like the sound of it," Hugo chimed in.

"If you don't like it now, give it a minute. I guarantee you're going to hate it," Shane added with a hint of sarcasm.

Hugo raised a questioning brow. "Then why are we having this conversation?"

"Because," Shane interrupted, "this situation involves Pierce."

"All right then," he said, raising himself slightly in his chair, giving the impression that he was bracing himself for whatever Shane had to say.

"Hugo, you know I wouldn't ask if I could handle it alone . . ."

"I know man." He nodded. "Now what's up with Pierce?"

"Pierce has gotten himself mixed up in a situation with a woman that I think the Carrabocas are looking for."

"You can't be serious," Hugo said, shaking his head.

"And he won't listen to reason. You know Pierce," Shane said almost brooding as he turned and stared at the dark storm clouds which were now rolling in. Hugo listened to Shane's account of the past few days' events while he attacked his morning meal. His faded T-shirt pulled itself tight around his huge bicep each time he raised the fork to his lips. Hugo and Shane had been friends since they were both eight years old in Oklahoma. As far back as they could each remember, Hugo had been Shane's muscle. From their early years together on the playgrounds to the times when Shane took care of problems that Wichita's privileged and powerful wanted handled quietly. Hugo was always there to make sure that Shane walked away unscathed. Shane took care of the rich and Hugo took care of Shane. No matter the problem, Shane could always count on Hugo to have his back. They lost touch briefly when Shane left for law school. About a year later, Hugo enlisted in the Army and served two tours in Afghanistan. He was a highly decorated member of a Special Forces detachment. During his second tour, Hugo led a small but extremely effective counter-terrorism unit that specialized in tracking and neutralizing terrorist operations behind enemy lines.

* * *

THE DOWNPOUR STOPPED and the ominous rumbling sounds made by the thunder were now muted and sporadic. Hugo finished his breakfast and was now clutching a cup of coffee. The picture which

Shane had just painted made him uneasy. Dario Carraboca was not someone you tangled with. Not unless you were a drug enforcement agent with the firepower of a government behind you. Shane could tell that Hugo's mind was busy exploring all of their possible options. From the lines which formed along the fringes of Hugo's eyes, Shane knew that there couldn't be many good ones.

"Who is this woman that Dario Carraboca supposedly wants to find?" Hugo asked.

"Her name is Alexis LaPorte . . ."

Hugo reacted like ice water had suddenly been poured down his back.

"What the fuck!" He blurted out, shaking his head in disbelief. "Not Juan Carlos's wife."

Hugo gave Shane a look that he instantly understood. Shane lowered his eyes almost in shame as if he was the one responsible for Pierce's faux pas.

Hugo couldn't get over Pierce's stupidity. "This is no good," he said, under his breath.

He remembered seeing Juan Carlos at several events where he had been in charge of security.

Setting his apprehension aside, Hugo asked, "The guy who got arrested and is awaiting extradition to Guadeloupe, please tell me it isn't Juan Carlos?"

Hugo's eyes widened before Shane could finish nodding. Everyone in Hugo's line of work knew Juan Carlos was Dario Carraboca's right hand man. Since leaving the army, Hugo supervised protective security services for executives, dignitaries and celebrities around the world. Over the years, he developed a reliable network of security firms and agents. However, he couldn't think of a single firm that would be willing to help with a case like this. That meant there was no one he could call to bail their asses out if things went bad. Hugo understood his was not a risk free business, but that didn't mean he gambled with his life. He took several gulps of coffee while he considered the odds of surviving any job where he stood in the way of Dario Carraboca. When he was done, Hugo threw up his hands. "Man! Shane, I don't think you realize what you're asking me to do. If Dario wants Alexis for insurance, the only thing we are going to do if we get in the way is get ourselves killed."

Shane continued to nod his head in agreement. Hugo acted like he wasn't sure who he should be more pissed off at, Pierce for getting himself into this mess or Shane for asking him to help get Pierce out of it.

"Shane, if we hide Alexis, we're putting an even bigger target on Pierce," Hugo was almost pleading with him to understand the gravity of what he was saying. "The Cartel is going to assume that Pierce knows where she is or how to get in touch with her. Meaning Pierce becomes the target," Hugo emphasized the last word.

"I know," Shane gave an exasperated sigh.

"Do you?" Hugo glared at him.

Hugo looked at Shane with dread in his eyes knowing that he really had no choice in the matter. If he didn't get involved, he was sure that if Shane and Pierce were lucky, they might both end up on the wrong end of a bullet. If they managed to piss off Dario Carraboca, it might be weeks before a forensics team could piece their severed body parts back together.

"I understand the situation," Hugo nodded in a calm and disappointed voice. "Give me some time to check out a few things . . ." Hugo paused almost in mid-sentence, suddenly distracted by the mental image of three unmarked graves in the Florida Everglades.

He shook his head and said, "We also need an emergency plan, just in case this whole thing goes to hell."

Shane nodded in agreement.

Hugo clapped his hands to make a point. "If we fuck up and don't handle our business perfectly, you realize it's going to be lights out motherfucker."

Shane frowned. "We've always handled our business."

"We have," Hugo almost smiled, but his eyes weren't smiling.

Shane gestured to the waitress to bring him the check. He paid it, left an ample tip and raised himself from the bright red booth.

"Pierce already left for Curacao to see Juan Carlos."

Hugo whispered a string of curses under his breath. Shane kept talking over him. "He should be back in town in a couple of days. I'll call you as soon as I hear from him," Shane said as he got ready to leave.

Hugo gave Shane a fist bump. "I won't be pissed off if I don't hear from you," he grunted.

Hugo stayed behind sipping a cup of coffee. He continued to weigh the odds of success and even relaxed the definition for this particular job. He turned his attention to what lay ahead and figured that any outcome where they all walked away in the end was a good one. However, he still couldn't give them more than a twenty percent chance of all walking away alive.

Chapter Nine

CURACAO

Pierce was sitting outside in a sidewalk café located immediately in front of the Hotel Curacao sipping a Latte. He carefully reread the police crime scene report and related investigative reports while he waited for local counsel. Supremely dedicated and sometimes competitive to a fault, Pierce was relentless in his preparation.

When he finished the last page, he flipped it over and closed the file. With a pensive look on his face Pierce, leaned back and took in the eighteenth-century buildings that had been beautifully restored and painted in bright colors alternating vibrant blue, red and orange hues which made up Willemstad's famed waterfront. They possessed a fluorescent and festive quality that reminded him of an old Hollywood movie set. The salty trade winds felt good against his skin, and the scent of the hibiscus blossoms coupled with the breathtaking view of the harbor completed a beautiful tropical setting different from anywhere else in the Caribbean.

* * *

A black Mercedes Benz pulled up just in front of the entrance to the café. Pierce watched as a man wearing a dark tailored suit, starched white shirt and black leather shoes stepped from the sedan. He looked rushed as he zigzagged his way around the tables and waiters. Marcus van Delft was a prominent criminal defense attorney from Willemstad. He had Scandinavian blood which explained his blond hair and clear blue eyes.

His stoic expression gave way to a broad smile. "Mr. Evangelista, I presume," he said, extending his hand.

Pierce stood, smiled and shook Marcus's hand. He was hoping to dispense with the polite small talk as quickly as possible. In his mind's eye, he had not travelled over a thousand miles to discuss Curacao's weather or beautiful sunsets. Pierce was pleasantly surprised when Marcus said, "We have to leave for Bon Futuro prison shortly, so why don't we spend the next few minutes discussing the case," in a cool and perfunctory manner.

Marcus reached into the side pocket of his suit jacket and pulled out a cigar.

He gestured to Pierce. "Would you mind terribly?"

Pierce smiled amiably.

"Splendid," Marcus smiled and sat down across from him.

Marcus puffed on his cigar while Pierce started to tick off a list of witnesses he wanted to interview. Marcus abruptly and impatiently stopped Pierce in mid-list and suggested that the interviews would prove to be useless.

"This drug trafficking charge is nasty business," he told Pierce in a grim voice. "But fundamentally an equally vexing problem is the missing money," he frowned. Marcus spewed out no less than a half a dozen theories in as many minutes on what might have happened to the money. The one that resonated most with Pierce was the possibility that the police informant never delivered the money and set up Juan Carlos to take the fall.

"Three million dollars can present too much temptation for some people." Marcus blew a stream of cigar smoke out of his mouth and regarded Pierce thoughtfully through the haze. Then he let out an exasperated breath. "We have a tough case Pierce."

Pierce took a sip of coffee and measured Marcus. "Really, you think so?" he asked. "The French government's entire case seems to be limited to two sworn statements. There doesn't appear to be any tangible evidence connecting Juan Carlos to a drug buy."

Marcus raised a cautionary finger. "None of that matters," he said with a sad laugh. "The French and the Dutch have to co-exist on a very small Island. The Public Prosecutor is not going to care about the strength of the evidence against our client or the truth for that matter."

Marcus, in the midst of relighting his cigar, exhaled a cloud of smoke and shook his head and said, "I know the Prosecutor very well. He will say whatever he needs to get Mr. Laporte extradited. The weight of the evidence and the truth are both irrelevant. Mr. Laporte's guilt or innocence will be up to the French court to decide."

Marcus turned and looked out over the water. "Powerful people are interested in what happens to our client. This makes the Public Prosecutor very nervous. He wants Mr. Laporte out of the Dutch government's custody as soon as possible by whatever means necessary."

Marcus could see that his assessment of how things worked in Curacao didn't sit well with Pierce. He could also tell that nothing he was saying was catching Pierce by surprise. Pierce had a look of awareness that suggested that the world held no surprises.

Marcus's expectation of the outcome of the extradition hearing was suddenly very clear. "Our client's extradition to Guadeloupe may be a good development. You may be able to put on a legitimate defense there."

Pierce supposed that there was some truth in his words; he simply had not considered the possibility that the hearing was merely a formality to maintain the illusion that his client had rights.

"Under the French legal system, circumstantial evidence might be enough to convict Juan Carlos," Pierce countered.

"Marcus winced at the thought. "I understand, but there you still have a chance. Trust me when I say that you want your client out of Curacao and, more importantly, out of Bon Futuro prison as quickly as possible."

Pierce silently asked himself if he should trust Marcus. He locked eyes with Marcus for a second before asking, "Have you ever represented the Carraboca Cartel?"

The uncomfortable look on Marcus's face gave Pierce his answer.

"You have to remember that Curacao is a small island and I'm one of the best . . ." he corrected himself, "the best criminal defense attorney on the island. So, the answer to your question is yes. I have occasionally represented their interests."

"And, are you representing the cartel's interests here and now? Pierce asked.

Marcus treated the question like an accusation. "Most certainly not, but I fail to see any conflict of interest at this juncture. Assuming the cartel had any business relationship with Juan Carlos, it would be safe to presume that their interests would be aligned in wanting to obtain his release," Marcus answered cagily. "And that is precisely what I have been hired to do."

Pierce was no longer unsure about Marcus. He was sure that he couldn't trust him.

"As I was saying," Marcus continued, "Bon Futuro prison is a bad place. What you don't know is that anarchy rules there. There are prison gangs that control parts of the prison," Marcus said shaking his head. "It's a violent place. Weapons and drugs are smuggled in. And as for prisoner hygiene . . . it's almost non-existent," Marcus frowned. "There have been so many brutal rapes and murders in the showers that the inmates know to stay away from there. It's a bad, bad situation . . ." Marcus looked like he was mulling over the prison conditions while taking one last puff of his cigar. He stood up signaling that it was time to leave and said, "Even though Juan Carlos is in solitary, he's not safe there."

Bon Futuro Prison was about twelve kilometers from the Hotel. Marcus van Delft's driver took a coastal road that passed several of the island's popular resorts. Pierce stared at the tennis courts and gleaming buildings, most flying hotel flags while he weighed the benefits of having Marcus sit in on his conference with Juan Carlos. The beaches were smaller and more intimate. They were not the long expansive patches of white sand that Pierce was accustomed to seeing in Florida. The majority of the coastline with its chalk rock formations was wild and untamed and beyond that an endless blue ocean. By the time the car came to a stop, Pierce had decided against having Marcus sit in. He could see the prison complex in the distance.

"We will walk from here. Marcus gestured.

The early morning sun was merciless. Pierce had taken no more than a couple of steps, and he could feel the beads of perspiration cascading down his back. Marcus began to explain how things worked at Bon Futuro Prison as Pierce stepped carefully along the dusty path teeming with broken glass and garbage.

"We have written permission from the Director of the prison to visit Mr. Laporte. He was gracious enough to arrange for a private room away from the general prison population," Marcus remarked.

"When we arrive at the desk, stand behind me, not next to me," Marcus instructed.

"Have your passport ready. All visitors are searched. Sometimes as lawyers we are extended certain professional courtesies. But then again, you are an American so it will depend on who is working the desk."

"Don't speak with any prisoner that you might happen to come across. You are cleared only to speak with Mr. Laporte. If a prisoner asks you for a smoke or spare change, ignore him. If you give them anything you will be escorted out," Marcus warned him.

"Your visit may be observed, remain seated during the visit at all times and do not hand Mr. Laporte anything, not even a piece of paper without first asking for permission."

Pierce nodded.

"Ok we're here." Marcus gestured for Pierce to follow closely behind him.

Chapter Ten

BON FUTURO PRISON, CURACAO

Pierce waited in the cramped windowless room for Inmate Juan Carlos Laporte to be brought in from his holding cell. The room was filthy and smelled like piss. Juan Carlos's face could not mask his surprise when he first set eyes on Pierce. He was much younger and not what he had expected. Pierce was handsome with a strong jawline, aquiline nose, thick black hair and fierce blue eyes that seemed to squint with intense, intelligent combativeness.

He started by explaining to Juan Carlos the extradition process that would unfold in the coming days. Juan Carlos feigned mild interest as he bided his time and sized Pierce up.

Juan Carlos's already narrow eyes grew more so, as he studied Pierce across from him. He leaned back. "The police reports," Juan Carlos interrupted.

Pierce stopped and gave him a curious look, waiting for him to finish his thought.

"Did they just talk about the drug deal or was there more?" Juan Carlos asked.

"The reports were surveillance reports. They detailed all your activities."

"All my activities," Juan Carlos repeated under his breath. He shook his head looking at Pierce with dread in his eyes. "So, they mention the gambling and women?"

Pierce nodded. "Yes, there are some parts of the reports that detailed those activities."

Juan Carlos eyed Pierce with suspicion. "Has my wife seen them?"

Pierce gave him a disappointed look and shook his head. “No, I didn’t let her see them.”

Juan Carlos persisted. “Does she know what they say?” He asked knowing how steadfast Alexis could be.

Pierce looked at his watch. Alexis didn’t need a surveillance report to tell her what she already knew. The constant arguments and repeated instances when she found condoms in Juan Carlos’s clothing or the lingering perfume fragrances on his shirts that didn’t belong to her were ample proof. Juan Carlos could have made it a point to be more careful, but he obviously didn’t see the need for any pretense.

Pierce wasn’t fooled by Juan Carlos’s questions. He didn’t think for a minute that Alexis knowing what was in the reports suddenly mattered to Juan Carlos. What he suspected was that Juan Carlos’s questions were some sort of test.

Pierce took a deep breath and exhaled slowly. “The reports were delivered to me from a confidential source, so your wife understood that they were for my eyes only.” He took a small amount of pleasure in adding, “I didn’t let her see the reports, or discuss what was in them, but I didn’t need to; she already seems pretty convinced that there are other women.”

Juan Carlos shrugged his shoulders. “It’s not safe for Alexis in Saint Maarten. I only get to see Alexis once a month. Those women are only casual distractions. They really don’t mean anything,” he said indignantly.

Pierce looked down at his notes and then back up to Juan Carlos. His eyes were cold, but the rest of his expression was neutral.

The face he put on for Juan Carlos did not jibe with his feelings. “I am not a Priest, Mr. Laporte, you don’t need to confess to me. I’m here for only one obvious reason . . .”

"Before we get to that," Juan Carlos cut Pierce off before he could finish his thought. "Did Alexis ever mention Jessica by name?" Pierce didn't like being asked these questions. Tapping the file, he said, "You mean your mistress in New York? No, I don't believe she mentioned her by name."

"Sure," Juan Carlos replied, not buying a word of it.

Pierce glanced down at his watch again; he was none too happy that he was spending valuable time on something that would have no bearing on the hearing, so he leaned in close and gave him a dead serious look. "I'm only going to say this once. How you treat Alexis is pretty fucked up, but it has no bearing on my case . . . In other words, if it doesn't help or hurt your chances of getting out of here, as far as I'm concerned it's irrelevant," he said in a calm but firm voice that made it clear that he was done talking about Juan Carlos's affairs.

Juan Carlos sat back and took a second hard look at Pierce. His lips were pursed in thought.

After a moment, he took a deep breath and said, "My mother trusts you . . . So I'm going to have to trust you as well," he added with some difficulty.

Juan Carlos leaned forward. "Don't say a word and just listen," he insisted.

"You already know that the French government wants to prosecute me," he frowned. "And if you're half as good as you think you are, you know that the Americans want me to cooperate with them in their investigation against the Carraboca Cartel."

Pierce listened intently, saying nothing.

"Well that brings us to the Carraboca Cartel." Juan Carlos told Pierce about the cartel's monopoly on the methamphetamine drug trade. He also admitted that he was responsible for moving the cartel's money and shielding its assets. Juan Carlos took a deep breath and let it out slowly. "The ugly side of my business is now that I'm in jail, I've become a liability to the cartel. And they are not going to put any of their operations at risk by hoping that I will remain loyal to them."

He didn't show it, but his nerves were frayed.

Juan Carlos also detailed for Pierce the cartel's connection to Iran, the Islamic Jihad and Hezbollah. He explained that the cartel supplied Hezbollah with Methamphetamine which they sold to fund their terrorist operations. He suspected that if the Americans were closely watching the cartel, they could deploy one of the terrorist cells to kill him.

"In other words, the only thing that is certain is that the cartel will eventually try to assassinate me. What I still don't know is when and how they will come at me."

"Sounds like a precarious situation," Pierce said dryly.

"It's more of a no-win situation," Juan Carlos said with a determined edge. "I've played out various scenarios and in every one, I wind up dead. In some scenarios I get killed sooner than in the others, but in every case, it ends the same." Juan Carlos gave a swift shake of his head. "If I'm extradited, the French won't protect me, the Americans can't protect me and Dario Carraboca is cunning and brutal but never merciful," he said in a matter-of-fact tone."

He stared at Pierce focused on a particular thought. "So, do you know what this means counselor?"

Pierce thought about it for a second, he wanted to tell him that he was fucked, but instead he nonchalantly said, "It means you need another option."

Juan Carlos arched an eyebrow. "Yes exactly."

"I need to get out of Curacao and disappear and you need to make that happen."

Pierce looked at Juan Carlos like he had lost his mind.

Pierce's eyes flashed. "What about Alexis?"

Juan Carlos made a foul face. It instantly registered that Juan Carlos was bothered by the fact that he and Alexis had been spending a lot of time together.

"What about her?" Juan Carlos asked derisively. "She's my wife. She'll come with me," Juan Carlos answered him. "I have enough money spread around in banks and brokerage accounts throughout Europe and Asia. None of it is traceable to me. So, we'll be able to live out our days comfortably and in anonymity."

Pierce didn't say a word. The glint in his eyes was the only indication he gave Juan Carlos that suggested that he would try and find a way to help them.

Juan Carlos thought for a moment, and then he leaned forward in his chair. "There's a great deal of money for you too, if you can help me get off this island; enough for you to retire."

Pierce dismissed the offer with a look of contempt. He could barely stand Juan Carlos, and it was only Dario Carraboca's reputation for killing family members of those who crossed him that prompted Pierce to consider helping him and Alexis disappear. "That's not necessary," Pierce said sounding seemingly incorruptible.

"Well, you are going to need cash, a lot of it if you are going to handle all of the black bag stuff to get me off this island. So, I need to tell you where to find it," Juan Carlos said in a low voice.

"I have a small interest in a nightclub in Miami. Next door was an Auto Parts business that my family owned. I still keep an office there in the back. Under the floorboard of my office directly below my desk is a safe. Here is the combination," Juan Carlos scribbled down numbers on a small piece of paper.

"I am a silent partner in the club. Very few people know I have an interest in it, not even Alexis," Juan Carlos said. "The Auto Parts business has been closed for a couple of years now, so it would look suspicious if you are seen going in. Go to the club, I have a man there that can get you into the store."

Like a Vegas dealer, Juan Carlos slid the paper with the combination to the side and wrote a note on a second piece of paper. "When you get there, ask for Domenic and give him this. He'll know what to do."

The tap on the door was immediately followed by Marcus's voice. "We need to start wrapping things up," he said, peeking his head in.

Pierce stood. "Anything else?"

Juan Carlos nodded at Marcus. "Give us a minute."

He stood up and stared into Pierce's eyes. Juan Carlos's face didn't so much as twitch. His eyes didn't blink. Only his lips moved. "I'll tell you a little secret about me. I'm not the forgiving type. If you fuck me or try to take what's mine or let me down in any way, my friends in the Russian mob will be paying you a visit."

Pierce's blue eyes turned to ice. "Now was that really necessary?" He asked with pathetic disappointment. "And as for your connections to the Russian mob, the people you know won't dare make a move without first checking with the people I know." There was no arrogance in Pierce's voice, only a calm certainty.

Juan Carlos laughed and tried to play it off. It was obvious Pierce was not intimidated, by him, the DEA or the cartel. "I'm starting to see why my mother likes you so much." Juan Carlos squeezed Pierce's hand, and then Juan Carlos and Pierce shared a look; a look that confirmed that each knew that they were in unchartered waters.

Chapter Eleven

On the flight back to Miami, Pierce looked out the window at the white clouds. His mind was filled with a menagerie of moving pieces and different scenarios as he sat back playing over and over in his mind everything Juan Carlos and Marcus had told him. Pierce analyzed every word and explored every possible outcome. After meeting with Marcus, he was sure that the Dutch wanted no part of Juan Carlos and would extradite him at the first opportunity. Beyond that, nothing else was black or white. He had been a lawyer long enough to know that what Juan Carlos described as a perfect storm could be the by-product of a client with an overactive imagination. But his telephone conversation with his DEA contact suggested otherwise. His source confirmed that something big was about to go down. Pierce's contact guessed that the big break in the investigation had something to do with Juan Carlos. While everyone in the agency was careful not to talk about it, there was an undeniable buzz in the office. With Juan Carlos's extradition hearing taking place in a little over one week, Pierce realized that he was sitting on a time-bomb. The Carraboca cartel had been conspicuously silent until now, but the American's growing interest in Juan Carlos would force its hand. Pierce suddenly felt a rush of anxiety when the idea struck him that Juan Carlos might be right. The only way to protect Alexis was to get Juan Carlos out of prison and help them run.

* * *

He used the remainder of the flight to prioritize his ever-increasing list of priorities. He made a list of what he needed to take care of to prepare for the extradition hearing. The other tasks had to be organized and kept in his mind. There could be no notes or files. There could be nothing that connected Juan Carlos's disappearance to him or his law firm. Pierce knew how to operate from the shadows. This wouldn't be the first time he had to delicately fix a problem without leaving any trace that he or his firm had been working behind the scenes. However, the stakes were dramatically different. At stake wasn't a drilling permit worth hundreds of millions or a regulatory agency's sanctions. In those instances, if Pierce failed to get results, no one died. But like most matters that required Pierce's unique skill set, this operation needed to be approached like a battle plan. It wasn't enough for Juan Carlos and Alexis to disappear. The cartel had to agree that Juan Carlos and his family were no longer targets. Pierce closed his eyes for a moment. In his mind's eye he figured that for the cartel to stand down, he would have to devise a plan that was both immune to the cartel's known tactics and one that would continue to keep them off balance. Looking out the window, Pierce also had another thought. If he succeeded in pulling this off, he had a feeling that he and Dario Carraboca were on a collision course.

* * *

When he landed, Pierce scrolled through his cell phone reading his text messages. The one from Alexis read, "*I'm anxious to hear how it went with Juan Carlos. Could we meet for dinner tonight? Alexis.*"

Staring at his cell phone, Pierce exhaled heavily. He wasn't sure what he was going to tell her.

"*Where should I meet you?*" He typed into his phone and hit the send button.

Seconds later his phone vibrated. "*Pick me up at my parent's home. 16048 SW 44th Lane at around eight.*"

* * *

At 7.55 P.M. Pierce pulled up to the home in West Kendall. Alexis was standing at the doorway waiting for him. The light which filtered out from the foyer behind her traced the contours of her frame and spawned a most alluring silhouette. The sleeveless summer dress she was wearing tastefully embraced the sinuous curves of her body leaving little to the imagination. The high heeled shoes made her long legs seem even longer and shapelier than Pierce had fondly remembered them. Alexis smiled and waved to him to follow her inside. Even though she was a married woman, her gesture confirmed that there was no getting around meeting her parents. For Pierce, meeting parents for some inexplicable reason was an act to be avoided until such time that it was no longer unavoidable. He put off meeting Jordan's parents for so long that they began to wonder if their daughter had invented an imaginary boyfriend. Jordan's sister even had a nickname for him. She referred to Pierce as figment, as in a figment of Jordan's imagination. Pierce walked past the neatly manicured lawn towards Alexis. When he got to the entrance, her eyes looked directly at him, and he felt a warm sensation. She took a step towards him and straightened his tie. It was clear that she wanted to do it. It gave her a reason to touch him without appearing too forward.

"You look handsome," she said.

"Thank you."

When Pierce was introduced to her parents, he could see that they were anxious and emotionally fatigued. Juan Carlos's arrest was more than two middle-aged immigrants who fled Castro's Cuba to give their daughters a chance at a better life. Alexis did her best to tactfully say goodbye ushering him through the door. Her father shook Pierce's hand

and told him that he was always welcome in their home. Alexis's mother was slightly more reserved. She just nodded politely appearing to go along with whatever her husband was saying. Pierce, however, wasn't fooled for a second. He could tell that she was bothered by something more than her son-in-law's incarceration. He noticed her apprehension with Alexis. He guessed that she didn't care much for how Alexis was dressed or how her daughter made no effort to hide how excited she was to see him. Pierce could tell just by the way she never took her eyes off him, watching his every move whenever he interacted with Alexis, that she was more unsettled by him and how he was starting to affect Alexis than she was by Juan Carlos's arrest.

"So, you're Jordan's husband?" She asked Pierce.

Alexis glared at her mother.

"Pierce smiled and politely said, "I used to be married to Jordan. We split up about two years ago and have been divorced for about a year now."

Alexis's mother made a face. "That's a shame," she said. "A good Cuban wife should stand by her man no matter what."

Alexis rolled her eyes. She looked like she wanted to say something, but instead she took Pierce by the arm and announced that they were leaving.

Pierce drove east on Kendall Drive towards Coral Gables. He wanted to tell Alexis that she looked beautiful, but he didn't know how to compliment a woman whose husband is sitting in jail without sounding lecherous. Pierce, who was well aware of Shane's vices, thought about what advice Shane might give him. Shane would tell him that vulnerable women are precisely the woman you complement.

Christy's restaurant with its crimson red awnings and large oak doorways had been located on the same corner on Ponce Deleon

Boulevard just outside downtown Coral Gables for over fifty years. The main dining room was dimly lit and decorated with rich wood furniture, thick curtains and paintings featuring hunting scenes.

* * *

PIERCE WAITED UNTIL after they ordered dinner before bringing up the subject of Juan Carlos. He fumbled nervously with his silverware and then with his water glass as he searched for the right words. Alexis smiled as she studied unreservedly the way Pierce's dress shirt pulled itself tight around his muscular chest and tapered down around his slender waist. It was such a nice change from Juan Carlos's large soft belly which over the years became larger and softer with repeated second helpings of black beans and rice. Her mouth curved into a smile as he raised his glass and offered a toast. His eyes seemed to dance when he spoke, and, when he slowly and deliberately reached across the table and gently touched her hand, she felt her stomach flutter. Alexis could feel herself becoming increasingly aroused. The pace of her heart quickened as it beat against her chest, and she felt a shiver of pure sexual thrill invading her body. It had been a long time since she'd been touched by a man her mind did not create.

Alexis felt a tight knot in the middle of her stomach embarrassed by the thought that Pierce might be aware of her aroused state. She took several deep breaths and stood up trying to stifle the thoughts that were running through her mind.

"I have to use the ladies' room," she said abruptly and left.

* * *

When Alexis returned, she looked Pierce in the eye and brushed a strand of hair behind her ear as she said, "Tell me everything."

Pierce first told Alexis about his meeting with Marcus and his belief that Juan Carlos's extradition was inevitable. He then explained that the DEA offered Juan Carlos a deal to avoid extradition if he would agree to testify against the Carraboca cartel. Alexis looked uncertain. "Why would the DEA think Juan Carlos could help them with anything having to do with the Carraboca cartel?"

Pierce frowned. "Because they believe that he works for the Carraboca Cartel."

Alexis was irritated by the accusation. "That's nonsense. They are obviously wrong."

Pierce shook his head. "They aren't wrong."

Alexis took a deep breath and told herself that Pierce was mistaken. "Juan Carlos is not a drug dealer. And he does not work for the Carraboca Cartel. He's clearly being set up," she said her voice colored with anger.

Pierce felt guilty at being the one to tell Alexis about her husband.

Pierce sighed heavily. "Juan Carlos told me himself that he works for the cartel."

Her fingers twisted as her hands worked at each other. She felt a lump in her throat.

"In exchange for his full cooperation, the DEA will place both of you into protective custody," Pierce said.

Alexis nodded, cleared her throat and asked in near disbelief "What exactly did Juan Carlos say?"

"He doesn't trust anyone, so naturally he's a little scared." Pierce took a sip of water and slowly put the glass back on the table. "I don't think he believes that the DEA can protect him."

Alexis gave an exasperated sigh. "My husband works for Dario Carraboca," she whispered mournfully.

Pierce nodded. “Juan Carlos is responsible for laundering the cartel’s money.” Pierce tried to put it as delicately as he could.

Alexis considered that for a moment and then said, “Juan Carlos told you that he launders the cartel’s money in those exact words?”

“Yes,” he said half-heartedly. Pierce didn’t speak another word. He didn’t have to. The restaurant suddenly felt small. Alexis felt paralyzed, pinned somewhere between nausea and disbelief. “So, if Juan Carlos agrees to cooperate . . .”

“In the past, those that have agreed to testify against the cartel have all been brutally murdered before they could give the DEA anything useful,” Pierce said, finishing her thought for her.

All the color drained from her face. “I’ve heard that they rape and torture family members of potential witnesses.” She said with some difficulty.

Pierce’s jaw clenched as was his habit when he didn’t want to talk about something. “I have heard the same thing.”

Alexis was becoming increasingly distressed.

Pierce leaned forward pushing aside the candlelight holder.

“Alex,” he whispered softly, trying to convince her that it was not a hopeless situation. Please believe me when I tell you that I am going over all our options and I am already making arrangements for your safety.”

“If they want me, they’ll find me and there really isn’t much that you will be able to do,” she said, lowering her eyes to avoid making eye contact with Pierce.

Pierce took a firm hold of her hand. His strong hands prompted Alexis to look up until her eyes locked on to his. His deep blue eyes and intense way made him seem invincible. However, she knew better, there were no longer knights in shining armor. But if they still existed, she was certain that Pierce would be one of them.

"I'm not going to let that happen," he said with a determined tone.

Alexis pulled her hand away. Her eyes were filled with sorrow and tears. There was a stunned, uncomprehending look on her face.

"I need some air," she stammered as she rushed towards the exit.

Pierce thought about following her, but he let her go.

* * *

When he left the restaurant, he spotted Alexis sitting on a bus bench across the street.

"Why are you still involved in this case?" She shook her head and turned her face away from Pierce's gaze. "You need to stop helping my husband," she demanded.

Pierce's eyes narrowed. "What do you mean?"

Tears streamed down her face and her throat felt constricted every time she tried to speak as if her words were choking her.

Pierce could see that she was confused and frightened.

"Juan Carlos will do whatever he has to save his own ass, even if it means putting you directly in the line of fire. I can't protect you without helping him."

Alexis felt numb. Her slight shoulders slumped forward. They looked like the weight of all those sleepless nights was finally too much. Alexis reflected on the countless sacrifices she'd made during her marriage for the sake of her husband and their relationship. She had misjudged her husband. "I chose this," she said in a hushed voice. "Nobody made me marry him." She turned to Pierce, looked into his eyes and bit her lip. "Walk away . . . You're risking too much." Her tone was flat and final.

Pierce started to say something, but Alexis stopped him with the wave of her hand. She was too exhausted to argue.

He wanted to tell her that he would never let anything bad happen to her. That he has never walked away from a fight. He just had to make sure when the fight came to him, it would be at a time and place when he had the upper hand and not Dario.

"I have a few ideas for getting Juan Carlos out of prison and making sure that both of you safely disappear," his voice shook her from her trance. Pierce paused to look around. "If the cartel believes that Juan Carlos is well hidden and poses no real threat, there's a chance that they will eventually stop looking for him," Pierce said, trying to comfort Alexis, even though there was a small part of him that didn't believe that Dario would ever stop looking for Juan Carlos unless he had a reason to stop. "But, for any plan to work, we are going to need money."

"I don't have the kind of money that you're talking about," Alexis said, unable to conceal her misery.

"Do you remember when I mentioned that Juan Carlos was given a down payment of three million dollars?"

Alexis looked at Pierce almost hopeful.

Pierce's eyes flashed. "I know where to find it."

Chapter Twelve

"It's been a long time since I've been in this area, but that street looks familiar. Turn here," Alexis said. Pierce and Alexis passed small and large vacant, trash-filled lots and abandoned warehouses in what used to be part of Miami's Warehouse district looking for Juan Carlos's club. Alexis counted more people sleeping on the streets than she did parked cars or pedestrians. This was a strange location for an upscale private club. "*No one in their right mind would walk in this neighborhood at night*," Pierce thought. On top of a two-story building was a billboard which advertised a new high-class, sophisticated South-Beach condominium. The billboard conveniently blocked the view of the blight for those travelling just above them on I-95. Pierce swerved the car to a complete stop in front of the only building that appeared to be occupied and had several valets standing by the entrance.

* * *

The urban decay covering several blocks where homes and stores and businesses once stood just north of downtown Miami and the debris and menagerie of discarded cigarette brands scattered along the street reminded Pierce of a place he had visited during the summer of his first year of law school. Pierce had just completed his last day of his eight week rotation at the Legal Aid Office in Harlem. One of the paralegals, a busty Puerto Rican girl with curly brown hair and an infectious smile named Yolanda asked him if he wanted to go out for a good-bye drink. He wound up having several vodka and cranberry juices before the late hour beckoned for him to take Yolanda home. She lived just south of the Bronx Zoo, he remembered. The neighborhood was a wasteland of scorched tenement buildings. If not for the overwhelming stench of old urine which made it all too real, her neighborhood could easily have been a movie set for one of those futuristic movies which depicted New York City as a ravaged and forsaken combat zone. Certain moments are forever etched in one's mind. For Pierce one of those was how Yolanda completely freaked out when she offered to call him a taxicab, and he declined saying the subway was only two blocks away.

"*You'll never make it alive*," he remembered her saying. He hadn't thought about Yolanda or that night for a long time.

Through the guarded entrance, a beautiful woman with large breasts and a beguiling smile waited to greet them. As they drew closer, Pierce noticed that the blue carpenter's outfit that hugged the contours of her supple body but came cheerfully short of covering her breasts was elaborate body paint.

"Welcome to Vellutato, my name is Mint," she smiled.

Pierce's face brimmed. "I think I know what type of club this is."

Alexis studied Mint's nakedness as though she was in some sort of competition.

"Are you members or is this your first time here?" She asked.

Pierce could not contain his grin. "No . . . no, we're not members. Actually, we're here to see Domenic," he said, trying in vain to contain the smile that was forming along the corners of his mouth.

Alexis was not amused.

"Oh, ok. You can wait for him inside, but you are going to have to buy a one-night membership. I am sorry, but I am not allowed to let you wait for him here."

Pierce nodded.

"That will be two hundred for the two of you," she said.

Pierce suddenly stopped smiling.

"You can wait at the bar. I'll page Domenic for you and if you're interested, I will be in the club in a little while," Mint said smiling at Pierce appraisingly.

Alexis caught Pierce's minute smile and shook her head at him. "You're ridiculous," she said.

* * *

When they entered the club, Pierce was surprised. He was not naïve enough to think that all swinger's clubs were necessarily seedy, but he did have certain preconceived notions. He was pleased by the club's welcoming social ambiance. The crowd was fashionably dressed, attractive and culturally mixed. The typical crowd one would see at other trendy clubs on South Beach, he thought. Inside, the club was tastefully decorated with tables, ample seating and plush red velvet couches. The club's décor also flaunted dance poles, cages and platforms which were all being made use of by people seemingly seeking a thrill slightly higher than that typically found at more conventional clubs. Along the walls were lush comfortable cabanas with day beds and ample curtains which could be drawn for privacy. In most instances, the curtains remained open as most of the participants seemed to enjoy being watched. Pierce waited at the bar with Alexis absorbing the sights around him. He didn't see any uninvited touching and grabbing that was typical at most other clubs and bars. While the end game for most people venturing out into Miami's social scene was probably the same, there appeared to be well articulated rules at Vellutato that were strictly enforced.

Alexis drank more glasses of whisky than Pierce cared to count. Fuming, Alexis concentrated on all the implications that surrounded Juan Carlos's ownership of Vellutato. She gripped her glass tightly, held it to her lips and took a gulp trying to drown out her husband and his secrets and his lies. Juan Carlos never went to great lengths to hide his unfaithfulness. In fact, that was his cunning. Alexis could see what was happening, but she was too young and naive. She thought that having children with Juan Carlos would bring them together again. A baby would make him want to spend more time in Miami, she thought. But by the time Alexis got pregnant, Juan Carlos seemed more anxious than blissful by the news. Five weeks later, Alexis was rushed to the hospital with severe vaginal bleeding and cramping. Juan Carlos flew back to Miami when he heard about her miscarriage. He stayed for a week and worked at being a sympathetic and caring husband, but he was unconvincing.

Sitting on the barstool, Pierce leaned into Alexis and said, "Don't forget why we're here. I need you to keep your wits about you."

Alexis shot Pierce a dark look. She dipped her face into the tumbler and drank agitatedly trying to forget her intolerable circumstances.

A few moments later Pierce was awe-struck by a freakishly tall dimpled, green-eyed blonde wearing a candy-red corset and seven-inch-high platinum leather boots. She had to be a regular, Pierce thought, because few people took notice of her as she cut across the dance floor towards the bar. Pierce nudged Alexis to turn around, but she seemed not to care.

"Are you the ones waiting for Domenic?" She shouted over the house music.

"Yes," Pierce nodded.

"Follow me," she gestured.

Pierce whispered in Alexis' ear, "It's time to go."

Alexis gulped downed her drink. He reached for her hand to help her off the barstool, but Alexis pushed his hand away.

"I'm fine," she snapped.

They followed the tall woman to the back of the building.

"Wait here," She instructed.

A wearily handsome, stubble-chinned man slowly and carefully peered out of his office.

"I am Domenic," he said.

Pierce introduced himself. Handing Domenic a piece of paper, "My client, Juan Carlos said that you would be able to get me into his office next door."

When Domenic finished reading the note, he looked up and glared at Alexis.

"The note only mentions you," he said suspiciously.

He looked nervous which in itself told Pierce something. Once Domenic discovered that Pierce was Juan Carlos's lawyer, he became even more uncomfortable. Pierce suspected that despite Juan Carlos's notion that no one knew he had an interest in the club, Dario Carraboca knew about it. Judging from Domenic's anxious behavior, Pierce was pretty sure that Dario's people had already paid Domenic a visit.

With an icy voice, Pierce replied, "Juan Carlos's hearing is in a week and I am not going anywhere without her. I'll be sure to tell him that we had a problem."

Domenic wanted Pierce out of his club. He was worried that someone might see them together. But the one thing that Domenic did not want was for his boss, Juan Carlos to find out that he chose to be intractable when given the opportunity to help.

"There's no problem," Domenic replied sheepishly. "Take this hallway; at the end is a door that connects to the auto repair shop next door."

Pierce nodded appreciably and turned towards the dimly lit corridor. With an unfolding gesture of his hand, Domenic added, "Please give me your valet ticket stub. I will have your car moved to the alleyway in the back of the buildings. You will be able to leave from there without anyone seeing you."

Alexis struggled to lift the latch to the unlocked door which had rusted shut.

"This place used to belong to Juan Carlos's uncle," she remembered.

"Please, let me," Pierce said as he eased his way in front of her. When he saw that the door was stuck, he gave it two solid kicks. The second one sent the door crashing off of its hinges. Startled by the noise made by the door when it slammed onto the floor, Pierce was worried it would attract attention.

"We better hurry. There's no telling who's likely to show up after all the noise we've made."

"Relax Sweetheart, it sounded just like a gunshot and that won't draw much attention around here," Alexis slurred her words, stumbling past the fallen door and swaying drunkenly towards the back of the warehouse. Juan Carlos's office was not visible from the general warehouse area. Alexis turned back towards Pierce as she got to the doorway.

"This used to be Juan Carlos's office," she said.

There was an old desk in the middle of the office. Alexis rolled back a piece of frayed carpet just below the desk. Under the carpet was a wooden board which had been used to level off the floor. Pierce lifted the wooden board and exposed a floor safe.

"Juan Carlos always kept some money here in case of an emergency," she said.

Pierce pulled out the piece of paper containing the combination.

Pressing on the flashlight application of his cell phone he handed it to Alexis and told her to point the light on the safe's dial.

Alexis held the light while she watched Pierce deliberately work through the combination. The tiny beam from Pierce's cell phone shook unsteadily as Pierce tried to focus on the dial's settings.

"Try and keep the light on the safe," he said.

"Sorry," she said with a loud hiccup.

The sound of a dog barking in the distance and the occasional blare of a passing car's stereo were the only other sounds which filtered all the way back to Juan Carlos's office. When the dial's setting stopped on the last number of the combination, Pierce paused and looked up at Alexis with a raised eyebrow as if to say, "here we go."

Pierce lowered the light to get a better look at the safe's contents. Whatever was in there was covered by a faded green thick canvas bag. He pulled off the bag exposing neatly piled stacks of one hundred-dollar bills. A feeling of dread overwhelmed Alexis. Stunned, her eyes widened at the same time as she exhaled. Pierce managed a small smile as he reached back for the bag. He began stuffing the packets of money into it. Alexis just sat there.

"Alex, we shouldn't press our luck," Pierce said trying to convince her that the faster they got out of the warehouse, the safer they would be. Alexis, still a little dazed, just nodded as the reality of her husband's double life had completely set in. She knew Pierce was right but at that moment her head was swirling. Her mind was a feverish montage of Juan Carlos's drug deals and infidelities. The whisky was also taking a toll and no longer just numbing her pain. Suddenly all of the color drained from her face, her stomach falling out from under her as if she were on a roller coaster that just made its first drop. In that instant she doubled over and threw up. Her body spasmed and reeled and retched. Alexis retched again and again. Pierce stopped putting the money into the bag and took a step towards her. Alexis flinched away from him. He ignored her and held her hair back away from her face. Between heaves, Alexis wept and with a childlike innocence murmured: "How could I have been so stupid?"

Clutching her stomach Alexis eased back onto the floor and eventually the nausea dissipated. When Pierce was satisfied that she had stopped throwing up, it took him only a few more minutes to finish packing the rest of the money into the bag. Pierce looked at Alexis closely to see if she was able to make it back to the car on her own. The rims of her eyes were red, the whites bloodshot. Pierce lifted the bag and stepped towards Alexis. Extending his hand to help her up he said, "We'd better be moving along."

Alexis nodded trying to avoid eye contact and drifted despondently towards the rear exit. Pierce could instantly tell that at that moment she was done. When Pierce looked at her, he no longer saw the seductive enchantress with the luminous eyes that first visited him in his office. Her eyes now belonged to a woman gazing into deep space and without a flicker of hope.

They stepped out the warehouse into a poorly lit alleyway. Pierce surveyed the alley to see if there was anyone loitering. He spotted a lanky twenty-something standing next to his car which had been parked in a pool of shadows. He flashed a one-hundred-dollar tip and thanked the valet for watching the car. The valet snapped to attention and hurried to the passenger side to help Alexis with her door. Pierce wasted no time securing the bag in the back seat. When he saw that Alexis was safely next to him, Pierce shifted the car into drive.

Alexis sat with her back slightly turned away from Pierce, staring quietly out of the passenger window. It was times like this that Shane's drunken theories about the futility of monogamous relationships didn't seem so preposterous. Love is such a precarious predicament, Pierce thought. Pierce's eyes drifted to Alexis, he recognized that look. It was not too long ago that he saw it every time he looked at his reflection.

Seeing her like that caused the not so welcome memories of his failed marriage to bubble up. He met Jordan during her freshman orientation in college. When he first laid eyes on Jordan, he was fiercely attracted to her. She was beautiful, a long-legged redhead with eyes as blue as seawater and a sharp mind. He didn't know if it was love at first sight, because he hadn't a clue what love was, but it was unlike anything he'd ever experienced. In the beginning of their relationship, it seemed like all they ever did was laugh and make love. They planned their entire life together. They discussed kids, ambitions and fears. Never once did Pierce think that they wouldn't spend their lives together. But what seemed like a blink of an eye, Jordan's priorities changed. She wanted to put off starting a family indefinitely. Arguments took the place of the laughs they once shared. Love making stopped being passionate and spontaneous and was nothing more than a thinly veiled attempt to sustain a relationship starving for real intimacy. Before their relationship could disintegrate any further, Jordan preemptively and inexplicably packed her bags and took a job in Philadelphia.

A flush passed over Pierce's face. "Alexis," Pierce's voice, though soft broke the silence.

"We need to talk," he said.

Her face was pinched with exhaustion and grief. "I'm tired . . . I just want to go home and get some sleep. Could we do this tomorrow?" Her voice was barely audible.

"Of course," Pierce nodded sympathetically. "But I think that it would be safer for you to stay somewhere else tonight," Pierce said.

Alexis shrugged her shoulders. She didn't seem to care either way.

Lifting the cell phone to his lips Pierce articulated a voice command, "Dial Four Seasons Hotel."

He arranged for a one-bedroom suite. Alexis waited by the bank of elevators while Pierce checked them into the room. She seemed lost and unfocused as she stood uncomfortably by the immense Botero sculptures that resembled sentinels guarding the hotel's elevator banks. She fought her hurt and stepped into the elevator. The two of them rode the elevator in uneasy silence. When the magnetic key unlocked the door, Alexis walked straight towards the bedroom.

Before closing the door to the bedroom, Alexis turned and faced him. "Can I ask you a personal question?" She said.

"Of course," Pierce nodded.

"I was thinking about that two-minute rule you talked about the other day?" Pierce could hazard a guess where Alexis was going.

"You said that a man decides within the first two-to-five minutes of meeting a woman whether he wants to sleep with her?"

Pierce nodded quietly.

"If our circumstances were different, what would you decide about me?"

Looking at her, Pierce felt something stir within him that he had not felt in a long time. There was a bewitching pull in her eyes.

He stared at her for another moment.

"A man would have to be a fool not to want you," he smiled.

"A fool," she repeated with a sad laugh. That's exactly what I've been," she said and closed the bedroom door behind her.

The telephone rang several times before Shane's wife answered it. She was annoyed by the late-night call.

"Kris, I'm sorry for calling so late, but Shane isn't answering his cell," Pierce said.

"You always are Pierce. Hold on while I go get him. He's probably laid out in the den pretending to watch T.V. while he's really sleeping."

Kris put down the receiver and traipsed across their home to the den where Shane was lounging on the sofa with his head propped up on the armrest.

"Are you asleep?" Kris asked in a surly tone which sounded more like an accusation than a question. Shane jumped up rubbing his eyes.

"Can't a man watch a ball game without being harassed?"

"Pierce is on the telephone for you. I told him you were probably sleeping, but he said to wake you," she said, turning and heading back to the bedroom.

"I wasn't asleep," Shane protested as if caught in the midst of a felonious act.

"Sure, you were. The game ended a couple of hours ago," Kris barked back without breaking her stride. As soon as Shane picked up the call, Pierce announced that he and Alexis found the three million dollars that the French police paid Juan Carlos.

Shane was completely awake and thunderstruck. "The three million, you found the three million?"

Pierce didn't know why Shane was surprised. He had been saying since the beginning that Juan Carlos had the money hidden somewhere.

"It was in a floor safe of an abandoned warehouse." Pierce paused for a moment. "Shane, we need to talk. I need your help with . . ."

"Shane cut Pierce off. "Not on the phone. Where are you?"

"The Four Seasons."

"I'll meet you tomorrow morning at six at Deli Lane. It's across the street from the hotel," he said.

Chapter Thirteen

BON FUTURO PRISON, CURACAO

In the early morning hours before the sun rose over the Caribbean Sea and most of the prison was still asleep, Marcus Van Delft arrived at the security checkpoint. The young woman that accompanied him made the prison guards envious. A guard with a clipboard stepped towards Marcus and gave him a knowing look.

"Who is this young woman you have with you Mr. Van Delft?"

Marcus slid a white envelope into the guard's hand. "This is Juan Carlos Laporte's niece. The visit has been approved by Mr. Jones, the Assistant Director."

The guard wrote nothing, took a step back, managed to say, "Wait a minute," and then left them. It occurred to Marcus that neither Rene Cabrera nor the cartel appreciated the considerable effort it took to arrange a conjugal visit for Juan Carlos Laporte.

Juan Carlos liked very young women and made it clear that he didn't want a professional. The girl that accompanied Marcus was not blond, but she was very seductive in a ripe wild way. She had a certain golden glow to her skin and long dark curly hair. Her faded blue jeans hugged her thick thighs and shapely ass. And when she walked, her round breasts bounced.

Marcus and the young woman were escorted inside the building, through a series of heavy doors, past more guards, and finally to a small isolated jail cell. The cell was no different than the rest of the prison building, dirty and poorly ventilated. Juan Carlos's cell consisted of a small bed, sink and toilet squeezed tightly into a narrow space. Spider webs hung from every corner like rotten drapes. The lack of any natural light made it difficult for Juan Carlos to know the time of day. He was isolated from the rest of the prison population and, except for the visits from Marcus, Hogan and the one visit from Pierce, he never left his jail cell. The air too was a prisoner. There was no draft. The humidity, trapped with the lingering cigarette smoke, doled out its own brand of corporal punishment.

Juan Carlos acknowledged Marcus before turning his attention to the young woman.

"What is your name," Juan Carlos asked politely.

"My name is Charlotte," She replied.

Juan Carlos nodded. His eyes darted to Marcus. He shot Juan Carlos a look which told him they had more business to discuss. On those occasions when Marcus previously visited Juan Carlos; they took place in his cell and the guards were paid well to make sure that there was no record of them.

"Give me an hour, then you can come back for her," Juan Carlos said.

Juan Carlos moved to the bed and sat down. His eyes strayed over Charlotte's body.

"Come here," he said.

Charlotte obliged and stood in front of him. He reached under her shirt and felt the warm softness of her breasts.

"Do you want me to take off my shirt?" She asked.

Juan Carlos smiled.

Her large swollen breasts jutted out proudly; two magnificent mounds capped by suntanned nipples.

"How old are you?"

"I'm seventeen."

Rubbing her large nipples; her nipples seemed to swell even larger. "So, tell me are you clean?" He asked.

"Yes, I'm clean," she purred.

Juan Carlos smiled. "Take off your pants." Charlotte pushed the denim down her lush thighs, and stood before Juan Carlos, a vision in black lace.

"Do you want me to take my panties off?" She asked.

"Everything," he said.

Charlotte stepped through her lace panties and unhooked her bra. Juan Carlos stood up and moved Charlotte to the wall.

He pressed her naked body firmly against the wall to restrain her from too much movement. His hands freely roamed, exploring the curves of Charlotte's body before he pinned her wrists above her head. His one strong hand was all it took to keep her still from the waist up. Fingers from his free hand slid deep inside of her. Charlotte bucked her hips riding his fingers. Aroused, Charlotte slipped one hand free from Juan Carlos's grip and groped his hardness through his pants.

They paid no attention to the guard's voices just outside the jail cell.

"Mmmm . . . You're so hard," she whispered in a breathless tone.

"Get on your knees . . . now," he demanded.

Charlotte knelt willingly before him and pulled his pants down. Juan Carlos's hand cupped the back of her head. Nudging her forward, he grabbed hold of her hair to anchor his grasp. "Suck me." he ordered in a low growl. Charlotte eagerly sucked him.

Turning her around to face the wall, Charlotte bent forward, arching her back to make it easier for Juan Carlos to slide inside of her. He spit on his hand and wet his throbbing muscle until it was moist enough to slide between Charlotte's ass cheeks. Surprised, she turned and glared at him. "Not there. Not in my ass," she said forcefully. Juan Carlos crushed her against the wall. His expression turned fierce. Juan Carlos didn't want to just fuck Charlotte; he wanted to dominate and humiliate her. Charlotte begged and frantically pleaded with him to stop. But Juan Carlos sadistically plunged into her backside.

She gave a yell of pain. Juan Carlos used his hands to keep her from twisting away as he pushed fully inside of her ass. Her tightness closed around his manhood squeezing it firmly in its grip. Juan Carlos shoved faster and deeper, tearing her anus. Charlotte screamed and squirmed around trying to escape. She bucked wildly, and Juan Carlos continued thrusting savagely into her tight opening. Charlotte twitched and made a noise, a gasping whimper before her body went limp. When she had no more fight left, he flung her on to the bed holding her hands over her head. He gave her a slap across her face before pushing his hard penis into her mouth. He held her there, going in and out as she gagged and struggled to breathe. Charlotte's face turned red and tears welled up in her eyes as Juan Carlos pounded her warm mouth. He pushed harder and deeper into her throat until he exploded. When he was finished, Juan Carlos removed his flaccid penis and wiped it clean across her face. A gasping sob of shame escaped her mouth. Charlotte began to cry, her body sweaty, convulsing. She sobbed uncontrollably. Dazed and her rectum dripping blood, Charlotte staggered towards her clothing and begged hysterically to be let out of the cell.

Chapter Fourteen

Pierce stepped into the bedroom for a brief moment before leaving. The room was dark. Alexis slept soundly under a comforter with her long brown hair draped across the pillow. Placing the "Do Not Disturb" sign on the doorknob, Pierce shut the door to the hotel room behind him taking great care to make sure the door locked. As he crossed the street, he noticed the shadows along the street beginning to evaporate as the Miami sun peeked out over the bay.

Inside the restaurant, business was slow; it would remain that way until 6:45 A.M. Shane was sitting at a table in the corner reading the Wall Street Journal when Pierce walked into the restaurant. He liked to be early. He had been that way since grade school. Shane's dark eyes, pencil thin eyebrows and shaved head gave him a menacing appearance. He had a hardness to his face that no suntan could conceal. Despite his Ivy League education, Shane's demeanor resembled one of a drill sergeant. He was surly, painfully honest and had little tolerance for excuses. Growing up, Shane had been in more fights than he cared to admit, but didn't believe in fighting. When confronted, however, Shane never hesitated. He was not a big fan of letting events play out. In his younger days, if threatened, he was prone to violence. He preferred to get the upper hand, so he always struck quickly and decisively.

Shane from behind his newspaper was sipping on a large cup of coffee.

"Good morning," Pierce said, offering a friendly smile.

Shane's eyes popped over the newspaper, his expression said, "*Fuck you for getting me into this*."

"Before we meet Hugo, I need to ask you one more time. Are you sure you want to do this?"

Pierce shot Shane a look, and Shane knew the answer.

"We have less than a week left," Pierce said looking so unconcerned that it made Shane irritable. The frown on Shane's brow became even more pronounced. Gesturing to the waitress to bring him the bill, Shane said, "I guess we have a lot to talk about."

"I guess we do," Pierce nodded.

Shane's eyes shifted to the couple sitting at the table immediately to his left. He shook his head in a curt way that told Pierce that this was not a good place to talk.

"What about breakfast?" Pierce asked.

Shane squinted and then smiled. "I already ate."

Pierce looked blankly at Shane for a moment, "I'm actually pretty hungry."

Shane stood up. "You can eat at the hotel. I reserved a conference room. Hugo's meeting us there in twenty minutes," he said.

Pierce checked his watch and gave Shane an affable smile. "Twenty minutes is plenty of time."

He glanced casually over his shoulder at the waitress and ordered a vegetarian omelet to go.

* * *

Mia Dawson, Hugo's partner in the executive protection company walked purposefully into the conference room. Her ash blond hair was stylishly tapered just above her shoulders. She was tall, halfway between lithe and muscular with a classically pretty face and the cheekbones of a Nordic goddess. She had large expressive eyes that were both curious and intelligent. Mia tended to dress conservatively; almost always wore her blond hair pulled back in a low ponytail. Most men found her irresistible, but to some, Mia's straight forward manner made her seem harsh and intimidating. Mia had been Hugo's partner since serving with him during his second tour of duty in Afghanistan, where she was part of his team that hunted and killed al-Qaeda and members of the Taliban. Having spent four years hunting anyone who posed a threat to the new U.S backed government in Afghanistan made the transition to security consultants an easy one. As partners, Mia and Hugo complimented one another. Mia was analytical and obsessed with detail. Hugo was an equal mix of intellect and intuition and extremely capable under pressure. Mia's intelligence and attention to detail satisfied Hugo's as well as all their company's needs. And when Hugo's needs were of a sexual nature, Mia fucked him. It was the best sex she'd ever had, and definitely the best sex he'd ever had.

When Mia saw Shane, she smiled wryly and hugged him. "It's so good to see you Papa Bear."

She turned towards Pierce revealing her blue-grey eyes; "Counselor, it's been a while. I wish we were seeing each other under better circumstances," she said matter-of-factly, in a voice that projected frankness.

Walking behind her was a large muscular man. Hugo towered over Mia, who was five foot ten inches tall. His thick neck, broad shoulders and powerfully built arms made him look like a professional athlete. To add to his mystique, Hugo moved with that rare mix of athleticism, grace and menace and acted like a man who needed a steady diet of danger in order to thrive.

When Hugo looked at Pierce, he shook his head solemnly.

Mia started by explaining that since speaking with Hugo she had been studying and familiarizing herself with the cartel's known operatives, including outside contractors that they might use. She detailed a variety of security countermeasures that her company could deploy to protect Alexis.

"They won't try to kill her, at least, not immediately. This is clearly a leverage situation," she said.

Hugo agreed. "If they kill her, they have nothing to barter with, this is a snatch and grab operation."

"Maybe," Shane interjected, "but have you considered there is a certain amount of pressure which the cartel can apply on Juan Carlos by killing Alexis. Juan Carlos has a mother and two sisters. Killing Alexis sends a very strong message," Shane reasoned.

Hugo answered quickly. "We're talking about the Carraboca Cartel. They don't need to send Juan Carlos a strong message for him to know they're serious. Killing Alexis would be a brash move and the cartel is patient and calculating. A dead body gives them less advantage than the threat of one," he said.

Mia shook her head. "Killing Alexis could have the opposite effect. Alexis's death could push Juan Carlos to cut a deal with the DEA in order to protect the rest of his family. The cartel is going to kidnap Alexis. That's the smart play," Mia nodded decisively.

Hugo shook his head in agreement. "That's the logical move. What surprises me is that they haven't done it already."

Pierce bit his lip. "Juan Carlos's hearing is in a week," he said with a sense of urgency.

Mia shrugged. "I know, the window is rapidly closing. They should be making their move any time now."

Hugo sighed. "Even if they kidnap Alexis, that's only a temporary solution to the bigger problem, which is Juan Carlos."

Shane's eyes shifted across the table from Pierce to Hugo and finally to Mia. "I don't follow," he said.

Seeing the confusion on Shane's face, Mia jumped in: "Holding Alexis hostage won't buy Juan Carlos' silence for a long period of time. Even if he refuses to talk for now, the cartel won't be satisfied. His situation is unpredictable and could change at any minute. I imagine that the DEA is going to put all kinds of pressure on him. Eventually the DEA will break Juan Carlos."

Hugo started to interrupt "So what we're saying . . ."

Mia shot Hugo a look which said: "*I'm not done*."

"What I'm saying is this isn't over until Juan Carlos Laporte is dead. When he's dead, he can't talk. Once the Cartel kills Juan Carlos, they will kill Alexis if they have her," Mia turned and shared a knowing glance with Hugo.

"No loose ends," Hugo added in a low somber voice.

Pierce cleared his throat and his expression became solemn.

"So, you've basically arrived at the same conclusion that I have. The best way to protect Alexis is to help Juan Carlos," Pierce paused. "So how do we help him?"

"We don't" Mia responded curtly. "We protect Alexis until the Feds move Juan Carlos or the Cartel kills him."

Pierce looked at Mia with disbelieving eyes. "So, we sit and wait for Juan Carlos to die? That's our plan?"

"You're hiring us to protect Alexis. Not to interfere with the DEA. Trust in the Feds, they will break him quickly. When he talks, the Feds will move him and Alexis into the Witness Protection Program," Mia shot back.

Pierce shook his head. "That's too risky." He could see Mia's legendary temper start to simmer.

Mia pulled in a quick breath and said, "The end game here is to keep Alexis safe until the Feds take her into custody. That's it. . . . no more."

Pierce looked across the table at Hugo and Mia. "How many witnesses so far that have agreed to testify against the cartel have the Feds been able to protect?" Before they could respond, Pierce held out the number zero with his middle finger and his thumb. “From what I hear that would be a big fat goose egg.”

Mia and Hugo looked at each other. Hugo spoke. “Do you have any idea what happens to us if we get between the cartel and the DEA?”

Pierce considered the question for a moment. “And if we don’t make Juan Carlos part of our solution both Juan Carlos and Alexis die.”

Mia rolled her eyes. “The only way to help him is to break him out of prison, and I know that’s not what you’re suggesting.”

“That’s exactly what I am suggesting.” Pierce snapped back.

Hugo sighed, eyes shut as though he needed to rid himself of an inner torment. “Do you understand that protecting Alexis is risky enough? I agreed to do this for you and Shane,” he said jabbing his immense finger at Pierce. “But this is bull shit. If we help Juan Carlos escape, all those mother fuckers will be coming for us.”

Pierce glared. “So, let’s give them a reason not to come after us.”

Hugo sat back and gripped the armrests of his chair, almost as if he was trying to hold himself back.

Shane could clearly see that the atmosphere was becoming increasingly explosive.

“Wait a minute Hugo! Hear him out,” he said. “What Pierce is saying isn’t completely off the mark. “Why would we risk our lives to protect someone when we know that once we turn her over to the feds, she’ll probably wind up dead anyway? If we’re going to do that we might as well let the cartel take her now and save everybody the trouble,” Shane said.

Hugo placed a big hand on the table. He tapped a thick finger and said, “That was exactly my point a couple of days ago when you asked for my help,” he barked at Shane.

“Okay, we are in agreement. So shut the fuck up for a minute.”

Shane turned his attention to Pierce. He was now completely focused on him; "what do you have in mind?"

Hugo and Pierce eyed one another.

"If we get Juan Carlos out of jail and he disappears with Alexis, the cartel may let him go if they are assured that the feds don't have him, and they can't extradite him back to the U.S."

Staring directly into Pierce's eyes, Hugo asked in a condescending tone: "And why would the cartel be okay with that? If they kill him," Hugo clapped loudly to make a point, "problem solved."

Pierce stared back at Hugo without blinking. "Because, Juan Carlos would now be the one with the leverage," he said.

When Pierce was sure he had their undivided attention, he conceded that on its face it appeared that the cartel's only option was to kill Juan Carlos to keep him from disclosing their secrets.

Hugo shrugged as if Pierce was wasting his time.

"What if, by killing Juan Carlos what the Cartel was trying to prevent, actually happens?" Pierce asked.

Mia narrowed her eyes gazing at Pierce speculatively.

"You're saying that if the cartel kills Juan Carlos, that's when he becomes a witness against them?" Hugo proclaimed more than asked.

"Precisely," Pierce said.

Hugo, Mia and Shane all looked at each other and then at Pierce with the same dubious expression. Shane searched Pierce's face wondering what he was thinking.

"Buddy, are you feeling alright?" Shane asked, trying not to sound confrontational.

Pierce nodded even though he wasn't listening. "We make a video tape of Juan Carlos that covers every detail that he knows about the cartel's operations, and we send a link to the video to the cartel. Once they've seen the video, we tell the cartel that if anything happens to

Juan Carlos, Alexis or their families, that video which includes every detail of their drug operations would be sent to the DEA. The DEA would now have all of the cartel's smuggling routes, locations of their safe houses and bank accounts."

Shane was processing what Pierce was saying. "What about the DEA?" He asked.

Pierce gave them the impression of having considered every angle. "If we move Juan Carlos and Alexis to a non-extradition country any threat the DEA presents is neutralized," he said.

Shane turned to Hugo with a *"could this fucking work"* look in his eyes and asked him if Dario was the type to negotiate if his back was against the wall.

Before Hugo could answer, Pierce answered the question for him.

"There is no way that Dario could risk the DEA getting its hands on the video. There's nothing to negotiate. Dario would have no choice but to take the deal we offer him . . . I have three million dollars to pull this off. Whatever we don't use you keep."

Hugo leaned forward slightly, placed his hands together on the table and looked at his partner. He couldn't argue with Pierce's logic or his offer. "What do you think?"

Mia appeared to be deep in thought as she considered Pierce's plan. The biggest flaw was that Pierce's plan wasn't really a plan but more of an idea since it didn't include any details. Extracting hostages was not something that Mia or Hugo had done since their days as Special Forces operators and the pensive look on Mia's face suggested that getting Juan Carlos out of Bon Futuro prison would be no easy snatch and grab. There were a lot of blanks to fill.

"I know a local contractor who knows more about how things work in Curacao than anyone. We'll need some local Intel before we can consider an extraction." Mia looked like she was still thinking about

Hugo's question. According to her, it was poor tradecraft to attempt an extraction without weeks of Intel and a well-developed plan. Maps had to be memorized, schedules scrutinized, and multiple modes of transportation put in place.

"We don't have a lot of time . . . actually we have no time so if we do this, we are going to have to wing parts of it." Mia folded her hands across her chest. "Meaning if something unexpected comes up that we cannot control, we have to abort," she said.

"So, what do you think?" Hugo asked a second time.

There was a slight delay and finally Mia said, "I'll need to get busy if this is going to work."

Chapter Fifteen

BON FUTURO PRISON, CURACAO

Juan Carlos sat on the floor flush against the dark stone wall of his dirty dank cell with his chin resting on his chest and head down between his knees. He sat motionless trying to steer his thoughts away from the oppressive heat and stagnant air that reeked of sex and cigarette smoke. In the days following his arrest, Juan Carlos started to wonder if he would ever see his family again. He found himself thinking incessantly about Alexis. It was ironic, he thought, how one comes to appreciate things they have long taken for granted when they're no longer at their disposal. He smiled as he thought about the time Alexis surprised him at Miami International Airport wearing nothing but a trench coat and her captivating smile. He hadn't thought about that time or Alexis in that manner for a long time. He had no explanation for "why" or "when" he stopped desiring Alexis. What he did know was that for quite some time he looked to other women to satisfy his sexual urges. Sleeping with his wife had become no different than taking care of his other marital obligations. His thoughts fast forwarded to Charlotte. As if on cue, he lifted his fingers, the ones that earlier had been buried deep inside of her to his nose and inhaled deeply as he took in her essence.

The cell door was yanked open and Marcus Van Delft stood at its threshold. A vein bulged in his forehead while he glared at Juan Carlos. Marcus was flush with anger. Juan Carlos lifted himself out of his daydream and up off the floor. Handing him a sealed Manila envelope Marcus said through gritted teeth, "I was instructed to give you this."

Still wanting to savor the recent memory of Charlotte's tight body, Juan Carlos flung the envelope onto the bed with an inaudible curse. He stepped to the small sink against the wall and washed his face with such force that water sprayed like a shower onto the floor.

His eyes glanced towards the envelope. Once he finished putting on his dog-and-pony show for Agent Hogan, he knew that Dario would send an assassin. What he wasn't sure of, was how long Dario would wait before he killed him. Would the cartel wait to make sure that the DEA took the bait? Juan Carlos's mind was whirling; he couldn't seem to catch hold of a single thought.

Juan Carlos took a deep breath. "So, when am I supposed to meet with the DEA?

"In two days," Marcus replied matter-of-factly.

Juan Carlos rubbed his neck. He could feel the tension starting to build in it: "Really, that soon?"

Marcus nodded. "Your friend wants this done quickly. If we put the DEA off any longer, they will get suspicious. You know how paranoid they can be."

A spike of anxiety washed over Juan Carlos. That feeling caused him to reach for the vodka.

"Rene asked that you study the information in the envelope and commit it to memory. It needs to appear as if it is second nature and not rehearsed. Otherwise, the DEA may have reason to doubt it," Marcus said.

"I know what I have to do," Juan Carlos scowled at Marcus. "Two days is plenty of time."

Marcus shook his head in agreement. He took it as a small victory that Juan Carlos didn't throw the bottle at him. He waited for Juan Carlos to consume a few ounces. When he looked relaxed enough, Marcus cleared his throat. "Is there anything else I can get you before I leave?"

Not knowing whether he would live to see the outside of his jail cell ever again, Juan Carlos wanted to indulge his sexual urges as much as he could.

"Another bottle of vodka and bring me a different girl," he demanded.

Marcus stared at him with his mouth open. He couldn't even begin to imagine what Juan Carlos could have done to a woman that was paid to have sex with him to cause her to scream and hysterically bang on the cell door to be let out.

"Rene asked me to arrange for a conjugal visit. He never said anything about more than one."

Juan Carlos's eyes closed for a moment, when he jerked them open again, his stare punched a hole through Marcus. He lunged forward and grabbed Marcus by the shirt. Their faces were only inches apart.

"Do you know what I need right now?" He asked in a clear determined voice.

"Um, no," Marcus said looking bewildered.

"To be distracted," he snapped. "When I'm having sex and looking forward to the next piece of ass, I'm not focused on this shithole I'm in."

Marcus jerked back. "I will try," he stammered. "But you brutalized the last girl. Curacao is a small place, word of what you did to her will get around."

Juan Carlos looked dryly amused. "Did or did you not pay her?"

Marcus shifted nervously.

"If you paid her to let me fuck her, I can fuck her how and wherever I please. That's all, nothing more."

"Marcus," A thin smile creased Juan Carlos's lips and he said, "Get me another one. And don't disappoint me."

Flustered, Marcus looked around the tight space and lowered his eyes towards the floor. His face was twisted with fear. He backed away and fumbled towards the door. Speaking quickly, his voice high and strained, Marcus assured Juan Carlos that he would find someone.

Chapter Sixteen

Alexis reached the conference room and knocked once before pushing the door open. Forgetting her manners, she stared at Hugo.

"I've seen you before," she said.

Hugo smiled. "I supervised the security at a Diplomatic event that you and your husband attended," he said modestly.

Extending her hand Mia said, "I'm Mia Dawson, Hugo's partner." When Alexis looked at Mia, there was a hint of recognition in her eyes.

Sliding past her, Pierce placed the duffel bag full of money on the conference room table. "And that's Shane," Pierce said with a nod.

Alexis stuck her hand out as a polite reflex. Shane looked up and glared at her in a manner that suggested that she had interrupted something very important. His stare made Alexis wobble as if she had lost her balance.

"Don't pay him any attention," Pierce said cracking a smile. "He still hasn't gotten over the fact that his five-year-old son has a bigger penis than he does."

A look of annoyance passed across Shane's face and he muttered, "Very funny Pizza man."

Hugo's laughter boomed off the conference room walls. "Maybe the boy is just freakishly large," he said with snarling amusement.

Holding his thumb and index finger only a couple of inches apart, Pierce lifted his eyebrows as if to say: *not really*. Mia made an impatient noise. She never found such banter very funny. "If you boys are through? We should get back to work."

Mia brought Alexis up to speed by explaining that since the cartel kidnaps family members as insurance against their people cooperating with law enforcement, she and Hugo were hired by Pierce to protect her.

Alexis put a hand on her temple and massaged it as if her head was aching. "When does this end?"

"When your husband is dead," Shane interjected cold heartedly.

Mia flashed Shane an angry look.

"The government thinks that Juan Carlos can help them with their investigation into the cartel's operations," Mia said in an effort to diffuse Shane's callous remark.

Alexis blew out an exasperated breath, "I know."

"If Juan Carlos agrees to testify, the DEA will move both of you somewhere safe."

"Does that place really exist?" Alexis shrugged looking around the conference room.

Shane opened his mouth, but before he could say a word, Mia waved him off. "The Witness Protection program works."

"Most of the time," Shane mumbled under his breath.

Mia glared at Shane.

Hugo recognized that look. He had seen it countless times when he and Mia served together in Afghanistan's desolate terrain.

"Take it easy player," Hugo smiled apprehensively.

"If Juan Carlos agrees to cooperate, both of you will be given new identities," Mia said in a clear and commanding voice.

"Are you fucking kidding me?" Shane returned her stare with a look of his own, not confrontational but unyielding. "I don't believe in sugarcoating things. She deserves to know what the hell is going on."

Shane could see that Mia was thinking about it, but he didn't wait for a response.

"Ok then," he launched right in. "Here's my take on things. The cartel has endless resources and they will never stop looking for Juan

Carlos. So, if you're thinking that you and Juan Carlos will settle down under an assumed identity . . . well that's not how it's going to play out. Bottom line is that you will probably have to get used to moving and changing identities often," Shane said, turning his attention to Mia.

"Am I wrong?" he asked.

"Shane could be right," Mia reluctantly agreed for Alexis's benefit. "Even in the program you'll probably never be able to put down roots."

Alexis's eyes went immediately to Pierce, she couldn't help it; he was the only person who could truly understand her predicament. Her face went a slow, dark red. "Breaking my heart wasn't enough. He destroyed my life," she hissed under her breath.

Pierce put his hand on her shoulder. "It's going to be okay."

"How can you say that?" Alexis asked angrily. "There's nothing left for me. I can be killed by the cartel, or I can live the rest of my life in purgatory with the man responsible for putting me there."

Pierce started to say something but stopped himself. "It's pointless Pierce," Alexis snapped. "This whole thing is pointless," she said, her voice remote and miserable.

Pierce sat quietly trying to figure out how best to reason with Alexis. It seemed surreal to him that to the DEA and the cartel she was nothing more than a chess piece in a high stakes game.

"There is another way," Pierce said, breaching the uncomfortable silence that had enveloped the room. Alexis didn't acknowledge him. It seemed as if his words bounced off her as if an invisible wall was surrounding her.

"We have a different way to go and Mia has already begun to lay the groundwork."

"A different way?" Alexis asked, not understanding.

Pierce thought through the likely scenarios if Juan Carlos was turned over to the French or the Americans. None of them ended with

Alexis walking away safe and unharmed. The smart thing to do was to take Juan Carlos out of play and see what the cartel would do if he no longer posed a threat. "If you and Juan Carlos disappear and the cartel is convinced that no law enforcement agency has Juan Carlos, you might be able to live your lives without running," Pierce said.

"If you're up for it, we even have an idea that we believe might work and ensure that the cartel leaves you alone," Mia said, punctuating her words with an emphatic nod.

Then Mia intuitively added, "This isn't a life sentence. For now, you and Juan Carlos would live together, but once everything stabilizes, you can stop pretending and move on with your life without him."

Alexis looked at Mia with a mixture of hope and trepidation. "But . . . What about the DEA . . . won't they still come after Juan Carlos?"

"Juan Carlos wasn't arrested by the DEA. He was arrested in Saint Maarten," Mia said.

Pierce nodded in agreement. "Mia's right. "But we're going to move you to a non extradition country just to be sure."

Pierce met Alexis's gaze and held it for a moment. Then he said,

"Both of you will be safe."

Alexis sank down further in her chair. She looked exhausted, drawn and confused: "I don't follow . . . how?"

"We're gonna get him out of prison and help the two of you disappear. When the cartel learns that the only remaining threat to them is if they hurt you or Juan Carlos, they will back off," Pierce said.

Alexis struggled to understand the implications of everything Pierce was saying but at that moment logic, intellect and common sense had all abandoned her. But not her instincts: She knew she could trust Pierce with her life.

"Okay, so how exactly are you going to free Juan Carlos?" Alexis asked, trying to steady her nerves.

Chapter Seventeen

Mia Dawson meticulously studied the map of Curacao. Sipping warm coffee but craving a glass of merlot, she also deliberated over the intelligence Hugo assembled concerning Bon Futuro Prison's operations and personnel. The extraction consisted of two parts. The first one was getting Juan Carlos safely out of the prison. The second was getting him off the island before the DEA and the cartel discovered Juan Carlos was missing. Mia knew that there was really no way to get off Curacao that didn't involve some degree of risk. Her military training taught her to keep her missions simple. The more elaborate the mission the greater the chance that things would go wrong. Mia never assumed that things would go wrong, she counted on it. Every operation contained variables. Some were controllable and she could plan for those. Looking for ways to minimize the effect of things she could not control covered the rest. The plan she devised to get Juan Carlos out of prison was uncomplicated, which is the way she liked it. She needed the attending prison physician and only one inside person. The physician during his routine visit to the prison would examine Juan Carlos and inject him with a drug that would induce a high fever. Before leaving the prison, the physician would leave instructions for the infirmary personnel to monitor Juan Carlos's condition. As Juan Carlos's fever spiked and his condition worsened, the prison infirmary would alert the officer in charge of the night shift that they had an extremely sick prisoner. Mia explained that he would be the inside person. Once the prison officer received the call from the infirmary, he would contact the physician in front of another guard and detail Juan Carlos's condition. At that point, the physician would advise them to transfer the prisoner to the hospital without delay. When Juan Carlos's disappearance is investigated, the prison guards and infirmary personnel would all tell the same story.

Mia was exquisitely trained and battle tested when it came to extracting businessmen, soldiers and government operatives from hostile environments. But this mission was different. The standard and acceptable solution for neutralizing problems on those missions was brute force. Her unit held nothing back and had the highest kill ratio among the Special Forces operators deployed in the Middle East. However, that was not an option on this mission which could certainly complicate matters if something went wrong.

Mia took another sip of coffee and organized her thoughts.

"Shane and Hugo will drive the ambulance," she said.

"Curacao is a pretty small island. The prison guards will probably know the usual ambulance drivers. You think two strangers can get past the prison guards at the gate without the guards getting suspicious?" Pierce asked skepticism coloring his voice.

Mia nodded knowingly. She shared the same concern, if the prison guards stop the ambulance and don't recognize anyone, that could complicate things. "It's a bit of a risk, but until I can refine the plan, that's where our guy on the inside earns his money. Our man will telephone down to the gate and order them to wave the ambulance through. It will be pretty dark. They shouldn't be able to get too close a look."

"Controlled turmoil is going to be our ally," Hugo spoke up. "For this to work, Juan Carlos has to appear to be so sick that the prison personnel's only objective will be to get him transported to the hospital as quickly as possible."

Shane took a hard breath and fired off an anxious question. "But what if one of the guards gets cute and tries to stop us when we are putting Juan Carlos in the ambulance?"

Mia and Hugo exchanged a knowing look. The answer was obvious.

"At the late hour a prisoner would only be transferred to the hospital if it was a serious emergency. The guards shouldn't be questioning anything when they have a prisoner that requires emergency medical treatment. Our man on the inside will be well compensated to make sure that no glitch occurs," Mia said.

Hugo patted the Glock 29 holstered under his arm. "But we are going in hot just in case. If I'm left with no choice but to take prison guards out, our inside guy will be the first to take a long dirt nap," Hugo said in his deep bass voice.

Pierce thought about how critical it was for the inside people to play their parts flawlessly. "Are you sure you can get these two individuals to cooperate?"

Mia nodded. "They have little risk, Pierce. No one is going to second guess either one's decision to move a prisoner to the local hospital in a life or death situation." Mia glanced at the duffel bag full of money. "Besides, like I said, they each are going to be well paid."

Looking for the holes in Mia's plan Pierce asked, "But what if they say no?

"They won't," Mia insisted. "Everyone has a price."

"How do you know you can trust them?"

"We don't, but it would be foolish for either one to double cross us."

"Why?"

"Because Doctor Hernandez has two children living in the United States. One at Brown University and the other works in New York. Mr. André Rojer, the prison guard in charge of the night watch has a young son."

Pierce reminded himself—again—that he was only doing this to save Alexis. But he couldn't hide the look of disapproval that flashed across his face. Mia recognized the mutinous set of Pierce's expressions.

"I know what you're thinking. But we're nothing like the cartel," she said trying to appease his concerns.

Pierce leaned forward. "You're using their families as leverage. How are you different?" Each one of his words was a precise clip of judgment.

Hugo looked like he was mentally counting to ten. "You're wrong. The families are our insurance should a problem arise not our leverage. If we can't pay Hernandez and Rojer to cooperate, we abort."

Mia's gaze sharpened. "Don't forget what you are asking us to do. We are risking our lives. We can't afford any fuck ups and that includes Hernandez or Rojer putting us in a compromised situation without a lifeline after they take the money. They need to understand that if they put my team in harm's way, there will be nasty consequences for them," Mia frowned.

Hugo put his huge hand that was the size of a small baseball mitt on Pierce's shoulder. "We are not going to hurt innocents to break out a drug dealer."

Hugo glanced over at Alexis as soon as he made the comment. "I meant no offense by that."

Pierce looked like he had to think about that. "So, tell me," he said leaning back in his chair. At the same time, he caught a glimpse of the map on the conference room table. "How are you planning on getting off the island?"

Mia stood up and bent over the map and in a conciliatory tone that suggested that there was no better option said: "We are going to charter a jet and fly him out of Curacao."

Shane didn't like it but initially said nothing waiting for a reaction from Hugo or Pierce. When they sat quietly, Shane looked at Mia with some frustration.

"That means we need to get Juan Carlos through Customs," Shane huffed with a bullish attitude. "The immigration records are computerized. Even if you get him through under an assumed identity, a flight leaving the island before dawn will be the first lead that the DEA follows."

"Yeah you are probably right, but that's the only way to get as much distance between us and Curacao before morning as possible," Mia said with a shake of her head.

Shane's face contorted. "Not leaving a trail for them to follow is more important. If we slip out by speed boat, there's no trace of us. If we fly out, we have to file a flight plan and leave a paper trail."

Mia peered over the top of her coffee mug at Shane. "I'm aware of that . . . I know that the feds will track the flight."

"So, the speed boat is a better idea."

Mia gave Shane an unhappy frown while she considered Shane's point. "And where would you go?"

"Any of the islands, Aruba for example and we can catch a flight from there."

Mia looked dubious. "You're complicating things Shane. You would still have to deal with customs in Aruba plus you now have to factor in the additional time it will take you to get to the states. This increases the risk. If we're lucky, we have a five-hour window at most before they realize Juan Carlos is missing."

"But," Shane protested. Before he could utter another word, Mia cut him off.

"It will take you almost two hours to get to Aruba by boat."

It only takes two and half hours to fly to Florida from Curacao. If we do it your way, we won't make it to the states for four-to-five hours. By then the FBI and DEA will have men at the airports waiting for all flights arriving from any of the islands close to Curacao including Aruba."

Shane pondered Mia's point.

"So, we don't take off from an airport. What about a rendezvous with a seaplane? We can meet in the ocean and take off from there. There's still no record of any plane leaving Curacao."

Mia drew on her patience but couldn't bite back her instinctive smartass reply. "Sounds like you have the makings of a great movie there."

"Excuse me?"

Mia instantly regretted her harsh comment. "Shane, you're right that there would be no hard evidence of Juan Carlos leaving Curacao, but there are too many things that can go wrong."

Shane shrugged his shoulders, "for instance?"

"Well for starters, a water landing in the ocean in the middle of the night isn't easy. It's going to be pitch black out there. Not many pilots are willing to land a plane under those conditions. There's also a good chance the plane could miss us. Like I said, its pitch black with nothing but a vast ocean. Any rendezvous point in the middle of the ocean is too risky. Even with GPS, we could lose precious time trying to find one another."

Mia winced and blew out an exasperated breath. "And if we don't make the transfer, we would be sitting ducks out there."

"Mia is right we could be in the U.S. in under three hours even if the feds go after the jet, we will be long gone by the time they get there. Hugo said without hesitation, while Pierce simply shook his head.

Shane rolled his eyes unconvinced but went along with it.

"It's settled," Mia said with a determined edge. "We take our chances in Curacao. All airports have services for executive jets. If I can grease the right palms, we should be able whisk Juan Carlos through customs and onto the jet. We'll hopefully have landed in Lauderdale before anyone even realizes Juan Carlos is gone.

"Why Lauderdale?" Pierce shrugged.

"Because we are leaving a trail that can easily be followed, so we want a relatively short flight so we can be on the ground covering our tracks as quickly as possible," Mia said. "Once we touch down in Lauderdale, we'll drive Juan Carlos to Boca Raton and have him on a chartered flight in less than an hour. Once we land in Dallas, we drive the rest of the way to Oklahoma."

Hugo looked at Pierce. "Pierce you'll drive Alexis to Oklahoma and meet us there."

Pierce nodded.

Sounding tense and confused Alexis asked: "Why Oklahoma? Why anywhere in the U.S. for that matter?"

Hugo smiled his razor smile. "Because everyone would expect Juan Carlos to make a run for Europe so the airports will be swarming with people looking for him. Juan Carlos has no ties to Oklahoma. Indian country is the last place they will look for him."

Shane nodded in agreement. "I grew up in and around Oklahoma. Full Blood Indians aren't afraid of anything. When they want to hide something, it stays hidden. Once the video tape is finished and we've cut a deal with the cartel, we will fly the two of you out of the country."

Pierce pushed the duffel bag towards Shane. "You'll be needing this."

Shane looked in the bag and closed it quickly as if its contents were contagious. Still not satisfied with Mia's decision, Shane asked about a contingency.

With a quelling glance at Shane Mia said, “Shane, you and Hugo will meet with Doctor Hernandez. I am waiting on a call from a local contractor who will confirm your meeting with Mr. Rojer, the prison guard in charge of the night shift. Our local contractor will make arrangements to get you in the ambulance—I will work with the executive jet service people to make sure that we have no problems with a late-night departure.”

Turning her attention to Pierce Mia said, “Pierce you and Alexis need to leave tonight. You can’t stay in Miami any longer.”

Mia grabbed the keys to her car and tossed them to Pierce. By now the feds and cartel know what car you drive, so drive this car. It’s a rental,” she said.

Mia walked over to the duffel bag and counted out five thousand dollars.

“Pay cash for everything. No credit cards,” she said handing the money to Pierce.

Mia looked at Alexis “Please give me your cell phone.” Turning towards Pierce she said: “If you need to make a call, use this phone. It does not have GPS, so the phone won’t give away your location. I will call you on this phone once we’re in Dallas and tell you where to meet us.”

A feeling of panic crept inside of Alexis. “I need some air,” she said and rushed out of the conference room.

Seeing her weakening resolution Mia gestured to Pierce.

“You better go get her.”

Chapter Eighteen

Alexis was sitting by the hotel pool staring out at the boats and the bay which shimmered around them. The first time Pierce saw her, Alexis was gazing out at Biscayne Bay from his conference room. Then he had been fascinated by her beauty. Now, what he saw was a deepening fracture in her very will to endure and eyes that had grown sick with misery. Alexis turned and smiled timidly at Pierce as he stepped towards her.

"I'm sorry," she said, her voice sounded tense and fragile like an over tightened violin string.

"It's all right. They threw a lot at you back there," Pierce said trying to console her.

Alexis shrugged her shoulders. "I need to tell my parents where I am," she said in a faint voice.

"Mia will take care of that. She will let them know that you're safe."

Alexis smiled at him; it was a sad smile with something else underneath. She sat quietly for a moment. It wasn't very long before her eyes began to tear. She took a long deep breath. "When I first met you," She awkwardly started. "I didn't tell you everything."

Her cheeks were flush, "I started to suspect that Juan Carlos was into something illegal, but he was very secretive, so I wasn't exactly sure what he was doing," she said, her voice quivering as she spoke.

Pierce didn't speak. He just shook his head and listened.

"When I confronted Juan Carlos about it, he swore to me that all he was doing was giving some people financial advice and helping them move money." Her face turned grave. "When I asked him who he was working for, he insisted that it was better that I didn't know," she sighed. "I got scared and begged him to stop, but he told me that his was not the type of arrangement that he could quit," Alexis said, her voice still trembling slightly.

Pierce assumed that Alexis may have turned a blind eye to the details of Juan Carlos's involvement with the cartel out of necessity. With a nod he asked, "When did you know that Juan Carlos worked for the Cartel?"

"I didn't. I never really knew who Juan Carlos worked for . . . Pierce, I'm sorry . . ."

He shook his head. "Are you?" He asked with a hint of disappointment in his voice.

"I am—"

Pierce looked around to make sure that no one was eavesdropping. "If you're truly sorry, you'll stop playing games and tell me everything you know."

Alexis bit her lip. Pierce saw her face streaked with dry tears. "Juan Carlos told me that he occasionally provided financial advice to some very dangerous people. He told me that was the reason he didn't want me living in Saint Maarten . . . It wasn't until last night that I realized that he was into a lot more than I ever imagined." Alexis stopped. She waited for a response from Pierce or at least some kind of sign that told her that he understood, but Pierce just peered at her over the top of his sunglasses. "You really shouldn't stay out here too long," he said, his voice was calm and professional and it irritated Alexis to no end.

"Pierce, please believe me, I didn't know," Alexis added quickly.

Pierce turned slowly back towards her. He looked like he wanted to say something, something in particular, but thought better of it and walked away without saying anything else.

* * *

Alexis jumped up and hurried to catch up to him.

"Look," she said trembling slightly in her anger and discomfort, "I didn't lie to you."

"No, you didn't," Pierce frowned. "But you weren't honest with me either."

She shot him an impatient look. "I told you what I was absolutely sure of . . . Yes, I could have told you that I suspected that Juan Carlos was into something illegal, but I didn't know he worked for the cartel."

Alexis had a disturbed look on her face. "Would you really have helped me when we first met if I had told you Juan Carlos laundered money for a drug cartel?"

Pierce shrugged but offered nothing more.

Alexis scoffed and shook her head. "I'll answer for you. The answer is no. You never would have agreed to help me."

There was a question that Pierce had wondered about but couldn't bring himself to ask, but in the heat of the moment he managed to say, "Why didn't you just leave him?"

Utterly frustrated, Alexis looked at Pierce in astonishment as she wondered if he had any idea what it was like to be a woman raised in a traditional Cuban family. "I did!" She snapped angrily. "I left him and moved to my parent's house. Juan Carlos flew back and begged me for a second chance. He filled my head with promises, and I believed him, so I went back."

Alexis drew a long-ragged breath. "A few months ago, when I discovered that he had been lying to me about everything including his involvement with those people, I moved out. I rented a small townhouse in Broward. I didn't tell anyone where I lived, but it didn't take him long to find me."

Pierce's eyes widened. "What happened?"

"Juan Carlos showed up every day and when that didn't work, he sent his mother and then my mother and they pressured me into taking him back," she said with a hint of regret.

Alexis nodded dismally. "I don't love him," her voice was tight. She stared up at Pierce with unfocused eyes and gave him a small, apologetic smile, "I don't think I can do this."

Pierce reached over and wiped the tears from her cheek. "You really don't have a choice."

Alexis shooed his hand away. "Don't tell me I don't have a choice."

Her pursed lips and the defiant tilt of her chin seemed to suggest that she'd reached a decision. She leveled her gaze and said, "You should go."

Pierce took off his sunglasses and leaned over and in close so that he was eye to eye with Alexis. "We need to go together."

"Listen to me Pierce," she bristled. "I don't want your help anymore," she said sharply.

Pierce laughed her comment away as if it was a harmless maneuver. "Are you firing me?"

"For Christ's sake," Alexis forced a smile through her watered eyes. "I could never fire you."

Alexis took a long breath and cleared her throat. "You're risking too much. I just don't want you to be involved anymore," she replied in a broken voice.

"I am seeing this through until you are out of the country safely," Pierce said.

"No Pierce!" she started sharply, her voice lowering to a whisper. "I couldn't live with myself if anything ever happened to you." Pierce looked at Alexis; his soft blue eyes coaxing her along. "Nothing is going to happen to me."

Alexis frowned and shook her head. “I can’t ask you to risk your life for something I don’t want . . . You don’t understand; I can’t spend the rest of my life with him. I hate him!” Alexis looked like she wanted to shout, but instead her voice was cool and unexpectedly bitter.

Pierce reached out for her hand. “No one is asking you to. You’re not being handed a life sentence. Once the cartel no longer has any reason to use you as leverage against Juan Carlos, you can leave him and start a new life for yourself. Until then, you’re going to have to trust me,” Pierce said.

Alexis looked up at Pierce. Her eyes glistened like the color of gold. “I do trust you. You are the only man I do trust,” she said.

Chapter Nineteen

FORT LAUDERDALE

The hypnotic drum of rain and lightning flashes made Shane edgy as he stared out of the passenger window into the darkness.

"Coffee?" Mia winked while handing Shane a Styrofoam cup. "Keep the lid on, it's going to be a little bumpy," she said.

Anxiously, Shane took a sip of his coffee and settled back into his seat. The high-pitched wailing sound of the Learjet 45 engines told him that the aircraft was poised to take off. Hugo made a sign of the cross, closed his eyes and offered up a prayer as the jet vertically climbed to thirty thousand feet. Mia smiled at Hugo and patted his thigh. She enjoyed his quirky mannerisms. The roar of the jet engines eventually softened into a whine as the jet reached its cruising altitude.

"Shane," Mia called out to him. "Come sit with us."

Mia sat in a thick leather chair and held a notepad with an endless list of things that needed to be done as soon as they landed in Curacao. Shane watched Hugo peer out of the window into the darkness. At thirty-eight years old, Shane suspected that Hugo had to be getting tired of living a life in the trenches protecting diplomats and rich businessmen and constantly putting himself in dangerous situations. While Hugo was not yet an old man, he wasn't a young man anymore. For Shane, it had been a long time since he had done anything like this. Ever since he agreed to help Pierce, his adrenaline surged, and he began to feel a whole range of emotions from anxiety to excitement. For the first time in a very long time, Shane felt like he was solidly in the moment, appreciative of each second. Over the last couple of days, he had been keenly aware of the clear sky, of the pleasant feel of the Miami sun, the flock of seagulls that fished off of the marina by his house each morning and the chorus of bullfrogs and crickets that serenaded him at the end of each day. Shane carefully cradled his coffee with both hands as he slid into the seat across from Hugo.

"It's like old times."

"Old times," Hugo grinned.

"So, what do you think?" Shane asked.

Hugo arched an eyebrow and glanced over at Mia. "We'll be okay."

She caught his look and smiled.

"When do we get the ambulance?"

"Tomorrow night right before you go in. Today you boys will meet with the doctor and the officer in charge of the night shift at the prison."

"What about uniforms?"

Mia nodded at Shane. "Curacao Emergency Medical Services has an exclusive contract with the government. I went on their web site and downloaded a picture of their uniforms. I picked up a couple of similar shirts and slacks at a uniform store in Ft. Lauderdale last night."

"Our local contact will bring us the patches to sew on to the shirts," Hugo said.

Mia focused on her list. "Your first meeting is with Doctor Hernandez at St. Elizabeth hospital. He will already be there conducting rounds. As far as anyone else is concerned, you have a wealthy client that would like to put on a fundraiser to raise money for the hospital, and you have been retained to handle security for the event."

"I got it," Hugo nodded.

Mia looked up from her notepad at Hugo. "Fine, after that you'll meet with Andre Rojer, the officer in charge of the evening shift at Bon Futuro prison at the Emerald casino. Our local contact set it up for us. Rojer goes to that casino on a regular basis. We're staying at that

Curacao Marriott hotel where the casino is located so our being seen there shouldn't raise any suspicion," Mia added.

Shane's brow furrowed. "There is one important item we haven't discussed."

"Really and what might that be?" Hugo asked.

"Our fee," Shane said.

Mia stopped going over the checklist and looked up.

Hugo's look told Shane that he had been wondering when Shane would get around to talking about money. It was obvious that something in particular had been on Shane's mind for quite some time. He grinned to himself and asked, "So Ponzi, what's on your mind?"

Shane made a sour face. He hated the nickname Hugo slapped on him when they were teenagers. The nickname stuck because Shane was always scheming and plotting how to use other people's money to further his own agenda.

Mia shrugged and stated the obvious. "I thought that was settled. We agreed to split whatever was left over of the three million."

"That's what Pierce agreed to . . . I prefer to do my own negotiating." Hugo made a groaning noise. "Here we go again."

Shane frowned as if Hugo was in no position to be cavalier when it came to making money. "With the payoffs and the cost of this jet, we are going to burn through one million easy."

Mia nodded as if she understood where Shane was going with his point. She had planned her fair share of clandestine operations in third world countries. "At least that much," she offered.

"That's not enough." Shane complained. "Juan Carlos has got millions parked in offshore accounts."

Mia agreed with Shane. This mission was different. The stakes were considerably higher. It was one thing to protect a prominent businessman traveling to a Third World country, but they were about to do something very illegal and piss off a superpower and the world's most dangerous drug cartel all at the same time.

She brushed a strand of her blond hair behind her ear. "So, what do you have in mind?"

Shane looked at Mia and then Hugo. "Let's be brutally honest," he took a deep breath and leaned back in his chair. "If Pierce's plan doesn't work, the cartel is coming after each of us. And if it does work, there's no telling what the blowback from fucking up a DEA investigation is going to be. My guess is that it's going to be bad."

Shane could tell from the look on both Hugo's and Mia's faces that they shared the same opinion.

His voice grew in intensity. "In other words, if we are going to have to look over our shoulders every day and go to bed at night wondering who is hunting us, we need to get paid and I'm not talking about splitting a lousy two million four ways . . . I'm not Mother Teresa," Shane declared.

Shane's last comment made Mia smile. "So, what exactly do you propose?" Mia asked, the intrigue in her voice obvious.

"Once we get Juan Carlos out of prison and on board the jet, I'll tell him that our fee to get him safely to the U.S. is ten million dollars."

"Here we go," Hugo mumbled to himself.

"Juan Carlos won't exactly be in a position to say no," Shane said.

Hugo flipped the comment around. "And if he does? It's not like we can put him back in jail."

Shane grinned but did not immediately answer Hugo's question.

"If he isn't willing to pay ten million, I can think of at least one person who would pay us that much."

Shane's comment made Mia cringe. He noticed the sheepish look on Hugo's face. "Relax, both of you." Shane gave them a satisfied knowing grin. "Juan Carlos isn't stupid. It's never going to come to that. It's not going to be a pleasant conversation, but he knows how things work. When he realizes that we won't hesitate to turn the jet around and fly him to Venezuela unless he pays us, he'll make the right decision," Shane smiled confidently.

Hugo and Mia mulled that over for a second, and then Hugo shrugged, "What about Pierce?"

Shane's face remained neutral even though he felt a twist in his gut. "What about him?"

"He'll never go for it."

Shane knew Hugo was right. "Pierce's principals sometimes are his own worst enemy."

After an uncomfortable silence, Shane responded in a manner that left no doubt that he was not going to be deterred. "He'll be somewhere between Miami and Oklahoma, so he doesn't need to know."

Chapter Twenty

BON FUTURO PRISON, CURACAO

It was almost sunrise before Juan Carlos dozed off while trying to commit to memory the smuggling routes through Central America that the cartel wanted him to use. He heard the rumble of thunder as he slept. It was faint, but enough to make him open his eyes. On impulse he grabbed a cigarette and lit it. Staring silently at the stone ceiling of his cell Juan Carlos recalculated his chances of success. It was painfully obvious that once Juan Carlos turned over the smuggling routes to the DEA that Dario had no further use for him. Juan Carlos realized that his greatest problem was one of time or the lack of it. At first, he wasn't sure when the cartel would make its move, but the more he considered various scenarios the more convinced he became that Dario would kill him soon after he finished delivering the fake Intel to the DEA. Juan Carlos needed to buy time. He hadn't heard from Pierce but held out the faintest hope that he would be his ace in the hole. With the extradition hearing only four days away, Juan Carlos had at most two, possibly three days left. By that time Hogan would have arranged his transfer, and he would have to go into protective custody if he wanted to come out of this alive. Juan Carlos inhaled deeply, holding the smoke inside of his lungs for as long as he could. He loved cigarettes and until Marcus Van Delft delivered Charlotte to his prison cell, they had been his only source of pleasure. When he was done, Juan Carlos tapped out the cigarette in the ashtray until every ember was extinguished; rose out of bed gathered his courage and prayed. Afterward, he wrote a note on a small piece of paper telling Hogan that his lawyer would report everything that was said back to the cartel. He asked Hogan to delay the official interview with his lawyer present. When he was finished, he slid the folded piece of paper between his leg and his sock and waited for the prison guard.

When the guard came for him, Juan Carlos flashed a one-hundred-dollar bill and asked the guard to arrange to let him speak with Agent Hogan alone before the meeting.

Handing the guard, the money and a business card Juan Carlos said: "Please call him on his cell phone and ask him to step out of the room, I do not want anyone one to see us talking."

Stone-faced the guard snapped, "two hundred."

Juan Carlos nodded. "All right, but after you make the call."

Agent Hogan was waiting outside the interrogation room when Juan Carlos arrived. Juan Carlos slid the note out from his sock and slipped it to Agent Hogan when he extended his hand to greet him. Hogan read the note, turned to the guard and directed him to wait a few minutes until after he and Agent Roy left before bringing in the prisoner.

Closing the door behind him, Agent Hogan turned towards Marcus Van Delft and said, "I have been called to the States. We are going to have to reschedule your client's interview."

Marcus shook his head and frowned. "But . . . the extradition hearing is in four days. I assume that you would want to interview my client before the hearing."

Hogan nodded. "Yes, we would, I will be back the day after tomorrow. We can interview your client at that time."

"Wait a minute," Marcus said, "let me check my schedule".

"Ah yes, I think I can move that," he mumbled under his breath. "How does one in the afternoon sound?"

"Fine," Agent Hogan said, "we will see you then." He looked over at Agent Roy letting him know that it was time to leave.

* * *

A few moments later, Juan Carlos pretended to be surprised when Marcus Van Delft informed him that his interview with the DEA had been postponed.

Juan Carlos gave him nothing more than a slight nod and told him that the news the DEA cancelled the meeting will make the cartel suspicious.

The corner of Marcus's mouth twitched, "The thought crossed my mind."

"So, when are we doing this?" Juan Carlos asked.

A troubled look skirted over his features briefly. "The day after tomorrow," Marcus scoffed. "Not good."

Juan Carlos shook his head in feigned disappointment, but in his mind, he was relieved to have bought himself precious time. He bit his bottom lip giving off the impression that this last-minute postponement was a problem. "So, what are you going to tell them?"

"I am going to tell them that the DEA cancelled the interview," Marcus said, his voice low, a little unsure.

Juan Carlos winced. "You don't want to phrase it that way."

Marcus gave him a curious look. "What do you mean?"

"Think about it for a second, if you tell Rene that the DEA cancelled the interview, he'll probably think that the DEA figured out what we were planning. Rene is naturally paranoid; it doesn't take much to set him off. He'll think that there was a leak." Juan Carlos's eyes bore into Marcus. "Rene will blame you even if you're not the leak . . . that could be very bad for you."

Marcus's right eye began blinking frantically. He squirmed for a moment and then anxiously offered, "You know Rene much better than I do, so how would you phrase it?"

Juan Carlos studied him for a moment. He was surprised at how easily Marcus took the bait. Juan Carlos sat quietly, giving Marcus the impression that he was carefully considering the best way to spin this latest development. Marcus paced while he waited. This was starting to look like a big mess.

"Tell Rene that the DEA informed you before I was brought in that they had a last-minute conflict, but they still wanted to try to and get started today."

Marcus rubbed his temple. "How does that help?"

Juan Carlos noticed the doubtful look in his eyes. In an effort to further assure him he said, "If something was wrong, there would be no need for pretense."

Marcus had a pained look on his face, "But—"

"No buts . . . if the DEA suspected anything they wouldn't have bothered to show up. Agent Hogan would simply have cancelled. And Rene better than anyone knows that to be the case."

Switching to a confident tone, Juan Carlos added, "You tell them the prison guard took over an hour to bring me into the room after the DEA got there. Tell Rene that Agent Hogan appeared sincere in his apology and made sure he rescheduled the meeting for the day after tomorrow before they had to leave. That should convince Rene that they don't suspect anything."

A touch of color returned to Marcus's face. "I understand. I will emphasize the fact that they insisted on scheduling the interview before the extradition hearing rather than the fact that they cancelled at the last minute," he swallowed hard.

Juan Carlos sat back in the chair and gave Marcus a sideways glance. The hint of a grin spread across his lips, seemingly satisfied that the story they would tell Rene would buy him time.

* * *

Later that evening, Juan Carlos followed closely behind the prison guard down a long narrow corridor. With each leaden step Juan Carlos took, he became increasingly aware of the harsh reality that protective custody might be his only viable lifeline. When he entered the small fluorescent-lit space, Agent Roy was busy fussing with his collar as the combination of starch and humidity caused a red welt on his neck. This time, Agent Hogan did not wait for Juan Carlos to get comfortable; this time he quickly took charge of the situation. The intricate information Juan Carlos had previously provided to the DEA would require that it expend considerable time and resources to verify the accuracy of Juan Carlos's claims. Assuming they were true, law enforcement would have to expend considerable resources on the investigation before it yielded quantifiable results. Agent Hogan's superiors, however, wanted something tangible that could be quickly confirmed as proof that Juan Carlos was in fact cooperating.

"You know that none of the information you gave us can be easily checked out," Hogan frowned.

Juan Carlos's eyes met Agent Hogan's glance. "So, what do you want?"

"The cartel's bank accounts and passwords," Hogan said.

Juan Carlos rolled his eyes. "What I gave you is just as valuable."

"Identifying the companies involved in the drug trafficking operation is very valuable," Hogan conceded, "But you're not a stupid man. You know we can't rush in. We're going to have to conduct our own detailed investigations and independently tie those companies to the cartel's operation. That will take some time. I need something that proves to me that you're not playing us." There was a hint of accusation in his words.

Juan Carlos could see where this was going. He shrugged his shoulders. "Why should I tell you anything else? I'm still here."

"Yes, and unless you give me the bank accounts, you can sit here and wait for the cartel to pay you a visit," Hogan said, sounding morbidly unsympathetic.

"I'll give you the accounts when I'm out of here."

"Not good enough," Hogan snapped.

Juan Carlos thought about the smuggling routes he had just memorized. "How about a compromise? I give you something like the locations of additional land routes and you put me in protective custody? Once I know I'm safe I'll give you all the banking information."

Hogan looked far from enthused. Agent Roy shook his head. "Once we can confirm the land routes, we'll put you on a plane to the U.S."

"That's not good enough," Juan Carlos said, shaking his head. "I need to be in protective custody right after we have our meeting with Marcus Van Delft. Once our meeting is over, he will contact the cartel and they will kill me before I can give you anything else." Hogan raised a suspicious eyebrow. "Why don't they just kill you now before we meet?"

Juan Carlos suddenly got the feeling that he lost the upper hand. He needed to say something to keep his only sure option intact, so he opted for the truth. "Because you're getting too close and the cartel wants me to feed you bogus information about their operations. Once I do that with my lawyer present . . ."

Hogan finished the sentence, "The cartel will kill you."

Juan Carlos winced at the thought. “So, if you want the bank accounts . . . you’ll get my ass out of here,” he said.

Hogan still wasn’t convinced. “So, what do you have to give us?” He asked.

Juan Carlos shook his head, his gaze impolite in its intensity.

“Do you have a map of Central America?”

I can pull one up on the laptop,” Agent Roy offered.

Juan Carlos identified the roads in Honduras, Guatemala and Belize that the cartel wanted him to give to the DEA.

He pointed to two areas on the map. Both of these points here,” he said, “are where we cross the border into Mexico.”

Agent Roy checked the screen on the laptop. “You’re pointing to the middle of the Guatemalan jungle.”

“Yes, there is a labyrinth of gravel and dirt roads that were used to smuggle weapons. They can be difficult to navigate since some appear to come to end abruptly and due to the dense vegetation, most can’t be spotted from planes or satellites. From there we head to one of two small border road crossings, at San Francisco and Corregidora Ortiz. Neither border crossing has any form of customs for either country. You should be able to confirm the existence of those roads relatively quickly,” Juan Carlos said.

Agent Hogan studied the map on the computer screen. “How do you move the drugs once you’re in Mexico?”

“Once we are in Mexico, we have several options. Some of the drugs are moved from there by ship to several ports in the U.S. or by submarine. Some are moved over land into the U.S.”

Hogan repeated the question. “So how do you move the drugs from Mexico into the U.S.?”

Juan Carlos hesitated. He knew that the DEA's discovery of the tunnels would deal the cartel a lethal blow. He also realized the tunnels gave him real leverage.

"The border patrols do not stray beyond fifty miles from the border crossing. Once we get within seventy-five miles from the border, we veer off to one of our tunnels,"

"Tunnels?" Hogan repeated not surprised. The DEA had discovered a few tunnels, but the U.S./Mexican border is almost 2000 miles long, and the cartels dug tunnels faster than the DEA could find them and shut them down.

"There are a few of them," Juan Carlos nodded. "As you know, they are in fairly remote areas and camouflaged by natural terrain," Juan Carlos said.

"How much product are you presently moving into the U.S. from these tunnels?" Hogan asked, trying to gauge the size of that part of the cartel's smuggling operation.

Juan Carlos barely hesitated, "We have a lot of tunnels but two tunnels in particular are sophisticated and equipped with rail. We move about six billion worth of meth a year through them."

Agent Roy slid a piece of paper across the table towards Juan Carlos and handed him a pen. "I want you to write down the locations of those tunnels."

Juan Carlos scribbled something on the paper and pushed it back towards Agent Roy.

In large letters Juan Carlos had written "FUCK YOU."

He glared at Agent Hogan, "I will give you the bank accounts and the tunnel locations when my family and I are safe."

Agent Hogan heard the urgency in his voice. He knew that the smuggling routes would be relatively easy to confirm, but he didn't care about them. Having the bank accounts and tunnel locations would shut down the cartel. Hogan nodded at Agent Roy and said. "We're done here for now."

Hogan stood up and told Juan Carlos, "I am going to run this up the chain of command and have them use back channels to get you released into our custody.

"How long will it take?"

"No more than twenty-four to thirty-six hours. We should be ready to move you the day after tomorrow," Hogan said his expression flat, his voice deadpan.

Juan Carlos shook his head, a gesture meant to tell Hogan that he was comfortable with the timeframe. He knew that the cartel wouldn't make a move until after his official meeting with the DEA. "I need to be in protective custody as soon as we have our meeting with my legal counsel present," he persisted.

"We'll have you on a plane before that time," Hogan reassured him.

Chapter Twenty-One

Alexis turned and reached for her bag. Pierce followed her out of the hotel room into the quiet, deserted hallway. When they got to the lobby, Pierce gestured to Alexis to follow him to the garage elevator.

"Aren't you going to check us out first?" Alexis asked in a mildly curious tone.

"My secretary will come by in the morning and take care of it. We shouldn't risk drawing attention to ourselves."

Alexis forced a smile trying to stay upbeat even though she found all the precaution to be a little unsettling. Pierce placed the two bags in the trunk of the sedan and slid into the driver's side. He took a deep breath before shifting the car into drive and easing the sedan out of the garage. He headed north on Interstate 95 until he reached the interchange for the Florida Turnpike.

* * *

DURING THE EARLY part of the drive, Alexis only occasionally made a half-hearted effort at striking up a conversation. She was content to sit quietly and stare at the silhouettes of the trees that whirled by as well as the occasional illuminated billboard advertising alligator wrestling, convenient food or motels with low room rates and free cable television. Pierce drifted in and out of random thoughts as the low background music coming from the radio twirled in his subconscious. He looked up at the night sky and for the briefest of moments wondered if anyone had ever bested Dario Carraboca.

It was almost four in the morning when he finally stopped for gasoline just south of Gainesville, Florida. Alexis was asleep, curled up against the passenger door. The drop in temperature and refreshing sting of the chilly night air felt good against his skin. He purchased a second cup of coffee, filled the car with gasoline and was back on the road in a matter of minutes. Alexis scarcely stirred in his brief absence. Pierce decided that the night air chill would help him stay alert and lowered one of the rear windows about a quarter-way. Alexis on impulse reacted to the cold air by turning and nuzzling up against Pierce as she searched for warmth while she slept. He lifted his right arm and slipped it over her, allowing Alexis to snuggle closer. Pierce occasionally stroked her hair and rubbed her arm and back throughout the night trying to keep her warm as he sped through the darkness. At one point she opened her eyes just enough to realize that her head was resting on his lap, but she was too tired to care about pretenses, so she closed her eyes and drifted back to sleep. Pierce glanced down at her while she slept. What Pierce felt for Alexis was warm and true and real. Under different circumstances it could certainly have been more. Part of him wondered, for a second, what it would be like to spend time with her under different circumstances. But just as quickly his thoughts shifted from his own feelings—to her predicament, confusion and pain and he knew that all he should be thinking about was keeping her safe.

* * *

IT WAS ALMOST eight-thirty in the morning before Alexis opened her eyes again. By that time, the morning sunlight poured into the car from all directions. Alexis sat up groggy and half-awake. Her voice slurred when she asked Pierce where they were.

"We're a couple of hours north-west of Atlanta. Did you sleep all right?" he added thoughtfully. His voice sounded husky.

Alexis smiled sluggishly, staring at the beginning of a beard which now shadowed Pierce's jaw line. She could tell that he was tired. His eyes moved slower and more deliberately.

"Yes, I slept fine. Thanks for the pillow," she said, playfully smacking her long fingers against his thigh.

She glanced out of the window. "Do you think we could stop soon? I could really use a cup of coffee?"

Pierce nodded. "Of course, I'll get off at the next exit."

He pulled into the parking lot of a restaurant which advertised several breakfast specials. Pierce sat alone in a small booth reading the Atlanta Constitution, while he waited for Alexis to get back from the restroom.

"Can I get you a cup of coffee while you wait on your Mrs.?" the waitress hollered at Pierce in a familiar manner from behind the counter.

Pierce flashed her with a warm smile.

"And your Mrs.? Will she be wanting some coffee?" the waitress asked in a charming drawl. In one fluid movement, perfected over years of practice, the waitress scooped up two mugs and the coffee pot in a single hand and meandered towards the booth.

"So, where are you folks from?" the waitress asked. Pierce could see that she had a very friendly and familiar way about her. He looked up at her name plate which read "Norma Jean."

"We're on our way to Tampa to visit family, down from Chicago. We drove all night . . ."

Norma Jean said wide-eyed, "No wonder you look like you've been ridden hard and put up wet. I'm gonna fix you up something special."
"Just some toast would be great," Pierce smiled.

"The hell it would. Now hush up and drink your coffee. I'll be back to take your wife's order just as soon as she's ready."

Pierce nodded. He couldn't help but like the way Norma Jean insisted on taking care of him.

A few minutes later Alexis returned from the bathroom. She glanced around before sliding into the booth across from him.

"Is that coffee I smell?" Alexis asked, wrinkling her nose.

Norma Jean allowed Alexis a few moments to look over the laminated breakfast menu before sauntering back to the booth. Pierce noticed Norma Jean raise her eyebrows and shake her head good naturedly as Alexis announced she was famished and then ordered a single grapefruit with a small side of cottage cheese. Pierce shrugged his shoulders solely for Norma Jean's amusement and followed it with a wink.

"Will that be all Ma'am," she asked in a tone suggesting that Alexis couldn't be serious.

Alexis lifted her eyes from the menu and studied the busty waitress. Norma Jean was a full-figured lady in her early forties who looked like she appreciated the finer attributes of three-square meals a day.

"Yes, a single grapefruit and a side of cottage cheese," Alexis repeated firmly but politely.

Norma Jean turned and mumbled something under her breath as she backtracked towards the kitchen.

Alexis looked at Pierce with an incredulous expression as if to say, "*what was that all about?*"

"A grapefruit coupled with a side order of glop is just not considered a real breakfast around here," he said, raising the mug to his lips and quietly sipping his coffee.

Alexis laughed without any amusement. "You are such a kiss ass. Do you even know the word no?"

Pierce shot her an extremely puzzled look. Alexis folded her arms and glared at him. "Don't sit there pretending that you don't know what I'm talking about," she snickered playfully.

Pierce seemed to be hiding a smile. His intense blue eyes never failed to send a tingle running through her body. "Just because I always say yes to you doesn't mean I'm incapable of saying no."

Rolling her eyes, Alexis sighed and leaned back onto the cool vinyl of the seat. "You are such a lawyer. Just go back to reading your paper," she smirked.

Alexis peered quietly over her menu at Pierce while he read the paper, looking at his tousled thick black hair which tumbled over his brow in disarray. His slightly closed sapphire blue eyes which cried out for sleep made her stomach flutter.

She thought about Juan Carlos. When they were first married, how he used to also sit across from her in the morning, drinking his coffee and reading the sports section. She mused about how content she was during that time and how things between them rapidly and inexplicably disintegrated. When Alexis first met Juan Carlos, she had been drawn to his confidence, but what looked like confidence was actually a façade of a cold, calculating, manipulative and selfish man. Pierce caught the resignation in her eyes. His eyes narrowed and he leaned forward across the table and wiped a tear that had rolled down her left cheek. Alexis let the wounded look fall from her face. She looked at him for a second and then protectively folded her arms across her chest. "What are you doing?"

"We should really kiss and hold hands." Pierce said, trying to shock her from her present state of mind. "After all, we are supposed to be traveling as a married couple." A smug smile tugged at the corners of Pierce's mouth.

Alexis wasn't sure if she wanted to kiss or slap it away.

* * *

Just then, Norma Jean returned carrying a large serving tray filled with smoked sausage, scrambled eggs, cheese grits, pancakes and a single grapefruit with a side of cottage cheese.

Alexis waited for Norma Jean to leave. “You could feed an entire family in Cuba with that meal,” she giggled.

Reaching across the table, Alexis used her fork to grope at his breakfast, “it all looks amazing,” she confessed.

Pierce tapped at the bottom of the bottle of hot sauce he held over his eggs trying to coax the red sauce from its home. Frustrated, Pierce gave the bottle one final hard smack sending hot sauce splattering all over his food.

A startled look flashed across his face. Alexis smothered her grin and focused on looking harmless.

So, when do we get to Oklahoma?” She asked, trying to contain her laughter.

Pierce reached for a couple of extra napkins to clean up the mess and gave an exasperated sigh. “If we stop in Arkansas tonight, we should get there tomorrow afternoon.”

“And when do the other’s get there? Alexis asked apprehensively, purposely not mentioning Juan Carlos by name.

“If all goes as planned, they should arrive the day after that,” he said matter-of-factly.

When they walked back to the car, Alexis offered to drive. She could see that Pierce needed rest.

“Are you sure?” He asked.

“I insist. Get some sleep.”

Pierce nodded. "All right, a short break would do me some good." Alexis put on her sunglasses and adjusted the driver's seat. She checked her mirrors before turning on the ignition key. When Pierce was satisfied that Alexis was safely on the highway, he closed his eyes. Alexis glanced over occasionally at Pierce as he rested. If looked at separately, each one of his facial features—the perfectly straight Roman nose, the curve of his full lips, his high cheekbones and curled black eye lashes-was almost too pretty, but something about the way they fit together and the addition of his five-o'clock-shadow transformed the prettiness from his face and made it remarkably gorgeous.

* * *

The sudden feeling that she was being watched made Alexis glance out her side window. Anxiety crept up on her as she noticed the markings of Georgia highway patrol car riding alongside her. Her stomach flipped at the sight of one of the uniformed officers staring at her openly. Alexis glanced at her speedometer, as far as she could tell she was going the speed limit.

"Pierce wake up," she said as inconspicuously as she could through gritted teeth.

The patrol car swung behind the sedan. Alexis tried to remain calm despite the gnawing sensation in the pit of her stomach that a traffic stop would require her to give the officer her driver's license. Once her license was punched into the computer, the DEA and perhaps even the cartel would know she was in Georgia.

"Pierce! Pierce! You really need to wake up," she said, jabbing him hard in his ribs.

Catching something from the corner of her eye, she glanced into the rearview mirror in time to see the patrol car, its lights blazing, swerve into the next lane and speed past her. Alexis took a couple of deep breaths.

"That could have been really bad," she muttered to herself. Ten seconds passed before her anxiety started to recede like the tide going out.

Rubbing his side, Pierce swallowed a groan. "What's up? Is everything okay?"

Alexis shot Pierce an edgy look. At that moment, she had a glimpse of what her life on the run living in constant fear of being discovered would feel like.

Chapter Twenty-Two

CURACAO

Hugo leaned against the window watching as the Lear jet approached the runway and touched down at Hato International Airport. Over the past decade, he had been part of many successful rescue operations. He stopped keeping track of his successful missions when he reached the number fifty. The couple of people, however, that he couldn't rescue, he never forgot. Those failures would haunt him for the rest of his days and the covert missions where he hunted and killed Jihad terrorists he tried to forget. No matter the circumstances, killing people was something Hugo never adjusted to, it was something he felt darken his soul. His general gaze as the jet taxied to a stop fixed on a metallic gray Range Rover parked on the tarmac. Hugo instinctively patted his Beretta holstered under his windbreaker. Mia also spotted the two men and a woman that had exited the Range Rover and were now walking towards the jet. She leaned over and placed a gentle hand on Hugo's broad shoulder as if to say they're with us. Hugo didn't break eye contact. His mood was dark and cautious. After all their years and missions together, Mia knew by the irritated face and the arched right eyebrow as he eyed the three figures standing just outside the aircraft with suspicion, that the switch in Hugo's mind had been turned on, and he was already in tactical mode. Reaching for her cell phone, Mia dialed the telephone number for her contact person at Curacao Air Terminal Services. She watched as one of the men pulled a cell phone from his belt holster.

"Good morning."

"Good morning Captain. It's Mia Dawson," she replied.

"Yes. I hope you had a pleasant flight. We are standing by just outside of your jet. You advised that you wanted us to facilitate your immigration clearance, so I have my assistant, Karina here to assist you."

Mia nodded at Hugo. "Yes, thank you. I am going to send my associates ahead with her. I want to meet with you to get started on the paperwork for our departure. We have a tight schedule tomorrow and will be leaving after our meetings, so I want to take care of the necessary paperwork today. I want to make sure that there are no last-minute delays."

"There won't be any glitches. We will arrange everything with Customs to make sure that everything runs smoothly when you're ready to depart," he said confidently.

"Excellent," Mia said. "We will be out momentarily."

Turning her attention back to Hugo, Mia said, "You have your first meeting with Doctor Hernandez at St. Elisabeth hospital in two hours. Give your bag and weapon to Karina. She'll make sure it gets through customs and then she'll give you a ride to the hotel. Tessa Bongard is the name of our local contractor. She will pick you up there." Mia looked at her watch. "You'll have a little time before she is supposed to meet you, so you have some time to grab something to eat."

"I'm not hungry," Hugo nodded with a confrontational edge while mentally going over the day's itinerary.

Mia leaned over and kissed Hugo on the cheek. "I will head to the hotel when I am through here. Mia eyed Hugo thoughtfully, "Make sure you eat something," she insisted.

Before exiting the aircraft, Mia talked to the pilots and reminded them to have all their pre-flight clearances completed and the flight plan filed, and the jet fueled and ready.

While they ate breakfast, Hugo talked with Shane about the local person they recruited to help them. Hugo explained that the local contactor came highly recommended by people that both he and Mia trusted. They were lucky to find an independent contractor with Tessa Bongard's connections on the island of Curacao and skill set. Despite the fact that she was a woman in a field dominated by men, Tessa had risen quickly through the ranks of the Dutch General Intelligence and Security Service known as Algemene Inlichtingen en Veiligheidsdienst (AIVD). She had been a very capable agent. In 2012 the Prime Minister of Curacao shut down the operations of the intelligence agency and implemented a complete reorganization under the guidance of a special, independent committee. The Prime Minister publicly condemned the widespread corruption in the AIVD and used that as the reason for reorganizing the country's security service. The new and improved security service, at the end of the day, was not that different from its predecessor. Both were corrupt to the core and both agencies served to line the pockets of those in power. As part of the reorganization of the agency, Tessa was offered a command post. However, Tessa had no fondness for playing politics and no stomach for looking the other way so she declined the promotion, inexplicably walked away and never looked back. Tessa was a powerfully built woman in her early forties, with black hair, eyes the color of coal and a coffee colored complexion. When she walked into the hotel's restaurant, she flashed Hugo with a smile the moment she noticed him.

"That must be her," Hugo said, gesturing in her direction.

Shane looked at her with curiosity. "A woman . . ." he mumbled under his breath.

"Bon Dia. You must be Hugo," She grinned. "Mia described the two of you perfectly."

Shane was staring at her. “What exactly did she say?” he asked, mildly interested.

“She said when I got to the cafe to look for two guys. Mia said one was as big as a house and the other one looked like he just took a bite out of a lemon,” she said. “Mia said that the one with the pissed off expression would be Shane.” Tessa grinned “That must be you.”

Shane frowned in the general direction of Tessa’s cleavage.

Tessa barely blinked and grabbed a chair. She ordered an iced tea and continued to keep the conversation light since they were in a public place where they could be easily overheard. Turning her dark eyes and ample chest towards the exit, she finally said, “I apologize for the short visit, but we need to get going if I am going to get you to the hospital on time.”

* * *

The weather was already very hot and sticky, and the Russian built jeep was not equipped with air-conditioning, so Tessa kept the side cloth flaps turned down to allow the wind to blow in. They drove along a narrow dusty road passing bright yellow houses punctuating flat, desert-like stretches. The cactuses that lined the road contorted themselves dramatically, like green pipe cleaners. The sun was so unmerciful that the jeep’s tarp provided little relief from the heat. Sweat began to instantly soak the back of Shane’s white shirt.

“Having a good time Mr. Shane?” Tessa shouted with a bright smile over the roar of the jeep’s engine.

“How much longer until we get there?” He asked, wiping the sweat from his eyes with a shrug of his forearm.

“Not long,” She said, “nothing on the island takes long to get to.”

Shane mentally played out numerous scenarios for convincing Doctor Hernandez to recommend Juan Carlos's transfer to St. Elisabeth hospital. Shane was a great persuader, which is why Hugo agreed to let him help. His days as a problem fixer were far behind him, but that particular skill set still served him well as a trial lawyer. Shane loved juries and they also loved him, but not because he was intelligent and articulate, but because he was a people person. He had extraordinary instincts when it came to reading people. Shane also had an uncanny gift for getting people to trust him. His attention to the smallest and seemingly insignificant details and mannerisms gave him unique insight into a person. There wasn't a jury Shane could not completely charm and as a result they were usually very sympathetic towards his clients. While he came from humble beginnings, Shane now enjoyed a successful career and marriage to a beautiful and intelligent woman. Shane worked out regularly, watched what he ate and didn't smoke or drink. By most accounts he was a man to be emulated. His sexual appetite, however, was a dark and formidable vice. Shane loved women, particularly young beautiful women. He was not the type to come home reeking of another woman's fragrance or indulge in any type of careless indiscretion. He respected his wife Kris too much. But he travelled often and had a penchant, if not a sixth sense, for coming in contact with beautiful women. He called his sexual liaisons "sport fucking" and he did it with gusto, but notwithstanding his frequent trysts, he still adored his wife.

* * *

Shane continued to dwell on what he would say to Doctor Hernandez to persuade him to cooperate. If he was unsuccessful, he knew he could always fall back on Hugo's blue-collar approach.

A few moments later, the jeep came to a rolling stop directly in front of a series of white posts which marked the pavement's edge.

Tessa turned to look at Shane. She smiled easily. "We are here, Mister Shane."

Hugo pulled out a roll of one hundred-dollar bills. Handing them to Tessa he said: "Pick up Mr. Rojer and take him to the casino. This should keep him entertained. We will meet you back there in a couple of hours."

Tessa nodded and said amiably. "When you're ready for him, call me and I will bring him up to your room."

Hugo was on his cell phone and Shane gazed down at the ocean for a full thirty minutes before Doctor Hernandez walked into his office. After introductions and social pleasantries Shane launched into a long selling speech. He talked about the famous and powerful people he knew and did business with. None of it had anything to do with why they were there, but it was the lure Shane decided to use to draw him in. He kept the conversation moving in the direction he thought best for his objective. When Shane finally broached the subject of Juan Carlos, Doctor Hernandez's initial cautiousness had dissipated. Shane would touch on Juan Carlos and then move to a funny story about him and a famous person or influential U.S. senator. But Shane kept coming back to Juan Carlos. Hugo enjoyed Shane's performance. Everything Shane said was with such confidence and brio that the doctor was fixated on his good fortune in meeting Shane and the future opportunities and contacts that Shane might offer him. It was right after Shane finished telling the story about a practical joke he played on a well-known professional athlete that Shane made his move and began to explain that Juan Carlos, a relative of one of his business partners was in Bon Futuro prison.

"Oh really," Doctor Hernandez replied.

"He's the black sheep of the family. If he's not guilty of whatever it is, they arrested him for, I am sure he's guilty of something else, but you know what they say, you don't get to pick your family."

Doctor Hernandez inclined his head respectfully indicating that he understood. A tinge of mild concern crept back into the Doctor's voice as he tried to figure out what Shane needed from him. "Very true," he agreed.

Shane was in the process of sipping a cup of coffee. "In any event, Doctor . . ."

"Keith, please call me Keith," he interrupted.

"Ok, Keith," Shane smiled. "I discussed Juan Carlos's symptoms and medical history with one of my partners, Doctor Michael Lerner at Miami Jackson Hospital. There are small traces of blood in Juan Carlos's urine. Doctor Lerner suggested that it is imperative that some tests be performed."

Doctor Hernandez gave a noncommittal nod. "I know Doctor Lerner by reputation, he's very good." Treading carefully Doctor Hernandez added, "I don't disagree, traces of blood in urine could be symptomatic of kidney failure, but we do not have the equipment at the prison to properly evaluate him."

"The last thing I want is for my partner's nephew to die in prison," Shane said with real vigor. "That's why we're here. You are one of the attending physicians at the prison. You could have him temporarily transferred to St. Elisabeth to run tests and then sent back."

Doctor Hernandez stiffened. He'd worked at Bon Futuro prison for almost six years. The prison administration was inflexible. Getting them to agree to move a prisoner even on his recommendation was a bit of a stretch.

Doctor Hernandez's voice was unsteady. "I do not have the authority to transfer a prisoner from Bon Futuro to St. Elisabeth. It would have to be a life-threatening situation and even then, the officer in charge at the prison makes the final call. It's very difficult."

Shane nodded. "I understand, but since you cannot treat him without first diagnosing him. All I can ask is for you to visit him and consider recommending that he be moved to St. Elisabeth for testing."

Doctor Hernandez's guard was up. He'd only just met Shane and what Shane was asking him to do was simply not done.

"Keith," Shane started before pausing, "I realize that what I am asking you to do is a tremendous imposition and extremely unconventional, but I hope you understand that we have a sick man in prison who is a family member of my business partner and dear friend."

Shane could see Doctor Hernandez's apprehension. He had a knack for seeing angles and an opportunity where others saw problems, and he had an uncanny sense of knowing when to make his move. Just then Shane lifted the briefcase and placed it on the desk. For dramatic effect and to make sure that the doctor's attention was focused on the case, Shane asked for permission to open it.

"Feel free," Doctor Hernandez nodded.

"My partners understand that what we are asking a lot and, while this does not begin to compensate you, we hope that you would accept this token gesture of our friendship," Shane said as he opened the briefcase containing two hundred and fifty thousand dollars.

"One quarter of a million dollars for one visit and one hospital evaluation," Shane gently nudged the case towards the doctor. "Can we count on you?"

Doctor Hernandez's face showed no emotion. "I don't think you understand. For me to move Mr. Laporte to St Elisabeth, it's going to take more than a few trickles of blood in his urine."

"Well," Shane said nodding his head vigorously, "You inject him with a strong dosage of Interferon. In this heat and humidity, he should rapidly develop a fever, chills, and general weakness. The infirmary's staff will have no other choice but to call you and report Juan Carlos's deteriorating medical condition. At that point you have what you need to justify his immediate transfer to St. Elisabeth."

Doctor Hernandez tugged at his mustache that drooped crookedly over one corner of his mouth, possibly a result of his tugging on it whenever he had to do some hard thinking. The thought of injecting a patient with a drug intended for chemotherapy in order to induce a high fever and debilitating symptoms twisted in his guts.

Shane's voice shook him out of his thoughts.

"The last thing anyone wants is to induce Juan Carlos with a fever when we don't know why he's urinating blood. But honestly Keith the only other option is to wait for his condition to deteriorate on its own and that is simply unacceptable. We would appreciate it if you could visit Juan Carlos tomorrow. Once he develops a fever, you can request that he be immediately transferred to the hospital tomorrow night. Can we count on you?"

Doctor Hernandez cleared his throat. He wasn't sure how he would do it, but he would figure something out. "I could recommend moving him, but the final call is still the prison officials to make."

"We understand," Shane plowed on. "I don't expect you to convince the prison official to take your recommendation. I am only asking you to request the transfer. Leave the other details to us."

Doctor Hernandez paced the cramped area of his office. He thought about what Shane was asking him to do. All Shane wanted was for Juan Carlos to receive competent medical attention and given his incarceration, inducing him with a fever was one way for him to get it. As far as everyone else was concerned, he would see a patient and later authorize his transfer once he was contacted by prison staff. Doctor Hernandez's gaze was repeatedly drawn to the briefcase and its contents. He couldn't see any real risk. When he weighed that against the two hundred and fifty thousand dollars staring at him, he couldn't think of any reason to say no. If he hadn't been star struck by Shane, perhaps he would have done more than just examine the superficial aspects of Shane's request. But the money and the promise of future riches was simply too much to ignore or over scrutinize. He pulled his attention from the briefcase back to Shane.

"I can give him a cocktail that will cause his fever to spike," Doctor Hernandez said, coolly keeping his voice low, "tell your partners that they can count on me. I will see Juan Carlos tomorrow and put everything into motion."

"Splendid," Shane stood up and slapped the doctor on the back. "Take my card, when you're in the states I would like to set up a meeting so that you can meet my partners and they can personally thank you for your accommodation."

A broad smile spread across Doctor Hernandez's face. "Yes, let's do that soon."

Chapter Twenty-Three

WILLEMSTAD, CURACAO

Andre Rojer was at the crap table, telling other gamblers to ride his dice. When the dice came to him, he barely shook them before letting them go vigorously so that they bounced off the opposite wall. Andre rolled an eight. He scooped the dice up, rattled them in his fist, and shot them across the felt table. The dice came up a six and two. Andre smiled, a little. Hugo took a place at the table and bet on Andre to win. Andre glanced up as he gathered the dice with the edge of his hand. He closed his fist around the dice and pressed them to his cheek, feeling their warm, rounded edges against his palm. There was a moment's pause as Andre breathed out, long and slow. He leaned back and with a violent twist of his wrist Andre whipped the dice across the table.

"Eight," The stickman announced over the screams as he grabbed the dice and held them momentarily so that other players could place their bets. Andre could not contain his grin. He couldn't remember a time when he had been on such a good roll. Andre Rojer was not a casual gambler. Gambling and in particular craps had been a problem since he was seventeen. He knew how to play the odds and when he kept his emotions under control he won or didn't lose too badly. It was those other times when he made bad decisions that left him without money for rent or food and in debt to people you didn't want to owe. Just one roll of the dice too many was usually all that it took to put him in a very bad situation.

Hugo studied Andre. He spent the last eighteen years of his life accessing and categorizing faces and potential threats. Andre was like a junkie who's next fix came each time the dice touched his palms. Hugo started to collect his stack of chips.

"Hey, you," Andre shouted good naturedly. "My winning streak ain't over."

Hugo finished picking up his chips and paid Andre a passing glance. He had a feeling the pendulum was getting ready to swing in the other direction. There are three ways to make an eight with two dice and Hugo figured that the odds of Andre throwing an eight for a fourth time before he rolled another number weighed heavily against him.

"Good luck to you," Hugo grinned as he walked away from the table.

A hint of a smile curved the corners of Andre's mouth. "All right then," he said, turning his attention back to the table.

Hugo knew how to read the signs. He could tell that it didn't matter whether Andre rolled another eight. He could see from the dark expression in Andre's eyes that all that mattered was the rush he was currently feeling. His tormented gaze fixated on the dice, Andre would ignore all the protests sent by his brain to quit and walk away with his winnings in favor of the rush which gave him a temporary escape from the drudgery of his island existence. Eventually, the odds would catch up with him. Hugo leisurely walked past several men in European button-downs and curly-haired, brown-skinned women in sundresses puffing on cigarettes and sipping martinis. In his wake Hugo heard a distant and collective groan as the stickman shouted three. When Andre Rojer crapped out, Tessa collected him and escorted him upstairs.

* * *

IN THE ELEVATOR, Tessa turned and faced Andre. She glared across the small space at him. "You have an enormous problem my friend."

Andre gave her a dismissive shrug. "I've been in a crack before."

Tessa looked him up and down and curtly said, "Not like this."

Andre read between the lines and understood what Tessa was hinting at.

Andre recognized that he had a problem. He owed a lot of money to the type of people that don't send courtesy letters or threaten to report you to the credit bureau when a payment is overdue. He had no illusion that he would win big at the casino and settle his debts. That ship sailed when the stickman yelled "three" earlier. Curacao is a small island, the people he owed money to would soon hear about his latest debacle at the craps table after being up a considerable amount. Very soon those very same people would pay him a visit and make him feel the type of pain that painkillers could not easily numb.

"So, what exactly do I have to do?"

Tessa glared at him. "Whatever it is you do it," she hissed.

Andre shuffled his feet behind Tessa down the long hallway to the hotel suite without speaking another word. When they reached the suite, Tessa knocked once before pushing the door open. Andre offered a friendly smile when Tessa introduced Shane and stopped smiling the instant Hugo walked into the room. He looked at Hugo with a sort of dark resentment as if Hugo had stolen his good fortune and taken it with him when he left the table.

"This is my partner," Shane said.

"Yes, we sort of met earlier," Andre frowned.

Hugo slid a beer across the table towards Andre.

Andre was a small man but with a wiry toughness that many islanders inherited long ago from their Dutch and African ancestors. Andre's eyes shifted uneasily between Shane and Hugo, as though he was unsure what would happen next. Beneath his calm demeanor he was as taut as a wire.

"I think you know why we wanted to meet you," Shane started.

Andre took a deep breath trying to control the tension that had been building up in him since he first stepped off the elevator. "Not really but I have an idea," he said disdainfully.

"For starters, Tessa tells us you are someone that can be trusted, and we are both in a position to help each other," Hugo lifted the bottle of Polar beer to his lips.

"Did she?" He said, in mocked surprise. "So, what exactly can I do for you?" Andre snarled, folding his arms across his chest.

Hugo didn't care much for Andre's tone. From what Hugo could see, Andre was self-indulgent and reckless. Both of those traits caused him concern. Hugo preferred not to work with civilians, especially an undisciplined one. Hugo sucked on his beer not sure whether Andre could be counted on to hold up his end.

"The people you owe money to won't carry you anymore."

Andre gave Hugo a curious look. "And how do you know that?"

Hugo's face darkened, "Because it's my job to know those things. And I'm good at my job," he scowled.

Hugo didn't feel like it, but he put a smile on his face. "We can take care of your problem if you do something for us." Then just as quickly as he put a smile on his face, Hugo took it off. "But if you get a last-minute case of religion or even worse you think you can fuck us, your problems just escalated to a whole new level."

As a prison guard, Andre had seen killers before, and Hugo had the same look in his eyes. Andre wasn't sure he wanted to see where this was headed and stood up to leave. "I think I'll pass and take my chances," he said cautiously.

Frowning Hugo pointed to the chair. "I'd have a seat if I were you."

Hugo made Andre nervous. Andre pointed his finger at Hugo. "I'm not scared of you."

Hugo scoffed and looked at Andre, who was inching closer to the door. "Then you're a stupid man."

Shane's eyes cut towards Hugo. "Ease up big man," he said, preferring a careful, deliberate approach to Hugo's sledgehammer tactics. Hugo didn't see eye-to-eye with Shane when it came to Andre. He was critical to the mission and a variable that could cost them their lives if not controlled. Hugo had to be sure that Andre understood what was at stake if he took their money and tried to trade information for another pay day. Andre had to understand that there would be brutal consequences if he didn't execute his part to perfection. The only way to be sure of that was a sledgehammer right between the eyes.

Hugo's voice turned sharper, more demanding. "What we want to know is whether you're willing to do what's necessary to protect your family?"

Panic crept into Andre's voice as he began to comprehend the gravity of the situation. "What does my family have to do with this?"

Shane walked over to Andre and rested his hand on his shoulder in a placating gesture.

"Not a thing. Why don't we take a step back and discuss what it is we would like to pay you to do for us," Shane suggested calmly.

Andre nodded, trying to remain calm.

"Relax, Andre, all we want is for you to make sure that someone at Bon Futuro prison gets the necessary medical attention that he needs, that's all." Shane smiled.

Andre gave them a puzzled look. "That can't be all," he frowned.

Hugo spoke in a deep baritone voice. "The prisoner is Juan Carlos Laporte."

Andre gave Hugo a strained smile. "I should have known," he grumbled under his breath. "You know, the Americans are keeping close tabs on him. So, what exactly do you want me to do?"

"We want you to approve his transfer to St. Elisabeth," Shane said.

Andre glanced up at Shane, his indecision clear on his face. What he was being asked to do was not a simple task.

"Transferring a prisoner to St. Elisabeth hospital is only done in extreme situations such as a gunshot or stabbing victim." Andre shook his head. "This is not an easy thing to do."

Shane leveled a determined glare at Andre. "You're in charge of the night shift. If Doctor Hernandez recommends the transfer, you have the final say."

Andre looked skeptical but didn't argue. "Even so, approving a transfer during the middle of the night is going to raise a lot of questions," he shrugged.

Hugo took a freshly opened beer and drained it in four big gulps. He set the empty bottle back on the table and said, "If this was easy, we wouldn't be clearing your debts motherfucker."

Shane tried to reason with Andre. "We know the Americans are interested in Juan Carlos. How would it look if he died on your watch and you could have done something to prevent it?"

Andre saw where Shane was headed.

"If Doctor Hernandez is willing to say that Juan Carlos's condition required an emergency transfer that would at least give me a reason for not waiting until morning for the Director's authorization," Andre reasoned out loud. "But I am still going to take a lot of heat," he sighed.

Shane's eyes locked on Hugo's. The look in Shane's eyes told Hugo what he was going to say before he ever spoke. Hugo shrugged letting Shane know that he should do what he felt he needed to close Andre.

"I am going to give you an additional hundred thousand dollars to ease the pain?" Shane said. "But I have to tell you, for the kind of money we're paying you, there can be no fuck ups. Everything better run smoothly."

Andre smiled, a tight unfriendly smile. "When do I get my money?"

"Tessa will make the arrangements to pay off your markers once Juan Carlos is transferred to St. Elisabeth," Hugo frowned.

Shane nodded. "As for the additional hundred thousand, Tessa will also pay you as soon as you've completed the job."

Andre took a deep breath as a multitude of thoughts flooded his mind. "So how exactly is this going to play out?"

Shane explained that Doctor Hernandez would examine Juan Carlos in the morning when he conducted his routine visit, he would give him something to trigger a high fever. At that point, Shane stressed that it was important for Andre to speak with the doctor in front of a witness so that the witness could corroborate that the Doctor diagnosed Juan Carlos's condition as life threatening and strongly recommended that he be immediately transported to St. Elisabeth.

"You will need to call down to the guard gate and order them to allow the Ambulance through without any delay."

Andre nodded.

"You are going to have to supervise the transfer to the ambulance and keep the number of personnel involved to a minimum. We don't want the guards asking too many questions."

"Why would they?"

"Well for starters, Hugo and I will be the drivers," Shane said.

Andre's expression hardened at the very moment he realized this had nothing to do with getting Juan Carlos medical attention.

"You are going to need to pay me more than one hundred thousand," he said. "I am going to be in a world of shit when everyone figures out your friend escaped, and I approved the request that cut him loose."

Hugo's eyes narrowed. "You owe close to eighty thousand dollars. So, we're already paying a ton of money."

Andre glared at Hugo. “It’s still not enough.”

Hugo’s frown deepened. “Your problem is you don’t know when to quit when you’re ahead.”

For a second Andre wondered whether he was over-playing his hand. Then the doubt melted away when he realized that he would be heavily scrutinized by his superiors for letting Juan Carlos go and once they were done with him, he suspected the cartel’s people would show up asking questions.

Andre looked around the hotel room, as though searching for something. “Here’s the deal,” he announced finally. “You don’t immediately clear my markers or else it will be obvious I took a bribe. You give me the money. I’ll take care of paying off my markers plus you pay me two hundred thousand dollars on top of that,” he said.

Hugo looked at Shane and then back at Andre. Then he cleared his throat. “I don’t care what the other’s say. I will only go as high as two fifty for everything. That means you walk away with one hundred and seventy thousand dollars after we settle your debts. If that is not good enough, I will kill you myself and pay your replacement half that much,” Hugo said.

Andre took a swig of beer, chewed on his bottom lip for a second, and then in a quiet voice said, “Fine . . . But you need to make a change to your plan. Yours won’t work. Even if I order the guards at the front gate to wave you through, they are going to spot Shane. Andre shot a breath from his nostrils, “The ambulance company we use doesn’t have any white employees. You are going to need at least one driver that my guards have seen before. Hugo can be a new guy or a trainee. Moving a high-profile prisoner even in an emergency without a regular driver will raise suspicion.”

Andre looked at Tessa. She knew he was right.

"I'd been thinking the same thing ever since Hugo told me earlier that Shane would ride in the ambulance," Tessa nodded in a cool and clipped voice. "I'll call the ambulance company and find out who is working tomorrow night."

Shane's brow crinkled; this last-minute development taxed his already over-stimulated brain. Hugo was accustomed to having to adjust plans on the fly. He sipped his beer and sat back in his chair patiently waiting for Tessa to make the call.

Moments later, Tessa hung up the phone and smiled at Hugo. "There are a couple of drivers we can work with. I am going to go see one and will give you a call with the details as soon as I've got everything worked out."

Chapter Twenty-Four

A single light bulb hung from the ceiling and cast a dull low illumination on a small wooden table, splintered and paint chipped. Tessa tapped her fingers on it.

"When was the last time you were offered ten thousand dollars to let someone ride with you in the ambulance?"

Leaning back in her chair, Marisa rubbed her temples and sighed.

"Tell me again why anyone would be crazy enough to offer that kind of money to drive around with me?" she said.

"Stop being a psychiatrist and be a businesswoman," Tessa snapped back.

Marisa didn't smile.

Again, Marisa shifted uncomfortably in her chair. "Tessa, you know I got two children. I can't afford to be getting in trouble and lose my job. If it wasn't you asking, I wouldn't even consider this."

Tessa smiled reassuringly. "You won't get in any serious trouble. You might get a little heat, but you can handle it."

Marisa stared at her. She was thin and bookish. Beneath the unruly black ledge of her eyebrows, her gaze was steady. Small round glasses magnified her eyes.

"How much heat?" She asked, giving Tessa a "go-on" look.

"Well for starters. You will be transporting a prisoner from Bon Futuro prison in the middle of the night."

"What the fuck Tessa?" Marisa said through a nibbling of her lips.

A clear reaction to the anxiety she was starting to feel.

Tessa half rolled her eyes. "A prisoner is sick and you get a call to transport him to the hospital. Why the attitude Missy. You just da driver." Tessa scolded her in a West Indian accent."

Marisa pushed the glasses up the bridge of her nose and said, "Yeah but if someone is paying ten thousand to ride along with me, we both know some shit is going down."

"It ain't like that Mari. All you have to do is respond to a call. Nothing else! In fact, you know nothing except that you got a call on the radio to go to Bon Futuro." Tessa reassured her.

"What about the ride along?"

"If the police question you, the other driver was a new employee."

Marisa's face soured. "Police . . . why would . . ."

Tessa cut Marisa off. "All you know is that he was in the proper uniform and told you he was new and assigned to ride with you. He was waiting for you by the ambulance in the parking lot, mentioned the night shift supervisor by the correct name so you had no reason to question it."

Marisa's thin lips pinched to the left, an expression that told Tessa that she was unsure.

"What's really going to happen? I need to know." Marisa insisted.

"It's better if you don't."

"I have a bad feeling," Marisa's voice was filled with gloom.

Tessa took an envelope from her bag and set it on the table. "How long have we known each other?"

Tessa, as impatient as ever, answered her own question. "Since you were ten years old; that's how long. And how many times have I saved your ass?"

Marisa looked down at the table.

"Look, if you don't want the money, just say so and I can ask Drew. He's working tomorrow night," Tessa snapped.

Marisa rolled her eyes. "Drew's a fuck up."

"What's to fuck up? You get a call; you drive to where you are told to go, and you pick up a patient." Tessa knew Marisa was right about

Drew which is why she wanted her behind the wheel of the ambulance. She looked around the small efficiency and shook her head. "For Christ's sake Mari, you need the money. Take it!"

Marisa looked solemnly at Tessa. "So, all I have to do is answer a call; pick up a prisoner and drop him off at St. Elisabeth and I get paid?"

Tessa nodded.

After a moment of reflection, Marisa looked down. It was obvious she was concerned about something.

"What's bothering you?"

Marisa shrugged. "What's not bothering me about this whole thing would be a more accurate question."

Tessa's jaw tightened. "Spit it out Mari."

"What . . . what about the police?"

Tessa threw the question back with disgust. "What about the police?"

"You mentioned something about questions," she said with a confused frown.

Tessa shook her head and said, "Stick to your story and you'll be fine.

Marisa looked down at the table and cleared her throat.

"So, do you want the job?" Tessa pressed in a clipped and cool tone.

Marisa's first thought was to say no. It was obvious that there was a lot more to this than Tessa was telling her. But she needed the money.

Tessa looked across the table at Marisa's preoccupied, dark brown eyes. She watched as Marisa nervously nibbled her thumbnail and tapped her leg against her chair. Tessa propped an elbow on the table and leaned in close. "Do you trust me?" she asked, startling Marisa with the question.

"What kind of question is that?"

“A simple one,” Tessa answered her voice thick and matter-of-fact. “Do you trust me?”

Marisa’s response was nerve-tinged, confused. “You’re the Godmother to my youngest.”

“That’s not what I asked.”

A memory surfaced, bobbing clear and vivid from the clouded depths of Marisa’s mind, where she’d anchored it safely away years before. In a gravelly voice just above a whisper, Marisa croaked out the words, “Of course I trust you. You were the only one there for me when Bryan was killed.”

Marisa’s husband had been scouring the island for work, taking on whatever jobs he could scrounge up. One-night Bryan didn’t come home. At first, Marisa didn’t pay it any mind because the only steady work Bryan could find was unloading and transporting packages in the middle of the night. When Marisa didn’t hear from Bryan for a couple of days she began to worry. Two weeks passed with no word. Then finally Marisa received a call. The forty-minute ride took an eternity. At the end of the twenty-mile stretch, the road narrowed and then abruptly disappeared. She arrived at an isolated drainage ditch. Tessa was already at the crime scene and tried to intercept Marisa before she could see the body. Bryan’s arm was detached from the rest of his body, and the fist of that hand was clinched. Dangling freely from his torso were his intestines, pulled out from a huge gash in his lower stomach area. Marisa wriggled free and edged closer. One of the investigating officers told her that the body was meant to send a message. The Carraboca Cartel had a monopoly on drug trafficking in Curacao and it would not tolerate any competition no matter how small and insignificant. Bryan was not a drug dealer. He was nothing more than manual labor but that didn’t matter to the cartel.

Tessa took care of Marisa and her children and helped her find a job. Marisa shook her head abruptly as if trying to clear her mind from a painful memory. The indecision on her face was readily apparent. There was a long stretch of silence and Tessa used it to pick up the thick envelope from the table and stand up. She realized that Marisa was prone to being skittish and it wasn't smart to push her into doing something she wasn't ready to do.

"No worries Missy. I'll handle it myself," Tessa snapped, her tone was brusquer than she intended.

Marisa flinched then cleared her throat. Her mouth dry and thoughts stuttering, "I'll do it," She swallowed nervously.

Tessa looked at the unsure look on her face. "Are you sure?"

Marisa gave her a nervous laugh. "No, but I need the money."

"I'll call you in a couple of hours and tell you where to meet your partner."

Tessa placed the envelope firmly in Marisa's hand. "Stick to your story and do what he says, and everything will be fine.

Chapter Twenty-Five

ARKANSAS

The storm flung itself at the car. Attacking, sometimes shrieking, it buffeted the vehicle until Pierce was forced to turn on his hazard lights and slow to a crawl. His windshield wipers were all but useless. Sheets of water folded over the car's windshield. Pierce strained to see the road.

"Maybe we should pull over and let the storm pass," Alexis nervously interjected.

"This road is under construction. There isn't much of a shoulder and if I stop, we could get rear ended. So, it's safer to keep moving," Pierce replied before forcing his complete attention back to the road.

"Okay," she said, offering Pierce a smile she did not feel.

Using both hands, he battled for control of the vehicle. The car crept forward, its tires losing traction, the rear pulling against the front, and both threatening to take the wheel from his control.

Pierce eased off the gas and tapped the brakes lightly, turning the steering wheel as he battled to keep the front of the car traveling in a straight line.

A truck careened just in front, brake lights flashing. Its mud flaps sprayed water against the windshield like waves breaking against the shore. Momentarily blinded, Pierce strained to see through the rain-soaked windshield. His grip on the wheel tightened. His tires lost traction for an eternal moment. Then they grabbed again. Alexis sat in complete silence, her heart pounding, staring out through the windshield, hoping, praying that Pierce was able to see the road in front of them better than she could. Once Pierce felt that he had navigated through the worst of the storm, he turned off the hazard lights and carefully picked up speed. Alexis expelled a sigh of relief. Her grip on the overhead handle slowly eased as her nervousness and fear began to subside.

Pierce leaned back in his seat, hands clenched on the steering wheel, "The worst of the storm is behind us. Why don't you jump in the back and get some rest?"

Alexis grabbed his jacket which was draped along the backseat and covered herself with it. "I can sleep here," she said. Alexis felt safe around him. Like his very presence instilled a sense of calm in her.

* * *

Alexis could smell traces of Pierce's cologne on his jacket. The scent of his cologne was light and reminded her of fresh cut flowers and citrus. Curling around it like she'd once curled around her favorite blanket when she was small, she closed her eyes and drifted off.

* * *

In her dream, Alexis was happy again. She was dressed in a colorful summer dress and on her left hand was a new wedding band. She was holding a little girl's hand. She was beautiful. She had Pierce's intense blue eyes and her mother's golden complexion. Alexis laughed and sung a song as she gazed out at the bay; the shimmering water spread out like an endless mirror that reflected the bright Miami sunlight. Holding the little girl's hand, Alexis strolled towards the large drawbridge that connected downtown Miami and Brickell Avenue. At the base of the bridge was a monument portraying a Tequesta Indian warrior aiming an arrow towards the sky with his wife and child by his side. The son was covering his face for-telling their extinction. Just on the other side of the bridge Alexis saw Pierce smiling and waving to her and the little girl. His blue eyes sparkled.

"Daddy!" the little girl cried out. Alexis let the girl's hand go and she ran ahead. The sky began to darken as she drew closer to the bridge. Then suddenly she felt her entire body begin to vibrate. The vibrations were accompanied by a loud roaring noise as a large cargo freighter headed for the bridge. Red lights flashed and gates lowered just before the draw span rose. The raised draw span blocked her view. Alexis could no longer see Pierce or their daughter. When the bridge was finally lowered and Alexis could once again see across to the other side, they were gone.

* * *

Alexis woke up gasping, her hands knotted in Pierce's jacket. It was dark outside. The only light streaming into the car was the blue ethereal light beaming in from the full moon. Alexis sat up. Her head felt heavy and the back of her neck ached. She scanned the road for signs to get her bearings.

"You were having some dream."

"She nodded. Her mouth felt thick. "How long was I asleep?"

"Close to four hours."

"No! Really? Why did you let me sleep so long?"

"I thought you could use the rest. Besides, you were really in a deep sleep. You even drooled all over my jacket," he smiled.

Alexis raised her hand and wiped her mouth dry, "Sorry."

"So, how much longer until we get there?"

Pierce's mouth twisted into a pensive frown. "We're about half-way across Arkansas, so I think we have about six or seven hours to go."

Alexis nodded. "And how much longer until they . . ."

Pierce answered her question before she could finish it. "Juan Carlos should be here tomorrow night."

Alexis felt a sinking sensation in the pit of her stomach. At least, from the absence of Pierce slamming the brakes in reaction to her shrill, she felt safe in assuming that this time the soul-shaking scream she'd let loose had been all in her head. Thinking about seeing Juan Carlos again brought back a familiar sense of betrayal and resentment which settled in her stomach like a rock. Those were emotions, however, that she had learned to manage. Facing the fact that the day after tomorrow she would never see Pierce again was a feeling that crushed her.

Alexis pondered the possibility of not going with Juan Carlos. She couldn't comprehend how staying with him once he went into hiding assured his safety or her own. She quietly analyzed the various paths she could take. A small part of her preferred a quick end than a life of hiding with Juan Carlos. She believed that Pierce's plan of threatening to release computer files containing detailed information about the Cartel's operations if any harm came to her or Juan Carlos was an ample deterrent. All she had to do was remain hidden until Dario Carraboca understood what he risked if he came after them. Alexis convinced herself that there was no need to leave with Juan Carlos. The last few years of her life had been hell spent drowning in infidelities, lies and lonely nights. She needed more than a "do-over." Juan Carlos was hardly the type of person who would meet her half-way or even a quarter of the way. He was a self-indulgent man. When they were dating, Alexis didn't see any of the negatives. Even the first year of marriage went well. Then the business trips and prolonged absences increased, and she saw the ugly side of Juan Carlos. She needed to stop being the victim, the responsible wife that pretended everything was normal when her drug dealer husband came home reeking of women's perfume. It was incongruously clear to her that there was no way to live and that Juan Carlos would never change. Even if he could change Alexis didn't want him anymore. She wanted Pierce. She wanted to ask him if he felt the same way about her, to see his face, to reassure herself, but she needed to wait for the right moment.

* * *

As if on cue, Pierce glanced over at Alexis. There was confusion and anguish behind her eyes. He looked like he wanted to ask her if she was okay, but he already knew the answer. Instead, he reached over and took her by the hand. Alexis reacted tentatively trying to pull away, but Pierce held her hand firmly, warmly in his. Straightening herself in her chair, Alexis called on all her mental reserves to stop herself from touching him. Pulling away had to do more with self-preservation than anything else. She was in the middle of an emotional freefall. It was painfully ironic that the man she was being forced to choose was the one man who didn't want her. At least, Dario wanted her as insurance. And she believed Pierce, despite his bad habit of side stepping anything that remotely smacked of intimacy, had feelings for her. Pierce was careful to keep his desires under control. However, there were brief moments when he looked at her that his eyes betrayed him. At first, Alexis reacted the way she knew her family would want her to and politely avoided his gaze. Now, when Pierce looked at her, all Alexis could do was stare helplessly at him, confused, aroused and curious about the promise she saw reflected in his eyes.

Chapter Twenty-Six

MIAMI

Lloyd Hogan stepped off the plane in Miami wearing a blue oxford shirt and khaki slacks. By the time he landed, his team had already been assembled, fully briefed and ready to deploy to Curacao. The team consisted of five agents and one private contractor, most of whom Hogan knew, at least by reputation. Before leaving Washington D.C., Hogan received confirmation from the International Prisoner Transfer Unit of the Department of Justice that the Netherlands government agreed to turn over custody of Juan Carlos to the United States government. The operation had been assigned the highest priority. The objective was to safely transfer the prisoner from Bon Futuro prison to the United States before the Carraboca Cartel became aware that Juan Carlos was no longer a prisoner in Curacao. Hogan spent the last twenty-four hours carefully coordinating Juan Carlos's transfer with only senior government officials in the Netherlands. The Carraboca Cartel had high level informants in both governments. He was also sure that the cartel would not stand by and let the DEA take Juan Carlos out of Curacao. Hogan suspected that once the cartel discovered that the Netherlands agreed to turn Juan Carlos over to the United States, they would send their own team of assassins. Juan Carlos in U.S. custody backed Dario Carraboca into a deep corner. Hogan knew the cartel would move decisively to make sure that Juan Carlos didn't reach U.S. soil. The one thing that both Hogan and Dario Carraboca agreed on was that every man had his breaking point and that Juan Carlos was no exception. He would talk.

Lloyd Hogan stepped into a conference room and glanced around at the other members of his team assembled around a small table. Six faces stared back at him. He knew their names by heart, their backgrounds and where they'd received their specialized training.

"My name is Special Agent Lloyd Hogan. I'm glad you were all available for this operation," Lloyd Hogan began. As the others introduced themselves to Hogan, he opened the briefcase on the table.

"Some of you may already know that ten days ago Mr. Juan Carlos La Porte, someone we believe possesses valuable information concerning the Carraboca Cartel's operations, was arrested in St. Maarten. Approximately two days later, he was transferred to Curacao. Mr. La Porte is in a precarious situation. He is aware that his knowledge of the Carraboca Cartel's smuggling operations and financial infrastructure makes him a liability and therefore a target. Mr. Laporte has agreed to cooperate with our government in exchange for our protection. We have arranged for his transfer out of Curacao into our custody." Hogan cleared his throat and then added, "The Netherlands has waived the formal procedural requirements that routinely accompany international prisoner transfers."

Hogan looked around the room at the elite team of special operations, intelligence, law enforcement and personal protection personnel sitting at the table.

"This team has been assembled to secure the prisoner and safeguard his transport back to the United States. You're here because it's highly possible that the cartel will try to neutralize the asset."

The security detail consisted of three DEA agents, a specialist from the FBI, a counter-sniper and Ryan Collins, a retired Navy Seal Master Chief with 15 year's experience as a special warfare commando. His dark hair was still cropped in a military buzz cut and his eyes burned with a hardened determination only attainable from years of intense training. Lloyd Hogan and Ryan had a long history of working together against the Colombian drug cartels and he and Collins had a great deal of professional respect for each other. Hogan specifically asked for Collins. Two DEA agents along with Lloyd Hogan were going to serve as the inner protection detail closest to Juan Carlos. Ryan Collins and FBI Special Agent Justin Giles from the FBI Hostage Rescue Team would handle surveillance detection and keep an eye out for any overt or covert threats that could not be spotted by the inner protection detail. Special Agent Giles, Hogan thought, looked like a typical FBI Rescue Team agent, a hard charger, tough, mean, and lean. Victoria Macy, a striking brunette with cobalt blue eyes, had been summoned from the CIA's Kabul station for the mission because of her success rate in spotting and neutralizing snipers. Macy would take charge of the outer protection area. She was an expert at finding terrorist snipers in their hiding places and neutralizing them before they could shoot their intended target. The final member of the team was Special Agent Roy who assisted Lloyd Hogan in conducting Juan Carlos's interrogations. Agent Roy knew the island and would be responsible for driving the van that would be used for transporting the prisoner to the airport.

Hogan reached into his briefcase and distributed folders to each member of the team.

"Here is the Operation Plan."

The folders contained the plan down to the minute for transferring Juan Carlos back to the United States. It also included a summary of what most of the team already knew, such as Juan Carlos's ties to the Carraboca Cartel. It also contained detailed maps of Bon Futuro Prison, and Hato International Airport and the route that they would travel from the prison to the airport. A brief surveillance report for the past 48 hours for the airport was included which had limited value but might help a team member spot something that did not appear routine.

"Study it overnight. We leave for Curacao tomorrow morning," Hogan said.

The members of the team stood up and started to file out. Hogan caught Agent Macy's attention and motioned to her to stay. Agent Macy waited for the team members to leave the room and walked towards Hogan.

"How can I be of service sir?" She said.

"Have you been to Curacao before Agent Macy?

"No sir." Macy pointed to the aerial photographs of the airport which were on the conference room table. "I pulled up several maps of the airport and studied the 800-meter perimeter as well as several possible routes from the prison to the airport."

Hogan nodded. "What about the prison?"

Macy's face wrinkled in thought. "The airport is where we are most exposed sir. If they make an attempt on the prisoner at Bon Futuro it won't be by a sniper. The transfer of the prisoner should occur inside the prison. There would be no opportunity for a long-range shot." Macy's face twisted into a frown. "Unless of course, the cartel intends to take out the driver and the vehicle transporting the prisoner. Collins and Giles will need to conduct some advance recon of the perimeter right before you leave for the airport. However, once you are en route, there is very little in the way of defense if they use a rocket propelled grenade," she said.

Hogan gave Macy a slight nod that told her to continue.

"A sniper is more likely to set up its kill zone on the airport tarmac where the target will be exposed."

Hogan shook his head in agreement.

"Hato Airport is wide open," Macy shrugged. "If the cartel uses a sniper, it's only as a back up if they can't neutralize their target inside of the prison. If they are going to take a long range shot, it will be at the airport. It's the only place where the asset will be exposed and vulnerable."

Hogan studied the map for a long moment.

"There are no real obstructions. The shot could come from anywhere."

He watched Macy thinking about what she said, chewing it over in her mind, trying to break it down and make it digestible.

"A Special Application Scoped Rifle (SASR),.50 caliber can be effective up to about 2 and 1/2 miles away. However, most shooters have an extremely tough time beyond 300 meters. A kill zone for a field sniper, shooting on estimated ranges, from an improvised position is not likely to be extended beyond 300 meters, a planned "hit" where you know exactly how far you have to shoot, and can work from a prepared position might be something else, but only a handful of people can consistently hit their target beyond 800 meters."

Hogan's face twisted into a frown. He stood motionless for a minute or so, running the various possibilities through his head. Any way he looked at it, he didn't like what he sensed. "I want you to leave for Curacao ahead of the rest of the team and do some advance recon."

Agent Macy shook her head and, without another word, walked out of the conference room, picked up her gear and departed for Curacao.

Hogan dawdled over the cup of coffee he was drinking as he reflected on the mission he was about to undertake. He had no idea what type of assault the cartel would launch. His staff had been monitoring cell phone and radio communications of known cartel operatives for over the last twenty hours for any indication that the cartel may have been tipped off. There wasn't very much chatter, but Hogan knew better than to assume that information regarding Juan Carlos's imminent transfer had not already been leaked to the Cartel.

Chapter Twenty-Seven

BON FUTURO PRISON, CURACAO

When he entered the cellblock, Marcus braced himself for the clank of steel doors coupling, which produced in him a physical effect not unlike the dysentery he once contracted drinking bad water in Botswana. A long legal career had made him no stranger to prisons; yet the clank of steel on steel still coupled with the thought of another unpleasant interaction with Juan Carlos ripped through his insides like a disease bent on killing him, which it did, in its way, with every visit.

Juan Carlos was sitting on the floor of his filthy cell too battered to brush away the flies that pestered his open wounds. Marcus gestured to the guard to give them a moment of privacy.

"Five minutes is all we need," Marcus said. He only needed to convey a brief message to Juan Carlos and didn't want to be alone with him a second more than was absolutely necessary.

"Special Agent Hogan is scheduled to be here tomorrow to interview you," he started.

Juan Carlos raised his head. His face was bloody, one eye swollen nearly shut. A look of surprise flashed across Marcus' face.

Marcus guessed that it was retribution for what Juan Carlos had done to the young girl. He could only guess at what had driven Juan Carlos to sexually brutalize a woman that had been paid to have sex with him. Marcus was sure that psychiatrists might differ, but all would offer some theory that Juan Carlos's obsession with subjugating and hurting women had something to do with his unfulfilled ego or his insecure id or some fixation he had developed as a child. Marcus didn't care. He was less concerned with how people became who they were than simply who they are. And as far as Juan Carlos was concerned, he didn't care much either way because he would be dead in twenty-four hours.

"What happened to you?" Marcus asked with mocked surprise.

"Two prison guards paid me a late-night visit," he said reluctantly. "They caught me by surprise." Juan Carlos touched his rib cage, wincing. "I think they kicked in a couple of my ribs."

It was easy to hate Juan Carlos. He deserved what he got, Marcus thought. He tried to conceal the contempt he felt for Juan Carlos to appear sympathetic.

"What did you expect? Curacao is a small island. Everybody knows one another. What you did to that young girl was bound to have repercussions."

Juan Carlos shrugged as if anally raping the girl was a minor thing.

Marcus's eyes narrowed. "Frankly, after what you did to her, you're lucky to be alive."

Marcus took a deep breath before changing the subject to the purpose for his visit. "Special Agent Hogan will be here tomorrow.

"I hope you're ready. Everything is riding on you being able to get the DEA to bite on those smuggling routes."

Juan Carlos's expression darkened. He shuffled through the materials in the envelope without saying a word.

"I do have a bit of good news for you," Marcus added.

Juan Carlos half laughed, "And what might that be?"

"I have it on good authority that your extradition will be denied, and you will be released," Marcus said.

Juan Carlos looked up at Marcus once again. His blood on his face and the swollen eye looked ugly, streaked in black.

"Released?" Juan Carlos echoed as he slid the envelope across the floor towards Marcus.

Marcus swallowed hard. "Yes, if your extradition is turned down, there is no reason to hold you."

Juan Carlos smiled, but his expression seemed twisted and sinister. "I want another girl tonight," he demanded his voice lifeless.

Marcus considered that for a moment and then said, "After what happened to the last girl, the prison's hospitality has worn thin. "I'll see if I can change their minds," he offered, even though he had no such intention.

At that moment a prison guard appeared at the cell door and Marcus shook his head. Marcus took two steps through the cell door and turned back. "Ohhhh . . . I almost forgot to tell you that the doctor is in the infirmary today. You are supposed to see him right after we're done here. Your American lawyer has been pressing to get you some medical attention. Judging from your present condition, I'd say the doctor couldn't have come at a better time," Marcus said with a sad laugh.

The guard snapped at Juan Carlos. "Get up!"

Juan Carlos sucked in a breath as he labored to get to his feet. He stood at the entrance to the cell just as he did every time now, waiting for the guard to grant him permission to walk out. Juan Carlos coughed, and a small spray of blood splattered on the floor just in front of where Marcus was standing.

Marcus pretended not to notice. "Focus on tomorrow's meeting," Marcus shrugged unsympathetically.

* * *

The prison guard swung the door open to the prison infirmary and marched Juan Carlos to the examining room.

"Please have a seat on the examining table," Doctor Hernandez gestured. He stared vaguely off towards the corner of the room as he traced his hand over Juan Carlos's torso. The Doctor's eyes finally settled on the guard.

"This man has two broken ribs. I'm assuming it's another accidental slip and fall," he said trying to keep the impatience and disgust out of his voice. There was a flicker of uneasiness in the guard's eyes. "I don't know Doctor. I just started my shift." Doctor Hernandez smiled ruefully. "Of course. This man, however, is in bad condition and needs medical treatment. I'm going to need you step outside," he said before turning his attention to his notes. Noticing the guard's indecisiveness, Doctor Hernandez waved his hand in the air to dismiss him and said, "You can wait on the other side of the door."

And with a brisk nod the prison guard left the examining room.

* * *

Doctor Hernandez leaned in and pressed his fingers against Juan Carlos's side. He flinched. Speaking in a low voice the Doctor explained that while he had previously agreed to inject Juan Carlos with a drug that would induce a high fever and necessitate his transfer to St. Elisabeth hospital, he was reluctant to do so without knowing the extent of Juan Carlos's internal injuries. He was concerned that inducing a high fever might cause serious complications.

"I'm not sure how prudent it is to further compromise your current condition just so that we can get you evaluated at St. Elisabeth," Doctor Hernandez whispered in Juan Carlos's ear.

Juan Carlos began connecting the dots and, after a minute, he figured that the transfer to St. Elisabeth had to be a part of Pierce's plan.

"I've been urinating blood for almost a week. When I asked to see a doctor, I was ignored. When I complained to my consulate, I was beaten," Juan Carlos shook his head in disgust. "Induce the fever, I have no time. My extradition hearing is the day after tomorrow. If I am turned over to the French, it will be at least a month before they will let me see a doctor. To the French authorities, I will be nothing more than another prisoner who died of some illness contracted in a Dutch prison."

There was a knock at the door, "is everything okay in there?"

Doctor Hernandez responded quickly, "yes, everything is fine."

Juan Carlos lowered his voice to half a whisper. "I understand the risk involved, but I have no real choice."

Doctor Hernandez considered that for a moment and reluctantly agreed to inject Juan Carlos. "I'm going to keep you in the infirmary and ask the attendant to alert me as soon as there is a change in your condition. You are going to experience flu like symptoms. Hopefully, we will be able to get you moved to St. Elisabeth before your fever spikes too high," he said with a touch of concern in his voice.

"Thank you," Juan Carlos nodded in a manner that conveyed both his appreciation and desperation.

Doctor Hernandez reached into his bag and pulled out a clear vial.

Juan Carlos turned his head to the side, enough to see the blurred outline of a Doctor Hernandez's hand silently emptying the contents of a syringe into his intravenous line.

Chapter Twenty-Eight

VENEZUELA

Rene stood alone outside the double doors that led to Dario Carraboca's study. It was more like a library than a study. Old leather-bound books filled the shelves which ran along two of the walls. Exotic animal head trophies and artifacts adorned every square inch of the walls that weren't occupied by bookshelves. Animal rugs were strewn over marble floors and on the far wall an ornate fireplace. As Rene pushed the doors open and stepped through the vaulted portal, he half expected to see the same heads of the cartel that were there the last time he had been summoned. A hierarchy existed among them and Dario alone sat atop the food chain for the simple reason that he was the most ruthless among a group of men who left a trail of bodies in their wake on a whim. But this time, however, Dario Carraboca was alone.

* * *

He stood utterly still, deep in thought as he stared at the fronds of a coconut palm outside his window whispering in the tropical evening breeze. The reddish-purple leaves of a nearby bougainvillea added a papery rustle to the air. Rene was reluctant to break the silence and stared unblinkingly at the floor just in front of him. When Dario finally spoke, he sounded more like a weary friend than the head of a powerful drug cartel.

"Juan Carlos was an outsider. He wasn't one of us. Yet, I treated him like a member of our family," Dario sighed and turned back to the window, his eyes drifting out over the sprawl of his estate. The sun had ceased shimmering on the vast ocean leaving the sky a brilliant orange pink.

"These past few days have been extremely troubling," Dario shrugged in a way a man shrugs when he had been disappointed by a son. Then Dario's tone changed abruptly from congenial to suspicious and he said, "We cannot underestimate the lengths Juan Carlos will go to in order to save himself."

Rene wore a puzzled expression. "I don't understand. Juan Carlos is cooperating with the DEA as we instructed."

Dario glanced uncomfortably at Rene, "So, I've been told," he said disbelief coloring his voice. "But anyone who knows Juan Carlos knows that he is opportunistic and there's the possibility that he will try to cut himself a better deal. And to do that, Juan Carlos will have to offer them more than a few smuggling routes."

Rene knew better than to disagree with Dario, so he nodded in agreement. But silently he couldn't see what the Americans could possibly offer Juan Carlos to make him betray the cartel.

Dario's eyes remained locked on Rene. He could tell from the tense expression on his face that Rene was uncomfortable with the idea that Juan Carlos would parlay his knowledge of the cartel's affairs into a lucrative deal with the Americans.

"Tell me Rene, would you be willing to bet your life and the lives of your loved ones that Juan Carlos will remain loyal to us?" Dario asked without a flicker of emotion.

Rene felt his insides jump as if he suddenly touched a live current.

Dario gave Rene a few minutes to let his question root into his thought process. Then he gave him a slight nod.

"Use your brain Rene and put aside any loyalty you still feel for your friend. Juan Carlos is not unlike a rat. And what are rats? They are vermin that will do anything and everything to survive."

Rene got a bad feeling that he wasn't going to like where the conversation was headed.

"Doesn't it seem like an odd coincidence that Juan Carlos's wife has disappeared?" Dario proclaimed more than asked.

Rene's face looked shocked at that, his lips parting slightly in surprise. Dario shared a knowing glance with Rene and added a few more troubling observations. Then he went back to the subject of Alexis's disappearance.

"Ask yourself, why would Juan Carlos feel the need to hide Alexis unless he is cooperating or planning to cooperate with the United States government?"

Rene frowned and stood there unflinching, but in the end, he was still unsure whether Juan Carlos was planning something. Dario walked over to his desk while he continued connecting the dots for Rene. A few minutes later he said, "Once Juan Carlos provides the DEA with the smuggling routes, pay him a visit and leave him to a slow death. Let him be an example to anyone else who would consider betraying us," Dario's eyes were hard glittering beads.

Rene hesitated. He had learned to think very carefully before answering Dario when he was in one of his surly moods. With some trepidation he asked, "Shouldn't I wait to make sure that the DEA takes the bait?"

A thin sudden frown formed on Dario's face, as if Rene had said something that disappointed him.

"There would be absolutely no reason to wait. Once Juan Carlos provides the DEA with the smuggling routes, he has done what we asked him to do. Juan Carlos has no control over whether the DEA takes the bait."

Rene understood from Dario's tone that at that point in time, Juan Carlos was a loose end.

There was no emotion in Dario's voice, only a calm certainty when he said, "Every breath Juan Carlos takes after his meeting with the DEA tomorrow poses a threat to us."

Rene sensed the reality facing him. He knew better than to think Dario would spare Juan Carlos. What Rene had hoped for was a gesture of kindness. He had been praying that Dario would not order him to kill the man who had been like a brother to him. Rene never wondered whether he could kill Juan Carlos. The fact was that he was a trained killer and he was good at it. He knew he could kill him. But he preferred not having to go through life knowing he killed his closest friend.

"Tomorrow, Juan Carlos meets with the DEA. I want this matter taken care of right after the meeting. Have I made myself clear?" Dario's tone was flat and final.

Rene nodded. He pulled in a quick breath and said, "I'll leave in the morning. Once Marcus confirms that the meeting took place, I will take care of our problem."

Satisfied with Rene's response Dario reached into the humidor on his desk and pulled out two cigars and handed one of them to Rene. Rene shrunk back into the chair and breathed in the tobacco from the lit cigar. He gazed at the exotic animals that Dario had shot on his hunts and were now mounted on his walls. They served as a reminder that none of God's creatures were safe from Dario Carraboca.

Chapter Twenty-Nine

Hugo and Tessa waited in the shadows of a narrow alley lined on both sides by lopsided wooden buildings for Marisa and the ambulance to arrive. The alley was dark and smelled of stale beer, urine and sweat. At that moment the alley was deserted, but in a couple of hours drunks staggering home would collapse there for the night. Hugo checked his watch. The ambulance was supposed to meet them ten minutes ago. He wondered briefly if the driver had had second thoughts. Hugo didn't like working with civilians. They lacked the training to think ahead and consider the gamut of possibilities that could go wrong during an operation. He preferred professionals with military training or former law enforcement officers who had been conditioned to improvise when things in the field didn't go according to plan. Tessa's eyes swept the alley and fell on the headlights of a van meandering slowly down the narrow corridor towards them. The ambulance stopped 15 feet from where they were parked and flicked its head lights twice. Hugo and Tessa got out of the jeep and approached the ambulance on foot. Reluctantly, Marisa unlocked the door to the ambulance. Lowering her window, Marisa looked at her watch and whispered to Tessa, her face tense, "what time are we picking up the prisoner?"

Hugo stared at Marisa. Her forehead was drenched in sweat and he saw genuine fear in her eyes.

When Hugo said, "A little more than two hours," Marisa looked like she wanted to jump out of her skin.

Hugo's frown deepened. He cocked his head back with a little bit of concern and shared a look with Tessa that asked, are you sure about this one?

Tessa gave a quick nod that said she'd be fine and turned her attention to Marisa.

"All you have to do is drive the same way you always drive. The same thing you do every night," Tessa smiled trying to sound reassuring.

"I'll be fine." Marisa whispered, sounding more like a hiss.

Tessa held her hands up in mock surrender. "Okay then," she nodded and peered over at Hugo who had placed his black bag in the ambulance and had settled into the passenger seat.

"I'm going back to the hotel and pick up your partner," Tessa said, careful not to call Shane by name. The less that Marisa knew when she was questioned the better, Tessa thought.

"We are going to pick up what we need and wait for you at the rendezvous spot," Tessa gestured at Hugo before heading back to her jeep.

"Rendezvous spot?" Marisa repeated sounding surprised.

Tessa turned and gave her a stern look over her shoulder. "Nothing you need to concern yourself with."

"I can't believe this," Marisa muttered to herself. "This is insane."

While Marisa eased the ambulance back on to the road, Hugo withdrew his Beretta from the shoulder holster and checked the chamber. Once he was done Hugo opened his bag which was what he considered his lifeline, should things go drastically bad and inspected his gear. Inside was a custom colt .45 machine pistol with a collapsible butt stock. Hugo had fired every handgun known to man, and in his opinion, there was no better weapon to carry into a gun fight. The bag also contained two M84 stun grenades with timers, should he need a distraction to make a quick exit, a Kershaw Black Blur folding knife and a stun gun if he needed to incapacitate someone. Marisa was unnerved at the sight of all the fire power. Her eyes shifted uneasily from the road to Hugo's bag several times.

Marisa mumbled a soft curse and then added, "Routine pick up my ass."

There was nothing average about the job or the goliath who looked like he was capable of extreme violence sitting to her right.

Sensing her uneasiness, Hugo put the guns away.

"Relax this isn't my first rodeo. They're just for insurance," Hugo said.

Marisa shot him a worried look. "This isn't a routine pick up is it?"

Hugo considered the tense, anxious expression on her face. "For you it is. All you have to do is pick up a sick prisoner and drive him out of Bon Futuro prison. You'll be alright," Hugo said trying to calm her nerves.

Marisa nodded vaguely and said nothing. When she stopped at the intersection, she craned her neck to her right and studied Hugo. Even though the light had turned green, she did not move.

In a voice full of suspicion, she asked. "Who are you?"

Hugo smiled in his easy way and said, "Tonight, I'm just a new employee assigned to ride with you."

Marisa gave him a dubious look. "You, my friend, do not look like someone who would be driving an ambulance. You are going to stick out like a sore thumb . . . You might as well have a professional mercenary or hit-man or something like that tattooed on your forehead."

Hugo pointed in the direction of the green light. "We'll be fine."

"And if we're not? What happens if something goes terribly wrong?" She asked nervously.

The smile melted from Hugo's face. "Something always goes wrong," he said nonchalantly.

Marisa stopped short. "What!"

"Careful," Hugo snapped. He could see Marisa was a sea of emotions. He reached for her arm to steady her. Marisa's instinct was to pull back, but Hugo's paw was too big, and his grip was too strong.

He couldn't have her falling apart with only one hour before they were scheduled to drive to the prison.

"Listen to me," Hugo insisted. "You have absolutely nothing to worry about. All you have to do is drive the ambulance."

Marisa nodded meekly, tension ebbing from her body. With a look of uncertainty and her forehead covered in sweat every instinct that Hugo had was telling him she was all wrong for the job. He knew that in her present state she wouldn't be able to maintain her composure and she would make the guard at the gate suspicious. He needed her to appear calm in order to get through prison security. Andre made a good point when he said that an unknown ambulance driver showing up to transport a prisoner in the middle of the night would create suspicion. An extremely nervous driver who can't answer a question without stammering or who can't sit still would be just as suspicious. Hugo was accustomed to dealing with soldiers and experienced mercenaries. He was unsure what he could say to a thirty-something year old woman with no combat training to help her to focus.

"Relax," Hugo barked before catching himself. He started over, this time he spoke softly and loosened his grip on Marisa's arm.

"I know you're a little scared. It's written all over your face. Pull the ambulance over and let's sit for a while. We still have some time," Hugo said.

Marisa brought the ambulance to a stop on the side of the road. She felt a dull pang of nausea roll over her. She opened her mouth, then closed it again as her stomach lurched. Marisa paused almost holding her breath as she struggled to choke back the food she had eaten earlier. "I'm sorry," she paused, almost holding her breath, "this whole thing just scares me to death. There's more to this than Tessa told me," she whispered at last.

Hugo reached into his bag and fished out a small flask of Tequila. Handing it to Marisa he said, "Take a few sips of this. It will calm your nerves." Marisa hesitated. "Drivers are occasionally tested after their shifts."

Hugo laughed so loudly that it caught Marisa by surprise.

"I can assure you that your employer won't be testing you tonight. Now, take a few sips," he smiled. Hugo kept talking while Marisa slowly sipped the Tequila.

"Let me tell you how this is going to play out," he said in a stern voice. Marisa took another sip from the flask and half closed her eyes as the Tequila burned its way down her throat.

"Go on," she gestured, her voice sounding constricted.

Hugo went over everything with Marisa and answered her questions as patiently as he could.

"I've served two tours of duty with Special Forces and we were sent into pretty hostile territory and on every mission my team always made it back safely because they knew their roles. Tonight, will be no different. Your role is simple. Just keep your cool. We'll receive a radio dispatch directing us to pick up someone and deliver him to St. Elisabeth. That's all you know."

Marisa nodded, her eyes a bit wide. "But I've never transported a prisoner from Bon Futuro prison in the middle of the night before."

Hugo smiled politely. "If you get a call in the middle of the night it's your job to respond. Am I right?"

Marisa released a long-suffering sigh still a little skeptical. "What do I say if the guards ask me questions?

Hugo's smile faded and his chin dropped in frustration. "The only thing they could ask you about would be me since I'm new and they have never seen me before. You just tell them I'm a new guy. I'll take it from there if they continue to press that issue," Hugo replied.

"But what if they want to know about the radio dispatch?" Marisa persisted, wearing Hugo's patience down to a small nub.

"You tell them what you know, which is absolutely nothing more than you got a call to come to Bon Futuro prison to transport someone to St. Elizabeth. For all you know it could be a sick prison guard."

Hugo could see that Marisa's nerves were still on edge. He resigned himself to the fact that he would never be able to completely calm her down. Not without some help. Reaching with his left hand into his shirt pocket, Hugo pinched a marijuana blunt, put it to his lips and drew the lighter flame to the tip. He took a drag and looked at the hot glowing tip.

"This will help you relax," he said, handing the blunt to Marisa.

Marisa shot Hugo a disbelieving look. "Are you serious?" She said with disapproving disdain. Hugo put the blunt two inches from her lips. Marisa narrowed her eyes at him. She pushed his hand away from her face. "I don't smoke anymore." Her eyes flared.

Hugo shook his head. "You're wound too tight. If you can't keep it together, you're going to fuck things up and cause me to put large caliber bullets into some people. I'm not asking you to get baked. Smoke just enough to take the edge off," Hugo insisted putting the blunt in Marisa's hand.

Marisa hemmed and hawed for a moment. "Fine," she mumbled under her breath, even though she didn't think it would make any difference.

Marisa pursed her lips and sucked in deep, taking the smoke into her lungs and holding it. Moments later, Marisa began to recline in her chair. After a while, she felt a numbness work slowly through her unwinding the tight cords of tension that had been holding her together.

After taking several more drags of the blunt, her face relaxed, Marisa smiled faintly at Hugo.

Hugo looked at her. He still didn't think that she was suited for this operation, but at least she appeared to have her nerves under better control and was as ready as she was going to be. "It's almost time, he nodded. "We should get back on the road."

Chapter Thirty

Shane finished loading the containers of gasoline on the small trailer hitched to Tessa's jeep and jumped into the passenger's seat. Tessa checked her watch. "One more stop."

About twenty minutes later, Tessa pulled into a small gravel parking lot just beyond the hazy glow of the streetlight and switched off the engine. Tessa pulled out her cell phone and paged a number.

"Where are we?" Shane asked.

"The morgue."

Shane looked through the windshield at two men wheeling a body bag towards the parked jeep. He understood the reason for torching the ambulance, but the need for a dead body caught him by surprise. Shane cocked his head an inch to the left and asked, "What's the dead body for?"

Tessa's eyes darted from the two men moving in their direction to Shane. "The bodies will buy you time," she said. "If there are three badly burned bodies in the ambulance, it will take the police a couple of hours before they figure out that Juan Carlos isn't one of them."

Shane nodded and watched the two men who were now only about twenty feet away. Hugo had told him they were going to set the ambulance on fire to get rid of any DNA evidence, but he never mentioned anything about torching the ambulance with corpses inside. Three charred bodies could give them additional cover. The police would be busy trying to identify the bodies. If there was a possibility that Juan Carlos died in the ambulance, they would not be quick to conclude that he had escaped; meaning that they would be deploying their manpower investigating the crime scene rather than looking for an escaped prisoner. By the time the police figured out that none of the bodies belonged to Juan Carlos, they should have already landed in the United States.

"Not bad," Shane said in an admiring tone.

Tessa shrugged as if to say, "I know." "Glad you approve. Now stay here," Tessa told Shane as she stepped out of the jeep and walked towards the back of the trailer.

Taking orders was not Shane's strong suit and he was out of the door of the jeep in a shot.

Tessa pulled the tarp off the back of the trailer and pointed to where she wanted them to put the bag.

"I count one. Where are the other two bodies?" She asked.

One of the men paid Shane more than a passing glance before he said to Tessa, "You have our money?"

"When I get the other two bodies," Tessa snapped in a firm tone. "Now go get them."

A few moments later the men reappeared out of the shadows and tossed two body bags onto the trailer like two dock workers unloading sacks of flour.

"Easy," Tessa snapped.

"We didn't hurt him, I promise," one of the attendants laughed.

"One Hispanic male, one black male and one black female, right?" Tessa asked unzipping the body bags.

"We got as close as we could," the attendant replied. "We couldn't find any white or Hispanic "John Does" so the third one is a light skinned Mulatto."

Shane stared at the two men with a suspicious glare convinced that the simpletons grabbed the first three bodies that they found.

"You're telling us that in that whole morgue you don't have a single Hispanic male? I'll tell you what I think . . . I think that you didn't look very carefully. If I go up there right now, I bet you that I'll find what we want."

"You won't find a Hispanic male without any identification," one of the two men answered with a shake of his head while the other stared at him with a "who the fuck are you" look.

They stood in silence for what seemed like an eternity, but was in reality a prolonged moment.

During that moment, a myriad of responses flashed through Shane's mind, most ending with him breaking one or more of the man's bones, but in the end, he decided that would be unwise.

Tessa looked irritated and let out a ragged breath.

The older of the two men was missing at least half of his teeth. "It's the best we could do," he snapped at Tessa. He then said something in a gruff Papiamento. Shane didn't understand a word, but he didn't need to. It was clear that the man wanted to be paid.

Closing the zippers to the bags, Tessa tossed an envelope onto the cart. By the look on her face, she wasn't happy.

"Three thousand dollars," She grunted in a manner that confirmed her disgust.

The man did not make eye contact with Tessa, he simply picked up the envelope and nodded at the other attendant. "Ok we're done. Let's go."

Tessa threw the tarp back over the trailer and slid back into the jeep. She gave Shane a quick glance. "That's the last of it. Now we go to the rendezvous point and wait on the others."

Chapter Thirty-One

Juan Carlos's pain worsened with each hour. His legs and feet felt cold and numb. His fever was dangerously high, and his lungs began to feel like they were drowning in fluids. Gasping in pain, Juan Carlos's stomach churned as he was overwhelmed by unbearable nausea. Despite Doctor Hernandez's specific instructions, the prison infirmary attendant had not checked on him regularly. Juan Carlos lapsed in and out of consciousness. Laying there, he thought that he would surely die. Juan Carlos swallowed hard as he tried to beat back the nausea to get the attendant's attention. His tongue might as well have been coated in cement for all the good it did him. When the attendant finally got around to checking in on him, Juan Carlos let his eyes shut for a moment and float dizzily in the darkness. It was obvious that Juan Carlos's medical condition was steadily deteriorating along with his odds of making it out of Bon Futuro alive. After checking his vitals, the attendant darted for the phone and dialed the Assistant Director of Security and Operations, Andre Rojer.

The Attendant cleared his throat. "Sir the Prisoner, Juan Carlos Laporte, is in physiological decline."

Rojer let out a heavy sigh. "What exactly are you telling me?"

"The patient's temperature is up to 105 degrees and his respiratory rate has been steadily increasing . . ."

Rojer bristled, "Then I suggest that you call whatever doctor is on call this evening."

* * *

Moments later the phone in Rojer's office rang. "Sir," the attendant calling from the prison infirmary began.

"I'm putting you on speaker. Captain de Wolff is also here. Did you speak with the Doctor?" Rojer interrupted.

"Yes sir."

"And what did he say?"

"Doctor Hernandez wants the prisoner immediately transported to St. Elisabeth hospital" the attendant replied.

Rojer's tone hardened instantly. "Does he now? I think the doctor forgets who's in charge," he snapped.

"Yes sir," the caller agreed.

Rojer sat silently in his chair with his arms folded across his chest. He appeared to be carefully considering all the information. Rojer's behavior was consistent with what his officers would expect. He was a man who believed in rigid protocol.

Rojer redirected his attention to Capitan de Wolff. He exhaled. Pausing as though he was still considering the proper course of action Rojer drummed his fingers on his desk for a moment. "There are two options. The first is that we treat the prisoner here and reassess his condition in the morning." Rojer stared at Capitan de Wolff. "But if the prisoner dies, the Americans will make a big issue out of ignoring the physician's recommendation that he be immediately transferred to St. Elisabeth."

Capitan de Wolff bobbed his head as if he was agreeing with him.

"The second option is that we transfer the prisoner to St. Elisabeth."

Rojer played Hugo's words over in his head where Hugo warned him what would happen if he backed out. Rojer wore an anxious look on his face. He wasn't sure which one would be worse-double crossing Hugo or the shit storm he was about to dive into by letting Juan Carlos escape.

“Capitan, I want you to call Doctor—” He hesitated appearing to forget the doctor’s name.

“Hernandez,” the voice on the call interjected.

“Yes, thank you,” Rojer nodded. “And I want you to confirm that transporting the prisoner to St. Elisabeth is an absolute medical necessity.”

“What if the Doctor says that it is?” Captain de Wolff asked.

Rojer nodded vaguely but said nothing for a moment. He held up two fingers. There was reluctance in his voice when he said, “Then we go with option two.”

Captain de Wolff took that to mean that if the Doctor insists on moving Juan Carlos, he was to make the arrangements to transport the prisoner to St. Elisabeth.

“Yes sir.”

“One more thing Capitan,” Rojer interjected. Capitan de Wolf who had reached the doorway turned and faced the Assistant Director.

“I would like you to personally make sure that if we have to transfer the prisoner that it goes smoothly.”

Captain de Wolff nodded, “Very good sir.”

Thirty minutes later the radio in Marisa’s ambulance crackled. “Dispatch to Unit One.”

“This is Unit One.”

“Unit One, we have a call from Bon Futuro. They have an unconscious prisoner with an extremely high fever. They are requesting immediate transport to St. Elisabeth.”

“Ten-Four, Unit One,” Marisa responded.

For a brief moment, Marisa sat there expressionless as if gathering her strength. Gripping the steering wheel tightly, Marisa let out a deep breath.

Hugo patted her thigh trying to comfort her. "We got this," he reassured her.

Marisa's lip twitched. "I hope so." She looked skeptical. Marisa sat in silence while she drove. She took another deep breath moments later when the prison came into view.

When they were about ten yards from the blockhouse situated immediately in front of the gate an armed guard waved at them to stop. Marisa felt her stomach flip as the guard stepped towards the ambulance.

"Good evening," the guard said, shining a light into the front seat trying to get a better look.

Marisa had only been to Bon Futuro once before but by the guard's reaction she seemed familiar to him.

"We just received a call from dispatch to transport someone to St. Elisabeth," Marisa volunteered.

The guard peered into the ambulance and gave Hugo an odd look. Hugo pretended not to notice.

"We don't normally send prisoners to St. Elisabeth in the middle of the night. It's very unusual," the guard mumbled under his breath.

Marisa was flustered. "My first time up here at night, but I just go where they send me," she shrugged.

Hugo leaned slightly over Marisa so that guard could look into his eyes. "Why don't you check with whomever you need to check with to make sure everything is in order? We'll just wait. We're not the sick ones. We got time," Hugo assured him in a sarcastic tone.

The little friendliness the guard originally displayed disappeared from his face. This time when he looked at Hugo he didn't blink. "I haven't seen you before," his voice twitched.

"I'm new and I'd like to keep this job," Hugo said, trying to move him along.

The guard snapped his pen back onto the top of the clipboard. "Wait here," he grunted. Marisa's heart was pounding as her eyes followed the guard back to the blockhouse. She could see him talking and nodding in the office as he appeared to be writing something down.

Suddenly, Marisa felt a flicker of optimism when she heard the screeching sound of the steel bolt as the gate began to open.

"There will be somebody waiting for you by the loading dock," the guard said as he waved the ambulance through the prison gate. The ambulance rolled through a second gate leading to the main building. A young guard waiting by a side entrance signaled to them and shouted. Marisa saw him and parked the vehicle by the entrance. She turned towards Hugo and said, "Grab the gurney in the back and follow me."

Hugo slid out of the passenger's side and grabbed the transport gurney from the back of the ambulance before heading after Marisa.

A look of concern spread across Marisa's face when she examined Juan Carlos. His lips were almost bluish in tint and his eyes though open were unfocused. Marisa turned back towards Hugo and the young prison guard who were trailing behind her. Her voice carried down the hallway.

"Move it gentlemen. We have a very sick man here!"

"We're here to take you to the hospital. Do you understand?" Marisa said, trying to communicate with Juan Carlos.

It took as much determination for Juan Carlos to open his eyes as it did to beat back the lingering nausea, but he clenched his teeth tighter and forced himself to blink.

In one coordinated heave, Hugo, the prison guard and Marisa shifted Juan Carlos onto the gurney. Juan Carlos grunted and moaned when they lifted him. Hugo swiftly pushed the gurney towards the ambulance. He moved with extraordinary grace and speed for such a big man. Marisa followed closely behind. She jumped into the back of the ambulance with the gurney and immediately put a clear mask over Juan Carlos's nose and mouth.

"I'm going to increase the ventilation," she said, turning a large valve to increase the flow of oxygen. I'm also going to need to get more fluids in him. You are going to have to drive," she barked orders at Hugo.

Hugo nodded and opened the door to the driver's side. To his surprise, sitting on the passenger's side was a prison guard.

"I'm Capitan de Wolff," the guard said, introducing himself.

"*Fucking hiccups,*" Hugo thought.

"I've been ordered to make sure that the prisoner's transfer to St. Elisabeth goes smoothly. So, unless you have an objection, I thought that I would ride along." Capitan de Wolff said.

"None," Hugo smiled. "Would you mind handing me the black bag by your foot? Hugo asked nonchalantly.

"Of course," Capitan de Wolff replied, reaching down and handing the bag to Hugo.

Chapter Thirty-Two

Alexis saw Pierce signal a left turn. The only thing she could see on the left side of the road up ahead was a dilapidated shack. She figured he had to be making a bad joke. But when he started to slow the car down, she said, "Enough Pierce this isn't funny."

Pierce cocked his head as he pulled the car into the gravel drive. "This must be the place," he said, in a tone that revealed his surprise.

The small wooden house looked like a large broken-down tool shed that could collapse at any minute. Alexis looked horrified.

"Maybe the house is better inside," Pierce shrugged even though he wasn't very optimistic.

Alexis kept her eyes fixed on the decaying hovel.

"We are not staying here," she hissed through clenched teeth.

Pierce's eyes were scanning their surroundings. Despite her tortured expression he knew why Hugo recommended that they spend the night there.

"We'll be safe here. Besides, it's only for one night," Pierce shrugged. Alexis bit her lower lip and nodded. She stepped out of the car and walked towards the small house. She realized that Pierce was right. No one would look for them in that decrepit hole-in-the wall. But that still wasn't good enough for her.

Alexis was caught completely off guard and flinched when a tall Indian man with a worn face suddenly appeared in the doorway.

"Folks," he said amiably.

Pierce reached around Alexis and shook the man's hand. "I'm Pierce and this is Alexis," he said. "I'm guessing you're Tiger?"

Tiger fished out a cigarette. "Yep, that'd be me" he said. "Hugo told me to expect you.

Pierce smiled. “Thank you. We appreciate your hospitality.”

Tiger regarded Pierce for a moment before replying. “Don’t mention it. Hugo said you needed a place to stay. I figure you have to be pretty desperate if you want to stay here.”

Tiger looked at Alexis. “Ma’am I didn’t get a chance to clean up in there or put any food in the fridge for you.”

Alexis cleared her throat. “That’s fine,” she nodded, still feeling a little unsettled.

“Well . . .” Tiger shook his head. “You folks should know that everything here in Wetumka closes pretty early. Unless you want to get back on Interstate 75 and drive about 20 miles, I’d suggest you get over to Shellie’s Country Cooking Café on North Main street no later than 7 P.M.”

“May I go inside?” Alexis gestured to Tiger.

“Please make yourself at home.”

The instant Alexis passed through the small doorway the overpowering stench of cat piss blasted her senses and made her gag. The small room was blanketed by stacks of old newspapers and scattered garbage. The tattered pea green couch in the center of the room was peppered with cigarette burns and had a strong musty smell.

“*Nice touch*,” Alexis thought as she sidestepped empty bottles of Jack Daniels and masses of cockroaches that scurried around in undisciplined ways. In the bathroom she spotted a small cracked sink. A faint splashing sound caused her to peer over into the topless toilet. Alexis jumped back and screamed for Pierce. Pierce ran into the bathroom. In the corner of the small bathroom with her back hugging the wall, Alexis stood frozen, her eyes filled with fear.

Pierce’s eyes darted around the small room until he heard the same splashing sound and leaned over the toilet. There he saw a rattlesnake swimming in foul smelling yellow water. Pierce turned his eyes back to Alexis and reached for her hand. "It's okay . . . you're safe. Let's get out of here."

Alexis bolted out of the house with an anxious look on her face. "I can't stay here," she said in a low voice only Pierce could hear.

Pierce shook his head and frowned. "I know."

* * *

It was almost dusk when they finally settled on a large oak tree in the middle of miles of rolling green pastureland. The Oklahoma countryside was desolate with the exception of a few cows grazing nearby. Fashioning a make-shift picnic blanket out of his jacket and a couple of sweatshirts Pierce laid out two sandwiches, plastic cups and a box of wine.

"Thank you for this," Alexis chimed gratefully as she sat on the ground next to him.

Pierce smiled. "This is actually pretty nice."

"It is," Alexis cooed.

Pierce poured Alexis a cup of wine. "Here you go," he said with a smile handing her a drink. Alexis put the cup to her lips and sipped the sweet chilled liquid. She felt his eyes on her. Alexis debated whether she should just lean over and kiss him. She looked into Pierce's eyes and a tiny, barely audible moan slipped out. Blushing, she wondered whether he heard it.

The sun began to straddle the hilltops on the horizon as it prepared to disappear for the night. Resting his head on one of the sweatshirts Pierce drank in the soft glow of the moon and the stars as the sun faded from view. He blinked a couple of times and a few minutes later, Alexis heard the soft snoring and deep even breaths and knew Pierce had fallen asleep.

Alexis stroked his hair and let herself fantasize about what a life with Pierce might be like.

When it got so dark that Alexis could barely make out the car parked a few hundred feet away she decided it was time for them to head back. “Pierce,” she whispered gently twisting her fingers in his thick black hair.

His eyes opened briefly. He peered up at Alexis through half-closed eyes.

“We should head back to the car and settle in for the night.”

“Alright,” Pierce said, sitting up and rubbing the remaining vestiges of sleep from his eyes.

When Pierce and Alexis got to the car, he opened the back seat for Alexis and then reached for the front door. Her eyes widened. “What are you doing?” Alexis said shaking her head disapprovingly.

“Letting you have the back seat. It’s more comfortable.”

“We can share it,” she said.

Pierce didn’t move a muscle. Before he could respond Alexis grabbed his hand.

“I won’t bite you.”

* * *

The tight back seat made it difficult to get comfortable. Alexis nuzzled between his arms. Pierce held her close against his chest. She could feel his breathing and heartbeat as she settled in. Alexis closed her eyes, warm and contented, and then brought them open again at the thought that after this night she would never sleep in Pierce’s arms again. Suddenly, in a burst of boldness Alexis turned and faced Pierce. Her eyes were glassy. Alexis lifted her face to his, her lips slightly parted, “Can you just kiss me now?” she quivered in a voice she nearly didn’t recognize as her own. Initially caught off guard Pierce looked into her eyes. They flashed with a deep desire. Unable to restrain his impulse to kiss her, Pierce finally did something he wanted to do since he first set eyes on Alexis. He gave in to his own yearning and pressed his lips to hers and Alexis reacted instantly. Pierce gently kissed her top lip and then her bottom lip, then he placed both his lips on both of her lips and when he opened his mouth so did she. Pierce brushed his tongue against hers and gradually deepened the kiss. His mouth moved over hers, testing and experimenting. His tongue tasted her, and he wanted more. Alexis moaned softly deliriously lost. She wanted to belong to him. She kissed Pierce with such dark and primitive passion that all he could do was surrender to the moment. All notions of what was right versus wrong took flight like leaves on the wind. When Alexis opened her eyes and met his gaze, she couldn't help but smile. Pierce craned his neck back enough to look into Alexis' beautiful and beguiling eyes. Tracing her fingers over the contour of his bottom lip, Alexis smiled. *"I love you,"* she thought, her heart so full, she thought it might overflow or burst from her chest. If only she had the nerve to say the words aloud.

Chapter Thirty-Three

Hugo swerved the ambulance around a tight curve and bore down the narrow road. The old island road was riddled with potholes and cracks. A faded white dash in the center which veered and disappeared at random was the only dividing line from on-coming traffic. The headlights and the oscillating lights on top of the hood were the only beacons that illuminated the road and surrounding countryside which was otherwise pitch black. The ambulance bounced violently over the dips and bumps in the road and rattled so loudly that it felt as if it would shake apart. Capitan de Wolf rocked back-and-forth in his seat. Hugo deftly reached into the bag for his taser. He made it a practice of always having an alternate weapon for situations where non-lethal force was an option.

"There is something in the middle of the road," Hugo suddenly blurted out hitting the brakes. Capitan de Wolf flew forward. A split second later the metal hooks pierced the Capitan's neck and face and Hugo set loose a violent stream of intense electric voltage. The electric jolt sent the Capitan's face slamming against the passenger side window. Saliva and blood dripped from the Captain's mouth and nose. Hugo's eyes dissected the man before he delivered another shot to make sure he was completely incapacitated while he edged the ambulance along the side of the road. Hugo opened the passenger door, reached in and yanked the limp body out of the ambulance letting it collapse with a thud on the ground.

Marisa jumped out of the back and stared at the Capitan lying motionless in his own pool of blood with his hands and feet tied. She could tell from the amount of blood gushing from his nose that it was broken.

"What are you doing?" She stuttered anxiously.

Hugo shook his head. “My job; would you prefer that I kill him?”

Hugo asked, his voice was like stone. Before Marisa could react, Hugo asked her how the patient was doing.

Her eyes nervously darted from Hugo to the man tied up on the ground. “Better, but he is still pretty weak.”

Hugo handed her a cell phone. On it was an address. “I need you to get us to that address.”

Marisa reluctantly grabbed the phone. “What are you going to do with him?” She asked, looking at the Capitan.

“He’s coming with us. At least for the time being,” Hugo replied coolly as he picked up the body with little effort and moved it to the back of the ambulance. Marisa hesitated not knowing what to think of Hugo’s willingness to make Capitan de Wolf collateral damage. Hugo checked his watch.

“We need to move now,” he barked at her as if admonishing a child. Marisa flinched, shaken from her stupor. She slinked into the driver’s seat. Using the steering wheel to steady herself, Marisa waited for the sound of the ambulance doors slamming shut before easing the ambulance back out onto the road towards the rendezvous point.

* * *

SHANE WAS PACING back and forth, his footsteps utterly soundless. Tessa sat behind the wheel of the jeep keeping an eye on the gate which led to the back of the warehouse where they were parked. He heard the low whine of an engine before he noticed the headlights connected to a dark sedan as it rounded the building. Despite the years that had passed since Shane had worked as an enforcer, his instincts were as keen as they had ever been. Shane instinctively slipped into the shadows of the long-abandoned building. Staring at the silhouette of a car slowly creeping towards them, Shane drew out his weapon, a .40 caliber Smith & Wesson and eased forward. Tessa watched the car waiting for the signal.

"C'mon," she exhaled feeling a small degree of angst setting in.

Time lost all meaning as the dark sedan rolled slowly towards the jeep. Seconds felt like hours. Tessa caught the blur of Shane's shadow scrambling along the cover of the building towards the car. A vein twitched along her eye. "Flick your fucking lights already," she seethed.

As if prompted by Tessa's will, suddenly, the headlights of the sedan flickered twice. Shane stopped moving towards the car but remained crouched in the shadows and did not holster his weapon until he recognized Mia.

Mia cast a seasoned eye over Shane. He looked emotionally fatigued. He had been out of this game for a long time, and he wasn't used to working under these stressful conditions. From his body language, it was apparent that the adrenaline was gone, and the tension was clearly taking a toll on him.

"We're almost home," she nodded as she patted him on the back and walked past him towards the jeep.

Shane murmured something under his breath.

"Keep up Shane. Hugo will be here soon, and the asset's medical condition is tenuous at best. We have a lot to do in the next thirty minutes. So, get it together. You can rest on the plane," she barked orders at him.

Shane palmed his shaved head and took a deep breath. "I'm good," he said, he had been in tough spots before. Shane and Mia watched as Tessa unzipped the three body bags.

"Two males and one female," Tessa confirmed.

Mia began running scenarios in her mind. “Let’s get them out of their clothes,” she said.

“I’ll take the body on the end,” she said, pointing to her left. “You two strip down the other two.”

Shane smiled grimly. He hated handling dead bodies. Mia worked quickly while Shane unsteadily removed the articles of clothing from the dead body. Fighting off a wave of nausea, he took a deep breath and gave the pants a firm tug.

“Hold him steady so I can get these pants off,” he snapped at Tessa.

“I’m holding him. Stop being a pussy,” Tessa clucked angrily.

“For the love of God,” Mia groaned. “Get his fucking clothes off already!”

“Hey, I didn’t sign up for this,” Shane snapped defensively.

Mia’s eyes turned to ice. “We have a couple of minutes before they get here.” She grunted in disgust.

“We’re done. Clothes are off,” Shane said, suddenly feeling guilty. Hugo and Mia took a huge risk when they agreed to help. The last thing his best friend, Hugo needed was an assignment where, if he was successful, it could mean that he now had a target on his back. If they were discovered, Hugo and Mia would become the next targets of the Carraboca Cartel. Shane’s mind churned and at that moment he wondered whether he should have simply said no when Pierce asked for his help instead of asking Hugo and Mia for help.

* * *

The sound and sight of the ambulance coming up the drive jolted Shane from his thoughts.

Mia shot Shane and Tessa a sideways glance.

"We've got fifteen minutes to get the ambulance driver's uniforms on the black male and female bodies and the prison uniform on the lighter skinned male."

Hugo jumped out of the back of the ambulance.

"Big Fella," he called over to Shane in a deep baritone voice. "Over here," he motioned to Shane to follow him to the back of the ambulance.

"We had a small situation but nothing to worry about," Hugo said, opening the back doors. On the floor, contorted in agony lay Capitan de Wolf. He was blindfolded, and his arms and legs were tied with heavy rope. He was also gagged to keep him from crying for help.

Shane frowned. "How did this happen?"

"There's no such thing as a perfect plan buddy. The key to success is having the ability to adapt to any situation. The prison guard threw me a bit of a curveball when he asked if he could ride with me to the hospital. If I said no, he would have gotten suspicious. So, he really didn't leave me much choice. A small hiccup," Hugo explained.

Shane just nodded quietly, a little disturbed.

"Help me carry him over to the trailer," Hugo said. The Capitan thrashed and bucked as Hugo and Shane lifted him by his shoulders and legs and carried him over to the trailer.

"Unless you want a little more electric shock therapy, I'd take it easy," Hugo scowled at the Capitan.

A few feet away Marisa was bringing Mia up to speed on Juan Carlos's medical condition. She told Mia that when she first saw him, he wasn't lucid, so as soon as she got him into the ambulance, she put an oxygen mask on him and gave him a heavy dosage of ibuprofen to help relieve the pain and bring down the fever. When it became apparent to her that they would not be heading directly to the hospital, Marisa started an IV drip to help replace the fluids he had lost. Mia shook her head indicating that she understood and turned her eyes momentarily to Tessa.

"I need you to soak all the fingers in acid. I don't want any fingerprints on the bodies."

"No worries," Tessa nodded.

Turning back to Marisa, Mia asked if she had any more IV fluid in the ambulance that she could take with her.

Marisa suddenly looked confused.

"Yes," but I don't understand," Marisa started.

"The less you know the better." Mia cut her off.

Marisa's eyes showed concern. "He's doing better, but he still needs medical attention."

"Listen to me," Mia spoke with the authoritative rattle of a seasoned special-forces officer. "The patient will get medical attention. I need to keep him in a stable condition until then. Give me all the supplies you have, and, for your own sake, don't ask me any more questions."

Marisa nodded but looked troubled.

Mia's blue-grey eyes sharpened and probed Marisa. "How much do you already know?"

"Only that this was no routine ride-along. That's all I know for sure." Marisa's eyes fixed on Tessa hunched over the dead bodies lying on the ground dressed in EMT and prison uniforms."

"What I suspect is that you have no intention of bringing the patient to St. Elisabeth." Marisa said with a pang of anxiety. "And what I don't know is what you plan on doing with me and the prison guard tied up on that trailer behind Tessa's jeep," Marisa wiped her eyes.

Mia walked Marisa over to the back of the ambulance.

"Get in there and pull together all the medical supplies that I am going to need to care for the patient until I can get him proper medical attention."

Mia studied Marisa for a moment. "Marisa, we don't kill innocent people. The guard is tied up for his own protection. We are not going to hurt either one of you. You have to trust me," she said. "Now, I need you to focus and get me those supplies," Mia demanded, eyeing the rustle of activity that was occurring all around them.

* * *

WHEN SHANE FIRST laid eyes on him, Juan Carlos's pasty complexion, dark puffy eyes and gaunt cheeks gave him a reason to think that he might not survive the flight back to the United States. His body shivered as Hugo and Shane helped him to the sedan. When Juan Carlos lowered himself into the car, his body crumpled. He winced and let out a cry of pain, his body trembling. Hugo lunged into the car to hold him steady while Shane crouched down and slipped a blanket over Juan Carlos.

"You're going to be alright," Shane said even though he wasn't sure he believed it. Juan Carlos looked into Shane's eyes and gave him an anemic nod.

Hugo looked over to Mia and motioned that Juan Carlos was ready. "Hang in there buddy," Hugo offered Juan Carlos some encouragement. "We're almost home." Juan Carlos blinked letting him know that he understood and for the first time in weeks he felt a ray of hope.

Chapter Thirty-Four

Mia went through her mental checklist one last time while Hugo and Shane loaded the dead bodies into the ambulance. The body wearing Hugo's EMT uniform was put in the front passenger's seat. The other two were put in the back. Hugo noticed Marisa standing near the ambulance paralyzed with a look of desperation on her face. He took a moment to walk over towards her. When he put his arm around her, Marisa instantly stiffened.

"You did great," he whispered softly into her ear.

Marisa's eyes watered.

"The tough part is done," Hugo continued trying to reassure her.

She blew out an exasperated breath. "What happens now?" She whimpered.

"I want you to listen to me," Hugo said in an easy tone. "This will all be over shortly. I need you to keep it together like you did in the prison."

Marisa blinked several times fighting back tears. Hugo spoke slowly, deliberately as if to make absolutely sure that Marisa understood every word he was saying. "You are going to drive the ambulance," he said simply. "All you have to do is follow Tessa."

Struggling to keep her voice steady, Marisa asked Hugo if they were going to kill her and the guard. She needed to hear from Hugo that they were not going to hurt her.

Hugo took a deep breath and exhaled. "No! Of course not," he shook his head emphatically. "You are going to follow Tessa to a fairly isolated area and leave the ambulance there. After you drop off the ambulance, Tessa is going to take you and the guard to a safe house. A few hours later, Tessa will drop both of you off and make an anonymous call to the police giving them the location of where they can pick you up. The police will find both of you blindfolded and tied up but otherwise safe." Hugo explained that he wanted to make it appear that both she and the guard were victims.

"If the Police find you tied up and blindfolded, it will make it easier for you to convince them that you don't know anything," he said.

"Okay," Marisa bit her lower lip. Her eyes moved from Hugo to the jeep that was inching closer to them. Tessa rolled down her window and waved to Marisa. "Let's go," she said.

"One more thing," Hugo remembered. "Don't use your cell phone for any reason. Don't make or answer any calls or texts. Leave it in the ambulance."

Marisa nodded; letting Hugo know that she understood.

Marisa looked across the ambulance at the dead body propped up in the passenger seat and climbed in slowly like someone cautiously easing into deep cold waters. The jeep began to creep into the darkness down the long snaking road and Marisa followed close behind. She felt uneasy. No matter how hard she tried, she couldn't completely rid herself of the lingering feeling that whatever was going on here was going to have serious ramifications. As they slowly wound their way down the narrow road overrun by long grass and thick bush, it felt as if they were moving in slow motion. The dead body next to her swayed each time the ambulance rolled over a dip or bump in the road. There were no lights of any kind and the dense leaves of the trees, wreathed with tangles of vines, made it impossible to see more than just a few feet in front of her. The hanging vegetation thrashed against the ambulance's windshield making it seem like at any moment the road would come to an abrupt end. The road banked slightly northeast and suddenly broke into a clearing about thirty feet wide and nearly ninety feet long. Tessa turned the jeep and trailer around and stopped. She waved to Marisa to leave the ambulance parked at the other end of the clearing. Wasting no time, Tessa grabbed a container of gasoline and soaked the dead bodies. She then proceeded to scatter fuel over the entire interior of the ambulance. For good measure Tessa poured gasoline over the exterior of the vehicle.

"What are you doing?" Marisa asked knowing the answer to her question.

Tessa stopped and looked up momentarily. "Getting rid of anything that the police could use to connect us to the job," she said.

Marisa looked confused. "Why put dead bodies in the ambulance?"

Tessa cursed under her breath. "To give the police forensics fuckers something to keep them occupied."

"I don't get it," Marisa regarded Tessa with skeptical squint. "Why pour gasoline over the bodies? They are going to burn in the fire anyway."

Tessa paused for an instant and then said, "we need the bodies to char all the way through so that the police can't easily identify them. Now help me move the body in the passenger seat over to the driver's side." When they were done, Tessa resumed dousing the ambulance with gasoline. "It will take hours before they realize that none of the bodies belong to the missing prisoner. Marisa didn't realize it, but her mouth hung open in disbelief. She was astounded at how every detail was carefully calculated to buy the others as much time as possible to disappear.

Tessa jumped into the back of the ambulance and opened the valves to the oxygen tanks. She now had to work quickly. Setting fire to the fuel-soaked rag stuffed in the gas tank, Tessa almost stumbled as she tried to move faster than her body would let her. Sensing that she now only had seconds before the ambulance would ignite, Tessa glared at Marisa and yelled to her to run to the jeep. Tessa then lit a fuel-soaked rag which she used as a wick for a bottle filled with fuel and motor oil and launched the fireball into the back of the ambulance. Black smoke rose up like a venomous snake and disappeared into the dark sky. She didn't wait for the ambulance to catch fire. Tessa sprinted for the jeep never once turning her head. A wave of flames rolled over the ambulance. Tessa didn't care that she could scarcely see the road in front of her. She barreled through the vine infested road like a battering ram trying to put as much distance between her and the makeshift time bomb as possible. Seconds later a flash of orange followed by oxygen tanks exploding in their wake lit up the sky.

Chapter Thirty-Five

HATO INTERNATIONAL AIRPORT - CURACAO

Earlier that day Counter-Sniper Specialist Victoria Macy completed field reconnaissance of Hato International airport and approximately a six-hundred-foot radius of the surrounding property. Victoria carefully scanned the area for optimal firing positions. Using her binoculars, Victoria searched for objects that could comfortably serve as hide-sights where a sniper team could conduct surveillance. The airport's single runway backed up against the Caribbean Sea. The jets disembarked and boarded their passengers on a tarmac a couple of hundred feet from the terminal blocking any shot from the water. A sniper shot from the terminal building was also not a viable option since the building was patrolled making it impossible for a sniper to establish a position to get off a shot. Victoria concluded that a long-range shot would likely come from the east or west while the asset walked from the airport terminal to the jet. She determined that the west provided the most favorable angle. So, Victoria set up her hide-sight on the roof of a cluster of buildings immediately west of the airport terminal building. She hid between the air handling units. Anyone looking would have a difficult time spotting her. The roof gave her a clear line of sight to all activity from the airport terminal building north to the tarmac. In her vast experience, that area would be the most likely kill zone. After hours of carefully probing, Victoria was left with no evidence of a sniper. But she knew that the absence of evidence meant nothing. If a person was good, it was a simple thing to conceal a position that was six hundred meters away.

She planned to recommend to Hogan that his team drive the asset on to the airport tarmac up to the jet leaving a sniper a very small window to take the shot. She assumed that the asset would likely be dressed in civilian clothing like the agents making him difficult to single out. The team was experienced so Victoria knew that they would be careful not to treat the asset in any manner that would help a sniper spot his target. The asset would probably exit the van and walk up the jet stairs as part of the team. Given the small window to take the shot, and the difficulty which she predicted would be associated with identifying the target, Victoria assumed that given the low probability of success, the cartel would only use a sniper as a last resort. She figured that the cartel would probably use a well-coordinated assault once the van was en route to the airport or the cartel would use one of the local police on its payroll to kill Juan Carlos in his cell.

The night brought with it a welcome cool and by 11 P.M. most activity at the airport had stopped. Laying on her stomach with her night vision binoculars by her side, Victoria settled in on the rooftop. A couple of hours later Victoria was awakened by the whine of jet engines as a private corporate jet taxied onto the tarmac. From the shadows of the rooftop, Victoria monitored the pilot while he conducted his preflight inspection of the aircraft. Her eyes darted across the airfield and settled on two golf carts driving from the terminal building towards the jet. Concentrating on the passengers she noticed a driver, a woman and a white male with a shaved head riding in the first cart. Following closely behind was a second cart, Victoria spotted another male wearing a baseball cap and a large black male sitting in the back of the cart facing backwards. The man in the cap hunched forward making it almost impossible for Victoria to get a clear look at him.

THE SECOND CART rolled to a stop just in front of the stairway leading up to the jet. Hugo measured Juan Carlos trying to determine whether he could make the walk to the jet on his own.

"You have about twenty steps to board the jet. Do you think you can make it?" Hugo asked Juan Carlos.

"Yes, I think so" Juan Carlos's voice was barely audible. He held up his arm so Hugo could help him to his feet. Juan Carlos tensed his body and took a deep breath summoning all his resolve and willed himself out of the cart. Cautiously, he put his hand on Hugo's shoulder to steady himself. He started by taking a couple of slow deliberate steps. Hugo kept pace with Juan Carlos so he could use him as a crutch. Juan Carlos began working his way up the stairs towards the entrance to the jet. Above him he heard voices, but he couldn't make out what they were talking about. His head was spinning. As he pushed upward, his vision narrowed, and he felt as if his consciousness would slip away. Two steps from the top his legs buckled, and he began to lose his balance. Hugo, who was just behind him, used his strong hands to hook him under his armpits and hold him steady.

"A little help," Hugo shouted up to Shane.

Shane who was a few feet ahead turned and darted down towards them and draped Juan Carlos's arm over his shoulder while he wrapped his arm tight around his torso.

"Easy does it fella," Shane said. "I got you."

Juan Carlos and Shane climbed the last two steps together. Juan Carlos focused all his energy on getting to the top knowing that once he was on board his odds of surviving the night greatly improved. Over the last couple of days, he indulged himself in fantasies about what life with Alexis might be like if he made it out of Curacao. He knew that it would be difficult to regain her trust and her love. But he reconciled himself to the idea that if given a second chance he would resist his sexual urges for young women and try to recapture the feelings he once had for Alexis. When he got to the top step, his hopes surged, and Juan Carlos turned and gave the island a fleeting glance.

At the very moment Juan Carlos stepped through the entryway the bite of a stern tongue snapped at him.

"Don't take another step," The voice echoed. "Now hold out your hands," Mia ordered Juan Carlos placing rubber latex gloves on his hands, a surgeon's mask over his mouth and a shower cap on his head. Pointing to a seat draped in plastic film, Mia directed him to sit there. Mia knelt next to Juan Carlos.

"How are you feeling?" She asked him, taking his arm and feeling his pulse.

"A little better, but those steps took a lot out of me," he gasped through the surgical mask. Mia nodded detecting the pain in his voice.

"I'm going to start another IV to help get more fluids into you," she told him.

Juan Carlos nodded and felt a prick in his left arm. Mia told him that she wanted him to stay seated for the duration of the flight. She explained that the law enforcement agencies would follow every possible lead. A chartered jet leaving the island in the middle of the night within hours of the time Juan Carlos disappeared would certainly become a target of their investigation. Law enforcement would eventually trace the jet leased by the front company she used as her company. Mia was familiar with the DEA's standard operating procedures. She suspected that a forensics team would sweep the jet and it mattered little whether the evidence was admissible in court. If they found any physical evidence that put Juan Carlos on the jet, the blowback from the DEA would be merciless and decisive. If no physical evidence was uncovered, then at a minimum Mia knew that both she and Hugo would be subjected to hours of interrogation simply because of the questionable coincidence. As former members of the United States Special Forces both she and Hugo received survival training in the event they were captured by enemy forces. Mia and Hugo were each put through mock-prison training where they were hooded and roped together. Special Forces instructors serving as interrogators put them through carefully choreographed chaos designed to disorient and break them. As part of the resistance training, they were each subjected to sleep deprivation, blaring music and semi-starvation. When the DEA's few leads evaporated, they would begin grasping at straws which meant that DEA would become relentless in its efforts to connect them to Juan Carlos's disappearance. But in the end, Mia knew that without any hard evidence she and Hugo would overcome anything the DEA threw at them. No interrogation methods deployed by the DEA would shake either one of them.

* * *

SPEAKING INTO HER headset, Victoria Macy called Lloyd Hogan. Her voice never rose above a whisper. She provided Hogan with as much detail as she could observe about the private jet and the four civilians that boarded it. Victoria's report filled Hogan with a sense of dread. After thirty-one years working for the DEA, Hogan had learned to trust his instincts, and a chartered jet leaving Curacao at two in the morning was too suspicious to ignore.

"Can you confirm that the asset is not one of the three men boarding the flight?" Hogan asked.

"That's a negative sir. I can rule out two of them, but the third male is wearing a baseball cap. I couldn't get a good look at him," She replied.

Hogan frowned.

Victoria offered an additional piece of information. "The man wearing the cap needed help climbing the stairs. I couldn't determine if he was physically impaired or ill."

Hogan grew increasingly uncomfortable. His brain struggled to find a way to stop the flight before it took off, but he knew there wasn't enough time. Victoria watched as the jet sped down the runway and disappeared into the darkness. Hogan heard a muffled rumbling sound not unlike the sound of distant thunder.

"What's that?" He asked.

Victoria looked in the direction of the flash.

"It appears to be an explosion about five *klicks* southeast from my position."

The initial explosion was followed by a second blast. Victoria watched as flames began to engulf the area where the explosion took place.

"*Jesus*," Hogan thought, tension ebbing from his body. As he quickly played out all the plausible scenarios in his mind, the notion that this could all be a series of coincidences was not a thought that stuck. Hogan could now make out the faint sounds of sirens over the phone. A wave of dread shuddered through his very core.

"Until we know more, maintain your position and surveillance," he ordered.

The line crackled, "Roger . . ."

There was a moment of dead air, and then the phone connection went bad.

Hogan wasted no time moving to his landline and calling Bon Futuro prison.

The phone rang at Bon Futuro prison for nearly twenty minutes before someone answered. Hogan picked up on the fact that the prison officer spoke to him in a more guarded and careful tone than usual. He knew the meaning of that tone. It meant that something had seriously gone wrong. As soon as Hogan asked to speak to the commanding officer, the voice on the other end of the call put Hogan on hold. When the guard finally took Hogan off hold, he rattled off a series of nonsensical reasons why his commanding officer was unavailable. It had now been fifty-four minutes since Hogan had first placed the call and he grew angrier and more impatient by the second.

"You do know who you are speaking with?" He asked, speaking through clenched teeth.

"Yes, I know who you are," the prison guard shrugged. "My commander is busy with an urgent matter and cannot be disturbed," the guard insisted.

"Put him on the phone!" Hogan yelled into the telephone.

Hogan heard a muffled and excited exchange take place, and then a click followed by dead air and a sharp beeping sound.

"Un-fucking believable," Hogan cursed under his breath as he slammed down the phone. Next, he dialed the United States Consulate. "This is Special Agent Lloyd Hogan. I need to speak to the Consulate General," he insisted.

"Agent Hogan, it's three in the morning."

"This is a matter of National Security. Wake her!" He responded in a forceful tone.

The phone rang next to the bed of the Consul General. Dazed the Consul picked up the receiver.

"Hello?"

"Madam, this is the Consulate. I have a Special Agent Hogan from the DEA on the line, and he insists on speaking with you."

The Consul General sat up in her bed and tried to clear her mind

Squinting at the digital clock which flashed 3:06 A.M. she said, "That's fine put Agent Hogan through."

"What's wrong Lloyd," the Consul said. She could barely focus.

"That's exactly what I'm trying to find out," Hogan started, but I can't communicate with anyone at Bon Futuro about an American prisoner who is currently incarcerated there."

"A groan escaped the Consul's lips. "Lloyd, it's three in the morning. We can barely get them to cooperate during normal business hours when they are at full staff."

"This is different," Hogan fired back. "When I identified myself and asked to speak to the commanding officer, they refused to put me through, and when I insisted, they hung up on me."

The Consul General was skeptical since she was very familiar with the prison's lack of cooperation.

Having no desire to hear any excuses, Hogan didn't give the Consul a chance to talk. "Juan Carlos Laporte is no ordinary prisoner," Hogan started before stopping in mid-sentence. "Valerie, we need to speak on a secure line."

"The line in my study is secure. I can text you the number."

"I'll call you back in two minutes."

Reluctantly, the Consul General put on her robe and walked to the study.

"Mr. Laporte is the most important lead we have ever had in our investigation of the Carraboca drug cartel. The Dutch have agreed to a prisoner transfer and are turning him over to us tomorrow," Hogan explained when the Consul finally answered the line. The Consul General tried to gather her thoughts.

"I haven't been advised of any prisoner exchange."

"And you wouldn't have been in this specific instance if not for the fact that I need your help."

The Consul considered Hogan's request. Standing in the dim light of the study, she put her hand on her temple and massaged it as if it were aching.

"I'm not sure I can get access to the prison at this time of night.

"I will be in Willemstad in four hours. Use whatever political capital you have at your disposal and get into the prison to see him," Hogan pressured her. "Valerie, I wouldn't ask for this if it wasn't important."

The Consul stood silently wondering exactly how she would get in to see a prisoner in Bon Futuro prison in the middle of the night. Curacao had two levels of government. The Insular government had jurisdiction over territorial affairs which included the prison in Willemstad. They rigidly followed protocol, and, except for Hogan who traded on personal favors, they were not very cooperative when it came to the American government. As a result, in the past, her office had only been granted limited access to American prisoners during normal working hours. The Consul's thoughts were a blur as she tried to think of who could effectively intercede on her behalf.

"I will call the Justice Minister, and see what he can do," she exhaled suddenly, feeling very inadequate.

Chapter Thirty-Six

The tinged air behind Tessa and Marisa was full of smoke and leaping flames. Tessa plowed through the thickly branched dirt path swerving and skidding along the tight turns as she tried to put as much distance as possible between them and the pillar of smoke and flames bursting behind them. The dirt road veered off and abruptly ended at an intersection. Tessa barely slowed down, jerking the jeep up onto the paved road and accelerating towards the safe house. Her plan was to hold on to Marisa and the prison guard tied up in the trailer hitched to the jeep until early afternoon before leaving them bound and gagged where the police could easily find them.

Marisa's head was still spinning. She stared at her reflection in the window and asked herself how she had gotten into such a ludicrous situation. It was the money of course, and the fact that she owed Tessa a debt. Tessa had been purposely vague when she described the job. But it was now clear to Marisa that she had been roped into an elaborate plan to help someone escape from Bon Futuro prison. The moment she met Hugo she knew that he was no ordinary ambulance driver. Mia's attention to detail and control at the rendezvous point also told Marisa that both Mia and Hugo were former military or at minimum had some kind of professional training. Then there was the matter of setting three dead bodies along with the ambulance on fire to destroy evidence and make the police think that the prisoner she was supposed to be transporting to the hospital was killed in the explosion. It was in that moment that Marisa experienced clarity and rid herself of any doubt concerning the chaotic events that took place earlier that evening. Despite the frenzied dance of activity at the rendezvous point, she could now see that it had an air of precision and a certain logic to it. Everything with the exception of the prison guard's last second decision to ride in the ambulance, Marisa assumed had gone according to plan. And even the matter of the guard was handled with such efficiency that it appeared Hugo had anticipated something might go wrong. From what Marisa could see, the team was made up of extremely capable and seasoned professionals. So incredibly proficient that it made Marisa worry about the identity of the individual she had just helped escape from Bon Futuro prison.

Marisa glared at Tessa trying to bore a hole through her with her eyes. "Do you think I'm stupid!"

Tessa's expression didn't change. Her eyes were fixed on the dark road ahead.

"Don't you have anything to say to me?" Marisa screamed.

Tessa flinched. "Easy," she said, blowing out an exasperated breath.

"What are you worried about?" Tessa asked.

Marisa just stared at her, wordless. Tessa's eyes darted from the dark road to Marisa and back to the road. Marisa knew Tessa was holding something back and wondered if Tessa had even an inkling of how angry she was.

"I told you from the very beginning that there would be police and questioning," Tessa said firmly.

Marisa's eyes narrowed. "You didn't tell me everything."

"That was for your own protection," Tessa shot back. "All you need to know is that you got teamed up with a new driver. There's nothing unusual about that. Tessa said in a cool and clear voice.

Marisa scoffed and shook her head. "There's more to it than that . . ."

"Yes," there's more to it," Tessa said, interrupting her. "But you can't talk about what you don't know. All you can tell the police is that you were training a new driver when you got a call from dispatch to pick up someone at Bon Futuro and drive him to St. Elisabeth."

Marisa returned to the question that was chewing on her nerves. "Who was he?"

Tessa took a long breath and said, "Its better if you didn't know." Marisa shook her head in semi-disbelief. "I'm not a fucking mushroom, so stop keeping me in the dark and feeding me bullshit. I risked my life back there. I don't want to hear that it's better that . . ."

"I told you the deal," Tessa snapped defensively. "The police are going to question everyone . . . Shit, you and the prison guard were the last two to see the prisoner. So, in other words you two are the police's best leads."

Marisa kept her mouth shut and only offered a slight shake of her head while she considered Tessa's point.

"When the ambulance left the prison and pulled over, you were forced at gunpoint to cooperate. All you saw was the guard tied up and blindfolded. Then you were blindfolded."

"I understand," Marisa said in a subdued voice.

"Keep your wits about you and watch what you say to anyone. The Police aren't going to be the only ones asking questions. The Cartel will probably put a big bounty on his head, which means you can't trust anyone."

"Excuse me?" Marisa asked, not quite sure she heard right. She felt a pang in her stomach. "The Car . . . tel," she stammered. Why would they be . . ."

Tessa knew dancing around the issue would only make it worse, so she blurted out, "The prisoner worked for the Carraboca Cartel."

Marisa didn't hear the rest of Tessa's explanation. Her mind hung on the part where the Cartel was looking for the same person she just helped escape from prison.

"No, this can't be happening" she said dropping her head into her hands."

Tessa remained silent.

Marisa made no effort to conceal the look of disgust on her face.

"How could you get me mixed up in this after what the cartel did to my family?"

Tessa sighed inwardly. "It wasn't supposed to go like this." She said in a low apologetic voice. "We were going to pay Drew to sit in a bar while we borrowed the ambulance."

Marisa nervously chewed her lower lip. "Why didn't you?"

"You said it yourself, Drew is a fuck up and we needed at least one driver that the guards at the prison had seen before. Two new drivers would have been too suspicious."

All the color left Marisa's face. She stared right through Tessa, didn't speak for ten seconds, and then said, "They butchered my husband. What do you think those scumbags will do to me if they find out I was involved?"

"Shit," Tessa said under her breath as she struggled to find an answer. The amount of money she was getting paid gave her no reason to consider Marisa's plight. Tessa needed an ambulance driver and Marisa had the evening shift.

Marisa's light mocha complexion became blotchy with anger. "How could you expose my children to this?"

"I'm sorry, I didn't think."

Marisa had experience with the Carraboca Cartel. She knew that the cartel would torture everyone until someone talked. As though preparing herself for what she was certain would happen, Marisa closed her eyes and took a deep breath. Letting it out slowly, she took another deep breath. Marisa took several deeper breaths trying to compose herself. The Cartel was not an organization you crossed swords with, because they would send assassins that would hunt everyone involved down to the end of the world, if necessary, to settle the score. If the Cartel wanted the prisoner that she had just helped escape from Bon Futuro, hell was coming for her and everyone involved including their families. A lot of people would end up dead and bodies would soon start popping up in canals and along the sides of roads. The hair on the back of Marisa's neck bristled with fear. "You need to get my children off the island today. Somewhere safe."

Tessa shook her head.

Marisa's voice hardened. "Do it today!"

Chapter Thirty-Seven

Two hours after taking off, Juan Carlos partially opened his eyes. His eyelids fluttered; it took his eyes a moment to adjust to the dimly lit cabin. His senses were coming back slowly like a computer booting up programs. From what Juan Carlos could see, he was still on the jet with a catheter still inserted in his arm. The medication and fluids that had been delivered intravenously were working and his temperature was only slightly elevated. Shane leaned over and looked at Juan Carlos. A pinkish color was starting to return to his cheeks.

"Mind if I sit?" Shane asked as he handed him a bottle of water.

Juan Carlos nodded numbly.

"You're looking better," Shane started.

Nearly every part of Juan Carlos's body still ached, and the pain in his ribs stood out. "I still feel like shit. But yeah, I'm doing better," he grunted, his face shining with perspiration.

"Give it time. It's only been a few hours," Shane casually sat down and turned his cold calculating eyes on Juan Carlos. "Mind if we talk a little business?"

Juan Carlos glanced over at Hugo and Mia.

"So, I assume Pierce sent you. Who are you guys?"

"Names aren't important," Shane said with a finger over his mouth. "All you need to know is we are the people that got you out of prison and for the time being keeping you safe."

Juan Carlos looked up at Shane. He recognized the tone in his voice. Juan Carlos spent much of his life leveraging people, and, when the hunter realizes that he is about to become the hunted, it's a feeling that's impossible to ignore. "Well . . ." Juan Carlos shook his head. "Get on with it."

"The three million you advanced to Pierce to break you out of prison and get you out of Curacao and away from the Cartel . . . it's not enough."

Juan Carlos took a long breath. "What's your point?"

"It's simple math really," Shane nodded. "The cost of this operation and paying off everybody that needed to get paid to get you out took a big chunk of the money you advanced."

"Not my problem," Juan Carlos shook him off, no longer interested in the topic of conversation.

"You can't be serious?" Shane asked, more amused than upset. "It's not your problem now, but I promise you it can turn into a huge problem for you if you don't cooperate. You can be stupid or smart. I've heard that you were a smart guy."

Juan Carlos's eyes narrowed. A vein bulged at his temple.

With a tinge of anger in his voice, Juan Carlos leaned forward and said, "It's really not smart to threaten me. You have no idea who you're fucking with."

Shane flashed one of those confident smiles that only a person who is holding all the cards can pull off.

"Let me guess . . . this is the part where you tell me that you're a very important man with very dangerous connections," Shane said.

"You might think you're still connected . . . but rumor has it that those very same connections are probably looking for you now. It's no secret that the cartel wants you dead."

Juan Carlos sat up in his seat and gripped the plastic covered armrest. He glanced uncomfortably at Shane. Two things struck him at once. First, this wasn't the first time Shane shook someone down. He was clearly experienced, and, from what Juan Carlos could tell, he had figured out most of the angles. And second, Shane was not like Pierce. Shane was greedy, hardened and ruthless.

With his mind hunting for options, Juan Carlos scoffed. "I already negotiated my fee."

Shane digested his final answer with a crooked grin. "You call that a negotiation? I took that to be a first offer with a good faith deposit. I'm not looking to fuck you. I just want this to be worth my while. We both know this doesn't end for my team when you disappear. There is a very real possibility that both the DEA and the cartel end up at our doorstep. We are not spending the rest of our lives worrying about what is waiting for us around every corner for a few hundred thousand dollars apiece," Shane said.

Juan Carlos thought about that for a moment and then took a sip of water. "And if I say no?"

"You won't.

"And why is that?"

"Because you won't like what happens to you if you do," Shane said with absolute confidence as he reached across and handed Juan Carlos a piece of paper. "Ten million wired into this account before we land."

Juan Carlos looked at Shane as if he had lost his mind. "I don't have that kind of money."

Shane didn't blink. He knew Juan Carlos was lying. He was one of the financial masterminds behind the cartel's operations. While he had no idea as to an exact number, Shane was pretty sure Juan Carlos parked at least fifty million in cash in offshore accounts.

Shane gave Juan Carlos a minute to think about his offer, then the congenial smile melted off his face. "Listen here, douchebag. Now is not the time to play games. I really don't care how many millions you've stashed away offshore. But if ten million dollars isn't in this account," he said pointing to the piece of paper, "I'm sure Dario would be willing to wire me twice that much if I offer to deliver you to him."

Juan Carlos almost came out of his chair and then his eyes caught something in Hugo and Mia's demeanor, something that told him that they preferred a way out and the only thing keeping them from turning him over to Dario and collecting a big pay day was Pierce. Juan Carlos prided himself on his instincts. When he looked at the three of them, he got the ominous feeling that they knew that Dario would pay them twice that amount, and they would cut out most of the risk that went along with helping him disappear. Suddenly the ten million didn't mean very much. He had a lot more stashed away, and it occurred to him that his only chance of living to spend it was to accept Shane's terms.

The vein bulged in Juan Carlos's head again, but he said nothing because there was nothing he could say. Shane handed Juan Carlos a laptop. Despite the anger that was coursing through his veins, Juan Carlos calmly took it.

"Oh, I almost forgot!" Shane slapped himself on the forehead. "Pierce doesn't need to know anything about—let's call it our performance bonus. Am I making myself clear?"

Juan Carlos half closed his eyes; he appeared to be concentrating on accessing one of his accounts. "Understood," he frowned after a pause. Squinting at the numbers written on the piece of paper, Juan Carlos typed them onto the laptop screen and authorized a wire transfer for ten million dollars. Afterwards, he shook his head in disgust which told Shane it was done.

"We'll be able to confirm the transfer before we land," Shane nodded.

Juan Carlos sighed and rubbed his temples. "It'll be there."

Juan Carlos looked at Shane and then over at Hugo and Mia. "Now that we have gotten that business concluded will one of you tell me exactly how you plan on keeping me alive?"

"Don't worry making people disappear into thin air is one of our specialties," Hugo said.

Juan Carlos stared at Hugo. Up to this point he had been too stricken with fever to recognize him.

"I've seen you somewhere before," Juan Carlos said.

"I was in the ambulance that picked you up at the prison," Hugo shot back.

Juan Carlos did a double take. "No, I have seen you before tonight."

Hugo nodded. "That's altogether possible."

Unsatisfied with Hugo's response, Juan Carlos continued to eye him suspiciously. Then it came to him. "You're former special forces, aren't you?"

Hugo shot Juan Carlos a quizzical look."

"It really wasn't that hard once I thought about it," Juan Carlos said as he wiped the droplets of perspiration from his brow and took a deep breath still dealing with the residual effects of the injection he received the day before.

"I recall one of my associates telling me that he hired someone to oversee the protective detail for his family. He described the man as a former special forces' operative with long dreadlocks and as big as an elephant. There can't be two of you walking around."

Mia knew exactly what Juan Carlos was talking about. The fact that Hugo did not blend into the scenery was a drawback in their line of work but his predatory instincts more than made up for it.

She took a short breath and pushed ahead. "We'll be landing in Fort Lauderdale in about thirty minutes. From there we are going to drive twenty-five miles north to the Boca Executive airport and take another private jet to Dallas."

"Why not just refuel and continue on to Dallas?" Juan Carlos asked.

Mia nodded. "You would be making yourself too easy to track. If we continued out of the Fort Lauderdale Executive airport, anyone looking for you could limit their search to Charter flights leaving that airport over a two-hour window. That would be about 30 flights."

Mia explained that taking the flight to Dallas from another airport made their trail much more difficult to follow. All that any airport personnel would be able to say if questioned was that the four passengers that arrived from Curacao got into a car and left the airport. Mia traced a grid on a notebook paper.

"That means that any tactical operations team looking for you will have to expand their search to include Miami and Tamiami airports to the south, Boca and Palm Beach airports to the North and Naples airport west of us; in the same two hour window that could be over 200 flights."

Mia traced a second larger circle on the grid while she continued to explain the tradecraft relied upon by the tactical operations teams for the FBI and DEA.

"The Tac-Ops teams will also have to account for the possibility that we drove to our target destination; meaning that everywhere from Key West to the south all the way north to Orlando will be a part of their immediate integrated search."

Hugo glanced over to Juan Carlos and grinned.

"For the next 48 hours, you're going to be the needle in the haystack."

Juan Carlos was pleased, after ten plus years of working for the cartel and successfully staying many steps ahead of law enforcement agencies he recognized talent when he saw it.

Juan Carlos looked out of the jet window into the darkness and then turned his attention back towards Mia. "What happens after we get to Dallas?"

"From there we are driving north about two hundred and fifty miles into Oklahoma."

"And after that?"

"That's where we will put Pierce's plan into play. It should make you untouchable as far as the cartel is concerned," Hugo said.

"*Untouchable*?" Juan Carlos repeated. He was skeptical. There were no guarantees in life and definitely none in the dangerous waters where they were swimming, but up until now everything concerning the plan to get him out of prison and off the island had worked.

"This I really would like to hear."

Mia nodded. "Pierce will explain everything when we get to Oklahoma."

Chapter Thirty-Eight

FORT LAUDERDALE, EXECUTIVE AIRPORT

The wheels touched down on the runway of Fort Lauderdale's Executive airport at 5:35 A.M. The pilot brought the jet as close to the terminal building as possible to shorten the distance that Juan Carlos would have to walk. When he exited the aircraft, Mia removed his gloves, surgeon's mask and cap. Juan Carlos felt a chill crawl up the back of his neck as the thought that he might get detained by Customs settled in.

"Here is your passport," Mia said, handing it to Juan Carlos. "Your name is Sergio Placido. You can see from the passport that I used your girlfriend's address in New York so it would be easy for you to remember.

Juan Carlos seemed lost for words. He stared at Mia for a long moment. The expression on his face said, "How could you know about her?"

"It's my job to know." Mia said with a quick shake of her head. And then she added, "If asked, you are in the import-export business. Stick to what you know. The only thing that's changed is your name. Can you handle this?" Mia put her words in the form of a question, but her tone made it obvious that it was an order.

Juan Carlos didn't flinch. He looked into Mia's eyes and gave her a nod. "Yes."

"That's the right answer. These gentlemen will accompany you through customs to make sure everything goes smoothly." Mia said pointing towards Hugo and Shane. "I'll catch up."

"Listen carefully," Hugo said leaning in close to Juan Carlos. "Wear your baseball cap low covering your eyes as much as possible without being too conspicuous. When you walk, stare at the ground five feet in front of you and don't look up for any reason. We don't want the surveillance cameras to have a clear shot of your face."

Juan Carlos gave a quick nod.

Hugo's voice sharpened like a laser. "And when you hand your passport to the Customs agent, do not avoid eye contact. That will make him suspicious. Look him right in the eye when he asks you a question."

Juan Carlos gave Hugo a small disbelieving frown. There was nothing that Hugo said that he hadn't already thought of.

"I'm a drug dealer, remember; I think I know how to get through customs . . . I got it."

Hugo dismissed the comment. "I'll lead the way. You go second and Shane will be right behind you."

Juan Carlos shook his head.

Hugo strode across the tarmac his gait military. Through the glass Juan Carlos could see the two Customs agents talking. When they got to the customs gate, Juan Carlos stood rigid like a soldier under intense inspection. He'd passed through customs a hundred times, but this time was different. He had never been on the run from the cartel before. Juan Carlos knew all too well the absolute brutality and hair-splitting agony the cartel would put him through before killing him if they got their hands on him. Those thoughts caused him to tense up as he got ready to hand the agent his passport.

Shane nudged him from behind. "Relax," his whisper sounded more like a hiss.

Instinctively Juan Carlos lowered his shoulders and took two deep breaths into his lungs. He started to feel his heart rate slow and his anxiety dissolve as he stepped up to the laminated desk.

"Passport please," the Customs agent gestured.

Juan Carlos slid the passport across the laminated surface.

The agent gave him a serious look and then carefully examined the passport.

In a voice devoid of any real interest he asked, "Early flight; what time did you take off?"

"I think it was a little after two in the morning." Juan Carlos replied.

"Business or pleasure?"

"Business."

"What kind of business keeps you working until two in the morning?"

"None if you're the boss or good at what you do. I'm in the import-export business."

The man let out a small laugh while he applied the appropriate stamps. He closed the passport and slid it back across the surface. "Have a nice day Mr. Placido."

"Thanks, you too," Juan Carlos said as he headed for the main door.

"Passport, please," the customs agent said in a steely voice as he turned his attention to Shane.

"What's that? The agent asked pointing to a faint bulge in Shane's shirt pocket. Shane removed a pair of reading glasses and cigar from his pocket. The agent took the cigar and examined it.

"We have a problem," he said calmly.

Shane frowned. He didn't like problems.

"What is it?"

The agent glared at Shane. He didn't care for Shane's tone. He held up the cigar. "Do you know what this is?"

"It's a Cuban cigar," Shane murmured under his breath. "I honestly forgot I still had it." He sighed.

The Customs agent nodded clearly displeased.

"Turn around please," the agent said.

Shane obliged, holding his arms out while the agent patted him down. Satisfied that Shane wasn't hiding any other contraband, the agent recited the provision of the law which required him to seize the cigar. Shane indicated he understood and accepted the custom agent's action with a crisp nod.

"It was an honest mistake," Shane said as he gathered his belongings and walked towards the white sedan where Hugo was waiting.

* * *

Mia finished wiping down the areas of the jet that Juan Carlos occupied or may have touched, gathered and folded the plastic coverings into a canvas duffle bag and hurried to catch up with the others. The Customs agent cast his seasoned eye on Mia and the contents of her bag and waved her through. Hugo pulled the sedan up to the front entrance of the terminal building and sounded the horn when he saw Mia exit the building. Once Mia climbed into the front passenger side, Hugo headed towards Boca Raton.

Chapter Thirty-Nine

OKLAHOMA

Alexis spent the night in the back seat curled up against Pierce. She had been lying there awake watching the clock count down the last few hours of the last time that she would be alone with him. Alexis shuddered at that particular thought. Under his soft snoring and deep even breaths were hard muscles that caused feelings and desires to stir in her that she knew she shouldn't have. Her body tingled and her pulse quickened as she replayed in her mind their first and only kiss earlier that night. The way his breath felt against her skin, the way he kissed her made her wonder what would happen if all the obstacles were suddenly stripped away and there was nothing keeping them from being together. It was a good memory; a potent memory that she would always have no matter what sad existence awaited her. Until that time, she would take her visual fill of him as often as she could.

* * *

She had been raised in a culture where daughters did not disappoint their parents. Her parents, Cuban immigrants, were very happy when Alexis cast aside her full scholarship and dream of studying journalism at Tulane University and stayed at home and attended a local college. A year later at nineteen she married Juan Carlos at the Church of the Little Flower in Coral Gables. Alexis tried in vain to meet her family's expectations by providing them with grandchildren. But as the years ticked by Juan Carlos's deceit, affairs and manipulations began to take a toll. Alexis secretly went on the pill. She couldn't fathom bringing another innocent victim into her hell. Instead, Alexis built up some very unhealthy coping mechanisms. She took up smoking cigars but the most destructive one of all was that she buried her feelings. The best way she could think of to not disappoint her family was to put her head down and keep her feelings to herself.

Alexis arched her neck and tilted her head to the side so that she could get a glimpse of Pierce sleeping in the rearview mirror.

Alexis watched as Pierce opened one eye.

"Good morning," Pierce smiled.

"You're awake," she said in a coy whisper.

Alexis sat up and gazed deeply at Pierce. The morning light accentuated the shadow on his face. Her anxiety grew with each passing minute as she realized that she was running out of time. Alexis could no longer keep her feelings bottled up.

"Can we talk?" she asked.

Pierce hesitated. Alexis caught the indecision in his eyes. It was obvious what she wanted to talk about despite the insurmountable obstacle that came in the form of a husband who was the target of both the DEA and the most dangerous criminal organization in the world. In a couple of hours, she would be reunited with him. In a day or two, Alexis would be out of Pierce's life completely. Pierce could see no reason for discussing their kiss or admitting the depth of his feelings for her. So, Pierce made a face, a face that gave her the answer to her question.

Alexis stared at him with disbelieving eyes. Something was happening between them, and she knew that he felt it. She wanted to believe that he wanted it as badly as she did.

"Why, won't you talk to me?"

A sense of pointlessness rippled through Pierce. The last thing he wanted was to let Alexis into his heart. The woman whose magnetic pull he couldn't resist belonged to another.

Pierce hated himself for not being completely honest with Alexis. It would have been so easy to tell her that he was falling in love with her; so much easier than remaining silent. But he realized that validating feelings that Alexis already suspected he had for her would only make things harder.

"Are you going to let me make the same mistake twice?" Alexis's question flew out of her mouth like a counter punch.

Pierce felt the tiny space of the car shrink around them.

"Did you for one minute give any thought to what I want?" she asked incredulously.

After an uncomfortable silence, Alexis said, "Of course you didn't."

Pierce was suddenly very aware of how close she was to him.

"I need to stretch my legs," he blurted out.

Pierce jerked the car door open and stepped out. He turned around to find Alexis sliding out of the car right behind him in pursuit.

He looked unsure of himself which she found confusing and a bit endearing because up until now Pierce had been a dynamic force and steady as a rock. The version of Pierce now standing across from her seemed vulnerable. Pierce nervously cleared his throat.

"This was settled. We agreed that you would go with your husband," Pierce said instead of what he really wanted to say.

Alexis crossed her arms. Her even complexion became blotchy with anger. "That was before!"

She looked for a sign that Pierce acknowledged that things had drastically changed between them. But Pierce didn't give her one. Instead, he shook his head and said, "It's too dangerous."

Alexis hung her head in despair. "I'd rather be happy with you for a few moments than in emotional purgatory with him."

Pierce took a step towards her. And then another until he completely erased the little distance between them. Alexis inhaled sharply. Her stomach rolled over with a wave of desire. She could almost taste him. The sunlight reflecting in his deep blue eyes made them look predatory as he zeroed in on her.

"The cartel won't stop looking. You have no idea what they will do to you if they find you."

Alexis's eyes widened slightly. "I'm willing to take that chance."

"But—"

"But nothing. That's my choice to make," she said with absolute conviction. Alexis held up two fingers. "You told me that you played baseball in college. So, let me put it in terms you can relate to. You've got two strikes. Are you going to take a third strike or swing for the fences?"

Pierce sighed as a wide swath of emotions spilled over him. "I'm not willing to take chances with your life."

Alexis started to say something else. But Pierce stopped her.

"I can't protect you."

"But what about your plan?" Alexis said in a pleading tone.

Pierce shrugged in an effort to convey what he was thinking, which was, "*We don't know if Dario Carraboca will even go along with it.* Even if he says yes, how do we know that we can trust him? Only time will tell."

Alexis tried to mask her emotions. She didn't want Pierce to know that the thought of not seeing him was twisting her into knots.

The expression on his face told her everything she needed to know. He was letting her go rather than risk any harm coming to her.

Her heart sank. "Strike three," she nodded with a tinge of disappointment in her voice.

Chapter Forty

BON FUTURO PRISON, CURACAO

Once the news spread that a prisoner from Bon Futuro and two paramedics died in an explosion, the prison switchboard was flooded with telephone calls. Sitting alone in his office, Andre Rojer tried to make sense of the information that he had been trickling in from the police at the scene of the explosion. The three charred bodies were believed to be the two paramedics and the prisoner Juan Carlos Laporte. His second in command Captain de Wolf was still unaccounted for, which was not a good sign. Andre sat at his desk in stunned silence unable to understand how a very simple plan had gone so horribly wrong. His private line rang several times. When Andre continued to ignore it, his cell phone rang.

Andre could feel his face muscles instantly tighten the moment he recognized the phone number flashing on the screen of his cell phone. He took a long deep breath.

"Rene, I'm surprised to hear from you at this late hour," Andre said.

"My sources tell me that an ambulance transporting a prisoner to St. Elisabeth exploded. They also told me that Juan Carlos was in that ambulance."

Andre paused understanding how critical it was for him to choose his next words carefully.

"Yes, Mr. Laporte was transported to St. Elisabeth hospital in the ambulance that exploded a couple of hours ago, but that's all we know."

"I know what you know," Rene snapped startling Andre. "What I want to know is why Juan Carlos was in that ambulance?"

Andre began to feel shaky as he tried to explain.

"He became violently ill during the middle of the night. The attendant at the infirmary contacted me and advised that his condition was rapidly deteriorating and nothing they tried was bringing his fever under control. He told me that the doctor who had examined Juan Carlos earlier that day left specific instructions that he was to be contacted if his condition deteriorated. So, I ordered the attendant to contact the doctor."

Rene looked at the calendar, his eyes locked on the circled date which marked Juan Carlos's extradition hearing. "And I assume that the doctor recommended that Juan Carlos be immediately transported to St. Elisabeth?"

"Yes exactly," Andre stammered. Sweat began to drip from his brow.

"Why didn't you contact my people the minute you decided to move him?" Rene sounded furious.

Andre flinched and did not offer an immediate explanation. He started to hem and haw as he tried to get the words out. Finally, he said, "I had my second in command guarding him in the ambulance. I was going to call as soon as the doctor examined him."

"And now your second in command is missing and Juan Carlos is either dead or also missing." Rene snapped caustically.

Andre felt a shiver of panic shoot through him. "One of the dead bodies was found in what could have been one of our prison uniforms. The police think Juan Carlos died in the explosion."

"Have they positively identified the bodies?" Rene asked, his skepticism obvious.

Andre was still trying to digest the snippets of information that had been filtering in. "No, not yet. The bodies are very badly burned making it difficult to identify them, but they are working on it," he said.

Rene remained silent, deep in thought as he tried to put the pieces to the puzzle together. When he spoke, his voice was startlingly calm.

"Andre please keep me informed of all developments as soon as you get them."

Andre loosened his white-knuckle grip on his phone. "Of course, right away," he nodded.

"One more thing," Rene said.

"Yes anything," Andre said, sounding relieved.

"What was the name of the doctor that recommended that Juan Carlos be transferred?"

Visions of reprisal seeped into Andre's mind. Andre didn't want to expose the Doctor's identity. He felt guilt-ridden revealing his name to the cartel, but he also knew that failing to do so would not protect him. Rene would eventually learn it. Andre also knew that it was important that he give them the impression that he was cooperating so that Rene wouldn't think he was directly involved.

Andre felt a lump in his throat. As soon as he told Rene the doctor's name the line went dead.

Turning to his men, Rene ordered two of them to go pick up the doctor. He ordered another to swing by the prison and bring Andre to him. He then looked at his two best assassins and directed them to put some men at the boat marinas and for the two of them to personally monitor the airport.

"The first flights leave the island in a few hours. Juan Carlos knows that the longer he stays on Curacao the harder it will be for him to get out. If he's still here, he will try to get off the island as soon as he can."

"So, you really think he's alive?" One of Rene's men asked.

Rene had considered that. He'd known Juan Carlos for over twenty years. He was nothing if not cunning and a master of deception. Rene would not believe that Juan Carlos was dead until he saw his cold body himself.

"I don't know. But we can't sit on our asses waiting for the police to identify the body. If he slips through our fingers, Dario will cut off our heads."

Rene's men nodded.

"If we find Juan Carlos, do you want us to bring him to you?" One of the men asked.

Rene exhaled sharply. "No," kill him and leave his body in a public place."

* * *

BETWEEN 8:15 AND 8:30 A.M. Doctor Hernandez left his home and got into a dark blue Mercedes Benz S class. Rene's men followed Hernandez in a gray van. After twenty minutes, the Mercedes pulled in headfirst into a parking lot behind the hospital. The van pulled up right behind the Mercedes making it impossible for it to back up. The two men sprung out of the car. The one that approached from the passenger's side was armed with an M4A1 automatic rifle. The man approaching on the driver's side was carrying a 9mm pistol. They moved so quickly that the first inkling that the doctor had that something was wrong was when he felt the barrel of a revolver pressing against his ribs.

"That's a gun you feel," the man said in a low but stern voice.

"Okay . . . Okay, please take it easy," Hernandez pleaded.

"Into the van and down on the floor," the man with the pistol ordered Hernandez. Hernandez crawled onto the floor and laid face down. The second man with the shotgun threw a heavy blanket over him and sat down with his feet resting on Hernandez's back. The man with the pistol jumped back into the driver's seat, slammed the door and sped away. Doctor Hernandez began to panic, his heart pounded, and he began to gasp for air like he was suffocating.

"Please," he panted and wheezed through the heavy blanket. "I can't breathe."

The man lifted the blanket off Hernandez's head. The doctor immediately filled his lungs with as much air as his lungs could draw in and exhaled slowly trying to regain his composure. The next thirty minutes felt like an eternity as the car navigated the morning traffic. Hernandez listened carefully for any familiar sound that might give away their location. Finally, it was the smell of hydrocarbons that wafted through the van that told Hernandez that they were passing the Isla Oil Refinery. A few minutes later the van slipped deftly into a warehouse located in the Curacao Dry Dock.

The men left Doctor Hernandez in a corner of a large warehouse sitting in a chair with his hands tied behind him and his mouth gagged. The doctor's heart was pounding, and panic was starting to cripple his senses. When Hernandez first saw Rene, he grew nervous and started crying.

"Relax, if I wanted you dead you would already be dead" Rene barked as if reading the doctor's mind.

Rene ordered his men to take the gag off and untie the doctor.

Rene squatted next to the doctor. "Listen carefully to what I am going to tell you," Rene started in a voice bereft of emotion.

The doctor stared at him in wide eyed terror.

"I'm only going to tell you this once," Rene offered. "Do you see my man behind you with the knife in his hand?"

Hernandez turned his head and nodded.

"When I ask you a question, if you tell me that you don't know, or that I have the wrong person or this is all a big misunderstanding, the man behind you is going to cut your throat before you draw another breath."

"Please," Hernandez cried. "I'll tell you what you want to know."

"Yes, you will." Rene stood and took a step back. He didn't have to torture the doctor. He knew from personal experience that fear could be a great motivator. "You are here because you examined Juan Carlos Laporte yesterday and a few hours later you recommended his transfer to St. Elisabeth hospital," Rene stared at Doctor Hernandez making him feel like he was studying him.

Hernandez's sniffles turned to sobs.

"I'm going to give you a chance to get out of this mess you're in with your life intact," Rene smiled. "But if you don't tell me everything I want to know, well then . . . you'll force my hand," Rene's smile faded.

"Are we clear?"

Doctor Hernandez shook his head emphatically.

"Whose idea was it to transfer Juan Carlos to St. Elisabeth?"

Hernandez thought quickly. He was worried that if he said it was his idea that the interrogation would be over and that his throat would be cut.

"A man claiming to be a family friend approached me and told me that Juan Carlos was urinating blood and was in poor medical condition."

"Hmmm . . . Why not treat him in the prison infirmary?"

"The man told me that Juan Carlos had a complicated medical history, and the family wanted him to undergo a series of tests before his extradition hearing."

"And you believed that bunch of shit!" Rene yelled.

Hernandez's pulse quickened. "Please," his voice trembled. "I . . . I am trying to tell you what you want to know."

Rene stared down the doctor and said, "Then give me a name."

Hernandez was too frightened to think clearly. "A name," he repeated clearly confused.

Rene's face twisted into a frown "The name of the person who approached you and requested that you transfer Juan Carlos to St. Elisabeth."

Hernandez desperately searched his mind trying to remember. Rene's eyes shifted towards his men. The one holding the knife took a step towards the doctor.

"Wait . . . for goodness sake, please give me a minute. I know this," he pleaded. "His name was Hamilton . . . yes that's it. The man's name was Shane Hamilton. I'm sure of it," he nodded eagerly.

Rene didn't recognize that name.

"What did you give Juan Carlos? Rene asked.

"I injected him with drugs that we give to cancer patients. That caused his fever to spike."

Rene shook his head. "I see."

"I am curious doctor about one thing."

"Yes, and what might that be?" Hernandez nodded.

"Why would you help this Shane Hamilton? You clearly didn't know him, or you wouldn't have struggled to remember his name?"

Before Hernandez could say a word, Rene answered his own question. His eyes widened like those of someone who had just gotten the card he needed to complete a Royal Flush in a high stake's poker game.

"He paid you a lot of money, didn't he?

Hernandez shifted uncomfortably. His body language suggested that he was ashamed to admit that he took a bribe.

"How much did he pay you?" Rene's tone shifted to that of a disappointed father.

"They left a suitcase with a quarter of a million dollars in my office."

"Wait! There was more than one guy?" Rene gave him a suspicious look. "You only mentioned one person," he snapped.

Hernandez began to stammer uncontrollably. His thoughts ran into one another. "I never got his name . . . He looked like a bodyguard or something . . . he just sat in the back."

"Easy!" Rene put his hand on his shoulder and played it off like it was no big deal. "Can you tell me what he looked like?"

"He was big, black . . . well over six feet tall and very muscular," Hernandez remembered.

"Is there anything else?"

Hernandez shook his head. "That's all I know."

Rene cocked his head to the side and looked at Hernandez speculatively.

"I can't help but wonder. Did you ever consider the possibility that you were being used as a pawn to facilitate an escape from prison?"

Hernandez looked deeply troubled.

"Come now Doctor, do you expect me to believe that you're foolish enough to think that someone would be willing to pay you a quarter of a million dollars for running some tests with no strings attached?"

Hernandez's expression changed to one of confusion. "But Mr. Laporte died in the ambulance."

"By injecting him and authorizing his transfer to St. Elisabeth, you made it possible for Juan Carlos to drive right through the front gate of the prison . . . We don't know if he died in the ambulance."

"What do you mean? Hernandez asked, trying to process the information.

"The police found three dead bodies. There were four people in the ambulance when it left the prison." Rene eyed the doctor suspiciously.

"I don't know if you were in on the plan, but either way this Shane Hamilton used you to get Juan Carlos out."

Rene nodded in the direction of his men.

Doctor Hernandez felt his heart flutter. The fear was plain on his face.

"Please believe me. I didn't know anything. I wasn't involved," he wailed and clutched for Rene's arm. Hernandez was so desperately trying to convince Rene of his innocence that he never felt the razor-sharp blade at his neck until after it had severed his artery. Hernandez instantly made a gurgling sound as blood began to fill his mouth and throat. His arms flailed about desperately as he made a futile attempt to stop the blood gushing from his neck. Consciousness soon faded and Doctor Hernandez slumped forward, toppled off the chair and hit the cement floor facedown: lifeless.

Chapter Forty-One

Special Agent Roy floored the van while deftly swerving around slower moving traffic. The Consul General had not been able to get any cooperation or information, and Hogan's police contacts could only confirm that Juan Carlos Laporte was in the ambulance that left Bon Futuro prison and subsequently caught fire in a desolate and densely vegetated area. Ryan Collins and Justin Giles rode in the van with Lloyd Hogan. The other two DEA agents were deployed to the scene where the ambulance exploded. Hogan rushed to the prison where he hoped to question everyone involved in Juan Carlos's transfer. He gazed out of the window deep in thought. The panoramic view of the Caribbean Sea from the coastal road provided little distraction as Hogan weighed a number of possibilities and scenarios. Ryan Collins and Agent Justin Giles were engaged in conversation in the back seat when Hogan's radio crackled loudly.

Victoria Macy's voice echoed throughout the van.

"Agent Hogan, we may have a possible situation at the airport."

Everyone in the van sat quietly listening intently to the radio.

"Go on," Hogan spoke into the radio.

"A FedEx truck pulled up and parked near the front entrance to the terminal building."

"And why is that unusual?"

"Well sir, the truck is just sitting there parked. No one has gotten out to pick up or deliver any packages."

"How long has the truck been parked at that location?" Hogan asked.

"About 20 minutes sir. I spotted two men. One appears to be using binoculars to observe everyone entering the terminal."

Collins flashed Agent Giles a sideways look. In twenty years as a navy seal, Collins participated in dangerous missions in the Middle East, Africa and Latin America. In each instance the one common denominator that he always encountered regardless of whether he was working with or against dictators, local warlords or terrorists was that they all operated by the golden rule that death was the solution to any problem. The way Collins saw it was that the two men in the parked truck could only be there for one reason.

Hogan suspected that the men in the truck worked for the cartel and that if the cartel was already there looking for Juan Carlos, they didn't think that he died in the fire.

"Keep tabs on the FedEx truck and radio me if anything changes," Hogan ordered Macy.

"Roger that," Macy signed off.

Agent Roy slowed the van down to almost a crawl when he was about one hundred yards away from the prison. Gathered in front of the prison was a human wall of journalists and onlookers which made driving any closer to the prison entrance close to impossible.

"What the hell are you doing?" Hogan snapped.

"Sir, there are too many people in front of us."

Hogan did not blink. "Honk your horn Agent and keep driving. They're not fucking sheep, they'll get out of the way." Hogan said forcefully.

Agent Roy blasted the horn and eased the van forward passing surprised and disbelieving faces. Standing just behind the gate surrounded by imposing walls stood five prison guards in full riot gear. One of the guards from the blockhouse stepped out and waved to the van to turn around. When he got to the van he tapped on the window. Agent Roy lowered the window. Lloyd Hogan smiled and flashed his badge and credentials. The guard expressed no interest.

"You need to turn around. We are not permitting anyone access to the prison facility today," the guard said with a note of hostility.

Lloyd Hogan leaned over Agent Roy making sure that the guard could hear him over the crowd noise. "We are here on official business," he said.

The guard glared into the van.

"All business today is cancelled."

Any trace of friendliness that may have existed quickly disappeared from Lloyd Hogan's face.

"We are representatives of the United States government. I have an order signed by the Dutch government transferring a prisoner into our custody. That makes him our prisoner. We have reason to believe that his life is in danger, so we're not going anywhere. Unless you want an international incident, I suggest that you let your commanding officer know we're here," Hogan barked.

The guard looked uncertain. Two more guards began to move towards the van. Collins made sure that the prison guard saw him pull his weapon out of his holster. Agent Giles followed suit and also readied his weapon.

"Understand that we are armed, and we aren't going anywhere without speaking with your commanding officer. You either radio your superior or you don't, and we see how this plays out," Hogan's face remained hard.

The guard rocked back and forth on his heels staring at his radio for 10 seconds not sure what to do. Suddenly, like a man awakening from a nightmare and coming to his senses, the guard waved the two other guards back and radioed his commanding officer. Moments later the guards unbolted the front gate and waved the van through.

Simon Groot, the prison manager was a man of unrelenting commitment to his profession. His family had long and deep roots in Curacao. He was a devout supporter of the Movementu Futuro Korsou (MFK) political party and was viewed by many as a rising star in the party and a future member of parliament. Simon had a particular fondness for anything American having spent the early part of his adult life in the United States getting his bachelor's degree in Political Science from Trinity College in Connecticut and his master's degree in Public Administration from the University of Central Florida. Two prison guards escorted Lloyd Hogan and his men through a labyrinth of long claustrophobic hallways lined with gun-metal filing cabinets. When they arrived at the manager's office, the guard knocked and opened the door. Simon looked up and removed his glasses revealing a pair of eyes that were a unique color of amber with flecks of russet tones. He was tall, slightly over six feet in height. His hair was dark with a touch of gray. He possessed an air of profound intelligence that made his current position as prison manager seem like a temporary stop towards a position far more important than that of a caretaker of men in need of rehabilitation.

* * *

Simon smiled warmly when Hogan and his men were introduced.

"Thank you for taking the time to meet with us," Hogan began.

"Of course," Simon said. "We are all trying to find the answers to the same questions," Simon said, frowning.

Simon looked troubled. "Unfortunately, there isn't much I can tell you. I have questioned the attendant who worked in the infirmary last night. All he could tell me was that the prisoner Juan Carlos Laporte had been examined by Doctor Hernandez earlier in the day. The Doctor left specific instructions with them that if Mr. Laporte's condition deteriorated that he was to be immediately contacted."

"Has anyone spoken with Doctor Hernandez?" Hogan asked.

Simon shook his head. "The police can't locate him. His car is parked at St. Elisabeth hospital. But he never reported for work this morning. They've tried his cell phone, but calls are going straight into his voicemail."

Hogan had a bad feeling. The men staked out in the FedEx truck at the airport and now Doctor Hernandez disappearing into thin air had to be more than a coincidence.

"What about the Assistant Prison Manger who was in charge last night? Hogan asked. "We would like to talk to him."

Simon offered a tight smile. "As would I. Andre Rojer had a family emergency about the time his shift was coming to an end so he wasn't here when I arrived this morning."

"And where is he now?"

Simon wore a look of exasperation. "I don't know. When he didn't answer his cell phone, I sent two men to look for him. Apparently, he never made it home. It appears that Andre Rojer is also missing."

Chapter Forty-Two

Andre Rojer lay on the floor curled up in the fetal position bloodied, battered and shirtless. He no longer wondered whether the cartel would kill him for letting Juan Carlos leave Bon Futuro prison—he was certain. Andre immediately felt an upsurge of dread when Rene finally walked in. Rene's gaze started at Andre's swollen face before locking in on his eyes. His look seemed to slice away any lingering hope Andre was still clinging to that he could somehow be able to barter for his life. Andre was no longer an asset to the cartel, but rather he was now part of a festering problem.

Rene waved at his men to lift him off the floor and put him in a chair.

"So, it would appear that you were the inside man," Rene accused him in a cold voice.

Andre choked back the gasp of surprise. "What—No, I only . . ." His throat tightened, cutting off the words he wanted to say.

"You have one chance to make things right so don't waste it trying to bullshit me." Rene never raised his voice, but his intensity tripled.

Andre's eyes widened. "Okay," he tried to deflect by saying, "I did approve Juan Carlos's transfer to St. Elisabeth, but only after Doctor Hernandez declared that his condition was critical."

Rene looked at Andre like a cockroach he wanted to step on. "You're wasting my time."

"What! Why? What do you mean?" Andre's voice trembled.

Rene kicked the chair sending Andre sprawling to the floor. "You knew!" He yelled.

Andre looked up at Rene with tears in his eyes. "What did I know?"

Rene's face twisted into a pissed off scowl. "You knew that Juan Carlos wasn't going to St. Elisabeth?"

Instantly the breath went out of Andre. It was like he had been punched in the stomach. Rene was a human bullshit detector. Andre feared that he would sniff out the cracks in his story and frantically searched his thoughts for something to say. Something that Rene might possibly see as a plausible reason for why Andre might choose to co-operate. Finally, Andre began to stammer. "Okay, I suspected that Juan Carlos was not going to St. Elisabeth. But the United States Drug Enforcement Agency and the French are the ones that want him. I honestly didn't think the cartel would care if he disappeared. In fact, I thought that they would be okay if Juan Carlos had gone missing." Andre's hands which were stretched and tied tightly behind his back began to throb.

Rene's eyes met Andre's. "A careful man would have first checked with us . . . But I misjudged you. You're a weak and devious man."

Andre's heart began to pound in rhythm with the throbbing in his hands.

"But if Juan Carlos can't cooperate with law enforcement, he poses no threat. I would never do anything to hurt the cartel. You have to believe me," he pleaded.

Rene exhaled heavily. Juan Carlos's memory was well known. The man forgot nothing which was a great advantage until it ended up in the hands of the DEA. "Juan Carlos is a loose end. A very dangerous loose end that cannot go unaccounted for," he said with a trace of impatience.

Sweat was dripping from Andre's body. The empty warehouse felt like a sauna. "Please tell me what I can do to make things right?"

After fishing out a cigarette and lighting it, Rene blew out a cloud of smoke and said, “You can start by telling me who was responsible for this.”

Andre licked his dry lips as a wave of regret formed in the pit of his stomach. The reality sunk in that anyone he implicated Rene would hunt down and brutally torture. He looked at Rene with resignation in his eyes knowing that he had no choice.

“I was approached . . .”

“By who?” Rene impatiently interjected.”

Andre flinched. “By Tessa . . . Tessa Bongard.” His words tasted like poison when they passed over his lips.

“Who is she?

Andre whimpered, “She’s a fixer, a private contractor.”

Rene’s forehead crinkled. “So why haven’t I heard of her?”

“Because she’s retired. But when she did work, she only worked with law enforcement,” he shrugged.

Rene glanced over at his men with a crooked grin. “Well then she’s not too smart. Everyone knows we pay better.”

Andre forced a nervous smile.

Rene pressed on. “When Tessa approached you, what did she tell you?”

“She told me that there were some people who would pay off my gambling debts and pay me some money if I cooperated.

Andre shook his head, “When I refused, they threatened my son if I didn’t authorize the transfer . . . I was supposed to approve the transfer only after I got a call from Doctor Hernandez. . .”

“We’ve gone over that part and I already got Doctor Hernandez’s side of the story.”

Andre's eyes followed Rene's to the blood and slurry of other fluids a few feet away. He buckled over and wretched when he made the connection between the blood stain and Doctor Hernandez.

"Who did Tessa introduce you to?" Rene snapped.

Andre whimpered trying to rid his mind of the barbaric images which dominated his thoughts. "Two men. I think they were American . . ."

Rene leaned over until he was only a few inches in front of Andre's face and leveled him with a cold stare. "I want their names?"

Andre's sniffles turned to sobs and his chin was coated with spit and tears. "I never got their names . . . All I know is that they planned to use a medical emergency to get Juan Carlos out of prison."

"Did they tell you that?"

Andre shook his head emphatically. "No . . . they didn't have to. Why else would one of their guys masquerade as a paramedic? I only agreed to go along with it because I didn't think the cartel would care if Juan Carlos disappeared."

Rene growled. "You got it twisted *Maricon*." Rene's anger reached a steady boil. "When you let him escape, you signed your death warrant."

Andre's battered body tensed. With Rene's words still hanging in the air, his men stood Andre up and forced a rubber tire around Andre's chest and arms and doused him with gasoline.

Andre's eyes were wide with terror. "Wait! Please, I honestly don't remember their names. But . . . Tessa she'll know who they are," he cried. Gasoline dripped from Andre's body forming a small pool by his feet.

Rene's voice seethed with feral intensity. "Did Juan Carlos fake his own death?" Andre was momentarily too stunned to speak. The possibility that Juan Carlos had faked his own death was not something

Andre had ever thought about. Nor would he have reason to. His part ended when Juan Carlos drove through the prison front gate. Sensing that he only had seconds left, Andre pleaded frantically for his life.

Rene looked at his men. His gaze was quick but absolute.

Andre rocked wildly trying to free himself. One of Rene's men lit a match and tossed it at the tire. The tire instantly burst into flame. Andre cried out as he smelled the choking scent of rubber and his own skin burning. His cries quickly transformed into blood curdling shrieks as the flames engulfed his body and burned away the flesh and muscles from his bones. Andre collapsed onto the floor. In his final minutes, he teetered in and out of consciousness. His eyes filled with agony gazed heavenward in a silent plea for mercy. But this time Andre was not desperately clinging to life, but instead praying for his soul to leave as his singed flesh fell away from his body like ash flicked from the lit end of a cigar.

Chapter Forty-Three

The guards at the front gate of Bon Futuro prison yelled orders and fanned outward pushing the crowd back and creating a path for Hogan's van to pull out of the main security post. Agent Roy swerved around people too slow to move out of his way. Once he got clear of the crowd, he accelerated towards the scene of the ambulance explosion. Hogan sat in the passenger's seat, questions whipping through his mind. Every witness that he knew of that could shed some light on the events leading to Juan Carlos's disappearance was missing. The cartel had a custom when it came to interrogation: they questioned the witness and when they extracted the information they wanted, they tortured the witness until they begged to be killed. There was another cartel custom when it came to killing: calculated and savage cruelty was their benchmark. Those killed by the cartel were to be made examples of to warn others. Castrations, beheadings and victims impaled upon greased stakes left to die slowly in extreme pain were trademarks of cartel ordered executions. Hogan was not one given to speculation, but sitting in the van staring out of the passenger window at cactuses and sand dunes that looked more like the American Southwest than the Caribbean, he could not rid himself of the foreboding feeling that Hernandez and Rojer were already dead. Even with his potential leads evaporating Hogan remained strangely calm. Missing witnesses were right out of the cartel's playbook. Hogan rationalized that if people that might know something about Juan Carlos's disappearance were suddenly missing the cartel was behind it, which was further proof that the cartel thought that Juan Carlos was still alive. Hogan's last and only lead to Juan Carlos's potential whereabouts was the flight that mysteriously left Curacao in the middle of the night. He decided that once he took a quick look at the scene where the ambulance exploded that he and the majority of his team would focus on tracking the flight and finding its passengers.

* * *

The Curacao police suffered from tunnel vision and were deploying all their resources on investigating the ambulance explosion. Not a single officer was assigned to investigate the flight that left Curacao in the middle of the night. It was clear to Hogan that the cartel was not completely buying into the notion that Juan Carlos was in the ambulance when it exploded which accounted for the two men in the FedEx truck.

Hogan gave Agent Roy a quick nod. “Get Macy on the radio.”

Victoria Macy reported that through her 40-power spotting scope she was able to confirm that both men in the FedEx truck were carrying firearms. Hogan considered his options. One was to order Macy to neutralize the possible threat. Without knowing if Juan Carlos was alive and on the island, Hogan realized that this choice was the most radical. If the two dead bodies were connected to the United States, Hogan risked an international incident. It occurred to Hogan that if Juan Carlos did try to sneak out on a flight leaving Curacao, the two men in the FedEx truck would see Juan Carlos and terminate him before Macy had time to react. The two men were 340 yards away from the barrel of Macy’s M24 rifle. A few years ago, a younger more patient version of Special Agent Hogan would have ordered Macy to stand down until they had better information. But Hogan had spent enough time with Juan Carlos to know that he was his country’s single best opportunity to cripple a drug cartel that had morphed into a mega-cartel. Hogan was committed to winning the war on drugs, which meant that there were things that he had to do that his superiors were better off not knowing.

With the information that Juan Carlos could provide the DEA, the cartel's operations would be exposed. Hogan couldn't risk losing Juan Carlos, so he ordered Macy to do what she was trained to do.

"Officer Macy, this is Special Agent Hogan."

"Yes, sir," Hogan's receiver crackled.

"I want you to confirm again that the men in the truck are armed."

Everyone sat silently while they waited for Macy. The only sound in the van was the anomalous hum of the radio. A few moments later, Macy's voice came across the walkie-talkie and echoed throughout the van.

"Sir, both men are armed. I have visual confirmation of two M-4s with suppressors," Macy said.

The assault rifles affixed with silencers removed any lingering doubt. Hogan didn't hesitate. "Put them down and then get the hell out of there and back to Florida as quickly as possible," he ordered.

"Roger that sir," Macy replied.

* * *

MACY HAD ALREADY calculated the wind-speed, direction and the distance of her targets. She crawled to the parapet of the roof and carefully scanned her surroundings before bringing the butt of the rifle to her shoulder. Her eyes bright and blue locked in on her first target through her power scope.

"There you are," Macy said with a smile creasing her lips.

She decided against a headshot to buy herself the additional second of time it might take for the second man in the truck to figure out that his partner had been shot. Macy's first shot sent a hollow point bullet slipping between two buildings on a downward angle and hit her target in the absolute center of his heart. The organ was decimated in a fraction of a second and death was instantaneous. The rifle jumped a quarter inch, but Macy immediately locked in on her second target. She hit her second target above his right ear as he spun around in reaction to the first shot. The hollow point bullet exploded through his skull and plowed through his brain and then exited in a violent stream of blood and bone fragments.

Chapter Forty-Four

It was almost noon. Tessa cruised along a red clay road which squeezed between limestone inlets overlooking a rugged coastline on one side, and clay soil sprinkled with green shrubbery and aloe plants on the other. Looking north, Marisa stared silently at the waves crashing fiercely on a black-sand beach. She was torn between horror and disbelief and a deep personal revulsion for letting Tessa con her into getting mixed up in Juan Carlos's escape. Marisa had a dark, ominous feeling that as the details about Juan Carlos's disappearance came to light, she would have to create as much distance as possible between her and her children. Marisa suspected that she would not see her children for a long time. That thought sent a surge of panic through her body even as she tried to dismiss it. Tessa drove past an ostrich farm and continued for about nine more kilometers before she got to the end of the road. There she brought the jeep to a stop and idled a moment while she surveyed her surroundings. There wasn't a soul in sight. Tessa swung open the driver's-side door and turned and looked back at Marisa.

"We're here. Now, help me with the guard," she said.

Together they moved purposefully lifting him off of the trailer. The guard did not put up any struggle as the two women carried him and lowered him onto the ground.

Tessa knelt next to Marisa and began tying her ankles together and then her wrists. Tessa made sure that she left enough give in the binding to allow Marisa to manipulate the cellphone. Before she was blindfolded, Marisa looked at Tessa and reminded her to protect her children.

"Remember your promise to me. Get my babies off the island," Her whisper was barely audible, but the desperation in Marisa's eyes made Tessa want to hug her, but instead she gave her a short nod.

"Don't worry about your kids, I will get them somewhere safe. You remember to keep your wits about you, and you will be fine," Tessa said as she slipped the blindfold over Marisa's head.

Tessa dialed the number to the police and placed the phone into Marisa's hand. Marisa felt an involuntary shudder crawl up her back. She waited for the police operator to answer, and then she asked them to track her cell phone.

"Dear God in Heaven," She prayed as she listened to the jeep gather speed as it drove away. "Please take pity on my children."

* * *

THE NARROW ROAD just ahead of the clearing where the remains of the ambulance was situated was littered with police cars, fire and emergency vehicles and television trucks. Hogan and his team of agents walked the last several hundred yards to where the ambulance and accident scene was roped off with yellow tape. The two agents that Hogan sent ahead briefed him on the status of the investigation. The accident scene was noisy and disorganized. Hogan sidestepped bits of glass that were sprinkled everywhere while he personally surveyed the damage. The ambulance looked like a pile of black twisted metal. The blast caused by the oxygen tanks blew a gaping hole through the roof. The bodies in the back of the ambulance were in the direct path of the force of the explosion. It ripped the bodies apart spraying severed limbs and organs throughout the entire area. The body in the front seat was charred and grotesquely mangled. The forensics team was still busy canvassing the area collecting body parts. Given the remoteness of the location, Hogan's first thought was that the scene looked like a professional hit. But Hogan quickly dismissed that scenario as unlikely. There were just too many things that didn't add up; such as Hernandez and Rojer going missing. If the cartel ordered a hit on Juan Carlos, they would most likely carry it out in Bon Futuro prison. Hogan ran the various scenarios and could not come up with a single reason for the ambulance being in this location.

Ryan Collins sipped on a cold cup of coffee as he walked alongside Hogan.

"What are you thinking?" He asked Hogan.

Hogan took a moment. "I'm thinking that I have more questions than I do answers."

Collins looked around the area which looked to be contaminated by sloppy police work.

"Well what do you expect? With all these people running around it's damn near impossible to recreate what happened here."

Hogan nodded. Nothing about the site made any sense to him.

Collins looked down and stepped around a sizable piece of charred metal. "This doesn't look like a random accident to me."

"I would agree with that," Hogan replied, his voice carried a trace of concern.

Collins took another sip of coffee as they walked.

"In all my years as a navy seal, I've seen more than my fair share of areas decimated by explosions and fires. I've also seen what they do to human bodies."

"Your point?" Hogan said with a surge of interest.

"In every other instance there was always blood. There should at least be some traces of blood splatter caused by the explosion. I didn't see any in the ambulance or anywhere else."

Hogan stopped walking and looked at Collins. He didn't know what to think.

"Let's take a walk back over to the ambulance," Collins suggested.

"What am I looking for?" Hogan asked.

"Hold your horses. Collins leaned into the hull of the rear of the ambulance and swept a UV light he pilfered from an unsuspecting member of the forensics unit.

"No blood. Not a drop."

"I still don't get it."

"If you believe this was an accident and three people died in the explosion there should be traces of blood in the back of the ambulance where Juan Carlos and one of the EMT's were supposed to be . . . but there isn't any."

"Come here," Collins walked over towards a body part a few feet from where they were standing. He leaned over what looked like part of a large intestine that had been collected but not yet bagged by the forensics unit. The intestine had not been completely charred. Collins guessed that the force of the explosion cut right through the body propelling pieces of it out of the ambulance before it could completely burn. Collins snapped on a pair of latex gloves and cradled the severed organ as if it were a bird with a broken wing. He brought it to his nose and smelled it.

"Just as I thought," he nodded with confidence.

"What is?" Hogan said, clearly looking intrigued.

"It has a very faint chemical smell," Collins said.

Hogan cracked a small smile. Collin's theory was slowly sinking in. "Don't believe everything you see. This was made to look like they died in the explosion. But they were already dead," Collins said.

Hogan ran all the information through his head. Putting on his conspiracy cap, he visualized the whole scene in his mind; the calculation, orchestration, deception and feints.

"The police think that Juan Carlos died in an accidental explosion because it's easier to stick their heads in the sand . . . Juan Carlos was just a prisoner waiting to be extradited and the harsh truth is the Curacao police and prison officials want to close the investigation." Collins eyed Hogan. "You know what I mean?"

Hogan didn't hear the question right away. His mind was elsewhere.

Hogan ran his fingers along his lips and nodded. "This whole thing was staged."

"Exactly," Collins snapped.

The relief Hogan felt instantly transformed into a sense of urgency as the thought occurred to him that they were being played. Hogan drew on his large database of real-life experiences. Whoever was behind this elaborate distraction was buying time for Juan Carlos to disappear.

Hogan turned and started in the direction of the van.

Collins looked up. "I guess we're done here."

"Indeed," Hogan said.

Collins rounded up the rest of the team and followed Hogan to the van.

As he walked towards the van, Hogan noticed the blinking message light on his cell phone. The Curacao police had located the missing ambulance driver and prison guard. Once they got off the deserted roadway Agent Roy made a series of turns darting through Curacao's back streets as he sped towards police headquarters.

Chapter Forty-Five

DALLAS

Hugo Jackson was the only person outside of the Muscogee Creek Nation that Keeper Bruner called when his baby brother Andrew Daniel was shot and killed. A.D. and Hugo developed a very strong bond when they served in the military together. When A.D. returned home to Oklahoma, he and his brother opened a smoke shop on their family's Indian land in Broken Arrow. The land was part of a restricted allotment given to their grandfather when the United States government signed a treaty with the Creek Indian Confederacy. Keeper was satisfied with the success of their smoke shop, but A.D. wasn't. He saw a window of opportunity to grow their business. By the end of their first year, A.D. and Keeper opened two more smoke shops on their family's other land in Tulsa. Shortly after, they entered into lease agreements with members of the Cherokee and Creek Tribes and within a couple of years A.D and Keeper were operating eleven smoke shops throughout the eastern part of Oklahoma. A D. stayed in close contact with Hugo after his honorable discharge. He repeatedly tried to convince Hugo to move back home to Oklahoma when he got out of the military and run the smoke shop business with him and Keeper. Hugo thought about it, but during his second tour of duty he met Mia.

* * *

While A.D. was stationed in Afghanistan, he and Hugo patrolled an area overrun with militant jihadists and took part in thirteen special operations together. The two Oklahoma boys instantly clicked. When they went on patrol together or on a mission, a quick look or nod of the head was all it took for them to be in perfect synch. No matter how dangerous the operation, A.D. handled his business with a calm focus and always came out of it without so much as a scratch. He often kidded Hugo that he had a great Indian spirit warrior watching over him. A.D. always had an instinct for spotting trouble. But on one December evening A.D was rushing to meet his brother at their nephew's wrestling tournament, and he didn't notice the meth addict slip into the store with a shotgun until it was pointed at his head. No one knows what happened after that. Keeper assumed that a junkie who was desperate to feed an addiction got spooked and shot his little brother in the face at close range. The shotgun blast blew half of his brother's face off. Keeper was already at the wrestling tournament when he got the call. As a retired police officer, Keeper knew better than to blame himself for his baby brother's murder but his sunken eyes and grim jawline told the world that his faith and happiness died with his brother. His brother's senseless murder haunted him every night when he closed his eyes. Keeper never again had a peaceful night. It was something that he accepted as his penance.

* * *

Keeper waited in a white Chevy Tahoe in the parking lot of the Dallas Executive airport for the private charter from Boca Raton to arrive. After a while, he spotted the confident and purposeful stride of a familiar figure making his way towards the truck a few steps ahead of Mia and two other people. Keeper swung open the driver-side door and waved at Hugo. When Keeper's eyes met Mia's, his granite demeanor briefly softened. It made him feel good to know that Hugo finally had a woman in his life. Keeper caught a glimpse of Juan Carlos who walked beside her. As a retired police officer who worked in the K-9 unit, drug dealers were his natural enemy. But for the next 48 hours Keeper decided to put his personal feelings aside and help an old friend.

* * *

The drive from the Dallas Executive airport to Ten Killer Lake was just over 250 miles. Juan Carlos yawned into his hand and began to drift in and out of sleep as the endless wheat fields and oil and gas wells had a hypnotic effect. Keeper looked in his rearview mirror and caught another glimpse of Juan Carlos this time while he slept. He shrugged and gave Hugo a side-ways look.

"I sure hope you know what you're doing."

Hugo nodded, but he wasn't completely sure. His silence told Keeper everything he needed to know.

Keeper's face wrinkled with a smile. "What have I stepped into?"

Hugo shrugged. "Some deep shit."

Keeper did a double take.

"We'll be out of your hair soon," Hugo reassured him. His expression turned serious. "Were you able to get everything on the list I emailed you?" Hugo asked Keeper.

Keeper shook his head. "It's all in the guest house at the lake."

Hugo went through his mental checklist. "What about access to the encryption server and software at your tribe's casino?"

Keeper took a deep breath and when he let it out slowly, he made a low whistling sound.

"That one took a little greasing. The tribe's head of gaming is white. He is a stickler for not breaking the casino's operating policies and procedures," he said. "I still don't know why a member of our Nation isn't running the casino," Keeper momentarily digressed before continuing.

"You know, the computer servers are the heart and soul of the casino operation. Without them the casino shuts down. So, they don't like to let anyone touch their system. In fact, No one other than authorized personnel are allowed in the casino's back-of-the house where the computer servers are located."

Hugo's eyes widened. "So how were you able to get it done?"

A devilish smile creased Keeper's lip.

"Our chief is a bit of a scaly-wag. For a few bucks in his pocket, he'd give you the keys to the kingdom."

"Good," Hugo shrugged. "Just let me know how much and we'll settle up."

Keeper waved off Hugo's offer. "Keep your money. It's fun to have a little skin in the game."

Hugo wanted to use the casino's sophisticated encryption technology to encrypt the video message that they would send to Dario Carraboca. His plan was to redirect the e-mail containing the encrypted link through several anonymous forwarding services before it reached Dario making the email close to untraceable.

* * *

Keeper turned off the main roadway on to a gravel stretch of road which wound its way up a gradual incline until it arrived at his property. The property was about 14 acres. The main house was a massive log home that sat on the highest point of the property overlooking the lake. The inside of Keeper's home had soaring ceilings and exposed timber trusses. The large fireplace in the great room with the brilliant blue waters of Ten Killer Lake and the Ozarks serving as the backdrop looked like a perfectly painted landscape one might find in a Thomas Kinkade painting. Shane scanned his surroundings and zeroed in on the kitchen filled with the inviting smells and sounds of food cooking. Completely disregarding social etiquette, Shane made no attempt to excuse himself. He banked hard to his right towards the kitchen abandoning the rest of the group. It was nearly four in the afternoon and Shane had not eaten anything substantial since leaving Curacao. He was starving. Shane was a creature of habit. His morning ritual included six egg whites, oatmeal and several slices of tomato on the side. Shane's stomach started doing somersaults somewhere over the Gulf of Mexico. When they landed in Dallas, Shane asked if they could make a quick stop to eat. Mia, never one to listen to anyone complain more than a second or two handed him a banana and told him to suck it up. They needed to get out of Dallas as quickly as possible. With some luck the FBI and DEA wouldn't begin to drill down on Dallas for a couple more hours. Shane casually read off the names out loud of restaurants advertised on the roadside billboards. Hugo smirked at his friend's childhood antics while the others ignored him. Starving and irritable, Shane did not wait for Keeper. He grabbed a plate and started filling it with chicken, flour tortillas, yellow rice and refried beans. Juan Carlos followed Shane's lead. Mia's expression darkened. She glared disapprovingly at Shane, but he did not seem to care as he squeezed a rolled-up tortilla between his lips.

"It's all right," Keeper placed a calming hand on Mia's arm. "I told these boys to make themselves at home."

Mia nodded clearly displeased.

"Why don't you get something to eat, and, when you're done, I'll take you and H down to the guest house where you can make sure that I got everything that you are going to need," Keeper suggested.

There was nothing else Mia could do. By this time Hugo had also joined in the feeding frenzy. Disappointed in their lack of manners, she strode in and joined the others.

The guest house sat down the hill on the backside of the property nestled under a canopy of tall spruce trees. Keeper led Hugo and Mia to a hallway and down a short flight of stairs towards the media room.

"I put everything you asked for in here," Keeper said as he opened the door. The room had no windows which was to both Hugo's and Mia's liking. In the center of the room were two portable office partition dividers, a desk, chair, laptop computer, video equipment and cabling. Hugo situated the desk to the left of a projection screen on the wall and set up the two partition walls on each side of the projection screen extending out past the desk. He then situated the video camera directly in front of the makeshift office while Mia was busy connecting the laptop to the projection equipment. Whatever they pulled up on the laptop computer would be displayed on the projection screen to the left. Hugo checked the screen shot on the camera to make sure that nothing outside the provisional cubicle was captured that could give away their location. When they finished setting up, they all headed back to the main house to wait for Pierce to arrive.

* * *

ALEXIS SAT QUIETLY waiting for the house to appear on the horizon.

"You okay?" Pierce asked, peering worriedly at her.

"Okay?" she repeated silently to herself. How could she be okay when she was about to spend the next few years of her life away from everyone she loved. She was sentenced to live in seclusion with a man responsible for all her heartache and humiliation. Biting her lip Alexis said nothing. Her anxiety increased as the sedan worked its way up the gravel road.

When the house was within sight, Alexis knotted her hands together in her lap. They were shaking. Finally, she let out a breath she didn't realize she had been holding.

"I need to go in by myself," she told Pierce her voice cracked with emotion.

Pierce eyed her thoughtfully. "Of course," he said.

He watched her walk tentatively up the stairs. When she arrived at the front door, Alexis glanced back briefly at Pierce. Her throat was dry, and her heart pounded as she rang the doorbell.

* * *

Juan Carlos was sitting by the fireplace when Alexis walked in. Her gaze swept the room, but everyone seemed to meld into a featureless blur. Juan Carlos stood up and smiled at her.

"Well hello," he said and took a step towards her. Alexis involuntarily stiffened her hands at her sides which curled themselves into fists. She stood motionless staring at her husband. It was hard not to feel like she was looking at a stranger. Her throat felt tight, almost too tight to speak. Shane touched her shoulder lightly.

"It will be all right," he whispered softly in her ear as he walked past her and headed outside.

Alexis shook her head, never taking her eyes off Juan Carlos. Mia sensed her desperation but stopped short of comforting her. Instead she gestured to Hugo and Keeper to follow her to the kitchen.

There was a long silence. Juan Carlos put his hand on her shoulder. Alexis spun around wildly, slapping his hand out of the way. Her amber eyes glared at him.

"Don't touch me again. You forfeited that right," she hissed.

"Just hold on a minute. I just want to—"

"Lie to me like you always have."

Gritting his teeth, Juan Carlos forced a smile. "I owe you an explanation."

"I don't want one."

"Alexis," Juan Carlos persisted. "The one thing a man has in prison is time. While I was in prison, I had plenty of time to think about the mistakes I've made and how poorly I treated you."

Alexis resisted the urge to scream.

"I started using drugs and everything quickly spiraled out of control. I lost it."

Alexis didn't want an explanation or promises; but Juan Carlos went on, the words pouring out of him like poison.

"The other women and the gambling were all part of that downward spiral. I couldn't stop." Juan Carlos's voice was flat and toneless, yet Alexis found herself shivering, dreading what he might say next.

"None of those women meant anything to me."

Her brain was racing, spinning dark scenarios, churning up clouds of pain.

"When you disappeared for a month at a time and finally came home reeking of another woman, I fell into a black pit. I just wanted to die," she shuddered. "Juan, I blamed myself for your indiscretions. I wondered what I was doing wrong."

Alexis looked like she was reliving a mistake. "And you just continued on while I slowly died inside."

Nothing, not a flicker of emotion passed across Juan Carlos's face. "I was in a drug and alcohol induced haze. I had no real control over what I was doing. I began to think I was untouchable."

Alexis was deeply troubled. Her heart fluttered. "You were cheating on me before the drugs."

Juan Carlos scoffed at her accusation. "That's not true."

"Stop lying to me," she said, shaking her head with pathetic disappointment.

Juan Carlos started to say something and then stopped and eyed Alexis suspiciously. "What did Pierce tell you?"

Alexis laughed at his insinuation. "Please . . . You think Pierce broke your so-called male code? No darling, I can assure you that he didn't. In the beginning, I was either too naïve or unwilling to read the warning signs . . . but let's just say after a while I had an epiphany."

Juan Carlos gave an exasperated sigh. "What signs?"

Alexis frowned and shook her head. "When we were first married, and we were apart, you always sent me text messages. At night you sent me one before you went to bed. And in the morning the first thing when you woke up was send me a text. You used to tell me that I was the last thing you thought of when you drifted off to sleep and the first thing when you woke each morning." Alexis sighed, her voice filled with emotion. "Then gradually the text messages stopped."

Juan Carlos frowned and started to say something in his defense.

"I'm not finished," Alexis snapped at him.

"You became very secretive."

Juan Carlos started to look annoyed. "If I kept things from you, it was for your own safety."

"The biggest red flag was when you stopped touching me. When we were first married, we had sex two or three times a day," she said with a trace of resentment in her voice.

Juan Carlos inhaled through his nose. "That was the honeymoon period."

Alexis leveled him with a cold stare. "Don't insult my intelligence. I know you, and I know your sex drive. We went months at a time without any intimacy."

Juan Carlos made a foul face. He was running out of patience. Instead of saying anything, he stayed quiet and stared into the fire burning in the fireplace.

After an uncomfortable silence, Alexis' lips trembled. "I started to feel ugly and undesirable."

Juan Carlos turned around and gave Alexis an uneasy glance.

"You're wrong", he said. "I never cheated on you until I got addicted to cocaine."

"Is that your excuse for cheating on me?" Alexis asked. The grief in her voice was raw and ragged.

Juan Carlos grunted. "Do you honestly think if I was in my right mind, I would have betrayed Dario Carraboca?"

Those words hit Alexis like a punch to the stomach. She felt shattered that her husband placed his loyalty to the cartel above his commitment to her. Alexis felt her voice rising. "Juan, I don't give a damn about the cartel. You betrayed me you bastard!"

There were so many things that Juan Carlos wanted to say, but instead he stuffed a cigarette between his lips and nodded in agreement. "I know, I know. I'm not saying I didn't fuck up. All I'm saying is my drug addiction clouded my judgment . . . When I dealt drugs on the side, I put your life and the lives of my entire family at risk. Alexis, you know me better than that. I may be selfish, but I'm not stupid."

The hatred that a few minutes ago boiled behind her eyes was replaced by doubt.

"Alexis, I won't use anymore. I've already hit rock bottom. And I know the warning signs. I won't do this to you ever again," Juan Carlos promised.

Alexis struggled to keep her voice steady. "But I don't love you anymore."

Juan Carlos exhaled a cloud of smoke as he studied her for a moment. He attributed her comment to her emotional state and decided not to believe her.

"Of course, you do. We've been together since you were sixteen."

Alexis shook her head. She felt tears prick her eyes and blinked them furiously away. The love she once felt for Juan Carlos now felt like a lifetime ago.

"No Juan" Alexis dismissed the thought of another chance as soon as Juan Carlos raised it. Alexis had grown tired of crying herself to sleep at night, of all the lonely nights wondering if each time he left the house for weeks at a time if he was in the arms of another woman. She was tired of all his deceitfulness. But most of all, she was just tired. Tired of everything. Their marriage was over and done with. Her only obligation as she saw it was to do what Pierce asked of her. She would leave the country for her own safety and live in obscurity with Juan Carlos until it was either safe for her to leave him or until she couldn't stand it anymore.

Alexis got that faraway look on her face as she thought about how they met, their marriage and their last few years together. She looked almost sheepish and her eyes glistened like beads.

"You will always have a place in my heart, but I can never love you again."

Chapter Forty-Six

Pierce sat on the front steps of the house, warming himself with a cup of coffee as the chill of the evening approached. Shane sat quietly next to him. He could tell that Pierce wasn't quite ready for any questions or comments. So, he simply sat next to his best friend and decided to leave him to his thoughts and the natural rhythm and beauty of Lake Tenkiller. He gave Pierce a sympathetic pat on the back. Shane had a sixth sense about these things, and he knew that Pierce never considered how hard it was going to be for him to say good-bye to Alexis until this moment. The sun dipped behind the Ozark Mountains sending a chill across the porch. It was getting late. Pierce picked up the cup and finished drinking the last of his coffee and went inside the house.

When Pierce walked into the house, Juan Carlos had his back to the door. He noticed a visible shudder pass through Alexis. Something in her appearance changed. Her gaze turned wide and luminous and a reddish pink flooded her cheeks. Juan Carlos recognized that look, it was one he had not seen in a long time. He didn't bother looking over his shoulder. He had a strong feeling that the man who caused Alexis to go red in the face was the same person responsible for his freedom. Juan Carlos looked to Alexis and shook his head in disappointment. Then he strode towards Pierce and hugged him.

"Pierce my boy! You did it."

Pierce looked mildly surprised by Juan Carlos's gesture which seemed out of character.

"We're not out of the woods yet."

Juan Carlos could not stop himself from smiling. His expression seemed to say that he never thought that they would make it this far. Glancing back at Alexis, Juan Carlos added thoughtfully: "I also owe you a debt of gratitude for taking care of my wife." Pierce forced himself to put a smile on his face. "Of course." Pierce and Alexis shared an awkward glance and then she fixed her stare on the surface of the cocktail table just in front of her. Pierce was momentarily distracted by her watery gaze. Shane glanced around the room. He offered a shrug and said, "Why don't I get the others so we can discuss the next step?"

"Yes, let's do that," Pierce said, forcing himself to focus on the plan instead of Alexis.

Juan Carlos wore a dubious expression. "I've been curious about this plan of yours."

Pierce was starting to have second thoughts about the part of the plan where Alexis had to go with Juan Carlos. "It's actually pretty logical. We just have to manipulate our current situation so that Dario Carraboca wants . . . No, needs to keep you alive."

AN OMINOUS FEELING gripped Juan Carlos as he was starting to think that Pierce had grossly misjudged Dario Carraboca. He shook his head in a slow, critical manner. Juan Carlos speculated that he would be on the run, hiding from Dario Carraboca for the rest of his days. The voice in his head told him that Dario would never stop hunting him. And when they found him, they would torture him and mutilate him, turning him into a grisly example for others to learn from. Dario made it appear that he had given Juan Carlos a way of making reparations to the cartel and instead of going through with it he made Dario look like even a bigger fool.

The only thing that would interest Dario now was for Juan Carlos to suffer a brutal and dehumanizing death.

"I pose a greater threat to the cartel if I'm alive," Juan Carlos disagreed. "Dario offered me a way out and instead of taking it, I escaped." Juan Carlos took in a deep breath and let it out slowly giving the impression that he was pondering his fate while he poured himself a glass of Jack Daniels whiskey. "The cartel intends to make an example out of me. There is no way that the cartel will let me live."

Pierce nodded. "There is a way. Trust me."

Juan Carlos inhaled sharply. "I'm listening," he said, sounding skeptical.

Pierce looked at Alexis and said, "It's really quite simple, you have something that's important to them . . . knowledge about the cartel's operations . . ."

"Not some. I know everything about their operations. I know their smuggling routes and where all their safe houses that store their drugs and cash are located. I have access to all of their bank account numbers." The more Juan Carlos explained the more he felt his world slipping from him. He took a swig of Jack Daniels. "That's why the cartel wants to kill me . . . If I'm dead, I can't cooperate with the DEA and cripple their entire operation."

"Not exactly, Pierce shook his head. "What would Dario do if we flipped the script on him, and if he killed you, the DEA would have access to everything you know about the cartel's operations?"

Juan Carlos was caught off guard by Pierce's question. "What exactly do you mean?"

"We put everything you know about the cartel's operations on video. Then we send a link to Dario Carrraboca and tell him that if he kills you, or anyone of us, the information gets immediately released to the DEA, the FBI and INTERPOL . . . If he plays ball, you and Alexis disappear."

All eyes moved to Juan Carlos to see what he thought.

Juan Carlos's mind hunted for flaws. He considered Dario's need to make an example of him and weighed it against the threat posed by Pierce's plan. He was certain that Dario would see the bigger picture.

The specter of law enforcement agencies possessing information that could expose his operations was not something Dario could let happen. He would have to temporarily look past Juan Carlos's betrayal to avoid an outcome that could cripple the Cartel's operations. But Juan Carlos was also sure that Dario's concession would only be temporary. He would play Pierce's game until he could find a way to dismantle the threat and then he would kill everyone which was Dario's way of tying up the loose ends. Juan Carlos gave Pierce a blank stare for a long moment and then said, "That might work, but only if we remain out of the DEA's reach. If the DEA gets its hands on me . . . we're back to where we started."

"If Dario's lawyers are any good, they will advise him that since you have not been charged with any extraditable offense in the United States, they have no basis for demanding that you be extradited," Shane said.

Pierce shook his head. "Just to play it safe, you are going to only reside in countries that do not have extradition treaties with the United States. That way, you are essentially untouchable as long as you don't step foot in this country."

Juan Carlos paced to the fireplace, exhaled a cloud of smoke, took a drink and then came back to where the others were sitting. He was still not completely convinced. He knew from experience that Dario Carraboca did not always react logically or predictably.

"Dario's not someone that is easily outmaneuvered. If there's a chink in your plan, he'll find it," Juan Carlos said.

Pierce's thoughtful gaze locked in on Juan Carlos. "Well then, if he doesn't take our deal, we'll all die, and the United States has everything it needs to destroy the world's most powerful drug cartel."

Juan Carlos considered Pierce's pronouncement with a crisp nod. He was impressed with Pierce's cold, calculated willingness to see who would blink first.

For the first time since his arrest, Juan Carlos had a reason to be hopeful. Turning towards Alexis, Juan Carlos looked momentarily star-struck.

"You chose well," he told her. His comment startled her. She reeled as if knocked backward by the message's hidden meaning. Hugo reached for her. "Are you all right?"

Hugo could see in her eyes a profound exhaustion.

"I'm just a little light-headed."

Alexis looked tired. Hugo shot Pierce a look which told him to wrap things up.

"It's my fault," Pierce said, sounding contrite. "We've been pushing pretty hard to get here."

Alexis heard Pierce, but his words barely registered. She was emotionally drained.

Juan Carlos didn't bother to look over at Alexis. "She'll be fine," he said callously without a hint of concern. "So, what time do we start videotaping?"

Hugo's voice sharpened. "We'll start tomorrow morning at six."

Alexis felt herself flush. She was embarrassed for causing the meeting to end abruptly.

Pierce stood up. "Good night, I hope you feel better," Pierce smiled, a small apologetic smile, as he exchanged looks with Alexis.

"I'll show Juan Carlos and Alexis to their room," Keeper said as he started walking towards the staircase. "Pierce, you and Shane can bunk in the guest house."

As soon as Juan Carlos and Alexis left the room, Shane spotted the same resignation and pain in Pierce's eyes that he saw when Jordan left him. Slipping his arm around Pierce's shoulder, Shane said with a trace of sadness: "I love you too much to tell you I told you so."

Pierce shook his head, frowning at the comment, but he didn't say a word.

Hugo's eyes were bugged in disbelief. "You just did, you asshole."

Mia opened her mouth to snap at Shane and closed it. Partly because she realized that she had been exceedingly tough on him since Curacao. And partly because there was a look in Shane's eyes that told her that he'd lived through Pierce's loss and heartache with him.

Chapter Forty-Seven

MIAMI

Jackie Hernandez sipped her morning tea and nibbled scones in her secretarial alcove located just outside of Pierce's office. Her organized gaze lowered on a list of matters that required her attention that morning. She had been given specific instructions to call local counsel on the Juan Carlos Laporte case and confirm the time and date of Mr. Laporte's extradition hearing. When she finally spoke with Marcus van Delft, he rushed her off the phone. All he would say was that the extradition hearing had been postponed indefinitely. Before Jackie could ask a question, Marcus van Delft hung up the phone. She raised an eyebrow, an expression which seemed to ask, "why are most lawyers such bad-tempered assholes?" Jackie then refocused on the computer monitor directly in front of her and pulled up Pierce's flight and hotel reservations. Once she cancelled them, Jackie decided to send Pierce a text message hoping to catch him before he started back for Miami. Pierce told her that he was going to be attending to personal business for a couple of days and that his cell phone signal would be hit-or-miss, but she wanted to let him know that his hearing was postponed and there was no need to rush back.

* * *

By coincidence, Marcus van Delft first learned of Juan Carlos's disappearance from Charlotte, the young woman he had hired to have sex with him. She took great pleasure in informing Marcus that her piece of shit client was dead. Even though the police at first were tight-lipped about the ambulance explosion, the brewing controversy of two EMT's and a prisoner's suspected deaths spread over the island like a wildfire. Marcus realized that the cartel had little tolerance for mistakes and customarily dealt with those responsible for making them harshly. It made no difference to the cartel that Juan Carlos may have died in the explosion. If Dario suspected that Marcus was responsible in any way for the decision to transfer Juan Carlos to the hospital, or if Dario decided Marcus should have known and failed to promptly inform the cartel of the development, the price for his role or oversight would be a slow painful death. Marcus sat in his office sweating; his face went white with fear when the voice on the intercom announced that Rene was on the line. Marcus stared at the phone for several seconds before he finally picked up. He cleared his throat discreetly. "Rene, my good friend, these new events are tragic indeed, shocking even," he babbled on nervously.

Rene sounded agitated. "I need help with a little problem," he scowled. Marcus did his best to make his voice sound normal even though his heart pounded, and his breath came in shallow gasps. "Anything, whatever you need. How may I be of service?"

"Do you know a woman by the name Tessa Bongard?" Rene asked. Marcus felt a shiver. He knew the name well having crossed paths with Tessa on more than a few occasions. He found it curious that Rene was inquiring about her.

"Yes, I know Tessa Bongard," Marcus heard himself say.

"Good," Rene replied. "Where can we find her?"

Marcus looked at his watch. It was just before one in the afternoon. "She usually hangs around the Emerald Casino, but it's a little early so she may still be home. If you give me a moment, I can give you her address," Marcus offered.

"No. You misunderstand me Marcus," he said, sounding pressed for time. "I want your people to find her. They know this island better than we do. When they locate her, call me and we'll take it from there," Rene's tone was final.

Marcus realized that he had no choice but to cooperate. "I understand," he said.

"I'm not sure you do. We think that she can help lead us to Juan Carlos."

"What the devil—" Marcus looked baffled. He was particularly unnerved by the thought that Juan Carlos might still be alive. Marcus wanted nothing more than to believe that he was dead. As he processed this latest development, the peril of his predicament closed in around him. If Juan Carlos was still alive that could only mean that he escaped and that he had help. It also meant that Juan Carlos still posed a threat to the cartel and that Dario would bring the wrath of hell down on everyone.

* * *

STOPPING TO PURCHASE a cup of coffee Tessa's eyes swept the street checking for a misplaced face or a suspicious gaze. She had no reason to believe that the cartel knew who she was. Still, she needed to be cautious knowing that in this slum any one of the men loitering in open doorways smoking cigarettes would gladly slit her throat if they thought it would make them some money. Satisfied her trail was clean; Tessa crossed the street and headed towards the school to pick up Marisa's children. The doors to the school were open, and inside the shadowy hall, was a matronly woman with untidy hair and an unhappy glare in her eyes sitting behind a desk.

Tessa stood over the desk and offered a friendly smile, "Good afternoon. Marisa De Meza asked me to pick up her children today," she said.

The woman looked up from her crossword puzzle and curiously eyed Tessa. "And who might you be?" Her eyes narrowed as she inspected her clipboard mumbling a few words to herself, shaking her head. "I don't have a note from their mother or the school stating that someone would be picking up the children," she said to Tessa.

Pressed for time, Tessa assumed that arguing with the woman would have little or no effect, so she decided on a different tactic. Tessa pretended to look confused.

"Please," Tessa said, extending her driver's license towards the woman. "I don't know what could have happened. With the ambulance explosion that occurred this morning all of the ambulance drivers got called into work. Marisa asked if I could do her a favor and pick up her children. It was a last-minute thing. I guess Marisa forgot to call the school."

The woman huffed at Tessa. "Ms. De Meza knows that we are very strict when it comes to our school's rules and procedures."

"Of course, I certainly understand," Tessa conceded. "I will call Marisa and tell her that she will need to pick up her children." Glancing at her watch Tessa bluffed: "I'm sure Marisa will be able to pick up her children in a few hours."

The woman was delirious with angst. "We close in 45 minutes. I can't stay any longer."

Tessa gave her a sympathetic nod. "You have my identification. If you ask the children, they will tell you that they know me."

The woman hesitated not knowing what to do. She stared at her clipboard as if it held some sort of answer to Tessa's offer. Marshaling her papers, she marched downstairs and returned twenty minutes later with two children.

"I kept a copy of your license. The woman's eyes were pinned to Tessa. "I'm going to trust you. Don't make me regret my decision."

Tessa nodded, "Thank you." Her words were rushed as she took each child by the hand and bolted for the doorway. Her eyes returned to the street. Scanning the intersection ahead, Tessa suddenly felt uncomfortable. She spotted a gray van parked just behind her jeep. Four locals dressed in baggy shirts and trousers walked impatiently towards her. Realizing that she would not be able to outrun them, Tessa looked back at the school building. A fifth man appeared behind her and blocked the doorway. Tessa loosened her grip on the children and pushed ahead of them putting herself protectively between the children and the four men. Sensing that they were in danger, the children began to cry. Frantically, Tessa looked around for anyone who might help her as the van barreled down on them. Tessa felt powerless. A man with a decidedly militaristic air jumped out. He raised a walkie-talkie and spoke into it. Then he moved towards her. Tessa caught a glimpse of a firearm under his jacket.

"Leave the children," Tessa barked in a bold voice. Before she could utter another syllable, the man gripped her throat and crushed her windpipe. Tessa tried to twist free, but the man's vice like grip cut off her air supply. Tessa clawed in vain fighting for a single breath. In a matter of seconds, everything became blurred, and like a deflating balloon, Tessa fell limp. The four men put Tessa's lifeless body in the van while the man turned his attention to the screaming children.

Crouching down to their eye level he said: "We are not going to hurt you. But you need to tell me if that is your mama?"

Sobbing uncontrollably, with a river of snot running from her flaring nostrils, Marisa's daughter trembled as she shook her head.

Turning to the driver the man said, "They are not her children." The driver lowered his sunglasses and cast a quick look at the two hysterical children. He weighed their value to Rene against the painful sound of two young children crying the entire ride back to the warehouse and decided to leave them.

Chapter Forty-Eight

Tessa Bongard had no idea where she was or how long she had been unconscious. When she opened her eyes, she found herself naked with her arms strung above her head and dangling precariously over an industrial size tank. There was a terrible smell coming from a corner of the warehouse like burnt flesh. She followed the smell to a remote part of the warehouse where her eyes spotted a lifeless form on the floor. Tessa caught glimpses of flickering flames heating the tank and instantly she knew how she was going to be tortured. She was going to be boiled alive.

* * *

The door to the warehouse swung open and Rene appeared. He stared at Tessa intently before speaking.

"Do you know who I am?"

Tessa shook her head. "Not exactly, but I have an idea who you work for."

"Good," Rene said in a satisfied tone. "Then you know why you're here."

Tessa's face was contorted in fear. She could feel the heat rising from the water a few feet below.

"I want you to give me the names of the people that helped Juan Carlos escape."

Tessa lowered her eyes and said, "I don't know anything about an escape."

Rene shook his head and gave her a disappointed look. He would take no joy in killing Tessa. She was a loyal asset who happened to pick the wrong side. In their business, foot soldiers were expendable but the brutal torture of boiling someone alive was something he preferred to reserve for traitors like Juan Carlos.

"Wrong answer . . . Tessa, listen carefully to me. If you don't tell me everything I want to know, I'm going to kill you."

Tessa's face was twisted with fright. "Who are you kidding? We both know you're going to kill me either way."

"Then you know how this works. After I kill you, I will find and kill your entire family." Rene gave her a considerate stare as he removed his pistol and flicked the safety. "It doesn't have to be this way. There's no need for you to suffer. I've seen people boiled alive. It's barbaric . . ." His eyes moved from Tessa down to the water. "But it doesn't have to come to this." Rene's brow furrowed. "I have no quarrel with you. "This," he said pointing to her and then to the tank filled with water is what we do to our enemies and people who betray us. You don't deserve to die this way . . . If you tell me what I want to know, I will kill you quickly."

Tessa glared at Rene. "I don't know anything."

Fear raged through Tessa as she gazed down and imagined the unbearable pain that was waiting for her a few feet below.

"I'll ask you again. Who hired you to help Juan Carlos escape from Bon Futoro?"

Tessa shook her head violently. "I don't know what you're talking about," she shouted.

Rene glanced at his watch. He was running out of time and patience.

He spread his hands palms up and gestured at Tessa with a 'see what you're making me do' look.

"And, I so hoped you'd cooperate."

Steam billowed up from the top of the tank. Tessa sensed the futility of her situation. "I'm telling you the truth. I don't know anything about any escape," she cried out.

Rene's face twisted into a grimace of disgust.

He looked at his men and said, "baje la cuerda," there was no malice in his voice as he gave the order, merely regret.

"You are going to tell me what I want to know sooner or later," Rene barked.

Fear raged through Tessa as she gazed down at the steam coming off of the water.

"Wait, I'll tell you what you want to know," Tessa pleaded frantically.

"I know you will," Rene's voice was tinged with a darkness that spoke of his past experiences boiling people alive. He was sure that the boiling water would loosen her tongue. His men lowered Tessa into the tank. Her head disappeared below the water as she struggled to gain her footing. The intense heat penetrating through the bottom of the tank made it impossible for Tessa to balance her bare feet on the floor of the tank for more than a couple of seconds. Rene leaned over the edge of the tank for a better look.

"I know you helped Juan Carlos escape from Bon Futuro. I want to know the names of the people who hired you and where they are now."

Tessa told herself to stay strong, but the water was becoming unbearably hot. "Please," Tessa started panting. "I only arranged for an ambulance driver to pick Juan Carlos up. After that, I don't know."

"One of the ambulance drivers was picked up by the police a couple of hours ago. Do you know anything about that?" Rene asked her.

Tessa shook her head. The hot water was making it difficult to breathe.

Rene glared at her. "Very soon the pain will become unbearable and you'll stop lying to me."

Tessa writhed violently within the confines of the tank. "I am telling you everything I know. I swear to you." She cried out.

"Tell me where Juan Carlos and his friends are, and I will put an end to this," Rene screamed over her cries. "Andre said there were two men. A man named Shane and a second man; a large muscular black man."

"I-I-I can't feel my legs," Tessa sobbed as tears ran down her face. Tessa was breathing in short gasps. "I-I-I-I told you," she stuttered. "I-I arranged for the ambulance drivers to pick him up and drop him off; nothing more."

Rene began to narrate what was happening to her hoping it would get her to talk. "You can't feel your legs because they are dead. Very soon your organs will start to shut down."

"Please," she gasped. "I'm telling you the truth . . ."

"Ahh . . . perhaps you are . . . But you know more than what you're telling me," he shouted at her.

The water came to a rolling boil. Tessa screamed out in agony as the scalding liquid attacked every cell of her being with growing intensity. Now breathing in labored pants Tessa waited to die.

"I don't know where Juan Carlos is . . ." her voice trailed off.

Rene checked his watch again and frowned. He could see that Tessa was getting unsteady and confused and was worried that she might soon lose consciousness. He had a feeling his window to get information out of her was rapidly closing. Rene considered pulling her out of the tank to buy more time, but assumed that if she wasn't willing to give up the identities of the individuals that helped Juan Carlos escape to stop the pain, she wasn't going to talk if he pulled her out. Even if Rene pulled her out of the boiling water, he had boiled enough people alive to know the intense heat had already cooked her from the inside, and she wasn't going to last much longer. Rene began peppering her with questions in a desperate attempt to learn anything he could before she died.

"Was Juan Carlos in the ambulance when it exploded?" Rene screamed.

Tessa's skin was severely scalded, and her muscles felt like heavy jelly. She twisted her head from side to side. Rene couldn't tell if Tessa was trying to answer his question or simply struggling to hold her head above the boiling water.

"Tell me the name of the black man," Rene pressed in frantic rapid fire.

"Did Juan Carlos die in the ambulance? Do you know where he is?" Rene yelled repeatedly trying to force a response. The intense heat was killing Tessa's brain cells.

Tessa gave a hollow gasp. "Soon you'll be in this tank," she managed a faint smile.

Rene was surprised by Tessa's intensity in her final seconds.

The skin on her face severely blistered; her vision blurred, Tessa concentrated and with calm in her cloudy eyes she looked up at Rene one last time. She made a gurgling sound, "Fuck you and fuck the cartel," as she slipped lifelessly below the surface.

Chapter Forty-Nine

At the Willemstad police station Marisa De Meza sat in a small interrogation room exhausted and hungry. She had been put through hours of questioning, retelling her story to an endless string of detectives and police officers. Her watch read 8:43 P.M. She prayed that Tessa and her children were already somewhere safe. She had been alone in the room for over an hour when she knocked on the door and asked if she could go home. The police officer guarding the door told Marisa that she would be able to leave after the Americans questioned her. Sitting idly in the small confining room, Marisa couldn't stop thinking and worrying about her children. She was desperate to speak with Tessa and hear that her children were safe. Ten minutes later Marisa banged on the door again.

"I need to make a telephone call," she said.

At first the officer ignored her, but Marisa persisted to bang on the door. The officer fixed Marisa with a gaze clearly intended to intimidate. Marisa did not flinch.

"I have two young children. I need to make a call and make sure that they are okay. Please," she pleaded.

"Wait a minute," he said before speaking into his radio. Moments later he opened the door to the room and directed Marisa to follow him to an office where she would be able to make a call. Marisa dialed Tessa's telephone number repeatedly. Each time the call went straight into her voicemail. Wispy feelings of worry quickly turned into a surge of panic.

Marisa exploded out of the office. "I need to leave."

The officer closed in on her. "You can't—"

"I can't reach the school or the person who was supposed to care for my children. I need to go and make sure that they are all right," Marisa said, trying in vain to slip by him.

"I can't release you until the Americans question you."

Marisa glared at the officer. The officer glared back.

"Where are they?"

He shrugged. "We sent them to St. Elisabeth's hospital to question Capitan De Wolf. They should be here shortly and then you can hopefully go home."

Marisa's patience evaporated. "Idiot!" She yelled. "I don't want to go home. Didn't you hear anything I've been saying? I have two small children. I don't know where they are. They could be hurt and lying in the street somewhere," she seethed.

It took two police officers to drag Marisa back to the interrogation room kicking and screaming.

"If you don't stop, I will put you in handcuffs." With that, the officer slammed the door, rattling the heavy glass and twisted the heavy deadbolt into place. Tears ran down Marisa's face. She persisted to bang on the door. The officer rapped on the glass motioning her to stop. But Marisa kept on screaming and kicking the door until two officers dashed in and put her in restraints.

* * *

Marisa looked, Hogan thought like a beaten woman. Her head slumped forward, her delicate arms handcuffed to the sides of the chair made her appear terribly fragile. Hogan turned and gave the police officer a disapproving look.

"Can you please take the handcuffs off of the witness," he requested.

"It was for her own safety," the officer replied slightly embarrassed.

"I'm sure," Collins rolled his eyes.

Marisa's eyes were red and swollen.

"You've been crying," Hogan knelt a foot from her. "What happened?"

Marisa took a shuddering breath. "My children . . ." She felt her eyes well up. "They're missing."

Before Hogan could say a word, Marisa made a gasping sound and burst into tears.

Hogan looked up at the officer.

"Have you sent anyone to look for her children?" Hogan asked knowing that he had no jurisdiction in Curacao but was still determined to get a response. The young officer frowned. "I was only ordered to guard the witness."

"*Unbelievable*," Hogan thought. He took a deep breath as he reeled in his thoughts.

"There are two children missing, and you are holding their mother." Hogan's tone was now challenging. "Don't you follow standard operating procedure here?" The young officer hailed his commanding officer on his walkie-talkie, and then he was gone.

* * *

A few moments later another officer reported that he had issued a citywide alert and was sending two men out to look for the children.

"That's good," Hogan said dryly.

"Where was your friend supposed to pick up your children?" Hogan asked.

"At school, my friend was supposed to pick them up after school."

Hogan nodded.

“Every time I call her it goes right to voicemail.”

Hogan could see the fear in her eyes. “How old are the children?”
“They are only five and six years old.”

Hogan put his hand on Marisa’s shoulder. You’re coming with me to the school,” he said.

Collins’s eyebrows shot up. “Sir, we don’t have time for this.”

The former Navy Seal and Special Agent Roy shared a worried look.

Hogan looked at Collins and Agent Roy and back to Collins again. He knew that Marisa would not tell him anything about Juan Carlos’s disappearance while her children were missing. Hogan didn’t say anything, he just turned around and left the station with Marisa in tow.

The van rolled slowly down the narrow street in front of the school. As usual, the only streetlight was out, and the street was black as pitch. Hogan and his men paid particular attention to areas where small children could easily hide. A shabby older drunk man sat slumped on the stairs of the school. Hogan gave the order for his men to fan out and look for the children on foot. He and Marisa moved purposely towards the main entrance of the school building and found the wooden door locked. Filled with desperation, Marisa hopped over the short fence and headed towards the back of the school. Hogan followed closely behind shining his flashlight in every crevice and dark corner he could find. While visually probing the grounds, a baseball dugout on the far side of the field caught his eye.

“The dugout could serve as a shelter, and it was the farthest enclosure from the street,” he told himself. Hogan called for Marisa, but there was no response. As he got closer, Hogan could make out the silhouettes of two small heads, limbs and torsos huddled together in a corner. He radioed his men to find Marisa and bring her to the baseball field behind the school. When he was about twenty feet away, he could hear whimpers and frightened murmurings. He was determined not to scare the children any further by shining a bright light on them. Speaking into his radio, Hogan smiled for the first time since arriving in Curacao. Calmly squatting down near the entrance, Hogan waited for Marisa to arrive.

"It's okay, I'm a policeman," he told them." Your mom will be here any second," he said trying to sound reassuring.

Marisa sprinted like a high-strung cat across the field. Wrapping both of her babies tightly in her arms Marisa cried tears of gratitude.

"Well done sir," Agent Giles said.

Hogan got to his feet. "Radio the Curacao police and advise them that we found the children."

Giles nodded. Collins, who watched the reunion of mother and her children, gave a slight shrug. They were all aware that after seventy-two hours their chances of finding Juan Carlos dropped considerably.

"We need to wrap things up here and get back to why we're here. We don't know for sure if Juan Carlos was on that plane, but it's our only viable lead right now and it landed in Lauderdale over 17 hours ago. Our window is rapidly closing."

That fact was already churning in Hogan's stomach. "I know," he grimaced. Hogan turned back to Marisa. "Is everything alright?"

"No," her voice was laced with concern.

Hogan's eyes narrowed. Marisa paused to regain her composure.

"Some men took the woman who was supposed to pick up my children. When they left the school, some men were waiting outside. They beat her up and shoved her into the trunk of a car."

Hogan was immediately suspicious. "Did your friend know anything about what happened to that ambulance and the prisoner it picked up at the prison?"

Marisa remained silent.

"This is no coincidence," Collins said under his breath.

In Hogan's mind the three disappearances were all connected. The cartel was still on the island which told him that they still hadn't learned about the chartered jet that left Curacao shortly after Juan Carlos rode out of Bon Futuro prison. Hogan and his men stood on the ball field in the darkness discussing what they should do with Marisa and her children.

Collins fumbled in his pocket for his smokes and lit one. Hogan glanced over at Marisa with her children. "They're not safe here," he said.

Collins and Giles nodded gravely.

Collins exhaled a cloud of smoke and said, "She clearly knows more than what she told the police."

Hogan studied Marisa.

"It certainly looks that way . . . But even if she doesn't, she was in the ambulance which makes her a target. We can't leave them on the island without some protection," Hogan said.

Giles shrugged his shoulders. "So, what do we do with them?"

Hogan took a step closer to Marisa: "The only thing we can do. We take Marisa and her children to the U.S. Consulate. The Perimeter of the Roosevelt house is guarded," he said. He knew that the cartel would not make a move against Marisa and her children as long as they remained there. Hogan moved closer taking stock of Marisa. "We are going to take you somewhere safe. But once we get there, I need you to answer some questions." Choosing his words carefully, he added, "And I need you to answer them truthfully."

Marisa avoided his probing look. Her eyes drifted to Hogan's men who stood by ready to leave. Sensing that she had no other option to keep her children safe Marisa agreed to cooperate.

Fifteen minutes after the children fell asleep, Marisa met Hogan in the foyer. She followed him down the corridor to the Consul General's office. Hogan sat behind the desk and without a word nodded for Marisa to sit. His experience with witnesses told him that Marisa had a well-rehearsed story. His instincts told him that she was not above resorting to deception or even outright lies to protect herself and her friend.

"Doctor Hernandez examined Juan Carlos Laporte yesterday and recommended his transfer to St. Elisabeth Hospital. He was the first to go missing this morning and the first to die," Hogan frowned.

Marisa looked uneasy. "You have no proof that he's dead."

Hogan didn't have proof, but he had a bad feeling about Doctor Hernandez. "You're right, we haven't found the body yet, but I know how the cartel works and the only trail they leave behind are dead bodies. If they took Doctor Hernandez to question him, chances are good he's dead."

As far as Doctor Hernandez was concerned, Hogan had already finished sliding the puzzle pieces in place.

"Andre Rojer, the prison officer in charge of the night shift, went missing a few hours later. He was the person who approved Juan Carlos's transfer out of Bon Futuro . . . And now, your friend Tessa," Hogan said with a hint of regret. "I'm willing to bet she was also involved," he paused instinctively watching Marisa for a reaction.

Marisa focused on concealing the fear that was clawing at her gut. Her voice was tentative. "I wouldn't know," she said brushing her fingertips across her cheeks.

"Maybe it was a case of mistaken identity," Hogan offered. "But I've been doing this a long time . . . too long to ignore my gut. And it's telling me that your friend was in the middle of this. If it turns out she wasn't, then maybe she was in the wrong place at the wrong time because from the sound of it the cartel snatched her . . . If they did, it's because they think she had something to do with Juan Carlos's disappearance."

Marisa shook her head refusing to come to terms with the likelihood that her friend may already be dead. "You don't know that they have her."

Hogan shrugged at the obvious. "I know how the cartel works. Anyone who crosses them winds up dead." Hogan gave Marisa a grave look. "I don't believe in coincidences, and I think the men who took your friend work for the cartel."

Marisa closed her eyes and sat silently for a long time. When she finally opened them, her eyes were drowning in tears. She counted herself and her children among the lucky and realized that telling Hogan everything she knew was a small price for keeping her children safe.

Marisa looked at Hogan with her brown eyes and swallowed hard. "Tessa paid me to let someone ride along with me in the ambulance."

"Who," Hogan fired back.

Marisa felt guilt-ridden. "I don't know his real name. He was American. That I'm pretty sure of."

"What else can you tell me about him?" Hogan pressed.

Marisa sighed and thought for a few moments. "He's black, pretty tall and very muscular. He had long dreadlocks . . . Wait," she said, suddenly remembering something important. "I remember something more. He told me that he served in the U.S. Special Forces."

"Of course," Hogan sat back in his chair. This made Hogan wonder about who was behind Juan Carlos's escape. Hogan knew that freelancers as good as the ones who extracted Juan Carlos's out of Bon Futuro prison didn't come cheap.

"Any tattoos?" He asked.

"None that I can remember."

Hogan sorted through his memory for any recollection of any mercenaries he could think of who might fit Marisa's description.

"Anything else?" He asked.

"At the place where we dropped off the prisoner, there were two others."

"What can you tell me about them?"

"Not too much. One was a woman. She was also tall and blonde. She also seemed like she had military training. The other guy was white with a shaved head. I never spoke with him."

"What happened after you dropped Juan Carlos off?"

"They moved the guard to a trailer that was hitched to Tessa's jeep and put the dead bodies in the ambulance."

Hogan nodded. "What happened after you loaded the dead bodies in the ambulance?"

"Tessa drove the jeep and I followed her in the ambulance."

"Did any of the other people you mentioned leave in the jeep or the ambulance?"

"No, everyone else including Juan Carlos left in a separate car," Marisa said.

"About what time was that?"

Mentally drained, Marisa had to force herself to remember. "I think it was a little after one in the morning," she said.

Hogan was intrigued. "Did they mention if they were headed to the airport?"

Marisa shook her head slowly. "I don't recall them saying where they were going."

Hogan frowned. "Where did you go after you and Tessa left the others?"

"We drove to a clearing in the woods where Tessa set the ambulance on fire. That was when she told me that setting the fire with the dead bodies inside would hopefully trick the police into thinking Juan Carlos died in the ambulance. Tessa told me that it was all part of the plan to buy them as much time as possible while they got off the island."

Hogan marveled at the simplicity and intricacy of the escape plan. It took about thirty seconds for Marisa's detailed answer to come together for him, but when it did, Hogan was certain that Juan Carlos left the island on that late-night flight.

"Did you know when Tessa asked for your help that she was planning to help someone escape from Bon Futuro?"

Marisa buried her face in her hands. She didn't trust her voice when all she wanted to do was cry. Hogan still had a few lingering questions, but Marisa looked completely worn down. The last 24 hours had been emotionally draining and now faced with the possibility that her friend was murdered by the cartel was simply too much.

Marisa's tears fell hard, and she blew her nose on a tissue.

Hogan stood up and stepped towards Marisa, smoothed her hair and promised her that she and her children would remain under the protection of the United States government until it was safe for them to return home.

"You're exhausted. Go, get some sleep," he said. Marisa stood up to leave. As she moved across the room, she felt an aching sadness. Tentatively, she reached for the doorknob and turned. Marisa looked back at Hogan. She didn't say anything as she shut the door behind her, but Hogan could see the gratitude in her eyes.

Chapter Fifty

OKLAHOMA

Hugo and Mia rushed down the darkened hall towards the screams and sounds of something smashing against a wall and crashing to the floor.

"You sanctimonious bitch," Juan Carlos screamed.

A half empty bottle of whiskey rested on the fireplace mantle. Juan Carlos was standing over Alexis who lay at his feet writhing in pain. Blood flowed down her face. Hugo stopped at the doorway and assessed the scene in front of him. Mia acted without hesitation wedging herself in between Juan Carlos and Alexis. Dazed, Alexis batted her eyes trying to gain her bearings. All she could see out of her right eye was a blur, a red blur. Juan Carlos continued to scream obscenities at Alexis as she rolled on to her stomach and tried to crawl away from him. He tried to follow her, but Mia blocked his path. In a low threatening voice Juan Carlos warned Mia not to interfere.

"This is between me and my wife," he scowled.

Mia stood her ground unblinking. Juan Carlos's breath was hot; Mia could instantly smell the liquor. He looked back for the fireplace poker, but a second glance at Hugo caused him to reconsider. Instead, he reached for the bottle of whiskey and took another swig. Hugo tried to help Alexis to her feet. The blood from her nose ran into her mouth as she tried to speak.

"You don't understand what the fuck is going on . . . so get out of my way," Juan Carlos slurred his words trying to push past Mia to get to Alexis. Once again Mia stepped directly in front of him stopping his progress.

"You need to go sleep this off," Mia ordered Juan Carlos.

Juan Carlos turned on Mia baring his teeth like a snarling animal, "Don't fucking tell me what to do bitch."

Mia took a step back and held up her hands trying to show Juan Carlos that she wasn't challenging him. Secretly, she was hoping he'd make a move. "I'm not telling you what to do. I'm only suggesting that you get some rest so I can take care of your wife," Mia said calmly.

"Fuck that bitch," Juan Carlos yelled taking a heated step forward.

"Enough," Mia snapped angrily.

Juan Carlos gave Mia an incredulous look. Feeling like a trapped animal, this time he reached down and grabbed the cast iron poker.

"Now get the fuck out of my way," he sneered, brandishing the poker over his head in a threatening manner. Juan Carlos never saw Mia's fist until it landed deeply in his gut doubling him over into a fast approaching knee to his jaw. The cast iron rod fell out of his hand onto the floor. Juan Carlos screamed and took a wild swing, but Mia easily moved out of the way and delivered a devastating kick to his exposed knee cap. Juan Carlos tumbled awkwardly rolling on the floor in agony clutching his knee. Hugo rushed over and wrapped his arms around Mia.

"He's had enough," Hugo said forcefully.

Mia nodded, still breathing hard from the heat of the confrontation.

"I'm fine, you can let me go," she told Hugo.

"Are you sure?" Hugo asked before releasing his grip.

Mia's eyes burrowed in on Juan Carlos like a lioness in the middle of a hunt readying herself to pounce on her prey. "Yes," she snapped back. "Now go find Keeper and ask him to find you a place to sleep tonight. I'm going to keep Alexis with me," Mia said.

Hugo nodded.

"One more thing H," Mia said. "Please help Alexis to our room." Mia turned and looked intently at Alexis. "I'll be right there." Her expression told Alexis that she wasn't finished with Juan Carlos. Kneeling beside Juan Carlos, Mia made sure he heard her cock her gun. He opened his eyes to the feeling of steel pressed against his ribs. Mia leaned over as close to his ear as she could get and whispered. "If you ever touch her again, I will put a bullet in you."

Juan Carlos could feel her warm breath. "You can't . . . You are bought and paid for," he scowled defiantly.

Mia made a noise of disgust. "Listen up asshole you paid us to get you off the island safely. Services have been rendered. Put your hands on her again, and I will personally deliver you to Dario Carraboca in a body bag."

A look of annoyance flashed across Juan Carlos's face. "Careful. You have no idea who you're fucking with."

Mia pressed the gun harder into his ribcage. Juan Carlos winced. "Actually, I have a really good idea. You're a selfish scumbag who gets his rocks off hurting women. The point is I really don't give a shit whether you live or die. So, you'd better give a fuck about who I am because I'm the most dangerous bitch you'll ever meet."

Juan Carlos said nothing.

"It's really very simple. Keep your hands to yourself," Mia said unable to keep the loathing out of her voice.

Juan Carlos was strangely silent.

Mia stopped at the door and took stock of Juan Carlos. "Now clean yourself up or don't. But you have a date with Pierce in a few hours, and you better sing like your life depends on it because in your case it does," Mia said and shut the door behind her with a click.

Alexis stood over the bathroom sink washing off the dried blood from her face. She stared in the mirror barely recognizing herself. Her right eye had swollen almost completely shut and the white towel which Hugo wrapped ice in to keep the swelling down was stained a light shade of crimson. Outside the door it sounded like Mia and Hugo were having a discussion. A few minutes later Mia walked into the bathroom, she put her hand on Alexis' shoulder, a gesture to let her know that she was not alone.

"Thank you," Alexis nodded.

Mia gave her an exhausted smile. She asked Alexis what happened to cause Juan Carlos to lash out so violently. Alexis removed the cold compress from over her eye. A small trickle of blood formed at her eye duct.

"Juan Carlos wanted sex. When I refused he became violent."

Mia suddenly looked like she wanted to go back into the room and put an end to his abuse. She did not try to mask the anger in her voice.

"This isn't the first time he beat you, is it?"

Alexis glanced up looking genuinely ashamed. Her amber eyes looked stricken. "No, this wasn't the first time," she nodded.

"How long?" Mia frowned.

"Not too long," Alexis said, trying to retain a shred of dignity.

Mia didn't want to think it, but there was one thing that usually caused men to behave violently. She gave her a look of admonishment. "Are you having an affair with Pierce?"

Alexis read Mia's expression and said defensively, "My feelings for Pierce had nothing to do with it."

Mia arched a disbelieving eyebrow. "My, my," she murmured.

"Oh my God, Mia! You know Pierce better than that. He would never have an affair."

Mia took a moment and withdrew her query. "You're right. But even Superman has his Kryptonite. And it's hard not to notice the way he looks at you," she said.

Alexis tried not to give herself away. But she couldn't completely conceal that whisper of affection in her voice whenever she mentioned Pierce.

"There's nothing going on between us."

Mia wasn't completely buying Alexis's story. But she didn't care. She felt sorry for Alexis. There was a moment of silence and then Mia asked.

"Does Pierce make you happy?"

For a second Alexis forgot the blood in her mouth and ignored her pain. "I feel safe with him."

Mia understood exactly how Alexis felt. She took an extra second and then changed the subject back to Juan Carlos and the events that occurred earlier that evening.

"What happened when you refused to have sex with your husband?"

Alexis shook her head in disgust. "Please don't call him that."

"Sorry."

"I had never refused him anything before tonight. I don't think he knew how to react, so he just stood there for a moment and stormed out. When he came back, he stared at me and said nothing. I could tell that he had too much to drink."

Mia frowned. "Then what happened?"

"He called me a whore, punched me in the face and threw me against the wall. After that, everything became a blur," Alexis said in a thin and devastated tone.

"What a fucking animal," Mia seethed. She saw in Alexis a wariness that looked unsettlingly like a broken woman stripped of her self-esteem and all hope. That played heavily on Mia's mind, and she began to second guess herself.

Chapter Fifty-One

Shane Hamilton was boiling under the surface. The deep wrinkles running the length of his forehead closed together when Hugo gave Shane the rundown of the events that happened after he and Pierce left. Shane and Hugo grew up in a small town, where folks attended the high school football games on Friday nights. On Saturdays they rooted for the Oklahoma Sooners or Oklahoma State Cowboys but not both, unless the other school was playing Texas, and on Sunday, they worshipped God. If you broke a written law, you were punished by the local judge. As for the unwritten laws, it was simple, those you didn't break. But for those who did, punishment was severe and administered swiftly by your neighbors. One of those unwritten laws was that a man did not hit a woman. Shane's thick chest rose and sank slowly, and his eyes took on a squinting expression that Hugo knew only too well. It was the same look that Shane had when he cut the ring finger off of a New York City agent and threw it into a wheat field when the agent threatened to keep his client from performing in a Kansas honky-tonk unless Shane's client agreed to pay him an extra ten thousand dollars. Hugo also saw the same expression when Shane stormed past a police barricade and talked a childhood friend, who was armed and strung out on Crystal Meth, into letting his hostages go free. Shane looked like he wanted to do something in particular to Juan Carlos, but knew that he couldn't, so instead he folded his hands and played out scenarios in his mind.

He tapped the surface of the kitchen counter with his forefinger. "We can't let Pierce see Alexis until after we finish and send the video to Dario or this thing is going to unravel fast."

"One step ahead of you," Hugo said. "Keeper is going to take Alexis and Mia out on his boat."

Shane let out a long-exasperated exhale. "Since we're both thinking about it, I'm going to get rid of the white elephant in the room," he announced as if wrestling with a guilty conscience.

Hugo was having similar feelings and wanted nothing more than to beat the hell out of Juan Carlos.

"I know buddy. But it is what it is. So, we don't need to discuss it further."

Shane shook his head. "No, he needs to get his ass beat but circumstances being what they are . . ."

Hugo shrugged his shoulders equally appalled.

* * *

SHANE TOOK THE stairs three at a time to Juan Carlos's room. When he got to the door, he opened it and looked in. Juan Carlos was asleep in the middle of the bed clutching a pillow.

Shane peered into the darkness of the bedroom. "Juan, it's time," he said.

Juan Carlos barely stirred.

"Juan, it's time to get up," Shane shouted a little more forcefully.

"Go away."

"Can't do that if we're going to keep you alive."

Juan Carlos blinked groggily at Shane, and then he frowned. "What time is it?"

"It's five thirty in the morning."

Juan Carlos groaned. "Jesus, don't you think it's a little early?"

Shane wasn't listening. He turned on the bedroom light and looked at Juan Carlos as if he were something he found growing under the sink.

Juan Carlos reluctantly pulled himself to the edge of the bed. He exhaled heavily, too hung over to think or argue, "I'm up."

"There's coffee downstairs. Meet us in the kitchen in five minutes," Shane shot back.

Juan Carlos muttered something but not loud enough for Shane to hear him. His injured knee throbbed like a pulsating heart; the surrounding skin was so puffy his kneecap all but disappeared. Juan Carlos had no memory of his confrontation with Mia. He didn't know what happened to Alexis—those were missing parts of the evening. He did remember arguing with Alexis and drinking. The more he drank the more pissed off he got at her. But he couldn't remember what they fought about. Juan Carlos saw stars the instant he staggered off the bed and put his full weight on his left leg. Swaying over the toilet, his half lowered puffy eyes caught a glimpse of his reflection in the mirror above the sink. He didn't care much for what he saw as he fretfully grabbed at his love handles and bloated belly. And when he leaned in for a closer look, he pissed on his feet.

* * *

A few minutes later Juan Carlos wandered downstairs to the kitchen on shaky legs. Hugo and Shane were sitting at a table across from one another engaged in conversation and each drinking a cup of coffee. Juan Carlos entered the kitchen with the familiarity of a man walking into his own home.

"Good morning," Juan Carlos interrupted in a low gravelly voice.

Hugo instantly noticed the pained expression on his face as he stepped past them and poured himself a cup of coffee.

"Good morning," he replied with a satisfied smile.

Juan Carlos winced as he slid down into a chair at the kitchen table.

He mentioned that he didn't remember the previous night, but that wasn't true. Bits and pieces were coming back to him as the fog around his head began to lift. His stomach rumbled.

"Do we have anything to eat?" he asked.

Hugo shook his head. "Keeper went into town to get some donuts. He'll drop them by the guest house."

Hugo took a gulp of coffee before walking over to the refrigerator. "I saw a few yogurts in the fridge . . . Let's take them with us," he said, his tone was urgent. Hugo wanted to get out of the house before Mia came downstairs. Something inside of Mia snapped the previous evening. The murderous glint in her eyes after she sent Juan Carlos crashing to the floor in agony told Hugo that Mia wasn't done. If he hadn't been there to slow her down, giving her a few seconds to momentarily disengage and clear her head, Hugo wasn't sure what Mia would have done. The one feeling he was certain of was that at that moment, when Mia stopped Juan Carlos from attacking her and Alexis, it wouldn't have taken much more for her to put him down permanently.

When Mia served with Hugo as a special-forces commando, she was viewed as a bit of an enigma–tall, blond and very feminine, Mia did not look like someone who specialized in infiltrating enemy occupied areas and neutralizing terrorists. She was completely fluent in Dari and Pashto, the two major languages of Afghanistan as well as several of the dialects spoken in the regions. She was also well versed in the intricacies of the Afghani culture. Since Afghani culture does not permit women to interact with men in public, as the only female member of the Delta Force unit, Mia became integral in the counter-insurgency tactics that they deployed. The members of her unit drew the attention of the male villagers and children while Mia approached and spoke with women in villages believed to be supporting or under the control of the Taliban or Al-Qaeda. She was very adept at eliciting information concerning hidden locations of terrorist leaders and enemy activities. Mia was also equally careful not to appear to get too friendly with anyone, mindful that insurgents were always watching and would certainly notice. On raids, Mia typically volunteered to gather the women and children and watch over them. The combat and rescue missions gave Mia ample opportunity to indulge her strong protective instinct and desire to kill terrorists. Both were the most therapeutic things Mia had ever done in her life. Given Juan Carlos's bruised ego and Mia's quick temper, Hugo had a premonition that one sideways glance or a derisive remark and their exchange would ignite into something explosive.

Juan Carlos gave Hugo an odd look. "What's the rush? I've barely had any time to drink my coffee."

As if reading Hugo's mind, Shane moved to the kitchen door.

"Take your coffee with you. We have a lot of ground to cover today, so we need to get out of here and make this day count for something."

Shane's lips split into what passed for a smile as Juan Carlos struggled to get up from the chair.

* * *

JUAN CARLOS FOLLOWED a few steps behind them down the grassy slope towards the guest house. To Juan Carlos, it felt more like he was traveling down a tunnel with a blinding white light. He had no idea how the events would ultimately unfold. What he was sure of was that Dario Carraboca was not a man that easily capitulated to leverage. He was the most ruthless, lethal and diabolical assassin in the world. Astute and patient, Dario would not immediately kill Juan Carlos if it threatened to make the cartel vulnerable to law enforcement agencies. Under those circumstances, Dario would reluctantly accept the terms of Pierce's deal. However, he would instantly devote an extraordinary amount of the cartel's resources and manpower towards eliminating the threat posed by Pierce. How much time Pierce's plan bought Juan Carlos depended on how long it would take for Dario to neutralize the threat. Once he succeeded and the video no longer presented a danger, Dario would move to kill him, and everyone involved. He was certain that Dario would respond in this manner because Dario trained him and that's exactly what he would do. Living on borrowed time was the game Juan Carlos was playing with the cartel. He suspected that Pierce, Shane, Mia and Hugo would all die horribly. While a heavy price to pay, Juan Carlos was willing to sacrifice them all if it bought him a year or two. Dario would kill them first because they would be easier to find. Like the proverbial canary in the coal mine, their deaths would serve as a warning to him that it was time to make a deal with the DEA. At that point in time, Juan Carlos realized that he would be out of options and would have no choice but to give up his garish and hedonistic life for a bleak existence under the witness protection program.

Chapter Fifty-Two

Juan Carlos's rise through the ranks of the cartel from someone who started out by waiting in the open sea to retrieve time released buoys attached to drug shipments to one of Dario Caraboca's most trusted advisors was unprecedented and meteoric. The fact that Juan Carlos was not Venezuelan did not stop him from earning a place in the cartel's inner circle. He got his first exposure to the financial side of drug trafficking when his childhood friend, Rene, asked if he could help him out of a bind and launder a modest amount of drug profits through his family's appliance export business. Money fascinated Juan Carlos. He loved everything about it from making it to the high roller lifestyle it afforded him. When it came to business, Juan Carlos Laporte was a savant. Like any exceptionally gifted prodigy, Juan Carlos needed an outlet for his talents, and Rene supplied it. With Rene's support, Juan Carlos was given the chance to develop elegant paper fronts to funnel profits from the cartel's Miami operations. Soon those business models were utilized by the cartel to move money along the entire east coast of the United States. It took Juan Carlos just two years to rise from a small business operator to a millionaire and three more to get Dario Caraboca's attention. Before Juan Carlos put his stamp on the cartel, it predominantly used banks in Latin America to launder money. Juan Carlos changed how the cartel did business. As far as Juan Carlos was concerned, the sale of drugs was not significantly different from the sale and distribution of any commodity. To expand the cartel's operation, it needed an efficient and dependable supply chain. He was not ignorant to the fact that the cartel's particular commodity was illegal. But to Juan Carlos, that didn't change the business model he needed to put in place to be successful. It simply presented a few wrinkles. Once he began to implement his business model, the days of dropping drugs in an uninhabited desert by plane and using GPS locators on the ground to find the shipments came to an end.

* * *

Juan Carlos stopped concentrating the cartel's deposits in Latin American banks and started targeting banks outside of Latin America that he could control as well as those patronized by the CIA. The CIA was no different than the cartel; they were both engaged in covert activities. Those banks that funneled money for the CIA to fund their operations had the people and systems in place to meet the cartel's needs. He moved the cartel's deposits from banks the U.S. had under investigation to banks they couldn't or wouldn't target. Using this business model, it only took Juan Carlos six years to fully integrate the cartel's drug profits into the global banking system.

* * *

The cartel's profits totaled $20 billion annually and were now processed through Deutshe Bank in Europe, J.P Morgan Chase in the United States, HSBC Bank in the United Kingdom and Industrial and Commercial Bank of China. The Carraboca Cartel owned controlling shares in major banks and multinational corporations. It became impossible for anyone to distinguish the cartel's money from the normal workings of finance capital.

* * *

Sitting behind a desk inside a small cubicle, Juan Carlos waited for Pierce to give him the signal to begin. While he waited, Juan Carlos downloaded decryption software necessary to access a private account that he maintained in a cloud storage service that offered client-side encryption. Juan Carlos's account contained detailed information concerning all the cartel's financial holdings. Every bank and brokerage account and password were listed. The laptop computer was synced to the large monitor to Juan Carlos's left so that the information on the laptop was displayed and easy to see. Juan Carlos took his time describing each account, the bank officers in charge of the account and the various sources and activities which funneled money into the account. Pierce sat behind the camera out of view, but every so often he asked Juan Carlos a question picking up on a particular point or requesting that he elaborate on a specific piece of information. It took several hours for Juan Carlos to identify every cartel bank and brokerage account. When he was finished, Juan Carlos listed all the companies and financial operations controlled by the cartel. He laid out extremely complicated flow charts which illustrated how ownership and profits trickled up to the Carraboca Cartel. Juan Carlos illustrated how the number of intermediate shelf companies and asset protection measures he put in place between any particular operation and the cartel made it impossible for bank regulators in charge of monitoring operations to find anything that violated regulations concerning money laundering. Juan Carlos created an elaborate business model to provide the banks with legal cover. However, he suspected that most of them would have taken the Cartel's 20 billion in annual profits even if the money had been wired in from Dario Carraboca himself. Juan Carlos next pulled up and displayed the addresses of the warehouses and safe houses in North America, Europe, Asia, Australia and Africa where cash and drugs were stored.

Juan Carlos had been talking for most of the morning without a break. As he tried to remember particular facts, he began to realize that his mind wasn't engaging as quickly as it had been a few hours earlier. Looking past the camera, Juan Carlos raised his index finger and slid it across his throat signaling Pierce to stop recording.

"I need to stop, my mind is mush," he declared.

Pierce nodded. "Take a break and get something to eat. We'll pick it back up in an hour."

Juan Carlos shook his head. "An hour isn't enough time. I'm spent. Let's start again in the morning. I'll do better with some proper rest."

"We have to finish today." Pierce's tone was sympathetic but still unyielding.

Juan Carlos took a deep breath and let out a frustrated moan. "We have a little time. There's no need to rush."

Pierce stared back at him, not entirely enthralled with his lack of urgency. "We don't have any time to spare. You have to assume that the DEA and the cartel both know by now that you got out of Curacao on that jet that took off for Florida in the middle of the night. Both will be working non-stop and using every resource at their disposal to find you."

"True, but your team did a good job in covering our tracks." Juan Carlos's voice was calm, almost flirtatious.

"We covered your tracks. We didn't eliminate them," Hugo interjected. "Up to this point we've managed to stay one step ahead of the DEA and the cartel, now would not be the time . . ."

"I don't think one more day to make sure that we don't leave anything important out of the video is going to make any difference," Juan Carlos snapped defensively.

Hugo's jaw dropped. "We don't have days; we have hours to pull this off."

Pierce agreed. "Twenty-four hours could be the difference between Dario feeling he has no choice but to accept our terms or stalling for time if he feels he's getting close."

Juan Carlos made a face. "We are in the middle of fucking nowhere! I doubt that either the DEA or Dario will be looking for us anywhere near this time zone in the next 48 hours," he scoffed.

Hugo's tone hardened instantly. "It really won't take them long to figure out that you took a flight to Dallas."

"Ok, but we're not in Dallas," Juan Carlos conceded.

Pierce managed a smile. "No, we're not in Dallas. But once they track you there and confirm through security surveillance that you didn't board another flight, they will make it impossible for you to fly out of any international airport within 1000 miles of Dallas."

"They will cut off your means of escape and use traffic cameras to tighten the noose," Hugo chimed in.

Juan Carlos had fallen silent. Pierce hoped he'd refocus his energies on the task at hand since they were working with an incredibly small window of time.

"I understand, but I'm afraid that as the day goes on, I'm going to forget to talk about a few things . . . important things," Juan Carlos stressed.

Pierce expected him to become more forgetful as he wore down. "You've already covered the financial part. When we come back, we'll have you start pinpointing the main smuggling routes. After that we'll go as long as you can. It's more important that we finish today and run with whatever we have."

Pierce looked at Juan Carlos with a hardened determination brought on by his intense desire to protect Alexis. "You put your trust in me to get you out of prison and somewhere safe. Let me do my job."

Juan Carlos sat back down behind the desk, folded his hands and sighed.

"Have someone bring me a sandwich, a carafe of coffee, a couple of aspirin and a pack of cigarettes," he exhaled.

* * *

When they resumed taping, Juan Carlos sorted through his computer files and typed in specific longitude and latitude coordinates into a Global Positioning System to locate random spots in the middle of the deserts and hills where the tunnels used to smuggle drugs into Texas and California were located.

"The cartel's fastest and most efficient system for smuggling drugs into the United States was the tube freight transportation system." Juan Carlos explained that the cartel developed strategic alliances with the Sinaloa and Gulf cartels to develop two fully automated underground tube systems that transported high volumes of drugs in unmanned capsules from warehouse terminals in Mexico through underground tunnels to terminals near San Diego and San Antonio.

"Sort of like a pneumatic tube you see in a drive-thru at a bank where you put your checks in a clear container and it gets carried up to the bank teller," Hugo interjected, sounding intrigued.

Juan Carlos exhaled patiently. "Conceptually, yes but the system used to transport the drugs from Mexico to the U.S. is far more sophisticated. For instance, the system you described uses compressed air to move the tube. The cartel's capsules are propelled by linear induction motors which are much faster and far more reliable, he said.

"How much product could you move through the tubes?" Hugo asked.

Juan Carlos gripped his coffee mug and wondered how many more distractions he would have to endure.

"The tube is about 3 feet in diameter. Each capsule can carry about 2,000 pounds of product and travels at a speed of about 60 miles per hour. Practically speaking this system can move more product than a boat or airplane can."

Hugo looked mystified. "I'm curious how the cartel was able to bury the lines in the U.S.?"

An uneasiness crossed Juan Carlos's face. Pierce sensed that Juan Carlos was becoming increasingly agitated by Hugo's questions which added little to the information that he needed to put into the video. "How the system worked is not important. What's important is the locations of the terminals," Juan Carlos grunted before exhaling a raspy beleaguered breath. "Most of the excavation of the pipelines was done in rural areas. Work crews typically had permits for repairing water lines or installing fiber optic cable."

Hugo looked unsettled. He was having a difficult time believing that the cartel could construct such an intricate system on U.S. soil without the government having any knowledge. Pierce was wondering the same thing. Hugo started to ask another question, but this time Pierce did not let him finish his thought.

"Can you show us the locations of the terminals in Mexico and in the United States?" Pierce asked.

Juan Carlos proceeded to identify the companies and displayed the addresses of each of the terminals on the monitor. Accessing the Global Positioning System software on the internet, Juan Carlos also displayed satellite photos of the transportation system terminals.

When he was finished identifying all the smuggling routes and operations, Juan Carlos lit a cigarette and poured himself another cup of coffee.

Next, Juan Carlos began to identify the individuals who did business with or collaborated with the cartel. The names included government officials, law enforcement personnel and members of terrorist organizations.

Shane shifted uncomfortably while Hugo whispered under his breath a dozen well punctuated curses, and then he threw in a few more for good measure.

"Are you sure about those names?" Hugo asked. His voice was beginning to take on an edge. "There are a few on there that have direct access to the President."

Juan Carlos took a long pull on his cigarette and exhaled a cloud of smoke into the lights above the desk.

"Yes, I'm sure."

Juan Carlos broke down the list of names, describing which government officials were on the cartel's payroll and those which did not work directly for the cartel but had been paid to perform a discrete task such as obtaining highly classified information. Hugo and Pierce listened with stunned attentiveness until he was finished.

It took Pierce only a brief moment to realize that the DEA would never be able to protect Juan Carlos and Alexis. A few of the names identified by Juan Carlos were high ranking government officials which he assumed had top secret security clearances, which meant that they were cleared to see almost anything, including the new identities and locations of individuals in the witness protection program. Without exposing the names of those officials, Pierce had a sinking feeling that the DEA would not be able to prevent Juan Carlos's new identity and location from being leaked to the cartel. Glancing back over the powerful positions held by some of the people on the list, Pierce wasn't sure that a purge was even possible. It was all starting to make sense to him why Juan Carlos blindly put his life in his hands. Juan Carlos knew that he had no other choice.

Chapter Fifty-Three

FORT LAUDERDALE

In Fort Lauderdale, Hogan's task force had swelled into a veritable army of federal agents. Dozens of law enforcement personnel assigned to provide tactical support scrutinized the data assembled from the vast network of video surveillance cameras watching the surrounding highways, airports, bus and train terminals. Hogan was in the middle of sifting through a stack of documents when he heard a knock and turned to see a young agent standing in the doorway.

"Pardon me sir, but we have confirmation that the asset boarded a flight in Boca Raton bound for Dallas."

Hogan turned around encouraged. Up until that point in time all he knew was that Juan Carlos landed in Fort Lauderdale and then disappeared. Hogan had been alerted by several confidential informants that there were already people on the streets and freelance teams made up of former CIA looking for Juan Carlos. That could only mean that the cartel also knew about the flight that left Curacao in the middle of the night bound for Fort Lauderdale.

The agent explained that one of the airport's security cameras got a picture of the license plate leaving Fort Lauderdale airport. The license plate was registered to a local car rental company. The DEA agents utilized the car rental company's GPS tracking system to find the car parked at Boca Raton airport.

"The target is still travelling with the same two men. We have them on surveillance going through the Boca Raton airport," the agent added.

"Do you have photographs of the men travelling with Mr. Laporte with you?" Hogan asked.

The agent nodded as he handed Hogan a folder. Inside he found a stack of surveillance photographs. Hogan glanced at the pictures before passing them one at a time to the agents sitting around the table.

Looking over the top of his reading glasses he said, “Send the images ahead to Dallas. Have our people begin dissecting all the airport’s surveillance footage.”

Hogan remembered Marisa telling him that there was also a woman at the rendezvous point in Curacao.

“One more thing,” Hogan said.

“Yes sir,” the agent stood rigid waiting on Hogan.

“Did you happen to see a woman traveling with them?” Hogan asked.

The agent thought for a moment before nodding. “That’s very possible sir. There was a woman who passed through customs shortly after the target.”

Hogan clenched and then flexed his hands in agitation.

Collins who was sitting closest to the door thought he knew what was coming, so he slid his chair back a bit to get out of the way.

“Then why wasn’t her picture included in the file?” Hogan’s face twisted into a scowl.

The agent’s face turned a touch ashen. He looked across at Collins and the other agents sitting around the table. Every one of them averted the young agent’s gaze. Before he could respond, Hogan cut him off.

“Have a forensic team sweep the car for prints and run their photographs . . . including the woman’s . . .” he said with a healthy dose of irritation in his voice, “through our facial recognition software and every database and let’s see if we can I.D. them.”

The young agent managed to compose himself just long enough to add a pathetic nod. “Yes sir.”

The rest of the agents sitting in the room began powering down their laptops and packing up as they prepared to leave for Dallas. Collins lingered behind while the others left the conference room.

Hogan hunched over and examined the pictures, palms flat on the table and brow furrowed. "What's bothering me," Hogan pushed his glasses up on his nose "is that nothing about this makes any sense. Why would Juan Carlos decide to run only to hide in our backyard?"

Collins nodded his head in agreement. "You'd think Juan Carlos would go anywhere but here."

For almost a minute, Hogan didn't speak. His mind filtering through all the possibilities. "They didn't arbitrarily pick Dallas. There's a reason they're still in this country . . ." The more Hogan thought about it, the more he wondered. The only thing that he was reasonably confident about was that the people who orchestrated Juan Carlos's escape were true professionals skilled beyond question. They would not pull off such an elegant extraction only to put themselves somewhere where the DEA or the cartel could easily pin them in. "Whatever it is that brought them there, they're not going to stay there long. From everything we've learned so far, these guys are pro's . . . they'll keep moving."

Collins nodded in agreement.

Hogan realized that he needed to learn as much as he could about the men in the photographs and the woman as quickly as possible and connect one of them to the Southwest before Juan Carlos disappeared again. Hogan looked harrowed as he appeared to wrestle with his thoughts.

"We'll find them," Collins told him because he felt he needed to say something supportive. Hogan didn't respond. He didn't need a motivational pep talk.

Collins stared at Hogan's tired face. "What are you thinking?" he asked.

Hogan let out a deep breath. "Questions . . . I have a bunch of questions running through my mind; unfortunately, I've got only hunches and theories and no clear-cut answers."

Collins had worked with a lot of men and women throughout his career, and no one came close to having Hogan's intuition.

"So we follow your hunches. They have gotten us this far."

Hogan slid the photographs into a folder and with a terse nod of his head asked Collins to follow him. When they were outside of the building, Hogan led Collins to a Cuban restaurant just around the corner on East Oakland Park Boulevard.

"Have you ever tried Cuban coffee?"

Collins shook his head. "A few times."

Hogan ordered two Cuban coffees and carried the small white ceramic cups to a table.

Collins observed Hogan with a practiced eye. The way Hogan gave his coffee a violent stir told him that something else was troubling him. The fact that they were sitting in a Cuban restaurant when the rest of the team was busy preparing for Dallas could only mean that whatever was eating at Hogan was something he didn't feel comfortable talking about in the office.

"Lloyd I've known you a lot of years. I can tell when something is bugging you," Collins pressed.

Hogan peered into his coffee for a moment. He couldn't shake a sense of unease. "A leak," he said, his tone disdainful. "I think that someone in the Agency is funneling sensitive information to the cartel."

Collins rolled his eyes in an exaggerated gesture. "Occupational hazard with your agency," he replied arrogantly.

Hogan grunted. "When you have the kind of money the cartel has, you can buy access and cooperation from anyone. The Pentagon included."

Collins folded his arms across his chest. "You have anything concrete to go on, or is this a case of professional paranoia?"

Hogan arched a disapproving eyebrow at Collins. He remembered every detail of a top-secret investigation that had inexplicably gone wrong and resulted in the brutal murders of two confidential informants.

"About six years ago I was working on an investigation. I had information from very reliable sources regarding the time and place of a very large shipment of drugs. The freighter docked in Port Everglades when my informants said it would. But there were no drugs on board. Instead, in the container where the drugs were supposed to be were both of my informants burned alive with their heads cut off. The bodies were deliberately left there to send me a message."

Hogan let out an exasperated breath. "I suspected that the cartel had inside help. They wanted me to know that they would always be one step ahead."

Collins finished swallowing his coffee. His voice bit with a tight military efficiency.

"If you're right about the leak, the cartel knows by now that Juan Carlos landed in Dallas." Collins continued to move the pieces into place. "If this guy Juan Carlos knows as much as you say he does about the cartel's operations, you can expect them to come to the party with a lot of fire power."

Hogan bobbed his head agreeing with him and said, "Precisely . . . this could turn out to be a bloodbath."

Collins acknowledged the warning with a crisp nod as he whipped out his cell phone. When he got Agent Roy on the phone, Collins said,

"Make sure everyone on the team is bringing full battle-rattle to the party. I'm talking tactical vests, body armor, goggles and MP-5s."

Chapter Fifty-Four

When Juan Carlos finished providing a detailed accounting of the part Dario Carraboca played in helping the Gulf and Sinaloa cartels infiltrate the Mexican Federal government and military to destroy the other cartels, Juan Carlos leaned back in his chair and reignited a half-smoked cigarette. He was satisfied that the video testimony he had just given would severely cripple the cartel's operations and possibly ignite a war with the Mexican cartels if it was ever released.

Before Juan Carlos could open his mouth to utter another word, Pierce, to everyone's surprise, walked around and stared directly into the camera. Juan Carlos's face was a combination of shock and wonder. He started to slowly rise from his chair, but Pierce laid a hand on his shoulder and gestured to him to stay seated.

"This is fucking madness," Shane muttered under his breath staring at Pierce's face, looking for twitchy-eyed indicators that he had lost his mind. Pierce looked over at Shane, his blue eyes resplendently sane. He was clearly in control of his faculties and was fully aware of what he was doing. Pierce intended to send Dario a message; one that he would not misinterpret or soon forget. Hugo could feel himself leaning forward in his seat. He sharpened his eyes on Pierce, as though he thought he was hallucinating. He wasn't sure if Pierce was on a suicide mission or trying to improve their chances of success. Dario needed to be convinced that if he did not agree to the terms, Pierce would not hesitate to release the video link to law enforcement and the Mexican cartels at the appointed time. Pierce reasoned that the best way for Dario to regard the threat to the cartel as real was for Dario to be able to look into the eyes of the man who would push the button and let all hell break loose. When Pierce began to deliver the terms, his voice was remarkably firm and calm.

"Mr. Carraboca. This video will remain confidential and in safekeeping as long Juan Carlos Laporte and his wife, along with their families, remain safe and unharmed. By now, I assume that you have learned the identities of the people responsible for helping Juan Carlos. The second condition is that there be no retaliation against any of them."

Pierce stepped forward cutting the distance between him and the camera.

"If any harm should happen to come to any of these people, I will immediately release the video to the DEA and INTERPOL."

Pierce held up a cell phone. "This is an encrypted cell phone. The number is displayed on the monitor to my left. I will turn the phone on tomorrow at 9:30 A.M. Eastern Standard Time. You have until 10 A.M. to contact me with your answer. If I do not hear from you, I will assume that we do not have an agreement and make a deal with the DEA."

When he was finished, Pierce walked around the desk over to the video camera and turned it off.

"That's a wrap," he said trying to lighten the suddenly somber mood. For a moment the faces in the room simply looked at each other in curious silence trying to make sense of what had just happened. A little frown of panic appeared in the gap between Shane's eyes which he tried, without success, to force away.

"What the fuck did you just do?"

Pierce could tell that, unlike Hugo and Juan Carlos, there was no flicker of understanding in Shane's eyes.

"I did what needed to be done."

Pierce immediately regretted his offhand remark and tried to rephrase it. Before he could utter another word, Juan Carlos jumped into the conversation. He looked as if Shane had asked an idiotic question.

"That's the trouble with you Harvard Boys; textbook smart but so fucking stupid when it comes to everything else. You asked what the fuck did he just do . . . I'll tell you. He saved your lives! That's what he did," Juan Carlos's voice boomed.

A number of smart remarks occurred to Shane, but he decided not to make any of them. Instead, he thought about what Juan Carlos had just said. Eventually Shane's eyes went to Pierce. Pierce could feel Hugo staring at him too, with the same expression of disappointment.

"Next time you decide to be a hero," Shane said calmly, "a little advance warning would be appreciated. We're in this together."

Pierce smiled. It was a smile that moved no part of his face other than his lips, and those only twisted slightly. It was a look that suggested that there was nothing to discuss.

"It was something that needed to be done if Dario was going to take the threat seriously. You would have tried to talk me out of it."

Shane's eyes tightened. "With good reason; up until now you were only Juan Carlos's lawyer. There was nothing connecting you to his disappearance."

"That would not have stopped Dario from coming after him," Juan Carlos interjected dismissively.

Pierce frowned. "No one knows for sure what Dario will do." Then he looked Shane in the eyes. "You, Hugo and Mia have already risked too much. I was simply trying to balance the scales."

Hugo shook his head. "There are no scales to balance when it comes to Dario. I understand why you felt you had to do what you did. If Dario takes the deal, we'll never know if your stunt was the difference maker." Hugo's eyebrows shot up. "But if he doesn't . . . I don't think I need to spell it out."

Juan Carlos nodded. "Dario has no choice but to accept the terms. Trust me . . ."

Shane cut Juan Carlos off. "Trust you? Why would we do that? You were one of Dario Carraboca's boys, and here we are in this mess because you betrayed him." Shane's tone was acid.

"And you are ten million dollars richer because of it." Juan Carlos reacted with a noise of disgust.

Shane flushed but said nothing. He avoided looking at Pierce.

Any other time Pierce might have been bothered by Shane's last-minute attempt to squeeze a few more dollars out of Juan Carlos, but not this time. Shane and the others had risked much so Pierce chose to ignore the comment.

"What time can we meet the IT engineer at the casino?" Pierce asked Hugo.

Hugo turned his wrist up and looked at the time. "They are ready for us now. All we need to do is swing by the house and pick up Keeper. He should be back by now," Hugo said.

"All right, let's go," Pierce said as he grabbed the laptop computer, the video camera and slipped out of the guest house.

Chapter Fifty-Five

"Wait here," Keeper told Hugo and Pierce as he walked through two heavy oak doors with a sign which read "*Casino Employees Only*". Keeper walked down a long corridor to a large frosted glass door. The security guard recognized him and pressed a code unlocking the door. The main security room bristled with banks of high-tech video surveillance monitors which displayed every angle of the casino. Keeper spotted Simon Tiger the head of security, a bulky leathery faced man whose normal expression possessed a hint of a scowl. The earpiece hidden discreetly behind his ear made him look like the U.S. Secret Service. Simon stood like a statute with his arms crossed as he watched a young man at the Blackjack table on one of the monitors. He had been keeping an eye on the bet levels to see if he was dramatically altering his bets after a run of low cards came out of the deck.

"Heschi Estonko," Keeper said, greeting Simon in Creek.

"Here Mahe Keeper," Simon's eyes flicked towards Keeper and then back to the monitor. His eyes bore into the monitor giving the impression that he was looking for something in particular.

"Card Counter?" Keeper asked.

Simon's voice was disarmingly hushed for such a large man, barely a whisper. "He didn't come up on our facial recognition software. But he's been winning big for a while now, so I wanted to take a closer look."

"Anything suspicious jump out at you?"

Simon shook his head. "He took a call about a minute ago on his cell phone and took his eyes off the table when the dealer was dealing cards. So, I don't see how he could have been keeping a running count. He's just having a good day . . . It happens from time to time."

Suddenly, Simon remembered why Keeper was there.

“Are your people here? He asked him.

Keeper nodded. “I left them by the door that leads to the back of the house.”

Simon maneuvered the computer mouse to switch cameras to one that monitored the area directly in front of the doorway leading to the back of the house. He sized up Hugo and Pierce for a moment before speaking.

“Are these your guys?” He asked dryly.

Keeper glanced over at the monitor. “Yes, that’s them.”

Simon radioed one of the security guards on the casino floor to escort the two men standing next to the employee entrance to the security office. Simon and Keeper watched the guard on camera carrying a clipboard as he strode over to Hugo and Pierce.

“You don’t need to sign them in,” Simon spoke into the radio. It occurred to him that he didn’t want any evidence that they were ever in the secured area of the casino.

Simon walked them over to a door and punched a code into the cipher lock beside the door. At the sound of the lock being released, Simon patted Keeper on the shoulder. “The IT department is at the end of this hallway. Good luck.” Simon said. His tone suggested that the Chief’s request would not sit well with Dode Alexander, the director of the IT Department, and he wanted no part of it. Keeper picked up on the meaning behind Simon’s comment.

“Yes, thanks we can get there from here.”

Compared to some of the chief’s other requests, this one was bland, but it still violated at least three of the casino’s operating protocols and Dode ran her department with an iron fist. The Chief and the Director of Casino operations gave her a wide berth because when it came to computers and operating systems, Dode knew what she was doing. She had a master's degree in computer science from Georgia Tech. After graduation, Dode worked for the International Bank of Commerce for ten years where she focused on computer-based fraud and preventing cyber-geeks from hacking into the bank's computer system. When the Director of IT position became available at her tribe's casino, the lure of coming back home was too strong to ignore.

Upon hearing unfamiliar voices coming from the corridor, Dode removed her reading glasses, spun in her chair away from her computer, and waddled out of her office into the hallway. The first thing she did was raise her hand up and stop the group leaving them in no-man's land.

Keeping her voice down but her intensity extremely high, Dode hissed, "Keeper, you know better than to bring people back here. This area is off limits."

Keeper retreated two steps. "Simon told us we could come back and see you. The Chief thought you might be able to help my friends." Dode rolled her eyes when Keeper mentioned the Chief.

"How much is the Chief's hospitality costing you this time?" Dode laughed without humor. Keeper shrugged and shook his head. Just then she caught a glimpse of Pierce. His chiseled features, thick eyelashes and dazzling blue eyes initially took her by surprise. Dode wasn't accustomed to seeing men that looked like Pierce wander through her hallway. In fact, Dode wasn't used to seeing men with Pierce's good looks anywhere.

Pierce and Dode exchanged a look. "It's a pleasure to meet you," Pierce said, extending his hand.

His voice was so rich and masculine that it made Dode shiver. She briskly acknowledged Hugo before turning her complete and unabashed attention back to Pierce.

"We need to send an email that is anonymous so that it . . ."

"It is completely untraceable," Dode said, finishing Keeper's thought.

"Can you do that?" Keeper asked.

Dode barely spared a glance at Keeper staring at Pierce while she spoke.

"Yes, I can do it, but we are not supposed to use our servers for anything other than running the games and supporting the casino's operations," she said.

Keeper started to explain to Dode that the chief had already authorized her to send the email when he felt Pierce's grip on his shoulder.

"The chief was gracious enough to offer your help. And we could really use it. If you'd like to call the Chief and confirm that he sent us over to see you, I'd understand," Pierce smiled at Dode. It was a self-deprecating smile that changed his ruggedness to something close to movie star handsome.

"That won't be necessary. I believe you," Dode batted her eyes. She couldn't remember ever batting her eyes at someone as handsome as Pierce.

Keeper, who had known Dode since she was in diapers, opened his mouth in disbelief. Hugo discreetly nudged Keeper and grinned at him. His expression suggested that this sort of reaction happened frequently when Pierce was involved.

Dode led them through a large room with a raised floor designed to manage and segregate large volumes of wires, fiber optic cables and other distribution systems. The room had a sophisticated climate control system which maintained the temperature at fifty-eight degrees. The room was filled with rows of tall black towers which warehoused the computer server network. This was the casino's nerve center. In a room adjacent to the network, programmers sat and monitored every aspect of the casino's operations from every bet placed in each slot machine and table game, to tracking the spending habits of every customer. The operation looked like a cross between a network news control room and an air traffic control tower. Behind that was a smoked glass office which allowed Dode to maintain a careful watch on everything that went on.

Pierce asked Dode how she was able to send an email that could not be traced to the casino.

"We can make the email untraceable by combining an anonymity application with anonymous remailers," she said.

Dode gave a slight shrug. "The anonymity application is really nothing more than a software application that allows you to access a network anonymously. What makes the message untraceable is the anonymous remailers."

Keeper nodded vaguely. "What exactly is an anonymous remailer?"

"It's a server like the ones we have here at the casino. I attach embedded instructions in the email on where to send the email. The server forwards the email to another remailer without revealing where it originally came from. The message then gets sent from one anonymous remailer to another to different jurisdictions around the world before it ends up at its intended address."

"Assuming that they could track the message, where would it take them?" Keeper asked.

"To the first remailer, the first server to receive our message is where the trail ends. They can't track it back to us," Dode said.

Keeper gave Dode a sideways look. "Humor me for a second," he interjected. "Are you saying they cannot track the email beyond the first remailer?"

Dode nodded. "That's exactly what I'm saying. The code that I write for the initial remailer appears as if the email originated there."

"Can you send the message several times? Each time sending the message to a different initial remailer so that each trail ends up at a different part of the world?" Pierce asked.

"Sure," Dode nodded. "But you're pretty safe with just one email."

Pierce wore a curious expression. "Let me ask you this . . . If you received the same email from several different email addresses located all over the world what would you think?"

Dode didn't have to think about Pierce's question very long. "I'd think that the sender was sending me a message that they took precautions to cover their tracks."

Pierce ran his hand through his hair. "Precisely, if the recipient of the email realizes from the very beginning that we went to great lengths to cover our tracks, they will hopefully focus on the contents of the email instead of wasting time trying to find where it originated from."

Dode liked the way his hair caught the light, then fell slightly out of place.

"Smart and pretty," she giggled under her breath.

Pierce powered up the laptop and opened the file containing Juan Carlos's video.

"This is the file that we need to send." Pierce handed Dode a sheet of paper. "And this is the email address that the video needs to be sent to."

"Okay, it will take me a few minutes to set up the anonymity application, write the code and transmit it to the anonymous remailers," she said.

Sitting at her computer, Dode typed a series of commands that allowed her to bypass the authentication protocol of the casino's servers. When she was done, she set up the anonymous account and uploaded the video to her computer. She double clicked on the icon and in nanoseconds pages with columns containing endless strings of numbers and letters strung together appeared on her computer screen.

Keeper leaned over Dode's shoulder to get a closer look. "What are those?"

"The I.P addresses to the anonymous remailers around the world," she said.

Dode typed at a furious pace, entering commands and prompts while she continued to explain how the process was going to work. "The first email is being sent to a server in Malaysia. From there it going to a different address registered under a different name to Reykjavik; from there to another address and name in Sao Paulo, then Tokyo, Los Angeles, Cape Town, London and New York before it ends up at this address," she said pointing the email address on the piece of paper Pierce handed her. Dode looked at Pierce and said, "Several copies of the same email are going to be sent, each appearing to originate from a different account located at a different offshore address."

When she was finished, she leaned back in her chair and stretched her arms over her head. Her gaze flicked to Pierce.

"We're ready to send," she said waiting for final confirmation.

Pierce tensed for a split second. His legs suddenly felt rubbery as he realized that once Dode pressed down on the button, they were about to find out if they could make one of the most powerful and ruthless killers in the world blink.

"Send it," Pierce said. His voice was steadier than his insides.

Dode winked at Pierce. "BOOM, it's done."

Hugo eyed Dode confused. "You just sent it once. I thought you were going to send it several times."

"I did. The recipient is getting twelve identical emails, all coming from different parts of the world."

"And, none of them can be tracked here?" Keeper asked, wanting one more assurance that nothing would come back to his tribe.

Dode let out a small laugh that said what she thought about the question. "Nope, as far as our servers are concerned, those emails don't exist. Nothing in those emails connects to our I.P. addresses. The trails will grow cold at each of the first anonymous remailers."

Dode slipped Pierce her business card. "I set up an anonymous account on a cloud-based server and parked your video file there for you. The login code and temporary password are on the back of my card."

Pierce's eyes lit up. "Thank you."

Depending on how Dario responded, Pierce thought he might need few additional safeguards in case Dario decided to double-cross him. "Can I call you tomorrow and possibly swing by to see you? I'd like you to help me with one more thing," he asked.

"Sure," Dode purred flirtatiously. "You can use me any way you want to."

Chapter Fifty-Six

VENEZUELA

Everything has a predetermined end and begins to die the moment it is created. This is what Dario Carraboca believed. Apart from the obvious reasons, this was why Juan Carlos's video deeply troubled him. It gave him a glimpse into the future. The actions he took this morning would either delay or hasten the cartel's fall, but regardless of the decision he made, Dario suspected that the video could one day lead to the collapse of his empire. He knew that unless the video was destroyed, the day would come when it fell into the hands of someone with the power and resources to use the information in it to cripple his operations.

* * *

Skeins of rain as fine as angel hair tapped softly against the window panes. As Dario turned over the details of the video in his mind, disquiet settled in his gut. He was apprehensive about how to proceed. He also had a feeling what his inner circle would advise him to do. Over the years, most of them succeeded in resolving the conflicts they encountered with extreme violence and brutality. For the most part, his advisers believed the cartel was invulnerable and capable of withstanding any threat. That was part of the reason that he didn't have much confidence in them. Members of the cartel lived by a well-established and inflexible code of rules. One of those rules was that the punishment for any act of disloyalty to the cartel had to be absolute. Allowing someone to live who had betrayed the cartel was unfathomable. Dario's advisors were loyal, but they were soldiers and they thought like soldiers.

None of them were particularly good when it came to diplomacy or formulating erudite solutions to problems. But it wasn't their lack of ingenuity that was troubling Dario this morning. Each time Dario replayed the video, his feeling that Juan Carlos was not the architect of this plan became stronger. Juan Carlos was a genius when it came to moving drugs and laundering money. But this was something else entirely; something outside of Juan Carlos's scope of expertise. This was about a different kind of leverage. And the person who negotiated the minefield and turned the tables on the cartel was someone who clearly understood how to play the game. A game which Dario himself had few equals. It was Dario's ability to never hesitate when he needed to apply leverage that had billionaires, politicians, sheiks and terrorists bending to the cartel's whims. When he saw Pierce on the video, it might have been his imagination, but Dario recognized a flicker in his eyes that told him that Pierce would not hesitate.

The bickering among his advisors drew Dario's attention. The squabbling instantly stopped, and the room fell silent when Dario walked in. The room seemed to hold its breath, waiting. Dario could feel his advisors studying him.

"My friends," Dario gave his advisors a solemn stare. "You have all now seen the video. Juan Carlos has revealed all our bank and brokerage accounts. He has divulged the locations of our safe houses throughout the world and made known the locations of all of our smuggling operations." Dario's stare intensified. "If this information is turned over to the United States, they will seize our assets and cut off our supply chains."

The tension in the room heightened. Dario scanned the eight men sitting around the long oval table.

"There is no question that Juan Carlos's actions are traitorous, and it goes against everything we stand for to allow someone who has betrayed us to live. But we need to consider the cost of killing him and having the video released."

Dario felt the stares hardening. Arsenio Mendoza, Dario's brother-in-law and longtime advisor cleared his throat, and everyone looked at him.

"The dog that betrayed us must die. And the fleas that helped him must also be exterminated," Arsenio's voice was hard and authoritative.

Dario drew a slow patient breath and locked eyes with Arsenio. "And what about the video?" He asked politely.

"We can transfer the money out of those accounts, and as for the smuggling routes, we go back to how we smuggled drugs before Juan Carlos changed everything. It may not be as efficient as the tunnels, but it worked."

Dario despised people who talked without considering the consequences. "We cannot move billions of dollars without calling attention to ourselves. Assuming, we can get our money out, where exactly are we going to move it to?"

Arsenio sank in his chair. "We own two banks and we have friends in the U.S. government. High ranking friends that can buy us the time we need to move our money. They can keep the CIA and DEA at bay for a week or even two if we need that much time."

Dario controlled his irritation and calmly looked around the table and said. "Does anyone agree with Arsenio?"

The room's tenor changed as uneasiness swept across the group. But no one said a word. It bothered Dario that it hadn't occurred to any of his advisors that most of the powerful friends Arsenio expected to rely on to help were the same people that were named in the video.

Dario had good reason to believe that most of them would be charged and prosecuted if the video was released. And the few that were so powerful that they were beyond the reach of the law would undoubtedly turn their backs on the cartel.

Finally, Dario grimly offered; "None of our contacts in Washington will help us. Most are named in the video and they will abandon us like rats fleeing a sinking ship. We will be on our own and at the mercy of the United States government . . . All of our money will be seized and our smuggling operations exposed."

"This is madness!" Arsenio seethed. "We will be perceived as soft if we do not kill Juan Carlos now. You should have killed him earlier when you had the chance," he challenged Dario angrily.

Again, the eyes watched Dario. With every point that Arsenio made Dario's face tightened. In his paranoid business, it was not just law enforcement that he had to contend with, it was also men in his organization that wanted his seat at the head of the cartel. In his aging face, intelligence and violence warred just beneath the skin, and when he finally realized that no amount of reason would make Arsenio understand, Dario's patience began to crack, like fractures in a frozen pond radiating out across the ice. To Dario, Arsenio had just become a liability.

The door opened behind him quietly. Dario glanced over his shoulder as Rene stepped into the room. Arsenio's face was outraged—unforgiving. "It appears that you've already made your decision."

Dario felt a rage rising in him. His expression changed—only a slight change, but Rene saw it, and knew what it meant. Arsenio was too engaged in openly defying Dario to notice his discrete gesture to Rene to hand him his gun. Dario moved deliberately towards Arsenio.

"You are misguided Arsenio . . . A disappointment to me," Dario exhaled. "If brutality is all that it takes to run a drug empire, the fucking Mexicans would be in charge."

For a moment Arsenio appeared speechless. Then he erupted. "If you don't handle this business as I'm telling you to do, it won't be long before the Mexicans are in charge."

Dario had no desire to listen to anymore. With Arsenio's words still hanging in the air, Dario pulled the linen table runner from the credenza situated just behind him and in one quick motion, like a cowboy throwing a lasso over a runaway calf, he slapped it around Arsenio's skull, covering his eyes and mouth and shot him in the back of the head. As Arsenio collapsed to the floor, no one dared to say a word or react. Dario had given Arsenio several chances to get in line before killing him. Everyone sitting around the table knew that. Dario had used the linen to cover the exit wound to control spraying blood and bone. Everyone sitting around the table knew that as well.

Chapter Fifty-Seven

Carrying a thermos of hot coffee and two mugs, Shane made his way down the grassy slope from the guest house to the lake. The pungent scent of pine was heavy in the air. Tree shadows were long and black, and the temperature was a crisp forty-eight degrees. Shane couldn't sleep, and when he checked on Pierce, he discovered that his cot was empty. He spotted his best friend standing utterly still in shadows of a towering pine tree by the edge of the water. Shane handed him a mug and poured coffee for both of them.

"I couldn't sleep either. I guess we'll catch another sunrise together."

Pierce sniffed the coffee. The warmth of the mug felt good against his hands. "Smells good."

Shane felt a moment of worry. "I've been thinking about what happens next if Dario doesn't accept our terms."

"Well, I suppose we'll each end up with a bullet in our head and our bodies dumped in a urine-scented alley," Pierce frowned.

Shane set the thermos down on the ground. "I don't recall you being such a smart ass when we were at Harvard."

Pierce grinned. "You were always stoned when we were at Harvard; I'm surprised you remember anything."

"I do remember thinking when I was asked to be your mentor, there goes another pretty boy. Then you saved my ass in that bar when I was too drunk to stand up straight, and those townies were trying to roll me."

Pierce's blue eyes swept out over the polished surface of the lake. The reflection of the moon off the lake seemed like a spotlight directed straight at him. "The good old days," he shrugged.

Shane tipped his mug towards Pierce. "To the good old days of alcohol and ideological intoxication."

Reminiscing about his law school days filled with drunken parties and pliable Wellesley college coeds momentarily distracted Shane, suddenly making him feel better. It reminded him of how fond he was of brunettes with silky unblemished skin, rounded thighs and lavish breasts.

Mia was out for a run and noticed two distant figures standing by the lake. Instinctively, her eyes darted around the trees and bushes looking for anyone else. Fluid as a cat, Mia moved in the shadows with her gun drawn until she recognized Shane's voice float in the darkness. At that moment, Mia stepped out from the shadows allowing Pierce and Shane to see her coming down the hill towards them. Shane instantly made a face.

"Doesn't anyone sleep around here?" he scoffed. Pierce waited for Mia to get closer and then he smiled at her. Mia commented on Shane's remark. "I always get restless before a mission," she said catching her breath. Mia turned nonchalantly and looked straight into Pierce's eyes. "I heard about what you did yesterday."

Pierce nodded expecting Mia to give him hell for appearing in the video, but he didn't get any.

"That was a ballsy move. Hopefully it pays dividends."

Shane rubbed his head, a habit he picked up when he stopped having hair to run his fingers through. At last, Shane gave into his nervousness and said: "I assume you have a plan for either contingency."

A reflective look crossed Mia's face. "Of course, however, since neither of you is coming with us, the less you know the better in case you are brought in for questioning."

Cold sweat drenched Mia's shirt and she began to shiver. Pierce knelt and poured hot coffee into his mug and handed it to her.

"This should warm you up."

Mia took a sip of the hot coffee. She could see that Shane was unsettled by not knowing what would happen once they knew Dario's decision.

"If Dario agrees to our terms, we have a jet already standing by at Tulsa airport. We will immediately leave and take Juan Carlos and Alexis out of the country. Somewhere that doesn't have an extradition treaty with the U.S. So, if the feds happen to find out where Juan Carlos is, they won't be able to charge him and try and extradite him." Mia gave Shane a stern look. "That's all you need to know."

Shane frowned. "That's not the plan I'm concerned about," he said. "I already knew that if Dario agrees, you will get Juan Carlos and Alexis out of the country. And Pierce and I won't wind up stuffed into 55-gallon drums of acid. It's the other contingency plan that I want to hear about," Shane said full of anxiety.

Mia completely understood. If Dario didn't agree to their terms, the cartel would hunt them down. Shane also made it known that he was worried about his wife who was still in Miami. Mia took a deep breath. For a moment, Pierce saw something flash across Mia's face – uncertainty, uneasiness – maybe even fear? Mia inhaled deeply. She had not said a word yet and Pierce still sensed that secretly Mia prayed that it would never come to the point where they would have to rely on the second contingency. She subconsciously pursed her lips looking dour.

"If Dario does not agree to our terms or fails to call, Hugo and I will drive Juan Carlos and Alexis along the back roads through Kansas and continue north. We'll disappear and keep moving until we hear back from Pierce that he has cut a deal with the DEA. In exchange for the video and Juan Carlos's cooperation, they will put him and Alexis in the Witness Protection program."

Mia glanced over at Pierce. "You will need to go into the program too," she said. "As for the rest of us, we will wait and see how things play out, but that will certainly be an option."

Shane looked ashen. Pierce patted him on the back reassuringly. "The first thing we do is make sure the feds send agents over to your house and pick up Kris."

Shane exhaled, some of the color returning to his face. "I really hope it doesn't come to that," he muttered.

"Me too," Pierce nodded. "But if it does, once the feds have the video, Dario will have his hands full with the DEA."

Shane felt an uneasy premonition. "But given all the names Juan Carlos identified—can we even trust the feds?"

Pierce and Mia exchanged a look. "Hogan was not one of the agents named by Juan Carlos." Pierce's clear blue eyes darkened with a hard resolution. "I will only speak with Special Agent Hogan and warn him about the people in his agency that are working with the cartel."

Shane nodded, but it was obvious from the look on his face that he was not the least bit satisfied with the second contingency plan.

* * *

The sun was starting to peek over the Ozark Mountains and the sky was slowly showing signs of morning. Mia looked at her watch. "I better get back; Hugo is probably up by now," she shrugged and with a delicate twist of her shoulders, Mia turned and started up the hill.

Pierce called to Mia as she strode up the hill. "We still have a couple of hours. I'm going to the guest house and taking a shower. I'll meet you up at the house in about an hour."

Alexis's bottom lip was still swollen, and she had a mouse under her right eye where Juan Carlos hit her. Mia did not want Pierce to see her bruises. She cast a quick look over her shoulder at Pierce.

"No, we don't know how the call with the cartel is going to go. We should spare Alexis any unnecessary drama. We'll come down to the guest house. Wait for us there," Mia's tone was polite yet firm. She resumed her brisk pace up the hill giving Pierce no opportunity to object. For a split second Pierce looked surprised. Shane decided to run additional interference.

"You know she has a point."

Pierce's desire to see Alexis was overwhelming. He missed the sound of her voice. Without warning, Pierce took off for the guest house ahead of Shane.

"I'm going to take a shower before you contaminate the bathroom."

"It's not my fault," Shane protested. "The fucking Mexican food out here is deadly."

"Yeah, that's it," Pierce added with a laugh.

Chapter Fifty-Eight

It was 9:47 A.M., Shane paced along the length of the family room. From the look on his face, he was unaccustomed to the feeling of angst that had a firm grip on him. Mia casually lounged on the sectional leather couch reading magazines to pass the time and Hugo sat next to her perched over a bowl of Cheerios, shoveling spoonfuls of the tiny shaped circles into his mouth. They were prepared for either course of action. Pierce occasionally stared at the cell phone in his hand. As the final minutes drew to a close, Pierce began to mentally put himself through the steps of meeting with Special Agent Hogan. He watched Shane as he sat down at the edge of the couch, fidgeted with random objects on the coffee table, sighed and stood up and resumed his nervous pacing. Mia looked up from her magazine and gave Shane a glance as he crossed in front of her but made no attempt to speak to him. Hugo eyed Shane's slow promenade across the room for a moment and then shoved another spoonful of cereal into his mouth. Over the years, Hugo worked security at a handful of events that Dario Carraboca attended. He saw some of the most powerful men in the world genuflect before Dario Carraboca. As far as Hugo was concerned, Shane's anxiety was in no way a sign of weakness. *He had good reason to worry*, Hugo thought.

* * *

A FEW MINUTES later, the cell phone in Pierce's hand began to ring. Pierce pressed down on the speakerphone button. The voice emanating from the speaker phone was distorted and metallic. Everyone in the room listened.

"Is this Pierce Evangelista?"

Pierce felt his muscles tighten. For a split second he felt a wave of adrenaline and dead fear come crashing all at once.

"Yes, this is Pierce Evangelista speaking," he responded, doing his best to keep his voice from wavering.

"So, you are the one responsible for threatening my operation," Dario conjectured.

"I don't see it that way. I'm the one who is presenting you with an opportunity," Pierce responded, sounding unrepentant. "The video link is nothing more than information. And I have presented you with the right to control it. If you agree to our proposal, the video stays buried."

"This so-called opportunity sounds more like a threat to me Mr. Evangelista," Dario sounded agitated. "And if I don't agree to the terms?"

Shane reacted to the question by shooting a concerned glance at Pierce. He looked strangely calm.

"Well, then I assume I won't live long enough to see all of the problems that releasing the video is going to cause you, your operations and assets," Pierce replied matter-a-factly.

"What you propose doesn't work for me," Dario sneered. "As long as the video exists, my operation will always be at risk. I need more than assurances from you. I need the video destroyed." Dario demanded.

Pierce dismissed Dario's stipulation as folly. Any butterflies that he felt at the beginning of the call had since dissipated, and he was now focused and engaged in the very thing he had been trained since his first day at Harvard Law to do: to out-think, out-wit and keep the other side off-balance.

Pierce had a feeling that Dario was trying to get him to make a concession. Asking for the video to be destroyed was something that he suspected Dario knew he would not be willing to do. But Dario would use Pierce's unwillingness to destroy the video to get something that he really wanted.

"Assuming for the sake of this discussion I agree to destroy the video. How exactly would I be able to prove to you that the video has been destroyed? I could easily conceal a copy," Pierce said.

Dario inhaled and thought about it. "True, that does pose a dilemma."

"It's only a dilemma, if I agreed to destroy the video which I haven't agreed to do," Pierce countered. "If you have no objection, let's skip this foreplay," Pierce coolly suggested.

"Very well," Dario said. Neither one seemed interested in extending the discussion any longer than necessary.

"Let's get to it. Juan Carlos has millions deposited in banks throughout Europe. You can have it all and in exchange all you have to do is give me an address . . . Turn him over to us and you and your friends walk away and live very comfortable lives without having to look over your shoulders."

Pierce hesitated for a moment to create the impression that he was considering Dario's counteroffer.

"That would defeat the purpose of our offer to you. Which is to save Juan Carlos's life," Pierce said. "As for not having to look over my shoulder, I was aware of the risks when I agreed to represent him. Your offer to turn him over in exchange for letting us walk away is not something I can do."

"Perhaps you should take another moment and discuss my counteroffer with the rest of your associates," Dario said in a gruff tone. "My offer makes you all very rich."

Shane's thin-lipped expression suggested to Pierce that he should think about the offer. Hugo cast a long guileless glance at Pierce which he took to mean that they didn't risk their lives to break Juan Carlos out of prison only to cave at the first hint of pressure from Dario Carraboca.

"While you and your friends consider my offer, keep in mind that Juan Carlos betrayed us. We gave him an opportunity to atone for his mistake and he elected to betray us a second time . . . And now you attempt to bargain for his life by threatening me with a ticking time bomb."

Pierce did not flinch.

"Juan Carlos's act of contrition was to bring the video to you and not take the deal that the DEA offered him," Pierce replied.

Dario scoffed at the comment and said, "If he was sincere about making things right, he would never have made the video."

"And your act of mercy would consist of what? Severing his head from his body while his family is forced to watch?"

"You are very arrogant Mr. Evangelista and needlessly risking your associate's lives," Dario glowered before catching himself. "You and your associates accomplished what my men didn't. You got Juan Carlos out of prison and away from the Americans. Why not be generously compensated?"

Pierce could see that he was getting nowhere and was suddenly distracted by a thought. He took a shot in the dark but a well-aimed one. "And Jesus said to his disciples, truly I say to you a rich man will reach heaven with great difficulty," Pierce prophesied.

As soon as Pierce uttered those words, Shane took his thumb and forefinger and pretended it was a gun, placed the imaginary barrel in his mouth and pulled the trigger.

Hugo and Mia both looked at Pierce completely surprised; concerned that he might be cracking under all the stress.

There was an uncomfortable silence as Pierce's words hung in the air like a blade. Pierce counted the seconds, waiting for a reaction from Dario.

"I see . . ." Dario mused. "You continue to surprise me, Mr. Evangelista. I didn't take you for a man of faith . . . We are all torn between two worlds . . . the real world and the divine," Dario sounded more intrigued than upset. "But still, you offer me nothing."

"No," Pierce calmly interjected. "I offer you something that you don't have . . . certainty. You have no assurance that your men will find Juan Carlos before the DEA finds him. If the DEA finds Juan Carlos before your men do, you can assume that he will cooperate with them in exchange for their protection. Our offer takes that possibility off the table."

"Only if you can get him out of the country," Dario retorted.

Pierce's voice sharpened like a laser. "We've managed to break Juan Carlos out of a prison and evade both your men and the DEA. We can manage."

Mia looked at her watch and held up eight fingers. Pierce knew that he had to cut off the call before the ten-minute mark in case Dario had someone tracking it.

"Time's up Mr. Carraboca. I need an answer."

Dario never really expected Pierce to turn Juan Carlos over to the cartel. He just wanted to press Pierce simply to see if his instincts were right about him. When he was satisfied, Dario ended the conversation.

"Mr. Evangelista, we have a deal," Dario said and was gone.

* * *

Pierce slumped in his chair as a fog of emotion that had been weighing heavy slowly lifted. Hugo nodded, looking impressed. "I underestimated you."

Mia wore an odd look as she reflected on the conversation. "I'm curious about one thing in particular," she said. "What possessed you to quote scripture?"

Pierce shrugged. "I played a hunch."

Shane finally stopped pacing and sat down next to Pierce. He was drenched in sweat and looked like he had just been waterboarded.

Everyone in the room seemed to ponder Pierce's hunch.

Mia offered an interested smile. "What was this hunch? Please share."

Pierce nodded focusing intently now. "Dario is a powerful man who can make anyone bend to his will. He expects to get his way and I realized that no logical argument was going to persuade him that we were intractable when it came to the terms of our offer . . . no logical argument," Pierce repeated for emphasis. "But religion is not about logic . . . it's about faith. Faith can be an extremely powerful motivator or deterrent depending on the circumstances."

"Yes," Mia smiled but what would make you believe that Dario was a religious man?"

"That didn't matter," Pierce said. "I just needed him to think I was religious . . . I grew up in a Catholic household where my mother and aunts prayed the Holy Rosary every day. I saw how fervently they believed, the sacrifices they made and their unyielding faith and devotion to Jesus. No power on earth could make them stray from their beliefs. Dario grew up in a country where the Catholic Church exercises extraordinary influence in politics and a near monopoly on religious beliefs and practices. Whether or not Dario believed in the Catholic Church was not important," Pierce said his voice deepening with deliberation. "He grew up with its influence and with friends and family who believed in the Catholic Church, so he had to have been exposed to people with strong religious beliefs."

Shane exhaled. "I'm happy it didn't, but that move could have backfired on you."

"Your point?" Pierce said coolly.

"My point is that you know there is a lot of controversy with the Church. What if Dario had issues with the Church?"

"The Catholic Church may be flawed because men are flawed," Pierce quipped. "Faith is altogether different," Pierce stressed emphatically. "If I could convince Dario that I believed I would be denied entrance into heaven if I turned Juan Carlos over to him, Dario would have to consider the possibility that there was nothing he could do to force me to turn Juan Carlos over. Not even threaten my life," Pierce reasoned.

Shane stared at Pierce and shook his head. "C'mon, you really think that's why Dario backed off?"

Pierce frowned. "I didn't say that. Mia asked me why I quoted scripture. I am merely pointing out that one of the few things Catholics don't fuck with is religion. In Latin America, death squads, paramilitary groups and organized crime all respect the Church, whether they believe in it or not. During raids in Latin America where entire towns have been wiped out, the Church and those given sanctuary by the Church survive. So, I played a hunch," Pierce said.

Hugo grinned. "Well played. So, where did you pull that religious quote from?"

Pierce smirked. "A little book called the Bible. You should read it sometime."

Hugo appeared to be hiding a smile. "I've heard of it." His gaze moved to Mia. "I'll go up ahead and tell Juan Carlos and Alexis to be ready to head out." Before leaving Hugo reached out and handed Pierce his cell phone.

"Keep it turned off until you get back," he said and then he hugged Pierce. "Don't worry about Alexis. She'll be fine," he whispered in Pierce's ear.

"I know," Pierce said with more confidence than he felt.

* * *

JUAN CARLOS STOOD alone on the porch chain smoking cigarettes while he waited for news. He watched as Hugo walked purposefully towards the house. Juan Carlos concentrated on Hugo's body language for anything that might give away how the call with Dario had gone. But Hugo had a physical strength in his movements that made him impossible to penetrate. When he reached the driveway, Hugo sharpened his eyes on him. Juan Carlos could feel his body leaning forward, waiting for Hugo to say something.

"Well how did it go?" he asked, his voice was tight.

"Dario agreed to the terms," Hugo said.

Juan Carlos showed no emotion putting a cigarette up to his lips and taking a long pull. "So, when do we leave?"

Hugo looked at his watch. "As soon as possible."

* * *

IN THE KITCHEN, Alexis placed her hand on the refrigerator to steady herself when Hugo told her that there was a jet waiting in Tulsa to fly them out of the country.

"I understand," Alexis replied in a low vanquished tone. She looked at Mia and Shane as they walked into the kitchen.

"Where's Pierce?" Alexis asked.

Mia looked at Alexis worriedly. She looked awful. Her face was full of cuts, her bottom lip was still swollen, and her eyes were sunken.

"He's not coming," Shane blurted out without giving an ounce of thought to Alexis's feelings.

Alexis looked stunned and shrank away into the corner of the kitchen. Her mind was swimming. She wondered in a panicked moment whether Pierce cared enough to want to see her to say goodbye. "What do you mean?" Her voice quivered.

Juan Carlos looked embarrassed by Alexis's display but resisted the urge to discipline her in front of everyone.

Alexis's lips were trembling so hard that she found it hard to speak. "Did he say that he didn't want to see me?"

Mia tried to reason with Alexis. "No, sweetie not at all," Mia gave her a smile. "I told Pierce that we needed to leave immediately, and I thought it would be better if he didn't come up to the house to say goodbye."

Alexis's mouth twisted and Mia saw something fracture behind her eyes. Mia looked at her sympathetically and glanced over at Hugo. Hugo shrugged. "We can wait a few minutes."

Juan Carlos suddenly grabbed Alexis by the arm and tightened his grip. "You heard Mia. We have to go," His voice rose while he shook her hard. Alexis felt her head rock back. She responded with a sound of disgust. "Don't touch me."

Hugo and Shane exchanged a quick look. Hugo took hold of Juan Carlos's arm catching him off guard and Alexis pulled away from him with a hard jerk. She slipped past him and sprinted out of the kitchen while Hugo still had a hold of him.

Juan Carlos took an angry step forward, and then another trying to follow her.

"Let her go," Hugo's voice boomed.

"Don't interfere. This has nothing to do with you," Juan Carlos snarled.

Shane flung an arm out cutting him off. His eyes bore relentlessly into him.

"Pierce saved both your lives. If she wants to say goodbye to him, you need to back the fuck off." Shane squared his shoulders. Juan Carlos recognized the look in Shane's eyes. He had the look of someone who was itching to hit someone. Juan Carlos's eyes darted from Hugo, to Mia, to Keeper and back to Shane. His face turned bright red. He felt humiliated and disrespected. Something he would not soon forget.

"Fine," he hissed. "Now, would it be okay if I got the fuck out of this kitchen?"

* * *

Alexis's heart began to pound against her chest the moment she first caught a glimpse of Pierce lounging next to a tree. Her eyes were wide and all she wanted to do was run into his arms. Pierce's expression changed as Alexis came closer. His smile when he first noticed Alexis rushing down faded the moment, he noticed her cuts and bruises. Alexis saw something flicker across Pierce's face, surprise, uncertainty, maybe even regret. Now face-to-face with Pierce, Alexis could feel her confusion growing to an obvious frustration.

"How could you let me leave without saying goodbye?" Alexis almost shouted.

Pierce averted her eyes. "I thought it would be easier for you."

His words sounded rehearsed. She could instantly tell that the decision to stay away from her was not his.

Her eyes began to moisten, gazing deeply at him.

"I know that you care about me, that I mean something to you."

Pierce's eyes glistened with a lucid determination. "*Something, no . . . not something, how about everything,*" he thought. His gaze passed over her face, down her neck, to her slender curves before rising back up to her face where it lingered on her mouth. Alexis felt his gaze as if it were a touch and took a step towards him. At that moment, nothing in the world mattered except him. She tilted her face up and Pierce kissed her. Their mouths pressed together. Pierce's touch ignited nerve endings in Alexis that she had forgotten she had. She could feel her legs starting to give out when the distant sound of the car horn blaring finally broke the spell and Pierce drew back. Alexis opened her eyes; she desperately wanted to tell him that she was in love with him.

The loud car horn sounded again blaring and reverberating all the way to the lake. Alexis turned her head for a split second and saw Shane walking towards them. When her gaze returned to Pierce the tears that had been threatening finally came and spilled down her face. Alexis didn't move them away.

Sensing her minutes slipping away Alexis asked Pierce if he knew where she was going. Alexis didn't care, but she hoped that if Pierce knew, it meant that there was a small chance that he would stay in contact.

"Alexis," he said. The sound of her name in his voice was so intimate that it made her body ache. "I can't know where you're going. If I'm questioned, they can't make me tell them something I don't know."

A feeling of confusion and then dread came over her. "Questioned by who, the cartel?"

Pierce smiled. "No, you don't have to worry about them anymore. You're safe . . ."

Alexis bristled. "I'm not worried about me."

"I was talking about the United States Attorney. They could argue that my knowledge of Juan Carlos's whereabouts is outside the scope of Attorney-Client privilege and require me to disclose where he is," Pierce said.

A hint of an exasperated smile appeared on her lips. "Would that be so bad?"

Pierce didn't need to be a mind reader to know what Alexis wanted. But facing the harsh reality that he might not ever see her again, Pierce realized that while telling Alexis that he loved her might make her happy in the present moment knowing how he felt would only torment her in the days that followed. So, Pierce remained conspicuously quiet.

Alexis glanced back at Shane who had been waiting about ten feet from where they were standing.

With a look of intense urgency Alexis threw her hands up in the air. "Dios Mio, Ayúdame!"

"Pierce," Shane called to him, losing his patience. "It's time."

Pierce nodded at Shane and gave Alexis a sad smile. "They are waiting for you," he said.

"Really? Pierce this is how you are going to say goodbye?" Her voice dripped in bitter disappointment.

Pierce touched her face gently with the back of his hand. Alexis brushed it away. She was starting to feel the angst that managed to disappear whenever she was with Pierce bubbling to the surface. Her heart sinking, Alexis turned and started back towards the house. Pierce was filled with guilt and doubt as he watched Alexis walk up the hill. When she got to the top, she took one last look over her shoulder directly at Pierce, her eyes were full of a terrible yearning. "It's all right," she whispered and disappeared from sight.

Chapter Fifty-Nine

Shane assumed that there was no amount of bourbon that would numb what Pierce was feeling. He expected to find him looking dejected or, at the very least exhausted, since they had been running on little food and no sleep. But instead, there was a look on Pierce's face that Shane unfortunately had seen before. Pierce's eyes burned with a haunting laser like focus as he compiled a list of the loose ends that needed to be tied up. The minute Shane recognized it; he began to worry. He had the same look in his eyes when Jordan left him. Pierce withdrew from everything except for work. His ability to take his emotions and bury them as far down in his subconscious as they could go and work each day to the point of collapse was nothing short of mind boggling. The one thing Pierce was exceptional at was getting results, and that cemented his place in his law firm as its rising star, but it came at a significant cost. It wasn't ambition that drove Pierce; it was his feeling of hopelessness. The divorce hit Pierce like turbulent waves of a hurricane, damaging his heart and soul. Pierce couldn't forgive himself and Shane wasn't sure that he would ever climb out of the dark hole he descended into the day Jordan left. For the first time, Pierce had shown signs of emerging from his emotional purgatory. All Shane wanted was to keep Pierce from crawling back in his personal dungeon. He wanted to say something, anything that might be supportive, but Shane knew any words of comfort would be brushed away. Pierce was never one to want to share his heartache, and he didn't want anyone including Shane feeling sorry for him.

"Listen, I know that you don't want to hear this right now, but I am sorry."

Pierce stared at Shane with his blue eyes, waiting for him to expand on his point. Shane waited for a second and then touched on the subject he promised himself he would stay away from. "What I'm trying to say is that I know it must have been hard to let her go. That's all."

Pierce eyed Shane coolly and after a long moment of thoughtful calculation he said, "Nothing to be sorry for; that was always the plan."

"Yeah . . . yeah . . . I know. But the plan didn't include you falling for her."

Pierce frowned. "Can we drop the subject?"

Shane took a hard breath. "Of course, . . . I called Kris and asked her to meet me in Vegas. Why don't you come along? We can grab a couple of suites, catch a few shows and eat some really good food. What do you say?" Shane's tone was upbeat, but his eyes couldn't hide his deepening concern.

Pierce subconsciously grimaced while he managed to nod. It was the gesture of someone who was familiar with the road he was about to travel on, whether or not he wanted to. "I still have a few things to take care of. I need to work with Dode over at the casino and have her put in a couple of additional safeguards just in case Dario gets any ideas that he could bury the video by getting rid of us."

Shane nodded, but Pierce's response struck him as a feeble excuse. "You can always meet us after you finish your work here."

Pierce smiled and put his hand on Shane's shoulder. "Thanks, but I need to get back to Miami."

* * *

DARIO OPENED THE FILE and looked at the photograph that lay atop the folder. It showed a tall, well-dressed man with dark black hair and handsome features standing next to Russian billionaire Alisher

Usmanov. Attached to the photo was a thumbnail biography, wholly unnecessary because Dario Carraboca could already recite the particulars of Pierce Evangelista's notable career from memory. Son of immigrants, graduate of Harvard Law School, golden boy at one of the most prestigious law firms in the country. Alisher Usmanov first took notice of him when Pierce orchestrated a strategic alliance between a handful of poor Native American Tribes rich in iron ore and the Brazilians and Chinese. Pierce skillfully orchestrated a deal that opened the door for the tribes to participate in the Consortium that dominated the spot and contract markets. Following that accomplishment, Alisher Usmanov retained Pierce to represent his company. Pierce started with small matters but eventually played a significant part in negotiating acquisitions of telecommunications, internet, and media companies worldwide which significantly expanded Usmanov's sizable fortune. Dario flipped to the next page, a glossy magazine quality picture of Pierce's ex-wife Jordan.

Dario tilted his head as he looked at the picture. "She is very pretty."

Rene leaned over Dario's desk to get a better look.

"Ah, the ex-wife, they were divorced a little over a year ago. She now lives in Philadelphia," Rene said.

Dario flipped through several more pages. Squinting at the information and immersed in thought.

"Do you want me to put a couple of men on Mr. Evangelista?" Rene asked Dario.

Dario leaned back and clasped his hands behind his neck. "I don't think Mr. Evangelista is going to lead us to Juan Carlos. Up to this point he has been careful . . . He won't contact him." Dario took a sip of wine and set down the wine glass. "What we need to do is focus on finding Juan Carlos."

Rene's expression soured since he viewed Pierce as his only real lead. "How can you be so sure?"

"Because he's smart . . . He made sure that email bounced all over the world before it got to us, and the cell phone had not been used before we called him. Our people couldn't find any tower usage history for the cell phone number he gave us. He knew we would try and track the email and call . . . he'll expect us to keep tabs on him so he'll keep a low profile and not give us anything we can use to find Juan Carlos," Dario reasoned as he weighed their options. "Now let's go over what we know," Dario nodded, focusing intently now. "We know that Juan Carlos left Curacao on a chartered jet. We also know that he took a second charter to Dallas."

Rene stared saying nothing.

"Mr. Evangelista assured me that once I agreed to their terms, they would get him out of the United States."

Rene felt lost; the lines in his brow deepening. "I understand Dario. But they could have gone anywhere." Rene's first instinct was to plant listening devices in Pierce's home and office and put the usual feelers out to their contacts around the world. "We will find Juan Carlos, but it will take time," he assured Dario.

Dario's tone hardened instantly. "No!"

Rene's face was an equal mix of confused and embarrassed.

"Focus on what we know and go from there . . . I want you to be smart," Dario insisted as he told Rene how to proceed. Dario's attention to detail was amazing. "First, you have to assume that Juan Carlos is within a one day's drive from Dallas. Secondly, that he took a charter to leave the country."

Rene followed along in silence as Dario explained his reasoning.

"The longer they stay on the road, the greater the chances of being spotted. They probably drove a few hours at most and got off the road.

If they drove a couple of hundred miles in any direction, that narrows it down to eight international airports that Juan Carlos could have departed from. I want you to check all eight for chartered flights that left the country in the last six hours."

Rene listened without interruption, but his better judgment screamed at him to stick with his plan of contacting the cartel's partners worldwide.

Rene cleared his throat. He wanted to tell Dario that basing the entire search on the idea that Juan Carlos departed from one of eight airports that happened to be geographically convenient to Dallas was a gigantic leap of faith, but the words would not come.

Dario fixed Rene with an adamant stare. His orders were clear.

Rene nodded, stood up and moved slowly towards the door like a wary animal instinctively sensing that something was wrong.

"Dario, just to be on the safe side, shouldn't I also put some feelers out? Rene asked the question before he could stop himself.

Dario's face hardened. "Why would you randomly contact our people around the world?"

Rene looked at Dario with a blank expression. Suddenly feeling awkward and unsure of himself.

A thin smile crossed Dario's lips as he stuck the end of a cigarette between his lips and struck his lighter.

"Once you assemble the information I've asked for, you can run with your idea. Reach out to our friends in Pakistan and ask them to discreetly look for Juan Carlos . . . But be careful. There can be no leak that we are looking for him," Dario cautioned.

Chapter Sixty

The Falcon jet roared into the sky climbing to thirty-nine thousand feet. Hugo felt a singe of anxiety as the jet jostled across some turbulence. He tried to imagine himself on a tropical island. The notion he realized was ironic since the events responsible for him sitting on the jet crossing the Atlantic Ocean started on a tropical island. Juan Carlos was watching him.

"Nervous?"

Hugo looked Juan Carlos straight in the eye. "What makes you think I'm nervous?"

"Just relax. We'll be there in . . ." Juan Carlos started to say before catching himself. "And where exactly is there?" He asked, realizing he had no idea where they were headed.

"Andorra," Mia replied. "But we cannot fly directly to Andorra, so we are flying to Barcelona and driving the rest of the way."

"Andorra?" Juan Carlos repeated with a raised eyebrow.

"They have no extradition treaty with the United States. Even if the DEA finds you, it won't be able to extradite you back to the U.S.," Hugo said.

Mia nodded. "Spanish is widely spoken there. Both you and Alexis are fluent in Spanish." Mia glanced at Alexis. "Not to mention, Andorra has a very high standard of living so you can live very comfortably there."

Alexis acknowledged Mia with unfocused eyes. She accepted the news silently. She couldn't possibly think about where she was going. All her mind could focus on was those she had left behind. She sat by the window staring out at the endless blue sky nervously twisting her wedding band. Alexis thought about her older sisters, cousins, nephews and nieces. She wondered about her parents. She had a picture of her parents resting in the palm of her hand and occasionally looked at it. Alexis had no idea if she would ever see them again. Would she even know when they were gone? She was told to leave her wallet, identification, passport, pictures and anything that connected her to her past life behind. But she could not bring herself to leave the picture of her parents.

"You won't be able to take that picture with you," Mia said.

Alexis swallowed hard feeling a lump in her throat.

"I know."

"You are now Mrs. Valeria Placido. Your husband's name is Sergio," Mia said handing Alexis her passport.

"Thank you," Alexis made herself smile wondering if the expression looked as fake as it felt.

"How long are you staying with us in Andorra?" Alexis asked Mia.

"Just a few days until we get you settled in," Mia said.

Alexis's lips became a thin line. Mia had seen that look of fright and uncertainty on Alexis' face before.

"Are you worried that Juan Carlos will hit you again?" She whispered in a barely audible voice.

"No," she said wishing that she could say no to all of this. But instead, Alexis used the veiled response she rehearsed in her mind.

"Juan Carlos and I talked. He felt horrible about hitting me. He promised it wouldn't happen again," she paused for a second and then added, "And I believe him." Her voice sounded normal. Amazing that she could do that given her fear of Juan Carlos and what he might do to her in another fit of rage.

Mia studied her as if she could tell Alexis was lying just by staring at her.

"Yes, I made a terrible mistake," Juan Carlos interjected after overhearing Alexis. His tone was level but full of menace.

Alexis glanced over at Mia and bowed her head. Mia could see her disapproval and hatred for him.

Mia tried to ease the tension by offering more details about Andorra.

"I'm tired," Alexis cut her off before yawning into the back of her hand. All Alexis wanted to do was go to sleep.

* * *

IT WAS SHORTLY after eight when Rene finished collecting the information on all the private charter jets that recently left the U.S. from airports within a three-hundred-mile radius of Dallas. Dario was sitting in his study reading and wreathed in cigarette smoke when Rene stopped outside the door, reached for the knob, and froze with indecision. When you worked for a man like Dario Carraboca, this was one of those moments where Rene realized that he could end up with a 9-mm bullet lodged somewhere in his skull if Dario didn't like what he had to say. Rene handed Dario a ledger identifying every international flight that satisfied Dario's exact specifications. Dario stared at the ledger hoping that something would jump out at him. Nothing did. However, he was particularly curious about two flights. The flight that departed Oklahoma City for Moscow and the one that left Tulsa for Barcelona. The remaining international charters flew to locations such as Mexico and various islands in the Caribbean. Places that Dario did not suspect Juan Carlos would hide in.

"The flight to Moscow is scheduled to land in about forty minutes and the one to Barcelona in just over two hours," Dario said letting the urgency into his voice. “I want people on the ground watching those airports.”

Rene nodded. “I have men watching those airports as well as Mexico City.”

Dario handed the folder back to Rene. “Make sure that they are careful. We don’t want them to be conspicuous.”

“Yes Dario,” Rene said. “What about the lawyer?”

Dario folded his hands and said nothing while appearing to ponder Rene’s question.

“If it makes you feel better, wait for him in Miami. He will eventually head back there.”

“Do you want me to question him?”

Dario shook his head. He knew what Rene meant. To Rene questioning someone meant causing them so much pain that the person begged to be killed.

“No, we stick to the terms of our agreement until we know more.”

“I’m sure I can persuade him to tell us what we need to know to neutralize the threat of the video being released.”

Dario was only marginally surprised by Rene’s recklessness. He was a modern day assassin who excelled at murder and real torture but not much more.

“I’m sure he’s anticipated that possibility and is prepared for it. That could backfire on us,” Dario said. “Find, Juan Carlos and watch him closely.”

Rene made no reaction. There was a clinical detachment with the way he carried himself. He simply stared at Dario with his deep set brown eyes.

“Do not assume that Juan Carlos will let his guard down because we have agreed to the lawyer’s terms. Juan Carlos is paranoid. He will not put any trust in our agreement. Once he lands, he will disappear, moving constantly from one safe house to another making him almost impossible to find," Dario said.

Rene stared, a long-confused moment. "But what about the video? The information on the vid—"

Dario's patience evaporated. His eyes went white like a shark about to attack. "Forget about the video for now!" He cut Rene off in mid-sentence. "Juan Carlos is much more dangerous than the video. Before we can deal with the video, we need to know where Juan Carlos is hiding."

Rene nodded, focusing more intently.

"Tell me Rene, what do we accomplish if we neutralize the threat of the video, and Juan Carlos turns himself into the DEA?"

Rene gave Dario an apologetic glance.

"Now, go find Juan Carlos," Dario's tone was final.

Chapter Sixty-One

BARCELONA

Amid the bustle of tourists, medley of sights, smells and sounds, Hugo noticed a look of recognition in the eyes of two men when Juan Carlos walked past them. From eight years of tracking and being tracked by terrorists, as part of a Special Forces deep penetration unit, Hugo developed a knack for knowing when he or a member of his team had been targeted. Mia and Hugo exchanged a brief look; a look that told her that the two men at her 9 o'clock looked suspicious. Mia's eyes instinctively raked the crowd for more men. Hugo casually watched the two men as they pushed their way through the crowded airport trying to follow Juan Carlos from a safe distance. One of Hugo's talents was his ability to slow things down in his mind's eye. When he was in the midst of a potentially dangerous or chaotic situation, Hugo could filter out the fear and extraneous information, focus on what was important, and analyze the tactical situation and skill set of the group following him or preparing to take aggressive action.

* * *

Both men had black hair and dark Mediterranean features. From Hugo's vantage point, their features would allow them to pass for Latino, Indian or Middle Eastern. Hugo couldn't be sure without getting a closer look, but what he did know was that they weren't professional assassins. If they were, Hugo wouldn't have made them so easily. And if by chance Hugo had spotted them, they would have known it. Hugo worked with assassins for years. There were several opportunities as they made their way through the airport terminal where, if something was going to happen, professional assassins would have made their move. They weren't there to kill Juan Carlos. Hugo figured that they were freelancers the cartel hired to watch the airport. Nothing more than *spotters* hired to stake out the airport and report back if they saw Juan Carlos. Hugo assumed that the cartel probably placed *spotters* in every major international terminal hoping that Juan Carlos would eventually walk through one of them.

Hugo accompanied Juan Carlos outside of the airport terminal for a smoke while Mia rented a car. Juan Carlos reached into his pocket and fished out a pack of Stallion cigarettes. Hugo casually looked through the glass doors. He had a cool detachment that he had honed from killing enemies of the United States. Hugo never looked nervous but that never stopped him from constantly surveying his surroundings for threats. He spotted one of the men standing by a coffee shop across from the car rental booth.

After a deep pull off the cigarette Juan Carlos asked, "You seem distracted. Is everything okay?"

Hugo did not want to alarm him. "I'm no more distracted than usual. Everything's fine. I'm just covering all the bases," he said.

"Are you sure?" Juan Carlos sounded skeptical.

With a dramatic roll of the eyes, Hugo laughed. "Am I sure? Let me ask you this," Hugo said. "How many jobs do you know of that call for you to prepare and train every day for different scenarios where you could be attacked by someone you have never met?"

Juan Carlos gave Hugo a curious look.

"Because that's exactly what I've been doing every day for the last fifteen years." Reaching out he grabbed Juan Carlos's shoulder and said in his deep bass voice, "You're fine. Everything's going to be fine."

"Okay," Juan Carlos shrugged. "What's next?"

Hugo saw that Mia was ready and in a confident, nonemotional tone said, "Now, we drive to Andorra. It's a little less than two hundred kilometers from here, so it should take us a couple of hours."

Juan Carlos put out his cigarette and flicked it into the trash can.

Hugo memorized most of the main roads that would get him from Barcelona to Andorra. Mia programmed the GPS app on her smartphone as a precaution. Hugo's eyes darted from the heavy traffic ahead of him to the rearview mirror. He saw the same blue Nissan that followed him when he made a right onto Carrer del Dr. Aiguader about thirty feet behind. When he merged onto a roundabout Hugo purposefully missed his exit and circled a second time. The Nissan made no attempt to take any of the exits and circled along with him.

"We definitely have a tail," Hugo said under his breath.

Chapter Sixty-Two

ANDORRA

Sunrise was just a few hours off, and from the shadows of a small alleyway, Hugo observed the blue Nissan parked up the street from the Andorra Park Hotel. He scanned the empty street. Up to this point, Hugo saw nothing that would lead him to believe that the men in the Nissan intended Juan Carlos any harm, but he had to be sure. There was no room for mistakes in what he did. What he wanted to know was who and why they gave the order to follow Juan Carlos? As a general rule, the best time to kill someone or catch someone when they were most vulnerable was between dusk and dawn when the human race was trying to sleep. The witching hour as Hugo liked to call it, was that time of relative inactivity between three and six in the morning. It was the time that Hugo's high school football coach used to say, "nothing good happens." He silenced his Beretta and secured it in a shoulder holster under his right arm along with a double-edged four-inch combat knife sheathed at the small of his back. Hugo scanned the street a second time for the slightest evidence that anything was out of place and then moved fluidly in and out of shadows until he was behind the parked Nissan. He'd made up his mind that if the two men in the Nissan did not answer his questions to his satisfaction, they would not see another sunrise. Dropping to a knee, he stole a quick glance. Hugo heard the two men engaged in a discussion in Urdu. His angle and concealment were as good as he could hope for crouched behind the small Nissan out of sight of any of the mirrors. Hugo punctured the rear right tire with his knife. The man on the passenger's side exited the car to check on the loud hissing sound coming from the rapidly deflating tire. Without so much as the tiniest flash of hesitation, Hugo drew his Beretta and aimed the sight, so the man instantly spotted the red dot on his chest. He lifted his index finger to his lips signaling to the man to remain quiet. If his partner panicked and reached for his weapon, Hugo would have no choice but to squeeze off a quick shot and kill him. The unsuspecting man took a wobbly step backwards and raised his hands in the air. Hugo moved quickly using the man as a human shield putting the man between himself and the driver in case the driver made a move for his gun. The back seat of the car was only three steps away.

"I just want to talk," Hugo whispered in the man's ear.

The man sitting behind the wheel stopped short of reaching for the glove compartment when he heard his colleague's voice scream, "No!"

He glanced anxiously at Hugo and watched him push his colleague into the backseat. Hugo kept the combat knife pressed firmly against the man's rib cage as a warning against making any sudden movements.

"I just want to talk," Hugo repeated himself slowly.

"Do you speak English; hablan espanol; aites vous comprenez le français?" Hugo asked, trying to find a way to communicate.

The young man sitting in the front of the car nervously shook his head from side to side. "We speak English."

"Good, then I'll get right to it."

"What do I call you?"

"Salim."

"Why are you here Salim?" Hugo frowned.

The two men shared a look that Hugo construed as nervous.

The man sitting next to Hugo mumbled something quickly in Urdu to Salim. He glanced warily at Hugo and with as much conviction as he could muster, said "We are here for the same reason as you are."

Hugo's scowl deepened. He knew there was much more.

"Who told you to follow Juan Carlos?" Hugo said gruffly.

Salim looked at Hugo with nervous eyes.

Sensing that he might talk, the man in the back told him to stay quiet in Urdu. In broken Urdu Hugo asked, “Do you know who I am?”

Salim hesitated. His eyes searched Hugo’s face for a moment, and then he nodded.

“Then you know that I have killed many of your brothers and will not hesitate to kill both of you, if you do not tell me what I want to know,” Hugo said.

Salim blinked several times struggling to keep his composure.

Hugo raised his pistol and pointed it at Salim’s face.

Salim stared at Hugo, terror in his eyes.

“Tell me Salim, do you still get into paradise and collect your 72 virgins if you’re killed for being stupid?”

Salim struggled to get the words out. “We are not here to hurt him.”

“Then answer my questions or I’m going to blow your brains all over the windshield,” Hugo snapped.

Both men were quiet.

“This isn’t your holy war. So, why sacrifice your lives for an infidel?” Hugo said.

“What do you know about the Koran?” The man in the back seat scoffed.

Hugo grinned. “Wrong question. What you should be asking me is what can you tell me to keep me from killing you both?” Hugo increased the pressure of the combat knife against the man’s ribs and placed the red dot of the front sight of his Beretta on the bridge of Salim’s nose.

“Salim how old are you, nineteen or twenty? Hugo growled.

Salim was dripping in sweat and taking rapid breaths. “Seventeen,” his voice cracked.

Hugo looked Salim calmly in the eye and said, "In ten seconds my knife is going to cut through your friend's ribs to his heart, and he will bleed out. But you won't live to see him die because by then you will have two bullets in your brain."

Salim was shaking.

"I'll tell you what you want to know," he cried out with absolute sincerity.

* * *

Salim confessed to knowing very little. He received instructions and a photograph of Juan Carlos Laporte from one of his usual channels. He was told to watch the airport. If he spotted Juan Carlos, he was to immediately report in, follow him and report back on his location. Salim explained that he was told that the people interested in Juan Carlos would arrive within twenty-four hours and, until then, he was to keep a close watch on him. Hugo suspected that Salim probably didn't know much more. Hugo knew he could only push so far. Salim's contact appeared to be his terrorist cell's lifeline to whatever terrorist organization Salim was connected to so Hugo assumed that Salim would choose to die before he gave up his contact. Hugo briefly considered doing the CIA a favor by killing them, but he left that life behind when he received an honorable discharge and now lived by a different set of rules.

Chapter Sixty-Three

ATLANTA

An ominous squall line of thunderstorms rolled into Atlanta temporarily canceling all flights out of the airport. Lines snaked out from the gates to the terminal breezeway as the numbers of frustrated travelers stranded at the airport continued to pile up. Pierce found a small space on the floor in a corner anticipating that it would be a while before his flight to Miami would be cleared to leave. By the time Pierce left Oklahoma he and Dode had successfully put in place safety measures and protocols for delivering the video to the DEA in the event anything happened to him. Even so, Pierce couldn't keep his thoughts from careening towards the horrifying notion that he hadn't accounted for every possible scenario. As a lawyer, he had to learn to live with that feeling. There was no such thing as the perfect set of facts. Every case had its warts. His mentor used to say lead with your strongest argument but be prepared for opposing counsel to expose your weakness. How you respond once it has been uncovered is usually the difference maker. But in this instance the stakes were higher. This was an all or nothing exchange with Dario Carraboca, the Cartel's operations in exchange for the lives of Juan Carlos and Alexis. Pierce tried to drive his thoughts away from the crushing feeling that this ordeal would never be over until either Dario or Juan Carlos was dead. Until then, Pierce felt in his gut that Alexis's life would always be in danger hanging by the proverbial thread. He urged his mind towards a rational explanation that perhaps the doubts he was feeling had more to do with not knowing where Alexis was and not being unable to confirm that she was safe. Knowing that Hugo and Mia were with her was his only calming thought. He pictured Alexis's almond shaped eyes and felt himself smile. Every time she looked at him, Pierce felt them reach into his soul. Even when they looked at him disapprovingly, there was a bewitching clarity and tenderness in her eyes. He chuckled when he thought about the hard stare Alexis leveled at him when she felt he was paying too much attention to the tall Nordic blond wearing nothing but body paint, or the look on her face when she thought they were going to have to spend the night in that broken down shack in Wetumka, Oklahoma.

* * *

Pierce powered up the cell phone Hugo gave back to him just before he left. There were an alarming number of missed calls and urgent voice messages from his DEA contact, Leonard Williams. Pierce looked at his watch. It was almost midnight in Atlanta but only 9 P.M. in California. He punched in Leonard's number and, after a few rings, a deep voice answered. When Leonard recognized Pierce's voice, Pierce detected a flicker of relief in his tone.

"The last time we spoke, you were thinking of representing Juan Carlos Laporte, and I contacted Special Agent Hogan on your behalf to request that he provide you with some information on the case. Then Juan Carlos disappears under mysterious circumstances and I'm no longer able to reach you. I wasn't sure what to think. I didn't know whether the cartel had gotten you—" Leonard rambled.

Pierce shrugged. "They didn't. Nothing to worry about."

"I hope that you are completely out of it now," Leonard said.

Pierce didn't answer right away. His tired eyes caught sight of a young woman chasing after a young toddler running out of control.

"Yes," Pierce said, "completely."

"I sincerely hope so."

"Juan Carlos and his wife are safely out of the country," Pierce said. "It's over."

An uncomfortable silence passed, and then Leonard told Pierce that Juan Carlos's freedom came at a high cost. He ticked off the names of the four people on Curacao who were suspected of helping Juan Carlos and told Pierce that three were missing and presumed dead. A disbelieving expression formed on Pierce's face. His head was swimming with possibilities, none of them good. Leonard then added that Hogan was in charge of a massive manhunt to find Juan Carlos.

"You know, there is bound to be some fallout," he warned Pierce.

Pierce listened in his perceptive way, reading between the lines. "That wouldn't surprise me."

"Pierce," said Leonard. "Hogan will press wanting to know if you had any involvement in Juan Carlos's disappearance."

Pierce's jaw clenched. He needed time to process the news about the people who possibly lost their lives helping Juan Carlos. He was in no mood to think about what might happen to him or to talk about Hogan. "Let him press."

Leonard knew Pierce well. As well as he knew anyone. If he was in Pierce's shoes, he would take a vacation and disappear for a couple of weeks, but he knew there was nothing he could say to convince Pierce to take his advice.

"Pierce, the DEA has a lot riding on this one. I may not be able to run interference," Leonard sounded disappointed. "If Hogan thinks you know where Juan Carlos is, he will . . ."

"Do what exactly?" Pierce interrupted Leonard. "Juan Carlos was not formally charged with any crime in the U.S. He's not a fugitive under U.S. Law," Pierce said a little testily.

Leonard leaned back in his chair. He hated using phones. It came from knowing firsthand the capabilities of the DEA and NSA, but there was little choice given the hornet's nest Pierce was about to step into. He'd known Special Agent Hogan for over ten years. Whether Juan Carlos had been charged with a crime in the U.S. wouldn't matter to him. "He'll push you. When that doesn't work, he'll threaten you."

"Then he'll push and threaten me." Pierce's voice took on a harder edge.

Overhead the airline agent announced the last boarding call for the flight to Miami.

"My flight's about to take off. I better get going,"

Pierce ended the call; his mind was thousands of miles away.

The tone in Pierce's voice worried Leonard. He sounded emotionally empty.

* * *

THE COOL CRISP evening in the high Pyrenees was perfect walking weather, so that's what Juan Carlos did. He slipped a cell phone in the pocket of a leather jacket that Hugo paid cash for in a duty-free shop in the Barcelona airport. It wasn't exactly what Juan Carlos would have picked for himself, but Hugo didn't want him in front of store surveillance cameras. Juan Carlos walked along the narrow winding streets bordered on both sides by old stone buildings. After a couple of days, Juan Carlos was beginning to enjoy the ebb and flow of the small tourist attraction wedged in the mountains between France and Spain. He stopped by the entrance of a small specialty shop to light a cigarette; it was then that Juan Carlos noticed two men standing by a granite monument. Juan Carlos casually glanced at the two faces. He was pretty sure he recognized one of them. Over the years, Juan Carlos committed to memory the faces and identities of the specialists employed by the cartel. As he walked past them, Juan Carlos lowered his gaze, resisting the impulse to steal a closer look. He took his time walking back to the hotel. The fifteen-minute walk took forty as he stopped in several stores and made small purchases which allowed him to move his eyes in their general direction and confirm that they were still there as he exited the shops. The two men plodded methodically in the same direction but were gone by the time Juan Carlos stepped out of the pastry shop which was only a few steps away from the Andorra Park Hotel. Juan Carlos realized that their presence in Andorra was no coincidence. The only logical reason for sending men to Andorra was to kill him. That possibility made his heart pound against his ribcage. Even if their orders were to watch him, assassins excel at one thing: snuffing out human life. If they were sent to Andorra, Juan Carlos expected that it was only a matter of time before Dario gave the order. Despite the crisp bite in the mountain air sweat began to form on Juan Carlos's upper lip. Silently he cursed himself for not being better prepared for this contingency. The one thing he decided he would not do is stay in Andorra lying awake at night wondering when Dario would make his move.

As soon as he strolled into the hotel lobby, Juan Carlos took a seat next to the fireplace and the well-tended wood fire and made a call. When he was finished, Juan Carlos sat in silence staring at the crackling flames concentrating on how to proceed. After several minutes, he glanced over and made brief eye contact with the concierge before walking over to his desk.

"Good Evening Alain," he said, reading the nameplate on his lapel. The man's gaze was lowered towards a list of pending matters.

Alain took a moment to look up and acknowledge Juan Carlos. "Ahh Bonjour Monsieur Placido," he smiled warmly. "How may I be of assistance?"

"Alain," Juan Carlos leaned forward and in a low voice said, "Can I count on your discretion to handle a matter for me?"

Alain gave him a crisp nod. "But of course, Monsieur."

Juan Carlos smiled. "I am going to have a package delivered this evening or early morning. I want you to text me at this number when it arrives."

"It will be my pleasure sir."

"Alain, I will compensate you handsomely if you can help me with a small matter," Juan Carlos reassured him.

Alain looked at Juan Carlos and smiled.

"Alain," Juan Carlos continued. "I need you to arrange for a ride for me and my wife to the airport in Barcelona."

Alain nodded. "Of course."

Juan Carlos cleared his throat and appeared to be choosing his words carefully. "It's very important that we are able to leave the hotel without being seen . . . I'll pay you $10,000 Euros if you can arrange this for me."

Just then Juan Carlos's phone began to vibrate. The message on the screen read "1 AM."

"When would you like to leave sir?"

"Today, as soon as you can arrange it after my package arrives," he said.

Alain thought about it for a second and glanced at his wristwatch.

"The food deliveries for the hotel begin to arrive around five in the morning. The only exit that I can be sure of that you will not be seen leaving the hotel will be out through the delivery bay in the back of the hotel," Alain said. "I can arrange to have one of the truck driver's take you straight away to the airport if that will work for you?"

Juan Carlos nodded. "That should do nicely. We'll be ready."

"Is there anything else I can do for you?"

Juan Carlos shook his head. "No, that's all we'll need . . . I will be back down around 1 AM to wait on the package."

"Of course, Monsieur Placido."

Chapter Sixty-Four

At 1:45 AM the phone in Hugo's hotel room rang. The instant Hugo picked up the receiver, Juan Carlos began to ramble.

"They are coming," Juan Carlos cried with indisputable fear in his voice.

Hugo sat up in his bed and tried to clear his mind. "Slow down Juan. Who's coming?"

Juan Carlos spoke at an accelerated pace. "I recognized several of Dario's men in town. We should talk, have a plan, they are coming, they are going to make a move . . . we have to meet now," Juan Carlos blathered on.

"Now?"

"Yes, now. Don't you hear what I'm telling you? The cartel is here . . . There could be only one reason for that. I'm on my way up to your room," Juan Carlos said and hung up the phone before Hugo could respond.

Hugo slid out of bed and grabbed a pair of shorts sitting on the chair in the corner. When Juan Carlos knocked, Hugo unlocked the door. Mia was asleep twisted up in sheets, blankets and several pillows. Even though he was still half asleep, the instant Hugo saw the darkness in Juan Carlos's eyes, he knew something was wrong. His eyes were fixed and unblinking above a small odd smile. The extra nanosecond that it took for Hugo to spot the dull sheen of the silenced Glock 19 pistol aimed at him was all it took for Juan Carlos to squeeze off two quick shots. The hollow tip bullets struck Hugo in the chest flattening on impact and doubling in size as they tore through his heart.

The muffled sound of gunshots and the thud made by Hugo's body as it collapsed onto the floor jarred Mia out of a deep sleep. Wide-eyed and gasping, Mia tunneled under the blankets towards the nightstand to grab her gun. Juan Carlos fired off another round. The shot slammed painfully into Mia's ribs tearing the breath from her lungs. Her upper body fell backward, sending her head crashing with a whiplash effect against the nightstand. A dark pain spread quickly through her chest. Mia made a feeble attempt to reach for her gun. Juan Carlos's next shot hit Mia on her left cheek with tremendous force. The impact of the bullet caused her body to arch like a bow and then go limp. The outline of a man standing over her was the last thing Mia saw before everything went black.

Juan Carlos still had three hours before he was supposed to meet Alain. After tying her hands together and rolling her over onto her stomach, Juan Carlos took a seat and lit a cigarette. He sat in a chair opposite the bed, teeth bared in a snarl, staring at Mia, muttering to himself. When he was done with his cigarette, he put it out on Mia's back and slid his fingers between her legs. He buried his fingers deep inside of her vagina and brought them to his nose. Juan Carlos inhaled deeply savoring Mia's scent. Mia continued to lay there unconscious and bleeding while Juan Carlos carefully removed his clothing to avoid getting any of Mia's blood on them. All it took was one fierce drive for him to shove his penis completely inside of her. Juan Carlos latched on to her hips and brutally fucked her. Mia's eyelids fluttered and her body grunted in time with Juan Carlos's violent thrusts. When Juan Carlos came hard inside of her, breathing between his teeth he said, "I wanted to slit your throat for the other night, but this was so much more satisfying."

Juan Carlos got up from the blood covered bed and walked into the bathroom. He jumped in the shower and washed off Mia's blood. He didn't feel the least bit of remorse. Sacrificing Hugo and Mia was necessary. It was something he suspected that he might have to do at some point in order to escape from the cartel. If he and Alexis disappeared during the predawn hours, Hugo and Mia would discover that they were gone long before the cartel's men knew. Hugo and Mia would look for them. Juan Carlos was afraid that they would lead the assassins to Barcelona before he could safely get out of the country. Therefore, there was only one solution. This was why Juan Carlos decided that Hugo and Mia had to die.

Chapter Sixty-Five

Juan Carlos stood in front of Alexis's bed watching her sleep and waiting. Precisely at 4.30 A.M. he turned on the lights in the room. He decided thirty minutes was enough time for Alexis to wake up and get herself ready to travel. Any more time and she would start to ask questions.

"Alexis, wake up. We have to go."

Alexis made a sound of disgust and drifted back to sleep. After five minutes of waiting Juan Carlos tried again.

"Alexis wake your ass up. We have to go. There's no time," he snapped, this time his voice was deliberately harsh.

Alexis opened her eyes surprised to see Juan Carlos hovering over her.

"What is it Juan?"

"Dario has men in Andorra. We have to get out of here now."

Alexis rubbed her eyes trying to wake up. He told her that they needed to be downstairs in the lobby in twenty minutes.

Alexis sat up. "What about Hugo and Mia?"

"I just left them a couple of hours ago. They worked most of the night putting together a plan to sneak us out of here."

Juan Carlos spun a story that they spotted a few men last night that looked suspicious, and that Hugo and Mia believed that they were indeed Dario's men. Juan Carlos explained that as part of the plan Hugo and Mia were going to stay back and casually walk around town in the morning hoping to buy more time. He told Alexis that as long as Dario's men saw Hugo and Mia that they would probably assume that he and Alexis were back in the hotel. Alexis listened while she milled around the room gathering her things and getting dressed. She threw on a pair of old faded Levi's and a stylish sweatshirt that she had borrowed from Mia. Alexis went into the bathroom, washed her face, brushed her teeth, grabbed a black scrunchie and pulled her long chestnut hair back in a ponytail.

When Alexis and Juan Carlos stepped out of the elevator, Alain was standing by the concierge's desk waiting. Juan Carlos discreetly handed Alain a white envelope.

"Merci Monsieur," Alain nodded, sliding the envelope into his jacket pocket.

"Is everything ready?"

"Yes, the delivery truck arrived a little ahead of schedule. We have to move quickly. Please follow me." Alain replied sounding rushed.

Alexis scanned the hotel lobby and gave Juan Carlos a questioning look.

"Where are Hugo and Mia?"

"They are not coming with us. We went over this already," he snapped impatiently.

"I know," Alexis shot back. "It's just odd that they wouldn't be here to see us off."

Juan Carlos gave her an ambiguous smile. "See us off," he repeated with irritation in his voice. "Jesus Alexis! We're not going on a fucking cruise. They are probably not here because they don't want to draw attention to us."

"Please hurry," Alain motioned to follow him.

Juan Carlos cut Alexis off with a wave of his hand. "We have to go."

Alain walked quickly. He took a sharp left through two swinging doors into the hotel's kitchen. Without a sound, Juan Carlos and Alexis sprinted trying to keep up with Alain who weaved around the kitchen staff with the agility and speed of a world class slalom skier. Waiting by the entrance to the loading bay was a short middle-aged man wearing a black beret that did little to camouflage a large protruding forehead.

"This is your driver." Alain said, in a rigid and precise accent.

The driver went by the name of Pepe. The man gave Juan Carlos and Alexis a gray-toothed smile. "Buenas."

"Son Cubano?" The man asked in a thick Basque accent.

Juan Carlos shook his head. "Actually, my wife and I are from Argentina," Juan Carlos replied in Spanish.

The man blinked, confused. "I mean no offense by that. Your Spanish sounds Cuban to me." The driver coughed and wiped his mouth on a white handkerchief as he fixed his dull brown eyes on Alexis.

"This is the couple that I mentioned to you that needs to get to the airport in Barcelona as soon as possible," Alain nudged him, sounding harshly efficient.

Pepe seemed to be enthusiastic to be of service. "Yes, of course," he said, taking Alexis by the hand and helping her into the back of the truck.

Alexis huddled into the corner of the truck bed. Juan Carlos followed behind her and sat beside her bracing his feet.

"This will be over soon," he told her.

Alexis briefly rested her eyes on him and felt a shiver go through her as if something had plucked at her nerves. Pepe slammed the truck's doors behind them, and everything went black.

Alexis heard the muffled sound of the truck's engine and faint music coming from the truck cab. The truck ambled out of the loading dock and took a tight turn onto the narrow road and drove past a smattering of cars parked on the road. Alexis struggled to sit upright each time the truck turned. Two men sitting in one of the parked cars watched the truck as it drove past them and left the small country of

Andorra. Juan Carlos and Alexis sat in the sightless darkness and didn't say another word to each other for the remainder of the trip.

A couple of hours later, the truck came to a complete stop. Pepe banged on the trailer as he walked past it on his way to the back to open the doors. The morning light poured in all at once temporarily blinding Alexis. She turned her face away half-closing her eyes.

"Are we at the airport?" she asked, slowly turning around. Pepe was amiably standing at the entrance waiting to help Alexis out.

"No, we are about ten kilometers away," he said. "Come," he gestured. "Please sit in the front with your husband. It will be easier and faster for you to get out once we arrive at the airport."

Once they were safely through customs, Juan Carlos put his sunglasses back on his face and checked his watch. It was a quarter past eight. "Our flight leaves at 10:25 AM, so we have about an hour before we can board."

Alexis could not think of a single reason for Hugo or Mia to book them on a flight back to the United States. She almost asked Juan Carlos why they would send them back and then thought better of it. He appeared to be more preoccupied than usual. Alexis knew better than anyone about his violent nature. When Juan Carlos was stressed, he was susceptible to great mood swings and a seemingly insatiable desire to beat her. He had enough self-control to restrain himself from hitting her in public. But Juan Carlos kept a mental ledger. He hadn't always abused Alexis. When he first began to formally date her, Juan Carlos was a handsome and slender man. He had been a bit of a playboy, always attending the best parties that South Beach hosted. Back then, Alexis didn't mind, since she wasn't old enough to drink and her parents had her under a strict curfew. She assumed his behavior would change once they were married. Now almost forty, Juan Carlos wasn't the distinguished man that Alexis expected he would grow into, but instead he was a quick tempered, gluttonous tyrant.

Juan Carlos plopped down on a seat next to the gate.

"Are Hugo and Mia going to follow later?" Alexis asked.

"Later," he answered in a dismissive voice.

She could tell he was lying. Alexis glanced down and noticed goose bumps on her arms. She hoped it was merely because she was sitting near an air conditioning vent and not an omen of something bad.

"When?" She pressed.

Juan Carlos grabbed her hand and squeezed it. His voice took on an angry tone. "Do yourself a favor and stop asking me questions . . . In fact, why don't you make yourself useful and go get us a couple of coffees while we wait?"

Chapter Sixty-Six

Pierce sat by the Four Seasons pool sipping a cup of coffee and casually perusing the newspaper as another Sunday morning in Miami got under way. At first blush, he appeared to be relaxed, enjoying his morning, but his mood was tense and his patience short. With the sun quickly warming the cool morning air, Pierce let out a yawn. The voice of a woman drew his attention away from the paper and he looked across the pool. From his vantage point, all he could see were empty cabanas and chaise lounges, and then a blonde beauty came into view. Without warning she dropped her robe and stretched her sun bronzed arms above her head revealing a slender figure with a large pair of breasts. Pierce smiled as he went back to reading his paper. A few moments later his face turned serious. Lifting his eyes over the top of his newspaper, he saw a man standing directly in front of him.

"Excuse me, would you mind moving a little to the left? You're blocking my sun." And then Pierce went back to feigning interest in the paper.

"Mr. Evangelista, my name is Rene Cabrera. I'm sorry to disturb your Sunday morning, but I have pressing business that cannot wait."

Pierce did not offer his hand. He simply looked at the chair opposite him and nodded for his guest to sit. Rene nodded at the server and she immediately came over with a napkin and a fresh cup of coffee for him. Rene reached for the cup with the same hand that held a cigarette. Never taking his eyes off Pierce he said, "We have a situation. Two of your people have been shot and Juan Carlos and his wife are missing. My employer wants you to know that we had nothing to do with this."

Pierce gave him a skeptical look. "And why should I believe you?"

There wasn't a single characteristic about Rene that was memorable. At five feet nine, he was neither tall nor short. He had a thin mustache that served as a dividing line for an otherwise bland and forgettable face. The dullness in Rene's eyes gave Pierce a feeling that Rene was someone the cartel employed to deal with its problems in a final manner. Pierce imagined that Rene handled things for the cartel that most people didn't have the stomach for. Rene exhaled and fanned away some of the smoke and very matter-of-factly said, "Because if we did it, you would be dead instead of having coffee with me."

Pierce thought about Hugo and Mia and then asked. "What happened to my friends?"

Rene didn't answer for several long seconds. Finally, he said, "Mr. Jackson was shot twice at close range. Ms. Dawson was also shot twice. She is in a hospital in Barcelona in critical condition."

A gust of wind sent Pierce's newspaper flying. Two men suddenly appeared out of the shadows to help the server round up the newspaper pages that flapped along the pool area like loosely trimmed sails. Rene made a shooing motion and the two men were gone. He gave Pierce a moment to process everything before he spoke again.

"My orders were to fly to Miami and personally give you the news." Rene began nodding his head slowly. "And most importantly, to assure you that we have not broken our agreement."

So intense was Pierce's concentration that he did not hear the question from the young woman the first time she asked him if he wanted another cup of coffee.

Finally, he said. "Whoever killed Hugo probably has Juan Carlos and his wife."

Rene mulled over Pierce's comment for a second. He raised the cup to his lips and took a sip of coffee and set it back down. "Can I be brutally honest?"

"Please," Pierce nodded, intrigued by Rene's willingness to put some of his cards on the table.

"I've known Juan Carlos for the better part of twenty years . . . He is very smart and calculating, but he also has no conscience. Juan Carlos is . . . how you say . . . a virus. If someone can be useful to him, he uses him, and when Juan Carlos has used him up, he eliminates him."

Pierce kept his stare focused on Rene's dark pupils. "Are you saying that Juan Carlos shot Hugo and Mia?" Pierce asked more than a bit surprised.

"A dead body provides a useful distraction if he was trying to disappear . . . I'm saying it's a distinct possibility," Rene answered with a nod. "Whoever shot Hugo fired two rounds at close range. Someone with your friend's training doesn't get caught with his guard down unless he had no reason to suspect his assailant. All I'm saying is that I would bet money that your friend knew the person who shot him," Rene shrugged intuitively.

Stunned, Pierce put his coffee cup down. He wasn't expecting to hear that Juan Carlos was responsible for shooting Hugo and Mia. "When Dario accepted your terms, we made it clear to everyone that we do business with, that Juan Carlos and anyone traveling with him was not to be harmed," Rene explained.

Pierce leaned back in his chair. He looked out at the water. There wasn't a ripple on Biscayne Bay, and he said more to himself than to Rene, "Could the shooting be unrelated to Juan Carlos? Perhaps, connected in some way to when Hugo and Mia were with Special Forces?"

Rene shook his head. "No! We were very clear that no one was to be harmed. The terrorist groups that would have reason to kill your friends would not risk jeopardizing their relationship with us to kill a couple of former soldiers who were simply following orders."

Pierce felt guilt ridden and deepening horror as he played out possible outcomes in his mind.

"If you're right about Juan Carlos, why didn't he shoot his wife as well? If you know him as well as you claim to, then you know he doesn't . . ."

"Because," Rene cut Pierce off. "Alexis must still have some value to him. Make no mistake, the moment he thinks differently, Juan Carlos will kill her."

Pierce couldn't overlook how casually Rene treated the possibility that it was only a matter of time before Juan Carlos would murder Alexis. It was clear to him that he and the cartel had different agendas, and the cartel didn't care who died in the process as long as Juan Carlos disappeared for good.

A foreboding premonition hijacked his thoughts and Pierce said, "I'm coming with you."

Rene looked at Pierce, his eyes revealing nothing. "There's no need for that. We can handle this."

Pierce couldn't get the bad images out of his mind. "I don't think so. From where I'm sitting, one of my friends is dead, the other dying and Alexis's death appears to be perfectly acceptable collateral damage as long as you get Juan Carlos."

There was an awkward moment of silence and then Rene reluctantly said, "I will run your request by my employer."

"It's not a request," Pierce corrected him. "And while you're at it, let Dario know that if Juan Carlos did shoot my friends, I'm open to changing the terms of our agreement."

Rene did his best to contain his grin. Dario had predicted Pierce's response almost perfectly.

Pierce shot Rene a curious look. "Where are we going?"

"Juan Carlos has a mistress in New York. If he contacted anyone, it would probably be her. So, we are going to start there," Rene said.

Pierce wasn't buying it. In the little time he spent with Juan Carlos, there was nothing he said or did to lead him to think that a girlfriend in New York registered even a small blip on his radar or to make Pierce think that she would be the one person Juan Carlos would contact if he was on the run. "Sounds like a bit of a leap."

Rene made a face and then said, "I didn't go to Harvard, but I know Juan Carlos better than you do. If you have a better idea, I'm all ears."

Pierce shrugged. "I didn't mean anything by it. That just sounds very predictable."

Rene's voice was tinged with irritation "That's exactly why Juan Carlos would do it. He thinks he's too smart to get caught and he's always preferred to hide in plain sight."

Pierce frowned when the thought occurred to him that by hiding in the United States, Juan Carlos could always turn himself into the DEA if he suspected that the cartel was closing in. If Juan Carlos spilled his guts to the DEA, his leverage would be gone, and Alexis would surely die.

Rene pulled out a picture of a woman and an address and slid it across the table. "She is the only person that Juan Carlos trusts completely." Rene stopped talking and gave Pierce a stern look. "This shit is going to get nasty, if you don't have the stomach for it, I suggest you stay here in Miami."

Pierce returned the look. He suspected that it would be much cleaner for the cartel to kill Alexis. He was her only chance to come out of this alive.

"You don't have to worry about me. So, when do we leave?"

Rene didn't like it, but he didn't have a choice. With a resigned tone he said, "Right after I make a phone call."

Chapter Sixty-Seven

NEW YORK

Jessica Davis was nowhere to be found when they arrived at her two-bedroom Brooklyn Heights condominium. While Rene and his men fanned out searching the apartment for any clue that might help lead them to Juan Carlos, Pierce tilted his head to the side and squinted in thought. There was something about the way several articles of clothing were scattered across the bed that made him think that she had packed in a hurry. He took a moment to stare out of Jessica's bedroom window at the dockyards and the busy New York harbor in the distance, wondering if Alexis was safe. His body felt anesthetized.

With obvious displeasure on his face, Rene stormed into Jessica's bedroom unleashing a torrent of expletives meant to punctuate his suspicion that Jessica had also disappeared. Pierce turned around. Rene's bombastic behavior was not entirely unexpected. He had to report yet another wrinkle to his boss in Venezuela who was only interested in results.

Pierce thought about Juan Carlos. If he was as duplicitous and cunning as Rene contended, he would have expected Rene to come looking for Jessica and had gotten her out of New York before Rene could find her.

"It looks like she left in a hurry," Pierce said. Rene turned his glare onto Pierce. "There's nothing here. Are you ready?"

Pierce returned his look with a stoic expressionless face. "Where to now?"

Rene told him that the minute Jessica became more than a casual tryst, the cartel checked into her to make sure that she wasn't a law enforcement agent working undercover.

"Her parents live in Mamaroneck. That's about a ninety-minute drive from here. They'll know where to find their daughter."

Pierce anxiously tapped the fingers of his right hand on his right thigh while he was driven through the dark streets of a string of sleepy bedroom communities that made up Westchester County. It was a few hours before dawn, and the thought of torturing an innocent couple until they agreed to give up the location of their daughter made Pierce's skin crawl. He did not want to sink to those depths. To Pierce, torturing blameless people was monstrous and barbaric. But unfortunately, they were rapidly running out of solid leads and Rene held a different view.

* * *

THE DARK SEDAN turned left onto Sherman Avenue and circled the house twice checking for surveillance. It was almost 5 AM when the sedan rolled into the driveway. Like most assassins, Rene preferred to kill or kidnap his targets when they slept. His reason was obvious. People didn't think clearly and were the least prepared to defend themselves when they were yanked from a deep sleep. Rene's singular goal was to get Jessica's parents to talk by whatever means necessary. Turning towards Pierce, Rene said, "You'd better wait in the car. You won't like what's about to happen."

Pierce gave Rene a hard look. "You don't need to kill them."

Rene ignored his comment and placed a tiny transmitter into his ear. The other two men hopped over the small hedge and went around to the back of the house.

Rene waited for one of his men to cut the power and disarm the alarm system to the house before picking the lock to the front door. He scanned the house for the slightest evidence that anything was out of place. Rene moved in the darkness through the foyer and to the staircase leading to the upstairs bedrooms like someone who was familiar with the layout of the house. He could hear wheezing and snoring as he approached the master bedroom. He listened to the snoring for almost a minute before the voice in his earpiece told him that there was no one else in the rest of the house. Rene drew his pistol and slowly turned the brass handle to the door without so much as a click. He looked for the light switch and stole a quick glance of the bed trying to confirm two bodies before switching the light on. After turning on the light, he moved a step closer and leveled his weapon. One of Rene's men used the tip of his silencer to jolt the sleeping woman out of her slumber.

"The instant the woman opened her eyes and saw the end of a barrel of a gun inches from her face, she let out a scream.

"If you scream again, I'll put a bullet in your head," the man scowled.

The look on Mr. Davis's face was first one of shock then dawning horror as his eyes came to rest on Rene's gun. "What do you want?" he stammered.

Rene grabbed him by the collar of his pajamas and dragged him to the foot of the bed. "We want to know where your daughter Jessica is."

Wide-eyed and breathing rapidly Mr. Davis gasped, "I . . . I don't know . . . What do you want with her?"

His response caused Rene's eyebrow to rise half an inch. Rene checked his watch. He did not expect it to take long for him to break. From what he knew, Mr. Davis was a civilian with no training on how to handle pain.

"Mr. Davis, what you don't know is that eventually you will tell me what I want to know. I can make this quick and painless for you and your wife if you cooperate," Rene said.

Mr. Davis glared at Rene with bloodshot eyes. "I'm telling you the truth. I don't know where she is," he said firmly.

Rene brought his right hand around with blinding speed, slapping Mr. Davis so hard he knocked him off the edge of the bed sending him sprawling across the floor. Mrs. Davis screamed.

"You have one more chance and then I put a bullet in your wife!" Mr. Davis lay stunned on the floor. Panic set in and he threw his hands up to signal his surrender. Rene's man grabbed him by the throat and yanked him off the floor and threw him back onto the bed like a rag doll.

"I . . . I don't know what to say. If you want me to lie to you, I'll lie, but I don't know where my daughter is," Mr. Davis continued to repeat himself, desperate and pleading one moment and angry and antagonistic the next.

Rene gave Mr. Davis an almost sympathetic stare. "I'm only interested in speaking with your daughter because she has information that I want. I'm not looking to hurt her."

Mr. Davis buried his face in his hands and continued to insist that he did not know where his daughter was. Rene's expression contained a resolve that his patience had run out. Taking a step back, Rene fired his silenced weapon hitting Mrs. Davis in her collarbone propelling her backwards, slamming against the bed's headboard.

Mr. Davis looked up at Rene with disbelief and horror.

"Do you want your wife to live or die?" Rene barked.

Mr. Davis looked at him with honest confusion on his face, so Rene repeated the question, this time screaming it directly into his ear. "Do you want your wife to live or die?"

His eyes were wide with terror as tears flowed from them.

"You have five seconds before I kill your wife."

"Wait a minute, wait a minute!" he shouted. "I'll tell you but please don't kill my wife," he pleaded through sniffles and sobs.

Mr. Davis looked at his wife and mouthed the words "I'm sorry." And then he said in a low voice. "I know where she is."

* * *

Jessica's father shook nervously when he told Rene that he kept a boat at a marina on Sanibel Island just off Florida's west coast. He continued to weep as he told them that Jessica was staying on the boat with some friends.

Rene stared menacingly at him as he handed him a piece of paper and pen.

"Write down the name of the boat and the address of the marina."

Mr. Davis handed the piece of paper back to Rene and began to blubber. "Please don't hurt my baby."

When Rene was satisfied that Mr. Davis had told him everything he knew, he squeezed the trigger three times in rapid succession. Rene pointed the pistol and long silencer at Mrs. Davis. She covered her face with her hands. Rene was amused that she thought covering her face could stop a bullet. He fired two hollow-tipped rounds. The second bullet went through her hand and her left eye, cutting through her brain and exploding out of the back of her head.

Chapter Sixty-Eight

TAMPA BAY

On the flight from New York to Tampa Bay, Pierce reminded Rene that he and Dario needed to speak before the cartel could make any move against Juan Carlos. There was a moment of uncomfortable silence as Rene and his men all looked at each other. Rene didn't care to be bridled by an agreement between Dario and Pierce. Any technicalities or understanding that needed to be sorted out were for other people to handle, people who sat in comfortable leather chairs. Rene and his men were on their way to Sanibel Island to get a job done, and in Rene's mind, it was a job that should include taking care of Pierce and neutralizing the threat of any future leak of the video once and for all. After several seconds, Pierce asked, "Did you hear what I said?"

"Yes, I heard you," Rene answered Pierce. "But Dario agreed to your terms under the threat that you would release the video if he harmed Juan Carlos." Rene flashed a contemptuous smile. "Your friends in Spain are no longer a threat and we have you here with us. We know that Shane is in Las Vegas so who is left to . . ."

Pierce didn't blink or show the slightest sign of tension. It wasn't in his personality to get emotional; he had divorced intellect from emotion a long time ago. He knew that Rene was not a man to be taken lightly, but Pierce was far from intimidated, and he also knew that he couldn't ignore Rene's threat.

"Precisely why you should leave the negotiations to the big boys," he said, cutting him off. "You think by killing me you stop the video from being released?" Pierce couldn't help but express his amusement. "If I were you, I would get the go ahead from Dario before pulling the trigger on this plan. Because there's no coming back from that fuck up," Pierce said with a smug smile plastered across his face.

Rene gave Pierce a measured look. He never considered that an amateur like Pierce would develop anything sophisticated. "You're bluffing."

Pierce laughed. "I'll let you in on a secret. I punch in a code and answer a series of different and random questions every day . . . If I don't enter the code, or if I answer any of the questions incorrectly, the video automatically gets released to the FBI, DEA and INTERPOL.

Rene squeezed his drink so tightly his knuckles turned white. In his mind, he was swearing the same four-letter word over and over again.

Pierce, like all great tacticians, focused on the smallest of details without ever losing sight of the overall picture. "Kill me and the video gets released. If you torture me and don't get the code before the window of time expires to punch in the code, the video gets released. We both know that is a huge roll of the dice," Pierce smiled. "Then again, since I know you're going to kill me once I give you what you want, I may give you the wrong code. The only way for you to know is to enter it. And you know what happens if you enter the wrong code . . . Do you need me to describe the shit-storm of all shit-storms that happens after that?" He was still smiling.

Rene couldn't think of an adequate response. With a dismissive grunt he snarled, "Well that wouldn't be too good for your ex-wife."

Pierce's face gave away nothing as he pretended to be stumped. "You got me. Game over. You win. I'm going to forfeit my life and not release the video to save the life of a woman that divorced me," Pierce said in a sarcastic tone.

Rene wasn't amused in the slightest.

At that point in their conversation Pierce decided he had enough fun laying his traps and making Rene uncomfortable. His tone suddenly turned serious. He grew up in the slums of New York with drug dealers and gang bangers. No Ivy League education would ever let him forget the deadly nature of the streets where human life held no meaning. Those laws were not unique to the Bronx. They applied everywhere where drugs were used as currency. Instinctively, he always knew that the cartel would kill him the first chance they got unless he had them by the balls.

"The biggest difference between you and me is that I didn't underestimate the cartel. But you clearly misjudged me. I know what you are. But make no mistake, if you kill me, it's only a matter of time before the cartel is also dead," Pierce warned Rene.

Rene said nothing. He wasn't sure what to think, much less what to believe.

Pierce's face was only inches from Rene's. He could smell the sour stench of nicotine on his breath.

"So, are you going to call Dario?"

The darkness behind Rene's eyes began to turn red. An anger burned inside of him. If all had gone according to plan, Rene would kill Pierce once they found Juan Carlos in Sanibel. But now he realized that there wasn't anything he could do but arrange for a telephone call between Dario and Pierce and wait for his orders.

The city lights beneath them spread out in all directions as the American Airlines 737 floated downward, flaps extended into the Tampa Bay area. The minute the airliner's tires touched the tarmac, Rene sent off a text to Dario.

Rene entered Dario's number on his encrypted cell phone and waited until he got onto the Jetway before initiating the call. Rene then filled Dario in on the most recent development.

"Understood," Dario said. There was a moment of silence as Dario mulled over Rene's account of his conversation with Pierce. Then Dario said, "What does your gut tell you on this one?"

Rene replied tentatively. "I'm not sure."

Rene didn't sound like his sure and impetuous self, and Dario picked up on it. "What does he want?"

Rene shrugged. "I don't know. He insisted on talking to you."

Dario wasn't the least bit surprised by anything Rene had told him. "Put him on."

Rene walked back to where Pierce stood waiting and handed him the telephone. He kept his predatory gaze on Pierce as he was going over in his mind a list of possible ways to kill him. Pierce decided to start the conversation cautiously. If Dario picked up on his change of heart concerning Juan Carlos, he would not be agreeable to trade much in return. Ever since Juan Carlos identified people inside the U.S. government that were leaking highly classified information to the cartel, Pierce had not been able to rid himself of a nagging feeling. All he wanted in return was to keep Alexis alive and to turn over that segment of the video to the FBI.

Dario didn't give Pierce a chance to talk. As soon as Pierce put the phone to his ear, he began to speak.

"To give a man a second chance is a relatively noble thing to do. To give a man like Juan Carlos a second chance wasn't noble it was foolish. We've both made the same mistake of thinking that Juan Carlos is deserving of a second chance. Your mistake cost your friend his life."

Pierce swallowed. "I'll have to live with that." He spoke the words like an act of contrition.

"As much as you don't want to recognize it, you and I have more in common when it comes to Juan Carlos than you would care to admit," Dario said.

Pierce did not suffer from any illusion that he and Dario were suddenly on the same side.

"I'm not sure we do see eye-to-eye. Your man is here for only one reason and that's to kill him," Pierce said. "I'm not sure that's the only solution."

"I'm not in the rehabilitation business," Dario shot back. "We agreed to do it your way and Juan Carlos snapped. He's unstable and poses a bigger threat to us than the video." Dario took a deep breath. "I'm sure you realize by now that Juan Carlos also poses a threat to you."

Pierce could feel the collective glare of Rene and his men on him while he spoke with Dario.

His blue eyes flicked uneasily. "Nevertheless, what you now suggest is a very significant change to our agreement."

"One that ensures your well-being," Dario countered.

"With all due respect, that's how you see it."

Dario smiled his razor smile and said, "What is it that you want?"

Pierce didn't hesitate. "I want the remainder of our agreement to remain intact, meaning I want assurances that no harm will come to Juan Carlos's wife and his family. She cannot be a pawn that your men are willing to sacrifice to get Juan Carlos."

"And?" Dario demanded sensing that Pierce wanted something more.

"And, the opportunity to prosecute those individuals in our government that took bribes in exchange for providing the Cartel with confidential information."

Dario's eyebrows shot up. "How do you propose to do that?"

"I want to release only that portion of the video that identifies the names of the U.S. officials that worked for or with the cartel."

Dario cut Pierce off. "Don't be naïve, the FBI and the DEA will know you only gave them a small piece of the video and will press you for the rest of it."

"Let them press, they won't get any more than your people would if they tortured me," Pierce insisted.

"How can you be so sure?"

"Because only that edited portion of the video will be sent to them from an anonymous source, the same way it was sent to you. There will be nothing that connects the email to me."

"You ask for a great deal."

"And you get a permanent solution."

"I wouldn't call that a permanent solution. We still have the issue of the video."

"That's more of a non-issue. Think of it as nothing more than an insurance policy."

Dario wondered about an accidental release of the video. "Rene did the best he could to explain to me your elaborate process. But what happens if one day you are unable or forget to submit the code?" Dario tossed the question out like a hand grenade lobbed at an enemy position.

"That won't happen."

"How can you be so sure?" Dario pressed.

"The same reason someone suffering from a life-threatening illness doesn't forget to get treatment or take their meds. Self-preservation is a very strong instinct," Pierce replied. "Do we have a deal?"

Dario wasn't satisfied but decided to put off the issue of the video and Pierce to a later time and focus on his more pressing problem. To

Dario, dirty politicians and police officers were like cockroaches. Get rid of one and another will crawl out of some cesspool or crevice.

"Juan Carlos's life in exchange for releasing the names of few American politicians and police officers . . . yes, we have a deal."

Chapter Sixty-Nine

GULF OF MEXICO

Jessica wore a thong bikini that revealed a deep tan and toned body. She stood behind the wheel looking out through a pair of black Ray-ban sunglasses while her long red hair blew in the wind like a lion's mane, and the sixty-four-foot Princess Cruiser thundered its way through the early evening water at twenty knots. The sun was still brilliant and hot, as it sunk over the Gulf of Mexico. For Juan Carlos sitting in the back, this little sojourn out into the Gulf was anything but relaxing. He was on the run and staying several miles off the west coast of Florida seemed like the perfect place to go unnoticed until he could figure out his next move.

Juan Carlos kept Alexis below deck locked in one of the cabins, in a trancelike state induced by heroin. He had been pushing it into her veins for the past several days to keep her subdued and under control. After the first two days, Juan Carlos didn't have to force a needle into Alexis's arm.

* * *

Juan Carlos stared out at the open expanse of blue water considering his options. He was keenly aware that hiding in the middle of the Gulf of Mexico was a short-term solution and had come to the startling conclusion that he had only three options. One was the possibility of attempting reconciliation with Dario. After ten years of effectively running the cartel's day-to-day operations, Juan Carlos was the most qualified to protect the cartel's assets. While he was the best person to put into place safeguards and make modifications to their operations that would be seamless and untraceable, he knew that his former employer was as unforgiving as he was ruthless. Juan Carlos understood that even if Dario accepted his offer, he would kill him the moment Juan Carlos was finished or as soon as someone in the cartel's organization could take over. As a result, it only took Juan Carlos seconds to mentally cross off the first option. His second and safest choice was to agree to testify against the cartel in exchange for going into the Witness Protection Program. Juan Carlos's intimate knowledge of every facet of the cartel's operations would give the DEA more than ample ammunition to prosecute the Carraboca Cartel's leaders, seize most of their assets and bring the Cartel's smuggling operations to a standstill. He was also not ignorant to the fact that if he cooperated with the DEA, Dario would never stop sending assassins to kill him. Dario had men on the inside of every U.S. law enforcement agency. Even if their identities were discovered, Dario would buy others and would never stop until he was dead. Another factor which surprisingly played a big role in Juan Carlos's decision was the modest lifestyle he would be required to suffer through in the Witness Protection Program. Juan Carlos suspected that the DEA would stash him in a small isolated community. Gone would be his extravagant standard of living, five star restaurants, exotic trips and most importantly the endless supply of supple young women and nightly escapades. For him a life without having sex with different beautiful women wasn't worth the trouble. At best the Witness Protection Program would buy him two possibly three years before the cartel found him.

Juan Carlos's testimony alone would bring down the largest supplier of methamphetamine in the United States. As far as he was concerned, his cooperation in exchange for an obscure and meager existence hardly seemed like a fair exchange.

* * *

The third option, which consisted of coming to an arrangement with the rival Mexican drug cartel held the most appeal. Juan Carlos had proof that the Carraboca cartel conspired with the Sinaloa cartel to kill members of the Zeta cartel. While that information would be useful in gaining him an audience, his value to the Zeta cartel was not as an informant. His reputation for being an artist and visionary when it came to smuggling drugs and laundering money was legendary. He recognized that there were inherent risks in meeting with the Mexicans. The Zeta cartel could just as easily sever his head and send it to Dario as a token of goodwill as they could accept his offer to work for them. And yet, Juan Carlos counted on the fact that they would see that his value to them was greater than any goodwill they would garner from turning him over. If Juan Carlos could convince the Mexicans that he could do for them what he did for Dario, he could continue to partake in the lifestyle he had grown accustomed to living.

By working for a powerful rival, Juan Carlos still presented a threat to the Caraboca Cartel but not of the magnitude had he cooperated with a federal investigation. And certainly not one that Dario would be willing to start a war over.

* * *

Juan Carlos's plan was starting to come together. Something that looked like relief flashed across his face. He raised a glass of wine to his lips and took a sip. He looked up at Jessica, his eyes roving over her glistening body before settling on her round ass.

"Turn on the automatic navigation system and come down here," Juan Carlos called to her.

Jessica giggled and pivoted on the balls of her feet before removing her top and squirming out of her thin strip of a thong. Juan Carlos's eyes followed her beautiful twenty-two-year-old hips as they sashayed down the ladder. Their eyes locked and Jessica didn't need any direction. She leaned over, her luscious breasts hanging over, full and inviting as she deftly worked Juan Carlos's belt and the zipper of his pants. Then Jessica lowered her mouth on him and every nerve in his body was electrified. Jessica eagerly and hungrily devoured him. With an arch of his back followed by a thunderous explosion and a shudder Jessica was satisfied that she had coaxed every ounce out of him. Juan Carlos brought Jessica's face up to his and gave her a satisfied smile. Without a word, he slowly got dressed and headed below deck to schedule a meeting with the Zeta cartel. Before disappearing, he said, "If things go well on this call, we will need to cross the Gulf towards Mexico."

Chapter Seventy

Jessica stood in the threshold and watched Juan Carlos pull the needle out of Alexis's arm. Her eyes flashed a glimmer of recognition when they briefly fell on Jessica and then Alexis closed them waiting for the undertow of the Heroin to numb her senses. Jessica watched Alexis curl up like a ball on the bed.

"You're giving her too much. She is going to die of an overdose," she told Juan Carlos.

Juan Carlos glanced over his shoulder and said, "Wait outside."

Until that moment Jessica hadn't given Alexis much thought. She had been nothing more than a name on a marriage certificate that meant little to her and even less to Juan Carlos. Alexis was someone that Juan Carlos only mentioned when he needed to blame someone for something that had gone wrong. Jessica had an uneasy feeling about Juan Carlos's intentions and lingered in the doorway. He noticed her still standing there and pounded his fist on the nightstand.

"I told you to wait for me outside," he seethed.

* * *

When he was finished with Alexis, Juan Carlos asked Jessica how long it would take them to get to Tampico Mexico. Jessica studied her nautical maps and calculated that the shortest line between Tampico and Sanibel was approximately 900 nautical miles. She explained that they could safely cross the Gulf of Mexico and arrive in Tampico in about three days. When Juan Carlos pressed her to get there faster, Jessica refused citing the heavy commercial freighter traffic in the Gulf.

"A boat our size doesn't always get picked up by the larger ships' radars. There are also abandoned oil platforms that are unlit and hard to see at night. Our safest bet is to cover about 300 nautical miles a day and to stay close to the shoreline when we cross," she said.

Juan Carlos made a sound of disgust and stomped his foot on the ground like a petulant child. "When you say three days you really mean five."

"I am not an experienced boat captain," Jessica said, her voice like boiling lava, "I don't feel comfortable crossing at night and I'm not going into the commercial shipping lanes. So, we get across the Gulf my way, or you can fuck yourself Juan!"

Juan Carlos stared at Jessica for a long moment and then apologized. He gently brushed away a moist strand of red hair from her face.

"It will take however long it takes," he said. "We should get going."

Jessica sighed heavily. "It's too late to get started today. Besides we need to go back to Sanibel and refuel first."

"Juan Carlos nodded. "Okay let's go back and get some fuel and then we'll anchor out here overnight and get started at first light."

* * *

JUAN CARLOS STAYED below deck while Jessica fueled the boat and went into town to get supplies. Rene's men had been discreetly watching the marina. As soon as one of them spotted a boat named "***Just Add Wine***" he immediately called Rene. Rene ordered one of his men to stay with the boat and the other to follow Jessica. Pierce was on the balcony of a condominium staring out at the bobbing masts of sailboats docked in the marina when Rene interrupted his train of thought.

"They're here. They just pulled into a boat slip down in the marina."

Pierce felt his pulse quicken.

"My man followed the girl. She's in town buying a lot of supplies. They are either going somewhere or planning on hiding out in the Gulf for a while," Rene said.

Pierce was so focused on Alexis that he wasn't listening. "We have to go," he heard himself shout.

Rene was standing in his way. "We can't catch them by surprise in the marina. If Juan Carlos is on that boat, he's bound to be watching for anything suspicious. If he sees anything, he'll call the police and lock himself away somewhere where we can't easily find him. We need to follow them out into the Gulf and board them out there."

Pierce tried to make sense of Rene's plan. He didn't want to wait. He wanted to rush down to the marina and look for Alexis. The idea of letting them head back out into the Gulf made Pierce sick to his stomach.

* * *

RENE POINTED TO the water. "Out there, if we can make it onto his boat, there's no one he can call for help that can get to him in time. If you want to rescue her you have to trust me."

As a professional assassin, Rene wanted to hit him before he even knew what was happening and get it over with. But there was another part of Rene, the part that felt personally betrayed. That part desperately wanted to see the fear in Juan Carlos's eyes before he pulled the trigger.

Pierce had no idea what to think. "But if he sees us in the water, Juan Carlos will just outrun us. And then what?"

Rene sounded resigned. "If he sees us and runs, Alexis would still be alive. If we get into a firefight in the marina with Juan Carlos and the local police, her odds of making it out alive aren't as good."

Pierce asked a few more questions and tried to poke a hole in the plan, but he didn't try too hard, the plan was solid. He prayed that Juan Carlos still believed Alexis had some value to him and that he had not yet hurt her. Pierce looked at Rene and with some difficulty he said, "We'll do it your way."

Chapter Seventy-One

GULF OF MEXICO

A quarter-moon on the water provided the only light that Rene and Pierce needed to follow the sleek cruiser. The small launch ducked and bobbed over the waves like an amusement park ride while one of Rene's men used night vision binoculars to maintain their fix on Juan Carlos's boat. Noise traveled great distances and with great clarity on a relatively still night like this, so as soon as the cruiser dropped anchor six miles off of the coast of Florida, they shut off the small outboard engine and floated in near total darkness along the gulf stream currents waiting for the lights in the portholes to go dark. Pierce and one of Rene's men rowed the last mile slowly and in unison more interested in stealth than speed. With each pull of his oar, Pierce's played Hugo death over and over in his mind's eye. He'd envisioned a variety of scenarios where Juan Carlos might meet his death, but he didn't necessarily wish it. He cared only for Alexis's safety and well-being. Every pair of eyes in the launch scanned the deck as the small boat pulled alongside the yacht.

* * *

JUAN CARLOS AND JESSICA were asleep in the master cabin situated in the bow of the boat. Rene and his men carried an arsenal of weapons; none bothered to bring silencers. The launch swung around the starboard side. Each man pulled himself up onto the deck from the swim platform. The four men together on the swim platform barely rocked the boat. However, it was enough for Juan Carlos to open his eyes. Juan Carlos threw the sheet off himself with no regard for Jessica lying beside him. He placed his feet on the floor and reached for his gun. With his gun drawn, Juan Carlos moved slowly down the hallway, past the staterooms towards the galley. From the shadows, he saw the outline of one man pass and then another. He knew that in a matter of a minute or two they would be in position and closing in. Juan Carlos also suspected that they probably brought a lot more firepower than he had and that he would not be able to hold them off long enough for help to arrive. If Juan Carlos didn't engage them in a gun fight, there was a chance they might torture him before they killed him and that might buy him the time he needed. Juan Carlos tried to rid his mind of the panic that was threatening to take control of his thoughts.

"Think," he whispered to himself. Crouching in a corner, Juan Carlos slid his cell phone out from his pajama pants pocket and dialed Special Agent Lloyd Hogan. When Hogan answered, Juan Carlos told him in a rapid and hushed tone that he was in the Gulf of Mexico and that the cartel's men had just boarded his boat. Juan Carlos told Hogan that if he wanted his testimony, he needed to scramble his men and the Coast Guard because he didn't have much time. He left the cell phone on and hid it in the galley so that Hogan could track it. Juan Carlos then crept back to his stateroom and slid back into bed next to Jessica and waited. A half minute later the door to the stateroom opened with a click. Then the next sound he heard was Rene's voice.

* * *

He was not surprised to see Rene. In fact, he expected it.

"In a voice tinged more with disappointment than disdain Rene whispered, "I told you to do exactly what Dario wanted or I'd be back. You couldn't possibly think you were going to get away with it."

What Juan Carlos didn't expect was to see Pierce standing next to him. Juan Carlos stared at them both for a long moment. Then he took a deep breath and blew it out.

"Get away with what exactly?" Juan Carlos asked. "We have a deal with Dario."

Rene's scowl deepened. "And how long did you honestly think Dario would keep his word? You betrayed us; this can only end one way."

Juan Carlos raised an eyebrow at Pierce as if to say "did you catch that?"

Pierce did but didn't let on that he caught it.

"Is Alexis on this boat," Pierce interrupted.

"She's in the first stateroom next to the galley," Jessica whimpered.

Pierce noticed a fear in her eyes that he felt had nothing to do with Rene and the guns pointed at her and Juan Carlos.

"Show me where she is," Pierce demanded.

Jessica looked at Rene for permission to move. He motioned with his gun towards the door. "Go," he yelled at her.

* * *

JESSICA NERVOUSLY AND TENTATIVELY led Pierce down the corridor. When she got to the door, she hesitated. Jessica tried explaining that she had nothing to do with what Juan Carlos had done to Alexis. Pierce pushed past her and opened the door. The fetid stench of burnt vinegar mixed with urine and sweat was suffocating. Pierce rushed into the small quarters towards a figure lying on the floor in the corner. He tried shouting and shaking Alexis vigorously, but she did not immediately respond. Finally, her eyes fluttered open for a second then they closed again. Bewildered and desperate, Pierce's eyes scanned the room. His eyes blinked in disbelief as they settled on a discarded needle next to the nightstand. He stared at it for a long-confused moment. Then he turned his head back towards Jessica. With a merciless glare, his deep voice growled at her. "What did he give her?"

Jessica stood in the doorway paralyzed with fear. It took her a second to react. Then she started to sob uncontrollably.

"Look at me," Pierce insisted. "She's not dead. I just need to know what he gave her."

Jessica continued to cry. She could barely focus. Finally, between whimpers, he managed to figure out that she was trying to say the word heroin.

Pierce realized with fearful clarity that Jessica would die if he didn't take her with him. Lifting Alexis's head slightly, Pierce placed his hand under her neck and raised himself off the floor taking her in his arms.

"Help me get her off of the boat," he ordered Jessica.

* * *

At 3:32 A.M. a 33 FOOT Special Purposes Craft, Law Enforcement boat crew from Coast Guard Station Ft. Myers sliced through the warm Florida waters at twenty-eight knots, its twin engines rumbling toward the longitude and latitude coordinates radioed to them by Special Agent Hogan. Eight men wearing night vision goggles manning .50-caliber machine guns went through their final check. They had been briefed by their commanding officer that an important witness was being held hostage by an unknown number of cartel gunmen. Hogan stressed to the commanding officer that the cartel would murder the hostages if they got so much as a sniff of the Coast Guard boat. For the hostages to have a chance of being extracted, the insertion would have to be a complete surprise performed under cover of darkness. The Coast Guard's orders were to provide additional support to the SEAL assault team, twelve men total that was being dropped by helicopter into the Gulf of Mexico less than a mile from pinpointed location.

* * *

Meanwhile, Hogan and his men sped across I-75 from Ft. Lauderdale to Fort Myers. Hogan rarely took cases personally, but he felt an unusual amount of hatred toward the men who tortured and brutally murdered Doctor Hernandez, the physician who treated Juan Carlos, the security guard from Bon Futuro prison, Andre Rojer and Tessa Bongard. He couldn't even begin to grasp what type of men would cook a woman alive. That factored heavily into why he had no problem when he gave the order to kill anyone on the boat who did not immediately surrender. Hogan felt confident that he would lose no sleep over killing everyone on the boat if by the time they got there Juan Carlos was already dead.

Chapter Seventy-Two

The images around him blurred, drifting in and out Juan Carlos's eyes began to focus. His head was ringing, and his body felt like it had been run over by a truck. Juan Carlos was lying on the floor in his own vomit spitting up blood.

Rene stood there savoring his prize. "Pick him up," he ordered. His voice was firm and professional. Juan Carlos's eyes casually looked over at the clock on the nightstand wondering how much longer Rene would keep him alive. It wouldn't take too much longer before Rene got bored of pounding him senseless. He tried to drive his thoughts towards some believable story that would buy him more time and provide him with a short reprieve from the beatings.

Short of breath and struggling, Juan Carlos said, "You never asked me why I did it."

"I know why you did it," Rene sneered. "You're a pig. You're never satisfied."

Juan Carlos coughed up blood. "I can't argue that point. But you've known me for a long time. Tell me, when have you ever known me to do something stupid?"

Rene did not immediately answer Juan Carlos with words, but with laughter that spoke of unpleasant things to come. "I would put double crossing Dario on the stupid list."

He glanced warily at Rene and with as much conviction as he could muster, said, "Dario is finished. The Zeta Cartel is planning to make a move against him."

Rene looked at Juan Carlos, his eyes revealed nothing. "And how do you know this?"

"Because I've always made it my business to know what my enemies are up to so that I could stay a step ahead," Juan Carlos said.

Rene shook his head. "You're full of shit."

"I'm a dead man, what the fuck does it hurt to hear me out?" Juan Carlos asked.

"You're wasting my time." Rene and his men exchanged a brief look. One of them immediately unleashed an elbow strike that caught Juan Carlos on his mouth. The blow hit with such force that Juan's head snapped back.

Blood began cascading out of his mouth. Juan Carlos smiled through blood stained teeth. He could barely speak. "What fucking difference is twenty minutes going to make? Fuck it then. Shoot me," Juan Carlos surprised himself with his bold tone. "Just remember that I tried to warn you."

"Why do us a favor when we were going to kill you?" Rene asked in a suspicious tone.

"I'm not doing Dario a favor. I'm warning you Rene. Our differences aside, you've been like a brother to me," Juan Carlos said with feigned earnestness.

Rene scoffed. "We can handle the Zeta cartel."

"I'm not so sure." he shrugged. "Dario is going to have his hands full fighting the DEA with no allies and no money."

Rene shot him a curious look. "What are you talking about?"

"Pierce isn't the only one with the video."

"Bullshit!"

"The video was on Pierce's laptop. I uploaded it to my cloud server before he sent it to Dario."

Rene's eyes moved towards the door.

"Don't bother asking him. Pierce doesn't know. You've known me a long time Rene. Do you think I would have put my life in that Fucking Gringo's hands without having a backup plan?"

Before Rene could react, Juan Carlos said, "How do you think I bought my way into the Zeta cartel?"

"Are you saying that they have the tape?"

Juan Carlos shook his head. "Not all of it, I gave them a small taste; the part where Dario helped the Gulf cartel and the Mexican police execute a bunch of the Zeta cartel's men."

Rene's frown deepened and he mumbled a few curses to himself. "They don't have much," he grunted.

"They have enough to go to war." Juan Carlos's eyes searched Rene's face for a moment and then he nodded. "It wouldn't take much for Los Zetas to go to war with Dario."

Rene wore a look that Juan Carlos construed as nervous. "It wouldn't take much for them to go to war with anybody. Los Zetas are unstable. They are just as likely to fight among themselves as they are another cartel."

Juan Carlos shook his head in firm disagreement. "You go ahead and believe that. Los Zetas have reestablished its alliances with the Juárez Cartel, the Beltrán-Leyva Cartel, and the Tijuana Cartel."

Juan Carlos saw an opening. "You need to think about yourself Rene," he stressed. "It would be foolish to think that the tape won't eventually get leaked. Like every bomb, they all explode sooner or later. When the DEA raids and shuts down the Gulf's and Sinaloa Cartel's underground pipelines into the U.S. who do you think they are going to blame? Without the Gulf and Sinaloa cartels as allies, no viable way to smuggle drugs into the U.S. and no money, how long can Dario last?"

Rene was still unconvinced, but Juan Carlos's reasoning hit a nerve.

"We went into town to refuel and stock up on supplies. We were leaving for Tampico in the morning to meet with the leaders of Los Zeta Cartel. For Christ sake, Rene," said a wide-eyed Juan Carlos "the Carraboca cartel is finished. The smart move is to come with me and work with Los Zetas," he implored him.

Rene studied Juan Carlos intently. His face pinched in thought, like a card player trying to decide if he should fold or put everything in the pot. Suddenly, he flicked the safety off and pulled the hammer all the way back into the cocked position. Rene leaned forward looking directly into Juan Carlos's still dazed eyes and said, "I do not believe you."

Juan Carlos opened his mouth and flexed his jaw. Then he smiled at Rene.

"Well then, I expect that I'll be seeing you in hell sooner than you think."

Chapter Seventy-Three

Pierce and Jessica could hear Rene's and Juan Carlos's animated discussion coming from the Master cabin.

"We have to go now," Pierce's voice plunged to a compelling hush.

Jessica seemed momentarily paralyzed.

"Jessica," Pierce snapped stunning Jessica back to sobriety.

"Oh God . . . oh God," She let out a fearful gasp.

"We don't have much time. You will be fine if you listen to me, but we need to move!"

Jessica hurried down the corridor through the Galley and up to the deck. Pierce held tightly on to Alexis's limp body as he sidestepped through the narrow passageway. Pierce felt like he was moving in slow motion. When Jessica got to the deck, she turned and looked at Pierce for direction.

Pierce nodded. "The boat is tied up next to the swim platform."

Jessica ran ahead and jumped into the launch. When Pierce got to the swim platform, he steadied himself before lowering Alexis into the boat. Alexis felt like dead weight in his arms.

When he lowered her safely onboard, Pierce turned and jumped back on to the swim platform.

Jessica looked horrified. "What are you doing?" She cried out.

Pierce said from the yacht's deck breathless, "I need to cut the fuel lines to the engines so that they won't be able to follow us."

"It's too risky," Jessica stammered. Pierce could tell by the way her hands shook that her nerves were completely shot.

"We don't have a choice. Where's the engine room?"

Jessica pointed to the Galley. "Beneath the salon; the doorway to the engine room is in the Galley."

Pierce nodded and raced below deck. He entered the small compartment and immediately spotted and cut the two fuel lines that were connected to the fuel tank and compound gauges. He couldn't stop himself from thinking about Rene's earlier comment to Juan Carlos. Sensing what Rene's true intentions were, he wasted no time pulling two fuel containers and taking them with him. Pierce turned the gas on high for each of the stove top burners. They started to make a low hissing sound as propane gas filled the room. He slid his head around the corner and looked down the hallway for any sign of Rene's men. Working quickly, Pierce emptied one of the fuel containers on the floor of the Galley. Then he took a bullet out of the chamber of his gun and reached into the toolbox and used a pair of pliers to pull the bullet apart from the casing and poured the gunpowder out onto a puddle of diesel fuel. Pierce hoped that when the diesel fuel around the powder caught fire, it would create a flash big enough to trigger an explosion of the propane gas that was building up in the room. Pierce emptied the second container of fuel along the stairs leading down to the galley and on the deck the boat. He then dropped a match starting a small fire on the deck.

"We only have a few minutes," Pierce shouted as he jumped onto the boat.

Jessica gunned the small outboard engine towards the coastline pushing the boat as fast as it could go and getting as far away as humanly possible. For good measure, Pierce aimed and fired the flare gun at the entrance to the Galley. Staring intently at the yacht, Pierce saw the flames flicker and start to spread in the middle of the endless and dark expanse of the Gulf.

* * *

By the time Rene and his men smelled the gas it was too late. A flash appeared in the porthole. Then it happened. Blinding white light followed by a thunderous explosion. The deep and hollow shock wave descended on them like the wrath of hell almost capsizing the small boat and nearly sending them flying overboard into the water. Bits and pieces of debris rained down all around them. Jessica looked behind her and knew that Juan Carlos was gone. Her heart shuddered and she felt her tears begin to well. Pierce took control of the rudder and pressed towards the twinkling lights on the coastline. He glanced over at Jessica slumped forward, sobbing and at Alexis lying unconscious and he knew that he would always look back on this night as a defining moment in his life. He reminded himself of Rene's comment about Dario and of his suspicion that Juan Carlos killed his friend Hugo and left Mia for dead. He tried to convince himself that if he hadn't blown up the boat, Jessica would probably have been killed and Alexis would never be safe. But none of it made his decision to take human lives any easier.

* * *

THE SEAL ASSAULT team which had been moving towards the Cruiser was stunned by the blast. They watched in bewilderment as the sixty-four-foot luxury cruiser that had been anchored in the Gulf of Mexico less than a half mile from their position had disappeared and been replaced by a pile of incandescent reddish orange fire. They were close enough to feel the sudden rush of warm air when the boat exploded. None of the men that witnessed it harbored any illusion that anyone survived. When the Coast Guard Captain radioed in what he had just witnessed, Hogan had little reason to be optimistic. As a precaution, he ordered the Coast Guard along with the SEAL team to inspect the wreckage. Hogan's men weren't sure whether it was instinct or exhaustion that had the biggest influence on his decision, but without warning Hogan ordered the driver to turn the car around.

“It’s over,” he sighed and rubbed his stubble chin tiredly.

Chapter Seventy-Four

Jessica Davis sat in the front of the boat and wept. Pierce felt like he was in the middle of a bad dream. He waited until he caught a glimpse of the marina in the distance before trying to start a conversation. Pierce realized that there was little he could do to console Jessica, but without his help, she had no chance of surviving. He considered trying to barter with Dario, but he had nothing left to trade. Rene confirmed what Pierce always suspected. That Dario had no intention of honoring their agreement. Pierce suspected that he was already at work making changes to the cartel's operations, carefully moving his assets and putting safeguards in place to counter the impacts of the video should it be released. Dario wouldn't kill Pierce and Alexis until he was certain that the damage caused by video was manageable. Jessica Davis, however, was another story. She was a loose end. Pierce suspected that Dario would have her killed as soon as he discovered that she survived the explosion.

The moment Pierce uttered her name Jessica flinched.

She continued to face forward. "You didn't have to blow up the boat. They wouldn't have been able to follow us once you cut the fuel lines," she said. There was an aching sadness in her voice.

Pierce took a deep breath. "I don't blame you for feeling that way. But those men were there to kill Juan Carlos." Pierce heard the harshness in his own voice and tried to soften it. "I am sorry . . ."

Jessica turned around and stared at Pierce. Her face was streaked with dry tears. "Juan Carlos's dead because of what you did."

It took Pierce a long time to answer. Finally, he said, "You're right, I killed him, but he was going to die. I don't expect you to understand, but I had to blow up the boat to save you."

"Save me?" She sounded incredulous.

Pierce's face was grim. "Those men were there to kill Juan Carlos. They would have killed you."

He tried his best to sound calm but there was tightness in his voice that told Jessica that this nightmare was not over.

A dull pang of nausea suddenly rolled over her. "I just want to go home."

Pierce felt himself frown. "I wish that was possible."

"What do you mean?"

Pierce briefly looked back over his shoulder at the gulf behind him and wondered if Jessica would ever be able to go back home. "It's not safe."

Jessica stared at Pierce like a trapped mouse staring at a cat.

"What am I supposed to do?"

He let out a tired sigh. "I'm still working that out, but you can't go back to New York. If you do the cartel will kill you."

Jessica could feel herself starting to come emotionally apart. "I just can't disappear."

"*That was precisely what she was going to have to do*," Pierce thought, but said nothing he was no longer sure what to say, much less what to do.

This time, the silence lasted until they reached the boat dock.

Jessica didn't wait for the boat to get tied down before she exploded on to the dock and started to walk away.

"You are going to have to trust me," Pierce called out to her.

Jessica jerked her head back around towards Pierce.

"And why should I do that?"

"Because I could have left you on the boat," Pierce shouted back.

"Thank you for that," Jessica snapped sarcastically.

Pierce looked at her, surprised, and shook his head. “Suit yourself. I can’t force you to accept my help.”

Jessica stopped walking and looked over her shoulder at Pierce with growing curiosity as he dropped to one knee and gently picked Alexis up.

Alexis barely moved.

“He gave her a couple of sleeping pills along with the hit of H just before you got there, so she should be out for a couple more hours,” Jessica offered.

Pierce looked concerned. “Thank you.”

“How do you know her anyway?”

“She hired me to save her husband.”

Speechless for a second, Jessica nervously shifted her weight from one foot to the other. “The man you killed?”

“Ironic isn’t it?” Pierce shrugged, planting one foot on the dock and balancing the other on the boat before raising himself and Alexis up.

Jessica stood frozen with a troubled look on her face unsure of what to do next. She continued to watch Pierce through cautious eyes. Then her eyebrows shot up as her mind rapidly filled in the blanks. “You’re the lawyer . . . Pierce . . . I’m sorry I’m bad with names,” she said as she continued to give him a measured look.

“Evangelista,” Pierce’s eyes flashed.

“Yeah, that’s right.” Jessica briefly nodded before turning her thoughts back to her predicament.

“So, what am I supposed to do now?”

Pierce detected a tinge of fear in her voice. He knew that it would be tough for her to hear but there was no way to sugar coat what he was about to say. “You can’t go back to the life you knew. That’s over.”

His thoughts turned to Hogan; he could protect her. "I'm going to call someone that I think can help but first we need to find a place to stay."

"I have a place," Jessica said.

* * *

HOGAN'S MOBILE PHONE vibrated. Tension ebbed from his body as Hogan felt a deepening disappointment over the outcome of his case. His eyes flicked uneasily over the phone. His first instinct was to ignore it, but he knew that was irrational.

"This is Special Agent Hogan."

"Agent Hogan, this is Pierce Evangelista. You sent me some information on Juan Carlos Laporte's arrest a couple of weeks ago."

Hogan let out a pained breath. "I know who you are," he said, cutting Pierce off before he could get another word out. Hogan's voice was bitter. "I assume you're calling about your client."

"In a manner of speaking, yes, I am."

Hogan's eyes narrowed. He had no desire to talk to Juan Carlos's attorney and the knot in his chest told him that he could do without a verbal sparring session.

"Counselor, I'm out in the field right now. I'll have to call you back," Hogan said curtly.

"That won't work. We need to meet right now," Pierce persisted.

Frowning Hogan said, "That's not possible. If you call my office . . ."

"I was on the boat that blew up," Pierce cut Hogan short.

Hogan had always hated roller coasters, hated that feeling of his stomach dropping. The impact of Pierce's news hit him like a mule kick to the gut and felt ten times worse than any rollercoaster.

"You were on the boat?" Hogan repeated out loud.

Everyone in the car stopped what they were doing. They were now all focused on Hogan.

"Is your client with you?"

Pierce drew a long, ragged breath. "Not the one you're interested in. He didn't make it. But I have something for you that's almost as good."

Hogan felt a stab of disappointment "And what might that be?"

"I have Juan Carlos's testimony on video. There's enough on it to not only extradite Dario Carraboca and put him away but to decimate his entire operation."

Hogan seemed to soak the words in for a second and then he said, "Where are you?"

"I'm in Sanibel. I'll text you the address."

Hogan looked at his watch. "We can be there in about forty minutes."

The driver slowed the car waiting on Hogan to give him the order.

Hogan looked over at him. "What are you waiting for?" He grunted. "Turn the car around."

Chapter Seventy-Five

Alexis woke up in an unfamiliar bed gasping and disoriented. She looked around the strange room trying to get her bearings and figure out why snippets of Pierce and of her floating in a small boat that she imagined while she was high on Heroin felt more like recent memories than a dream. Her hair was plastered to her neck with sweat and the bruises on her arm ached along the track of needle marks that ran the length of her forearm. The bathroom contained clues of activities that occurred earlier that morning. There were soiled clothes shoved into trash and a smear of dried vomit in the sink. With a shudder Alexis ducked into the shower with a bottle of Apricot body wash and baby shampoo determined to scrub away her fears, worries and anxieties.

* * *

Afterward, she wrapped herself in a robe that she found hanging on the back of the bathroom door. Alexis heard the faint sound of voices coming from the other side of the bedroom door. She stopped just short of opening it not sure what she was going to find on the other side. She felt numb and hopeless. When Alexis finally opened the door, she saw a figure in the corner bending over a computer. She stood on the threshold stunned, unable to believe her eyes. Alexis let out a breath that she hadn't realized she had been holding. Pierce looked tired and worn down and yet he was still the most beautiful man she had ever seen.

"Pierce?"

He turned towards Alexis smiling as he walked to her.

Alexis started to tremble. Tears flowed down her face. "Oh my God . . . oh my God!"

Pierce wrapped her in his arms and kissed her. When their lips touched, it was a tender kiss filled with gratitude. Alexis pulled away and looked into his deep blue eyes.

Pierce kissed her again, more passionately, and she pressed against him, losing herself in his arms. Alexis closed her eyes. She felt weightless. Pierce's touch made her forget about all the pain and suffering that she endured the last few days. She didn't let go of him until they heard Jessica clear her throat and tell them that Agent Hogan and his agents were waiting.

* * *

PIERCE ACCESSED THE encrypted server and downloaded the video on to the laptop. When the video was finished, every agent experienced a private moment of wonder. The look that passed over Hogan's face was pure incredulity. The DEA had enough to destroy the Carraboca Cartel and cripple the smuggling operations of the Sinaloa and Gulf cartels. The names of the dirty politicians and law enforcement agents were more than Hogan could ever have hoped for. Hogan was not a religious man and believing in miracles had never been a part of his core beliefs, but Juan Carlos's video testimony was starting to feel like a miracle.

"My God," he said under his breath. Then his mind kicked into gear.

He drew a slow and patient breath and locked eyes with Pierce waiting for his tit-for-tat request. "What do you want for the video?"

"Nothing unreasonable," Pierce said. He and Jessica exchanged a look. "For starters I'd like you to put Ms. Davis in the Witness Protection Program. She was Juan Carlos's mistress and if Dario discovers that she is still alive, he'll come after her."

Pierce felt like a heel discussing the personal nature of Jessica's relationship with Juan Carlos in front of Alexis.

"Understood," Hogan nodded.

"Mrs. Alexis Laporte will need a new identity. She was also on the boat," Pierce continued. "As for Juan Carlos Laporte, I want the government to grant him immunity from prosecution."

Alexis looked confused by Pierce's request.

Pierce glanced over at Alexis. "If your husband is granted immunity, the U.S. government will not be able to seize the millions Juan Carlos has in his offshore accounts. The Department of Justice can only seize his money if they convict him of obtaining it from illegal drug activities."

Hogan agreed. "You have a deal."

The corners of Pierce's mouth turned up ever so slightly. "I know I do, but I'm not done."

Hogan did not respond at first, and then glancing sideways at Pierce he said, "My mistake, I thought you were finished. Please continue."

Pierce shook his head and looked at Hogan. "I would like for you to make arrangements and personally oversee the transfer of Juan Carlos's money into new accounts under Alexis's new identity."

Hogan appeared to consider Pierce's request. "How am I supposed to do that? Juan Carlos only identified the cartel's accounts. He never talked about where he had his money."

Jessica swallowed and then cleared her throat. "I know where he kept his accounts," she volunteered trying to find some way of repaying Pierce for saving her life.

Alexis looked at Jessica with blank shattered eyes. Pierce could tell that she was wrestling with a cyclone of emotions. He moved over to Alexis and rested his hand on her shoulder. Turning towards Jessica with sheer gratitude, he said, "Thank you."

“Yes, thank you, Alexis said very faintly, still looking troubled.

Pierce turned his attention back to Hogan and explained the terms and details of his arrangement with Dario.

“As I understand it, Dario knows that you were on the boat. For all he knows you died in the explosion,” Hogan said. “When we freeze all of the cartel’s assets and shut down the two tunnels, he’ll assume that the safeguards you put into place in the event he killed you were triggered.”

Pierce nodded in agreement.

“Which means,” Hogan continued “that we will have to give you a new identity.”

Pierce frowned ever so slightly. With Juan Carlos’s video testimony, Dario would have his hands full with the DEA, and if Hogan played his hand correctly, he could further cripple the Carraboca cartel by instigating a war with the Mexican cartels. Pierce had a hunch that Dario would be much too preoccupied to worry about him.

Hogan looked at Pierce “So is that it? Are we done?”

“Almost,” Pierce replied. “We still have to discuss the reward?”

Hogan gave him a dubious look. “Yes, there is a reward of two hundred and fifty thousand dollars for information leading to a seizure.”

Pierce gave Hogan a steady measured look. “You can do better than two hundred and fifty K, much better,” Pierce insisted.

Hogan made a noise under his breath and glared at Pierce. “I can’t help you there. The federal guidelines are set in stone. They cap a reward for information leading to a seizure at two hundred and fifty thousand.”

“A seizure?” Pierce repeated sarcastically. “I gave you the combination to the safe. On the video are the account numbers to hundreds of accounts, locations to cartel safe houses around the world and the tunnels which are responsible for billions of dollars of drugs being smuggled into the U.S. every year. You call that a seizure?"

"It will be a historic seizure," Hogan agreed.

Pierce took a sharp breath and stood up and looked around at the room full of agents. "I'm afraid we don't have a deal."

Hogan looked Pierce in the eye. "What's to keep me from confiscating the laptop?"

Pierce returned the look with calculating eyes and gestured gracefully, "Take it . . ."

Before Hogan could react, Pierce added, "The video was streamed from an anonymous and untraceable location . . . It's gone."

Hogan looked completely miffed. "What you're asking me to do is . . ."

Pierce's eyes flashed as if he could read Hogan's thoughts. "I'm asking you to think outside of the box Lloyd. Each bank account containing millions can be treated by our government as a single seizure. There is no law against that. Every four seizures equal one million dollars of reward money. I figure twenty million in comparison to the billions in those accounts is a fair reward."

Hogan's jaw tightened. He was rarely out-thought and out- maneuvered and like a brilliant strategist capable of calculating the ripple effect from making the wrong move, Hogan realized he had no choice. Getting the sign off on Pierce's last demand was going to require some heavy lifting on the Hill but he had the right allies to make it happen. Hogan let out a moan and shook his head, "Where do you want it?"

In a cool and clear voice, Pierce said, "I don't want any of it."

Hogan looked at Pierce thoughtfully. "Then where do we send it?"

Pierce leaned over to one of the agents. "You should write this down so that the old man doesn't forget it . . . I want the twenty million divided evenly between the victims, Marisa De Meza and the families of Tessa Bongard, Andre Rojer and Doctor Keith Hernandez."

Hogan looked at Pierce with an unwavering stare. Two miracles in one day were enough to make him possibly rethink his religious beliefs.

"Done," Hogan said as he stood and stuck out his hand. "Perhaps you'll consider working for us . . . a man of your talents could be a hell of an asset."

Pierce realized that the real battle against the cartel and the dirty bureaucrats and agents who occupied Washington's back rooms was only beginning and there was no way for him to completely sidestep or walk away from this fight. Until it was over, Dario would always be a storm on the horizon.

He thought about Hogan's offer for a second. "I'll get back to you."

* * *

ALEXIS WAITED for Pierce in the bedroom. When he walked in and saw her standing by the window, Pierce was mesmerized by her beauty in the same way he was when he first saw her in the conference room of his office. Alexis looked happy to see him.

"I do have a question for you," she smiled letting her robe completely slip off her shoulders and onto the floor.

Pierce's eyes lingered on her breasts and soft curves, drinking in her full lips and burning eyes. She was such a vision that he could barely think.

"What question is that?"

She started to count out loud. "One, two or was it three minutes?"

A ghost of a smile touched the corners of his mouth. "Ah, yes that question . . ."

Alexis looked into his eyes that sparkled like blue sapphires waiting for an answer.

"So, how many minutes did it take for you to realize that you wanted me?"

"It didn't even take a minute," Pierce laughed. "I wanted you the second I laid eyes on you."

"Come to bed," she said softly.

Coming Soon!

BREAKING ARROWS
BY
LUIS FIGUEREDO

Breaking Arrows is a courtroom battle and legal thriller involving a small Indian tribe's battle against a corrupt system. After his grandson dies swimming in a contaminated pond, Jeremiah Tiger, Chief of the Kialegee, knows he can no longer sit by and allow his tribe to barely subsist on minimal federal assistance. For any chance at all, the tribe needs to reclaim what is rightfully theirs and push back on 300 years of oppression . . .

For more information
visit: www.SpeakingVolumes.us

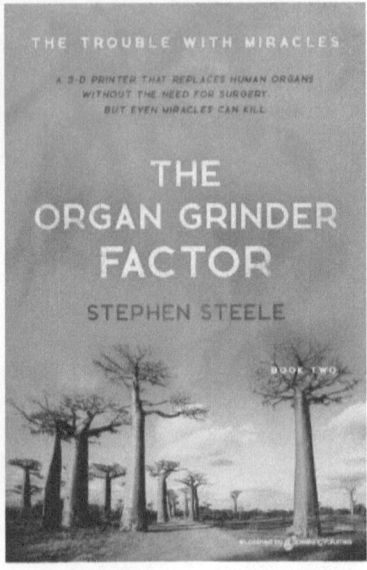

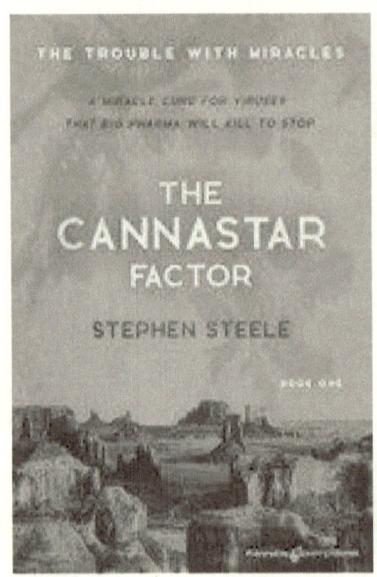

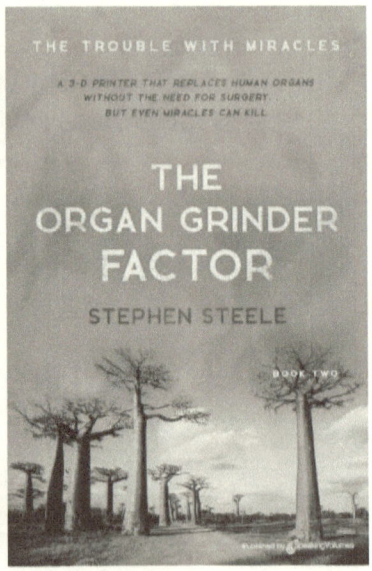

On Sale Now!

JAMES V. IRVING
JOTH PROCTOR FIXER MYSTERIES

"Irving's writing is relaxed and authentic and takes readers inside a compelling world of legal and social issues…"
—Bruce Kluger, columnist, USA Today

For more information
visit: www.SpeakingVolumes.us

www.ingramcontent.com/pod-product-compliance
Lightning Source LLC
Chambersburg PA
CBHW022203030726
47494CB00019B/114
9781645406099